A TEXT BOOK OF

CONTROL SYSTEMS

FOR
SEMESTER – II

SECOND YEAR DEGREE COURSE IN ELECTRONICS / ELECTRONICS & TELECOMMUNICATION ENGINEERING

Strictly According to New Revised Credit System Syllabus of Savitribai Phule Pune University
(w.e.f June 2016)

Ms. P. J. PARDESHI
BE. (E&TC), ME. (Signal Processing)
Assistant Professor,
Electronics and Telecommunication Deptt.,
MAEER's MIT College of Engineering,
Kothrud, PUNE.

NIRALI
PRAKASHAN
ADVANCEMENT OF KNOWLEDGE

N3573

CONTROL SYSTEMS (SE Elec. / E&TC)

ISBN 978-93-86353-05-4

First Edition : January 2017

© : Author

Published By :   Polyplate

NIRALI PRAKASHAN
Abhyudaya Pragati, 1312, Shivaji Nagar,
Off J.M. Road, Pune – 411005
Tel - (020) 25512336/37/39, Fax - (020) 25511379
Email : niralipune@pragationline.com

☞ DISTRIBUTION CENTRES

PUNE

Nirali Prakashan   :   119, Budhwar Peth, Jogeshwari Mandir Lane, Pune 411002, Maharashtra
Tel : (020) 2445 2044, 66022708, Fax : (020) 2445 1538
Email : bookorder@pragationline.com, niralilocal@pragationline.com

Nirali Prakashan   :   S. No. 28/27, Dhyari, Near Pari Company, Pune 411041
Tel : (020) 24690204 Fax : (020) 24690316
Email : dhyari@pragationline.com, bookorder@pragationline.com

MUMBAI

Nirali Prakashan   :   385, S.V.P. Road, Rasdhara Co-op. Hsg. Society Ltd.,
Girgaum, Mumbai 400004, Maharashtra
Tel : (022) 2385 6339 / 2386 9976, Fax : (022) 2386 9976
Email : niralimumbai@pragationline.com

☞ DISTRIBUTION BRANCHES

JALGAON

Nirali Prakashan   :   34, V. V. Golani Market, Navi Peth, Jalgaon 425001,
Maharashtra, Tel : (0257) 222 0395, Mob : 94234 91860

KOLHAPUR

Nirali Prakashan   :   New Mahadvar Road, Kedar Plaza, 1st Floor Opp. IDBI Bank
Kolhapur 416 012, Maharashtra. Mob : 9850046155

NAGPUR

Pratibha Book Distributors :   Above Maratha Mandir, Shop No. 3, First Floor,
Rani Jhanshi Square, Sitabuldi, Nagpur 440012, Maharashtra
Tel : (0712) 254 7129

DELHI

Nirali Prakashan   :   4593/21, Basement, Aggarwal Lane 15, Ansari Road, Daryaganj
Near Times of India Building, New Delhi 110002
Mob : 08505972553

BENGALURU

Pragati Book House   :   House No. 1, Sanjeevappa Lane, Avenue Road Cross,
Opp. Rice Church, Bengaluru – 560002.
Tel : (080) 64513344, 64513355,Mob : 9880582331, 9845021552
Email:bharatsavla@yahoo.com

CHENNAI

Pragati Books   :   9/1, Montieth Road, Behind Taas Mahal, Egmore,
Chennai 600008 Tamil Nadu, Tel : (044) 6518 3535,
Mob : 94440 01782 / 98450 21552 / 98805 82331,
Email : bharatsavla@yahoo.com

niralipune@pragationline.com | www.pragationline.com

Also find us on ⓕ www.facebook.com/niralibooks

Dedicated to ...

In Sacred Memories of
Late Smt. Maynabai N. Kaithe
Late Shri. Dr. Hiralal Kondiram Pardeshi

...... Prajakta

PREFACE

It gives me great pleasure in publishing this text book on "**Control Systems**" for the students of Second Year Degree Course in Electronics / Electronics & Telecommunication Engineering. This book is strictly written according to **New Revised Credit System Syllabus** of Savitribai Phule Pune University (2015 Pattern).

As per the policy of the University, Engineering Syllabi is revised every five years. Last revision was in the year 2012. New revision is coming little earlier, as university has introduced **Online System of Examination** from year 2012.

As per the **New Credit System**, the **Online Examinations** Phase–I will be conducted based on First & Second Units and Phase–II on Third & Fourth Units. The **Online** examinations will have objective types of questions with multiple choices. End Sem. Theory Examination will be based on all the six units and that will be conducted in traditional way and the Theory Course will have 4 credits.

Control Systems Engineering is the engineering discipline that applies control theory to design systems with desired behaviors. Control systems also plays major role in growth of Industrial Control and Automation Business. Modern day control engineering is a relatively new field of study that gained significant attention during the 20th century with the advancement of technology.

Main feature of this book is, **Complete Coverage** of the New Credit System Syllabus with large number of **Worked (Solved) Examples and Exercises.**

I have given Separate Book of Multiple Choice Questions (MCQ's) which will be very useful to the students especially for Online Examinations.

I take this opportunity to express my deep sense of gratitude to Dr. V.V. Shete (Head, E&TC, MITCOE, Pune) for his encouragement and support he has extended.

I would like to express my deepest thankfulness to my parents, Dr. Jagansing & Sadhana Pardeshi. I know that they are very proud of me. But I am even more proud to be their daughter as they provided me with the essentials to get the degrees: some basic intelligence and the spirit of never giving up. Their unconditional love and support has always been my inspiration. My Husband, Mr. Vishal Rajput for Struggling day and night with me in writing this book, last but not the least my dear friends and colleagues for their support in realizing my dream.

I take this opportunity to express my sincere thanks to Shri. Dineshbhai Furia, Shri. Jignesh Furia, Mrs. Nirali Verma and Shri. M. P. Munde and entire team of Nirali Prakashan namely Mrs. Deepali Lachake (Co-ordinator), who really have taken keen interest and untiring efforts in publishing this text.

However readers are always welcome for their invaluable suggestions to enhance the usefulness of the book for Suggestions and Queries you can mail at prjakta.pardeshi@gmail.com.

Pune   **Author**

SYLLABUS

Unit I : Control System Modeling (6 Hrs)

Basic Elements of Control System, Open loop and Closed loop systems, Differential equations and Transfer function, Modeling of Electric systems, Translational and rotational mechanical systems, Block diagram reduction Techniques, Signal flow graph

Unit II : Time Response Analysis (6 Hrs)

Standard input signals, Time response analysis of First Order Systems, Time response analysis of second order systems, Steady state errors and error constants, design specifications for second order systems.

Unit III : Stability Analysis (6 Hrs)

Concept of Stability, Routh-Hurwitz Criterion, Relative Stability, Root Locus Technique, Construction of Root Locus, Dominant Poles, Application of Root Locus Diagram.

Unit IV : Frequency Response Analysis (6 Hrs)

Frequency domain Versus Time domain analysis and its correlation, Bode Plots, Polar Plots and development of Nyquist Plots. Frequency Domain specifications from the plots, Stability analysis from plots.

Unit V : State Variable Analysis (6 Hrs)

State space advantages and representation, Transfer function from State space, physical variable form, phase variable forms: controllable canonical form, observable canonical form, Solution of homogeneous state equations, state transition matrix and its properties, computation of state transition matrix by Laplace transform method only, Concepts of Controllability and Observability.

Unit VI : Controllers and Digital Control Systems (6 Hrs)

Introduction to PLC: Block schematic, PLC addressing, any one application of PLC using Ladder diagram. Introduction to PID controller: P, PI, PD and PID Characteristics and concept of Zeigler-Nicholas method.

Digital control systems: Special features of digital control systems, Necessity of sample and hold operations for computer control, z-transform and pulse transfer function, Stability and response of sampled-data systems.

CONTENTS

CONTROL SYSTEM MODELING

1.1 INTRODUCTION

Why Learn Control Systems?

Control systems today have various uses. In the industry, these systems are used to control the production or working of other machines. Different types of control systems work on different purposes. Control systems manage the behavior and working of a machine.

The usefulness of control systems is in the precision and reliability of functions and equipment they can deliver. The field of control systems has its roots in industry and home appliances as well.

Automatic control systems have played an important role in the advancement and improvement of engineering skills.

From the devices as simple as toaster or a toilet, to complex machines like space shutter and power steering; control engineering is a part of our everyday life.

Control systems are found in number of practical applications like computerized control systems, transportation systems, power systems, temperature limiting systems, robotics etc.

Hence, it is necessary to get familiar with the analysis and designing methods of such control systems.

A control system is glue that sticks all the engineering fields together. Understanding fundamentals of control system opens the door to understand and solve many different problems, not just as an control engineer but as any engineer.

- **Electrical Engineer :** To design switching power regulator which are in almost every electrical device and relay on feedback they can be unstable if designed incorrectly.
- **Communication Engineer :** If you are building a automatic gain control circuitry that automatically increases the gain, weakens the signal and decreases it in strong signals.
- **Mechanical Signals :** You will be concerned with vibrations in your damping structure; for this you need to design isolation system in motor around for a system i.e. is sensitive to vibrations.
- **Civil Engineer :** Building active and passive damping system for tall buildings and earthquake zone.
- **Industrial Engineer :** Design robotic assembly or tune PID controller gains.
- **Aerospace Engineer :** Solve problem related to aircraft flutter (aerodynamics).

Control system theory is more than PID and inverted pendulum

- It is building models of your system.
- It is simulating predictions.
- Understanding Dynamic Interactions.
- Filtering and rejecting noise disturbances.

1.1.1 Requirement of Good Control System

Accuracy : Accuracy is the measurement tolerance of the instrument and defines the limits of the errors made when the instrument is used in normal operating conditions. Accuracy can be improved by using feedback elements. To increase accuracy of any control system error detector should be present in control system.

Sensitivity : The parameters of control system are always changing with change in surrounding conditions, internal disturbance or any other parameters. This change can be expressed in terms of sensitivity. Any control system should be insensitive to such parameters but sensitive to input signals only.

Noise : An undesired input signal is known as noise. A good control system should be able to reduce the noise effect for better performance.

Stability : It is an important characteristic of control system. For the bounded input signal, the output must be bounded and if input is zero then output must be zero then such a control system is said to be stable system.

Bandwidth : An operating frequency range decides the bandwidth of control system. Bandwidth should be large as possible for frequency response of good control system.

Speed : It is the time taken by control system to achieve its stable output. A good control system possesses high speed. The transient period for such system is very small.

Oscillation : A small numbers of oscillation or constant oscillation of output tend to system to be stable.

1.1.2 Feedback Loop of Control System

A feedback is a common and powerful tool when designing a control system. Feedback loop is the tool which takes the system output into consideration and enables the system to adjust its performance to meet a desired result of system.

In any control system, output is affected due to change in environmental condition or any kind of disturbance. So one signal is taken from output and is fed back to the input. This signal is compared with reference input and then error signal is generated. This error signal is applied to controller and output is corrected. Such a system is called feedback system. Fig. 1.1 below shows the block diagram of feedback system.

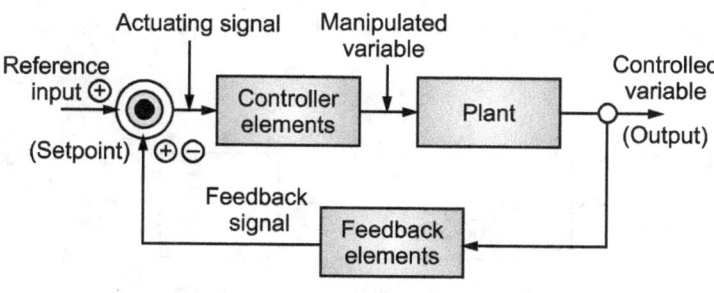

Fig. 1.1

When feedback signal is positive then system is called positive feedback system. For positive feedback system, the error signal is the addition of reference input signal and feedback signal. When feedback signal is negative then system is called negative feedback system. For negative feedback system, the error signal is given by difference of reference input signal and feedback signal.

Effect of Feedback

Refer Fig. 1.2 beside, which represents feedback system where R = Input signal, E = Error signal G = forward path gain H = Feedback C = Output signal B = Feedback signal.

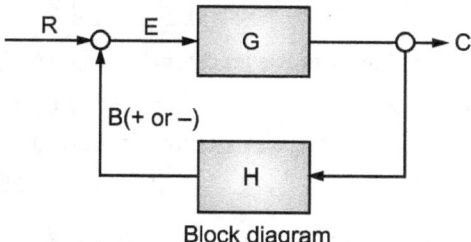

Block diagram

Fig. 1.2

- Error between system input and system output is reduced.
- System gain is reduced by a factor $1/(1 \pm GH)$.
- Improvement in sensitivity.
- Stability may be affected.
- Improve the speed of response.

1.2 BASIC ELEMENTS OF CONTROL SYSTEM

The Control System : The control system is that means by which any quantity of interest in a machine, mechanism or other equipment is maintained or altered in accordance with a desired manner.

Example : The driving system of an automobile.

Speed of automobile is a function of the position of its accelerometer. The desired speed can be maintained by controlling pressure on the acceleration pedal.

This automobile driving system (accelerator, carburetor, and engine vehicle) constitutes a control system).

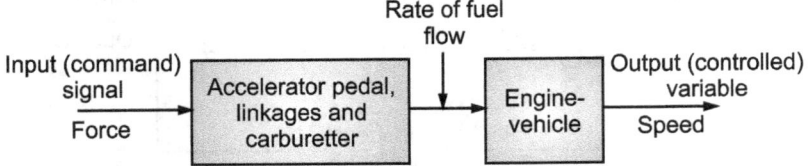

Fig. 1.3 : The basic control system

Fig. 1.3 above shows the general diagrammatic representation of a typical control system.

For the automobile driving system, the input (command) signal is the force on the accelerator pedal which through linkages causes the carburetor valve to open (close) so as to increase or decrease fuel (liquid form) flow to the engine bringing the engine vehicle speed (controlled variable) to the desired value.

The diagrammatic representation of Fig. 1.4 is known as block diagram representation wherein each block represents an element, mechanism, and device.

Fig. 1.4 : Generalized block diagram

Each block has an input and output signal which are linked by a relationship characterizing the block and the signal flow through the block is unidirectional.

Basic Definitions :

System : When a number of elements or components are connected in a sequence to perform a specific function, the group thus formed is called a system.

Control System : To control means to regulate, to direct or to command.

In a system when output quantity is controlled by varying the input quantity, the system is called control system.

The output quantity is called controlled variable or response and input quantity is called command signal or excitation.

Example : Classroom, professor and lamp.

In short, a control system is in the broadest sense, an interconnection of the physical components to provide a desired function involving some kind of controlling action in it.

Plant : The portion of a system which is to be controlled or regulated is called plant or the process.

Controller : The element of the system itself or external to the system which controls the plant or process is called controller.

For each system, there must be an excitation and system accepts it as an input and for analyzing behavior of system for such input, it is necessary to define the output of a system.

Input : It is an applied signal or excitation signal.

Output : It is the particular signal of interest or the actual response obtained from a control system when input is applied to it.

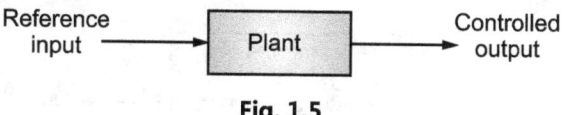

Fig. 1.5

Keynote :
Input → excitation
Output → response
Cause and Effect relationship

1.3 CLASSIFICATION

Classification of Control Systems :

1. **Natural Control System :**

- Biological systems are generally naturally systems.
- Systems inside human being.

Example : Perspiration system and temperature of human being.

2. **Manmade Control System :**

- System designed and manufactured by human being.

Example : Vehicles, various gadgets.

3. **Combinational Control System :**

- Having combination of natural and man-made together.

Example : Driver driving vehicle.

But for engineering analysis, control systems are classified as below :

1.3.1 Time Varying and Time in-Variant System

Time Variant : Time varying control systems are those in which parameters of the systems are varying with time. It is not dependent on whether the input and output are functions of time or not.

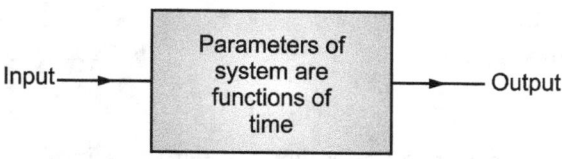

Fig. 1.6 : Time variant system

Example : Space vehicle whose mass decreases with time as it leaves the earth.

Time Invariant : Parameters of the system are independent of time.

Example : Network elements R, L, C.

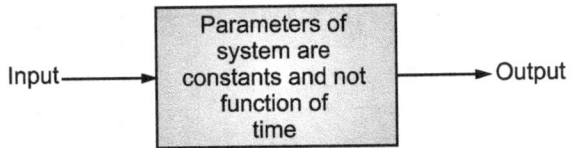

Fig. 1.7 : Time invariant system

1.3.2 Linear and Non-linear Systems

Linear Systems :

Linear systems shown in Fig. 1.8 obey superposition principle, additive property and homogeneous property. Another important property is that in absence of the input, the output is zero.

Principle of Superposition : It states that response to several inputs can be obtained by considering one input at a time and then algebraically adding the individual results.

Superposition is expressed in two ways :

- **Additive Property :** For x and y belonging to the domain of the function f then we have,

$$f(x + y) = f(x) + f(y)$$

- **Homogeneous Property :** For any x belonging the domain of the function f and for any scalar constant α, we have,

$$f(\alpha, x) = \alpha f(x)$$

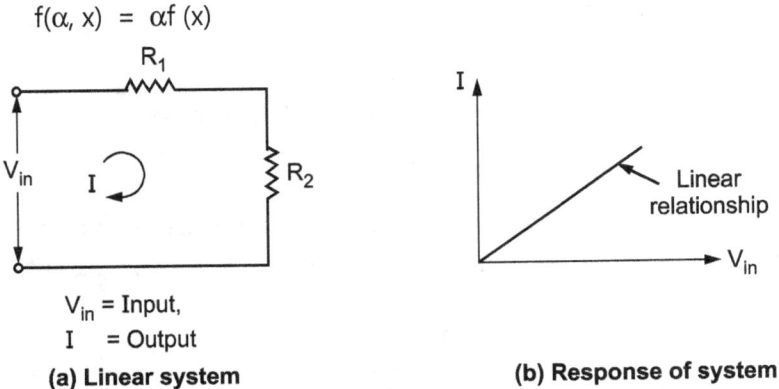

V_{in} = Input,
I   = Output

(a) Linear system   **(b) Response of system**

Fig. 1.8

Practically the output, i.e. response varies linearly with the input, i.e. forcing function for linear systems.

Non-linear Systems : In case of non-linear system shown in Fig. 1.9, principle of superposition theorem, additive property and homogenous properties cannot be applied i.e. it does not satisfies all these properties.

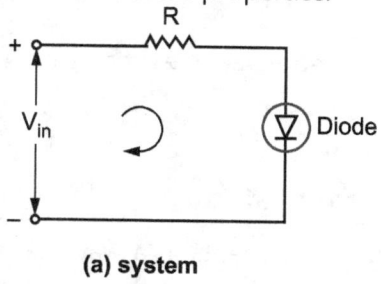

(a) system

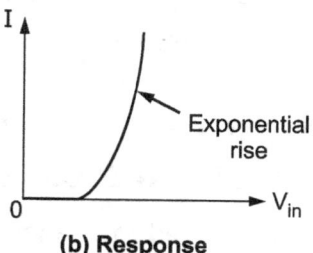

(b) Response

Fig. 1.9

The function, $f(x) = x^2$ is non-linear because

$$f(x_1 + x_2) = (x_1 + x_2)^2 \neq (x_1)^2 + (x_2)^2$$

and $$f(\alpha, x) = (\alpha, x^2) \neq \alpha x^2$$

where α = constant

The output does not vary linearly for non-linear systems.

The Element of the system has non-linearity's present such as saturation, friction, dead zone.

1. Saturation : It means if input increases beyond certain limit, the output remains constant; i.e. it does not remain linear depicted in Fig. 1.10.

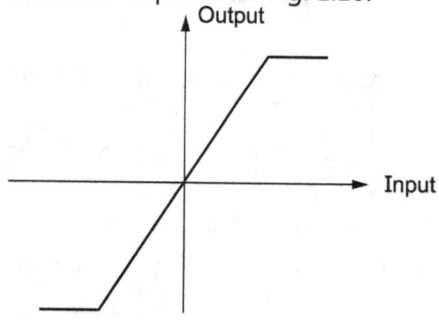

Fig. 1.10 : Saturation

2. Dead Zone : Though, force increases upto certain value, the value does not operate. So there is no response for certain limit time which is called dead zone seen in Fig. 1.11.

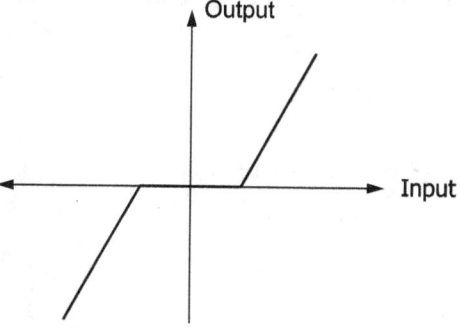

Fig. 1.11 : Dead zone

1.3.3 Continuous Time and Discrete Time or Analog and Discrete Time

- In continuous time control system, all system variables are function of continuous time, t.
Example : Speed control of dc motor.

- A discrete time control system involves one or more variables that are known only at discrete instant time.

Example : Microprocessor or computer based system.

1.3.4 Open Loop and Closed Loop Control System

Control systems are used to arrange and manage components in a way that the required condition or output is obtained. The word 'control' itself shows the command over any system. It is controlled when the system is stable.

There are two main attributes of control system.

- Stability
- Desired output

1. Open Loop System :

Definition : A system in which output is dependent on input but controlling action or input is totally independent of the output or changes in output of the system is called an open loop system.

Open loop → Which does not automatically correct for variation in its output.

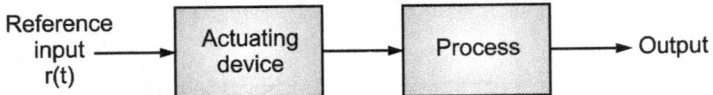

Fig. 1.12 : Open loop control system

An open loop control system utilizes an actuating device to control the process directly without using feedback as seen in Fig. 1.12.

An open loop control system takes input under the consideration and doesn't react on the feedback to obtain the output. This is why it is also called a non-feedback control system.

There are no disturbances or variations in the system.

Advantages :

- Simple in construction and design.
- Easy to maintenance.
- These are not troubled with problems of stability.
- Simple to design and hence economical.

Disadvantages :

- Inaccurate and unreliable.
- Cannot sense internal disturbances.

- To manage and maintain the quality and accuracy, recalibration of controller is necessary from time to time.

- In these systems, the output remains constant for a constant input signal provided the external conditions remain unaltered.

Practical Examples of Open Loop Control System

- **Flow of Traffic :** A traffic control system for regulating the flow of traffic at the crossing of two roads.

   The system will be termed as open-loop if red and green lights are put on by a timer mechanism set for predetermined fixed intervals of time.

   It is obvious that such an arrangement takes no account of varying rates of traffic flowing to the road crossing from the two directions.

   If on other hand i.e. scheme is introduced in which the rates of traffic flow along both directions are measured and are compared and the difference is used to control the timings of red and green lights, a closed loop system results. Thus, the concept of feedback can be usefully employed to traffic control.

- **Electric Switch :** This is open loop because output is light and switch is controller of lamp. Any change in light has no effect on the ON-OFF position of the switch, i.e. the controlling action.

- **Automatic Washing Machine :** Here output is degree of cleanliness of clothes. But any change in this output will be affect the controlling action or will not decide the operation time or will not decide the amount of detergent which is to be used.

- **Electric Hand Drier :** Hot air (output) comes out as long as you keep your hand under the machine, irrespective of how much your hand is dried.

- **Bread Toaster :** This machine runs as per adjusted time irrespective of toasting is completed or not.

- **Automatic Tea/Coffee Maker :** These machines also function for pre adjusted time only.

- **Timer Based Clothes Drier :** This machine dries wet clothes for pre – adjusted time, it does not matter how much the clothes are dried.

- **Light Switch :** Lamps glow whenever light switch is on irrespective of light is required or not.

- **Volume on Stereo System :** Volume is adjusted manually irrespective of output volume level.

2. Closed Loop System :

Definition : A system in which the controlling action or input is somehow dependent on the output or changes in output is called closed loop system. Sometimes, we may use the output of the control system to adjust the input signal. This is called feedback. Feedback is special feature of a closed loop control system.

A closed loop control system depicted in Fig. 1.13 compares the output with the expected result or command status, and then it takes appropriate control actions to adjust the input signal.

Therefore, a closed loop system is always equipped with a sensor, which is used to monitor the output and compare it with the expected result.

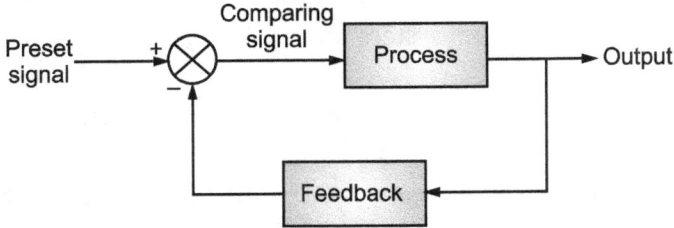

Fig. 1.13 : Block diagram of closed loop control system

The output signal is fed back to the input to produce a new output. A well designed feedback system can often increase the accuracy of the output.

Detailed Representation :

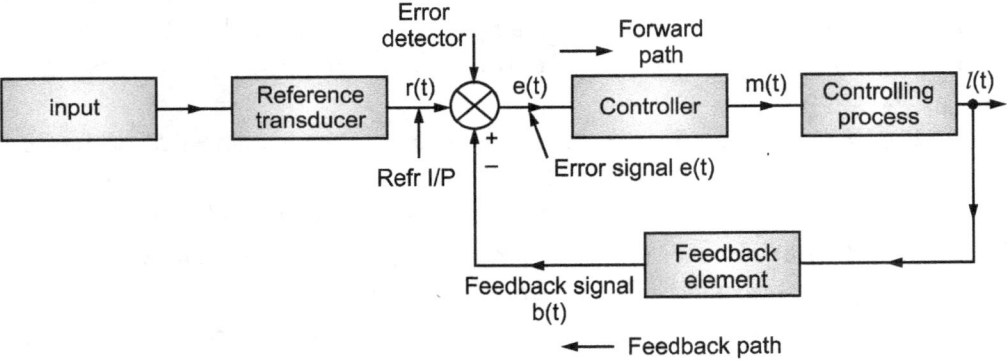

Fig. 1.14

r(t) = Reference input

e(t) = Error signal

c(t) = Controlled output

m(t) = Manipulated signal

b(t) = Feedback signal

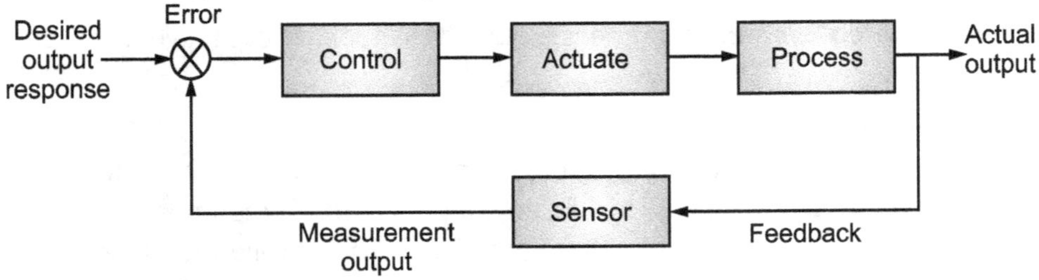

Fig. 1.15 : Closed loop feedback control system (with feedback)

Examples : Most modern appliances and machinery are equipped with closed loop control systems. Air conditioners, refrigerators, automatic ticketing machines, etc.

Advantages of Closed Loop Control System

- Closed loop control systems are more accurate even in the presence of non-linearity.
- Highly accurate as any error arising is corrected due to presence of feedback signal.
- Bandwidth range is large.
- Facilitates automation.
- The sensitivity of system may be made small to make system more stable.
- This system is less affected by noise.

Disadvantages of Closed Loop Control System

- They are costlier.
- They are complicated to design.
- Required more maintenance.
- Feedback leads to oscillatory response.
- Overall gain is reduced due to presence of feedback.
- Stability is the major problem and more care is needed to design a stable closed loop system.

Practical Examples of Closed Loop Control System

- **Automatic Electric Iron :** Heating elements are controlled by output temperature of the iron.
- **Servo Voltage Stabilizer :** Voltage controller operates depending upon output voltage of the system.
- **Water Level Controller :** Input water is controlled by water level of the reservoir.
- **Missile Launched and Auto Tracked by Radar :** The direction of missile is controlled by comparing the target and position of the missile.
- **Cooling System in Car :** It operates depending upon the temperature which it controls.
- **TV Remote Control :** It is operated by human hands which are controlled by Brain.
- **Air Conditioner :** An air conditioner, for example, uses a thermostat to detect the temperature and control the operation of its electrical parts to keep the room temperature at a present constant.

Fig. 1.16 shows the block diagram of the control system of an air conditioner.

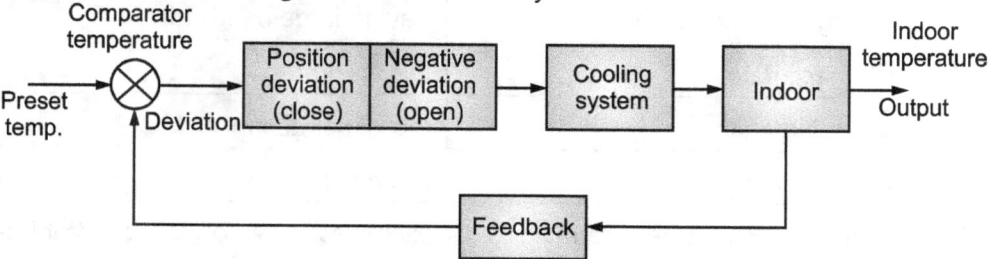

Fig. 1.16 : Block diagram of the control system of an air conditioner

- **Water Level Control System**

The level transmitter is a sensor and the valve acts as a final control element.

The liquid level of the tank can be compared by the desired level (set point) with the present level (controlled variable) which is measured by level sensor.

If there is any difference (error) between set point and controlled variable, the controller takes the necessary action to increase or decrease the value opening.

Fig. 1.17 shows the block diagram of the Water Level Control System

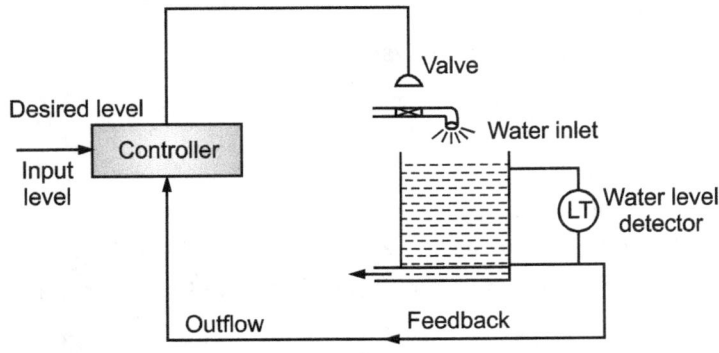

Fig. 1.17

Comparison of Closed Loop and Open Loop Control System

Sr. No.	Open Loop Control System	Closed Loop Control System
1	The feedback element is absent.	The feedback element is always present.
2	An error detector is not present.	An error detector is always present.
3	It is stable one.	It may become unstable.
4	Easy to construct.	Complicated construction.
5	It is an economical.	It is costly.
6	Having small bandwidth.	Having large bandwidth.
7	It is inaccurate.	It is accurate.
8	Less maintenance.	More maintenance.
9	It is unreliable.	It is reliable.
10	Examples : Hand drier, tea maker	Examples : Servo voltage stabilizer, perspiration

1.4 FEEDBACK CONTROL SYSTEMS

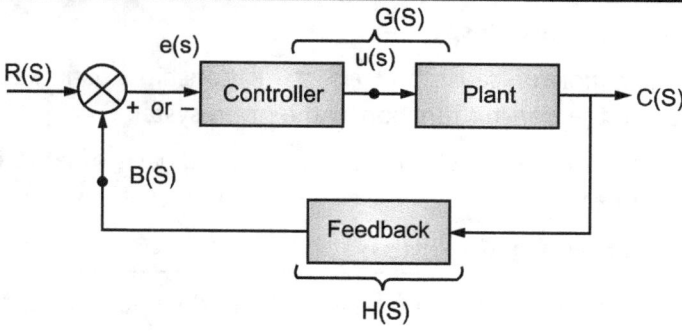

Fig. 1.18

where   R(s) = L.T. of reference input

C(s) = L.T. of reference controlled output

e(s) = Error signal

U(s) = Manipulated control system

B(s) = Feedback signal

G(s) = Forward path transfer function

H(s) = Feedback path transfer function

If,   B(s) is Positive – Positive feedback system

B(s) is Negative – Negative feedback system

UFSC : (Unity Feedback Control System)

If phase of input and output are same; unit feedback.

Example : Voltage stabilizer (input is voltage and output is voltage) (input and output units are same).

NUFCS (Non-unity Feedback Control System) : If phase is not same non unity feedback.

Example : Heater input voltage and output is temperature.

Positive (+ve) Feedback Characteristics :

• High gain system.

• Low BW system.

• Makes system oscillatory.

• Make system unstable.

Negative (–ve) Feedback Characteristics :

• Low gain system.

• High BW system.

• Make system stable.

• Make system less oscillatory.

1.5 DIFFERENTIAL EQUATIONS AND TRANSFER FUNCTION

Transfer Function and Impulse Response :

The mathematical indication of cause and effect relationship existing between input and output means to decide the transfer function of the given system.

In control system theory transfer function is defined on the basis of laplace transform which helps to analysis system easy.

1.5.1 Concept of Transfer Function

In any system, first system parameters are designed and their values are selected as per the requirement.

The input is selected next, to see the performance of the designed system, as seen in Fig. 1.19 below.

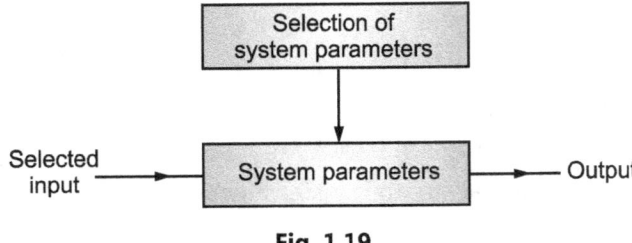

Fig. 1.19

Performance of a system is expressed in terms of its output as;

Output = Effect of system parameters on the selected input

∴   Output = Input × Effect of system parameters

∴   Effect of system parameters = $\dfrac{\text{Output}}{\text{Input}}$

Mathematically, such a function explaining the effect of system parameters on input to produce output is called transfer function.

Definition : Transfer function is defined as the ratio of Laplace transform of output to the laplace transform of input under the assumption that all initial conditions are zero.

Transfer function = $T(s) = \dfrac{C(s)}{R(s)}$

Symbolically system can be represented as;

Fig. 1.20

1.5.2 Transfer Function of Control System

Let us consider transfer function of feedback system as;

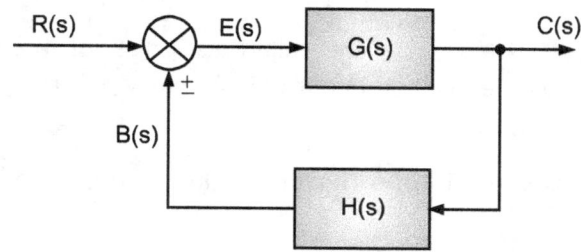

Fig. 1.21

$$C(s) = (R(s) \pm B(s)) \cdot G(s)$$

$$C(s) = [R(s) \pm H(s) \cdot C(s)] \cdot G(s)$$

$$\therefore \quad C(s) + G(s) \cdot H(s) \, C(s) = R(s) \cdot G(s)$$

$$\therefore \quad C(s) \, [1 \pm G(s) \cdot H(s)] = R(s) \cdot G(s)$$

$$\therefore \qquad \frac{C(s)}{R(s)} = \frac{G(s)}{1 \pm G(s) \cdot H(s)}$$

$$T(s) = \frac{C(s)}{R(s)} = \frac{G(s)}{1 \pm G(s) \cdot H(s)}$$

Keynote :

$$+ \rightarrow \text{Positive f/b}$$

$$- \rightarrow \text{Negative f/b}$$

is called closed loop transfer function of a system, while $G(s) \cdot H(s)$ is called open loop transfer function of closed loop system, or $1 \pm G(s) \cdot H(s)$ is called characteristic equation.

where, $G(s)$ is called forward path transfer function and $H(s)$ is called feedback transfer function.

Generally, transfer function is in polynomial form, which is mathematically expressed as;

$$T(s) = \frac{a_0 s^m + a_1 s^{m-1} + a_2 s^{m-2} + \dots a_m}{b_0 s^n + b_1 s^{n-1} + b_2 s^{n-2} + \dots b_n}$$

$$= k \cdot \frac{(s - s_a)(s - s_b)(s - s_c) \dots (s - s_m)}{(s - s_1)(s - s_2)(s - s_3) \dots \dots (s - s_n)}$$

$$= k \cdot \frac{(s - a_1)(s - a_2)(s - a_3) \dots (s - a_m)}{(s - b_1)(s - b_2)(s - b_3) \dots (s - b_n)}$$

where k is called gain factor.

Poles of Transfer Function :

The value of 's' that makes the transfer function value infinite is called poles of that transfer function.

For above equation, s_1, s_2, s_3, ...s_n are called as poles of the transfer function or (b_1, b_2, b_3, ...b_n) are called poles. Denominator polynomial = poles.

Zeros of a Transfer Function :

The value of 's' that makes the transfer function value zero is called zero of that transfer function.

Transfer function shows flow of signals through a system, from input to output.

For the above equation s_a, s_b, s_c ... s_m are called as zeros of the transfer function or (a_1, a_2, a_3, ...a_n are called zero).

Characteristic Equation of a Transfer Function :

Equating denominator equation of transfer function to zero is called characteristic equation of that system.

$$1 \pm G(s) \cdot H(s) = 0$$

Complete information is in denominator.

$$T(s) = \frac{G(s)}{1 \pm G(s) \cdot H(s)}$$

Complete behaviour is dominated by denominator.

Roots of characteristic equation are poles of transfer function.

Keynote :

Transfer function shows flow of signal through a system, from input to output.

1.5.3 Advantages

- It gives mathematical mode of the system.
- Laplace transform approach avoids integral differential time domain.
- 'S' variable simplify equation in simple algebraic equations.
- Once transfer function is known, one can compute stability and response of the system.
- Different equations can be obtain easily by replacing 'S' by $\frac{d}{dt}$.

1.5.4 Disadvantages

- Applicable to linear time invariant systems only.
- Effect arising due to initial condition is totally neglected.
- Does not provide information regarding physically structure of the system.

1.5.5 Procedure to Determine the Transfer Function of a Control System

- Write down the time domain equations for the system by introducing different variables in the system.

- Take laplace transform of the system equations assuming all initial condition to be zero.

- Identify system input and output variables.

- Eliminating introduced variables, get the resultant equations in terms of input and output variables.

- Take the ratio of laplace transform of output variables to get the transfer function model of the system.

SOLVED EXAMPLES

Example 1.1 : Find out the transfer function of the given network

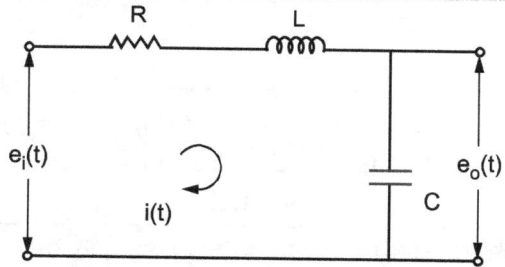

Fig. 1.22

Solution : Applying KVL, we get the equation as;

$$E_i = iR + L\frac{di}{dt} + \frac{1}{C}\int i\, dt \qquad \qquad ...(1.1)$$

$$\text{Input} = E_i; \quad \text{Output} = E_0$$

Laplace transform of $\int f(t)\, dt = \frac{F(s)}{s}$

and Laplace transform of $\frac{df(t)}{dt} = s.F(s)$

Taking Laplace transform of equation (1.1)

$$\therefore \qquad E_i\,(s) = I(s)\left[R + sL + \frac{1}{sC}\right] \qquad \qquad ...(1.2)$$

$$\text{or} = R.I\,(s) + sL \cdot I(s) + \frac{1}{sC}\,I(s)$$

$$\therefore \qquad E_0(s) = \frac{1}{C}\int i\, dt$$

$\therefore$ $\qquad E_0(s) = \dfrac{1}{sC} \cdot I(s)$

$\therefore$ $\qquad I(s) = sC \cdot E_o(s)$ $\qquad \qquad \qquad$ ...(1.3)

Substitute value of I(s) in equation (1.2)

$\therefore$ $\qquad E_i(s) = sC\, E_0(s) \left[R + sL + \dfrac{1}{sC} \right]$

Now, $\qquad \dfrac{E_i(s)}{E_o(s)} = sC \left[R + sL + \dfrac{1}{sC} \right]$

But transfer function $= \dfrac{E_0(s)}{E_i(s)}$

$\therefore$ $\qquad \dfrac{E_o(s)}{E_i(s)} = \dfrac{1}{sC \left[R + sL + \dfrac{1}{sC} \right]}$

$\qquad \left[\dfrac{E_o(s)}{E_i(s)} \right] = \dfrac{1}{RsC + s^2LC + 1}$

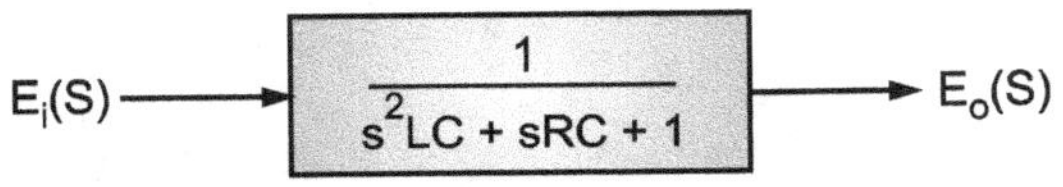

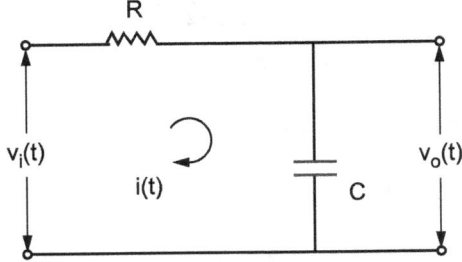

$E_i(S) \longrightarrow \boxed{\dfrac{1}{s^2LC + sRC + 1}} \longrightarrow E_o(S)$

Fig. 1.23

Example 1.2 : Find out the transfer function of the given network

Fig. 1.24

Solution : We can write time domain equation for system, by applying KVL as,

$$V_i(t) = R \cdot i(t) + \dfrac{1}{C} \int i(t) \cdot dt \qquad \qquad \text{...(1.4)}$$

and $\qquad V_o(t) = \dfrac{1}{C} \int i\,(t)\, dt$ $\qquad \qquad \qquad$ ...(1.5)

Taking Laplace transform of above two equation and neglecting initial condition zero,

We can write , $\qquad V_i(s) = R.I(s) + \dfrac{1}{sC} I(s)$ $\qquad \qquad$ ...(1.6)

$$V_o(s) = \frac{1}{sC} I(s) \qquad\qquad ...(1.7)$$

$$\therefore \qquad I(s) = sC \cdot V_o(s)$$

Substituting value of I(s) in equation (1.6)

$$\therefore \qquad V_i(s) = I(s)\left[R + \frac{1}{sC}\right]$$

$$V_i(s) = sC \cdot V_o(s)\left[R + \frac{1}{sC}\right]$$

$$\therefore \qquad \frac{V_i(s)}{V_0(s)} = \frac{1}{sC\left[R + \frac{1}{sC}\right]}$$

$$\frac{V_i(s)}{V_0(s)} = \frac{1}{sCR + 1}$$

$$V_i(s) \longrightarrow \boxed{\frac{1}{1 + sRC}} \longrightarrow V_o(s)$$

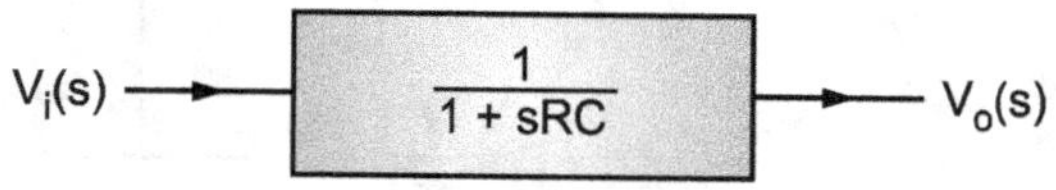

Fig. 1.25

Example 1.3 : Find the transfer function $\frac{C(s)}{R(s)}$ of a system having differential equation given below :

$$\frac{2d^2c(t)}{dt^2} + \frac{2dc(t)}{dt} + c(t) = r(t) + 2r(t-1)$$

Solution : Taking laplace transform of the given equation and assuming all initial conditions zero, we get

$$2s^2(s) + 2s(s) + C(s) = R(s) + 2e^{-s}R(s)$$

Laplace transform of delayed function is;

$$L\{f(t-T)\} = e^{-sT} F(s)$$

$$\therefore \qquad L\{r(t-1)\} = e^{-s.1} \cdot R(s)$$

Combining terms of C(s) and R(s) we get

$$(2s^s + 2s + 1) \cdot C(s) = R(s)(1 + 2e^{-s})$$

$$\therefore \qquad \frac{C(s)}{R(s)} = \frac{1 + 2e^{-s}}{2s^2 + 2s + 1}$$

Example 1.4 : Derive the transfer function of the system

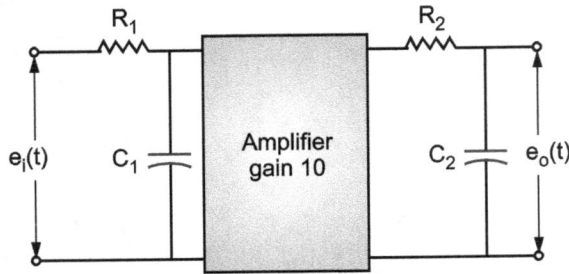

Fig. 1.26

Solution : Taking laplace transform of the network

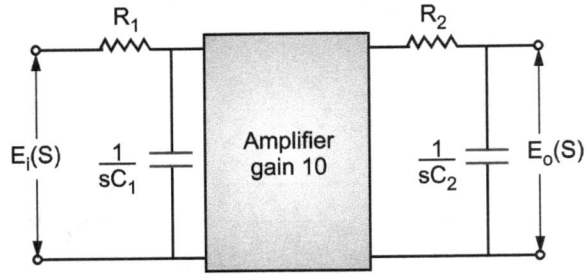

Fig. 1.27

Divide the network into two parts,

$$E_i(s) = I(s) \cdot R_1 + \frac{1}{sC_1} I(s)$$

$$= I(s) \left[R_1 + \frac{1}{sC_1} \right]$$

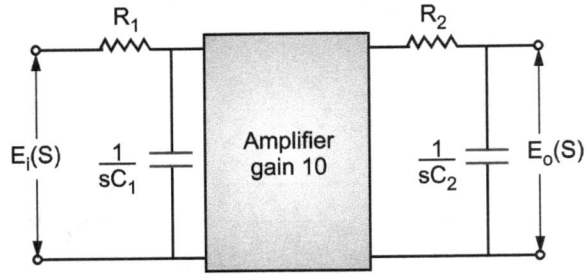

Fig. 1.28

But $\qquad V_1(s) = \dfrac{1}{sC_1} I(s)$

$\therefore \qquad I(s) = V_1(s) \cdot (sC_1)$

$\therefore \qquad E_i(s) = V_i(s) (sC_1) \left[R_1 + \dfrac{1}{sC_1} \right]$

$\therefore$ $\dfrac{V_i(s)}{E_i(s)} = \dfrac{1}{R_1Cs + 1}$

or $V_i(s) = \dfrac{E_i(s)}{R_1C_1s + 1}$

Part 2 :

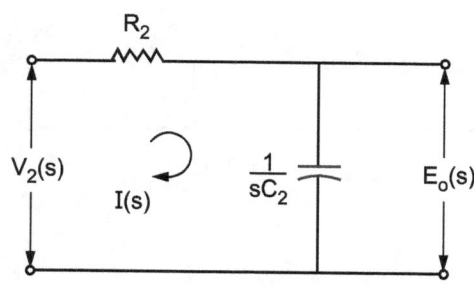

Fig. 1.29

$$V_2(s) = \left(R_2 + \dfrac{1}{sC_2}\right) I(s)$$

$$E_0(s) = \dfrac{1}{sC_2} \cdot I(s)$$

$\therefore$ $I(s) = E_0(s) \cdot (sC_2)$

$\therefore$ $V_2(s) = E_0(s) \cdot (sC_2) \cdot \left(R_2 + \dfrac{1}{sC_2}\right)$

$\therefore$ $\dfrac{E_0(s)}{V_2(s)} = \dfrac{1}{s_1C_2R_2 + 1}$

Amplifier gain = 10 ; hence $V_2(s) = 10\, V_1(s)$

$\therefore$ $E_0(s) \cdot (sR_2C_2 + 1) = 10V_1(s) = \dfrac{10\, E_i(s)}{(sR_1C_1 + 1)}$

$\therefore$ $\dfrac{E_0(s)}{E_i(s)} = \dfrac{10}{(1 + sR_1C_1)\,(1 + sR_2C_2)}$

Example 1.5 : Derive the $\dfrac{V_i(s)}{I(s)}$ and $\dfrac{V_0(s)}{I(s)}$ for the circuit shown in Fig. 1.30 below

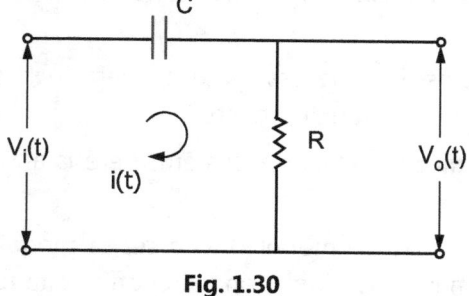

Fig. 1.30

Solution : The s-domain network of the given circuit is shown in Fig. 1.31.

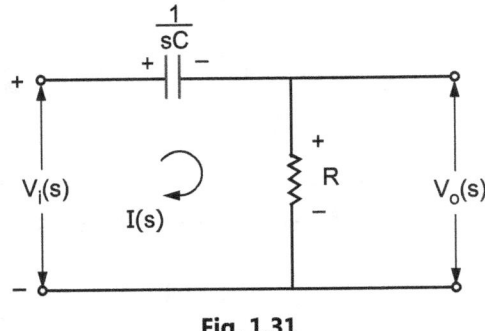

Fig. 1.31

Applying KVL to the loop

$$-\frac{1}{sC} I(s) - I(s) \cdot R + V_i(s) = 0$$

$$\therefore \qquad V_i(s) = I(s)\left[\frac{1}{sC} + R\right]$$

$$\therefore \qquad \frac{V_i(s)}{I(s)} = \left[\frac{1}{sC} + R\right] = \frac{1 + sCR}{sC}$$

and $\qquad V_0(s) = I(s) \cdot R$; i.e. $\dfrac{V_0(s)}{I(s)} = R$

1.6 MATHEMATICAL MODELLING OF CONTROL SYSTEMS

Mathematical Model : Mathematical representation of the physical model through use of appropriate physical laws.

Depending upon the choice of variables and the co-ordinate system, a given physical model may lead to different mathematical models.

Definition : The set of mathematical equations, describing the dynamic characteristic of a system is called mathematical model of the system.

- Obtaining mathematical model is the first step in analyzing a given system.
- Most of the control systems contain mechanical or electrical or both types of elements and components.
- To analyses such systems, it is necessary to convert such systems into mathematical models based on transfer function approach.
- We can show that for given mechanical system there is always an analogous electrical network and vice versa.
- A network, for example, may be modeled as a set of modal equations using Kirchoff's current law or a set of mesh equations using kirchoff's voltage law. A control system may

be a modeled as a scalar differential equation describing the system or state variable vector-matrix differential equation.

- The particular mathematical model which gives a greater insight into the dynamic behaviour of physical system is selected.

1.6.1 Analysis of Mechanical Systems

Mechanical systems and devices can be modeled by means of three ideal translatory and three ideal rotary elements.

In case of mass/inertia elements it may be noted that one terminal is always the inertial reference frame with respect to which the free terminal moves / rotates.

1.6.1.1 Translation Motion

A mechanical system in which motion is taking place along a straight line.

The following elements are dominantly involved in the analysis of translational motion systems.

(i) Mass (ii) Spring / elasticity (iii) Friction / Damper / Dashpot

> **Keynote :**
> - **Kinetic Energy :** Energy poessed by a body by virtue of its moment.
> - **Potential Energy :** By virtue of its positive.

1. Mass : This is the property of the system itself which stores the kinetic energy of the translational motion.

Mass cannot store potential energy; so there cannot be consumption of force in the mass.

The displacement of mass always takes place in direction of the applied force results in inertial force. This force is always proportional to the acceleration produced in mass (M) by the applied force.

Consider a mass 'M' as shown in Fig. 1.32 having zero friction with surface shown by rollers.

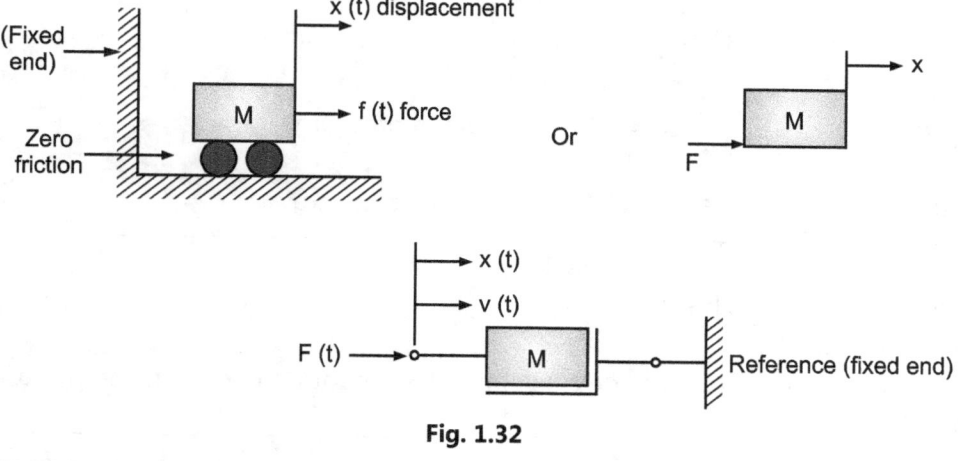

Fig. 1.32

The applied force f(t) produces displacement x (t) in the direction of the applied force f (t).
Force required for the same is proportional to acceleration.

$\therefore$ $\qquad$ f(t) $=$ M $\times$ Acceleration

$$f(t) = M \frac{d^2x(t)}{dt^2}$$

Taking laplace and neglecting initial conditions

$$f(s) = MS^2 x(s)$$

Consider two masses directly connected.

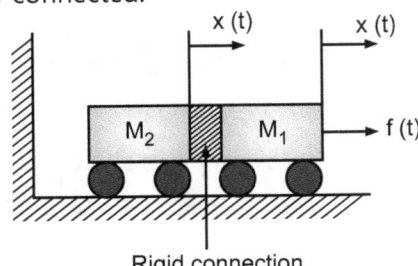

Rigid connection
(No friction and no elastic action)

Fig. 1.33

If force f(t) is applied to mass M_1 then M_2 will also displaced by same amount as M_1.

Due to mass, there cannot be any change in force from one mass to another hence no change in displacement.

Keynote :

Displacement of rigidly connected masses is always same.

Note : Mass/Inertia and the two kinds of springs are the energy storage elements where in energy can be stored and retrieved without loss and so these are called conservative elements. Energy stored in these elements is expressed as :

Mass : $\qquad$ $E = \left(\frac{1}{2}\right) Mv^2$ = K.E. (J) ; motional energy

Inertial : $\qquad$ $E = \left(\frac{1}{2}\right) JW^2$ = K.E. (J) ; motional energy

Spring (translatory) : $E = \frac{1}{2} kx^2$ = P.E. (J) ; deformation energy

Spring (torsional) : $\quad$ $E = \frac{1}{2} k\theta^2$ = P.E. (J) ; deformation energy

---

Keynote :

Mass does not store PE : It stores KE.

Spring Stores PE

Mass and spring are energy storage elements and dashpot/damper is an energy absorbing element.

---

2. Linear Spring : The spring behaves as a linear mechanical device. It stores energy during the variation of its shape due to elastic deformation resulting from the application of force.

When a force 'F' is applied to the spring, a restoring force f_k is produced, as shown in Fig. 1.34.

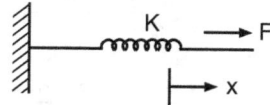

Fig. 1.34 : A fixed spring fixed at one end

This force depends upon the stiffness constant k of the spring and the displacement x.

The force is given by;

$$f_k = kx \qquad \qquad ...(1.8)$$

The force required to cause the displacement is proportional to the net displacement in the spring.

$$F = f_x$$

∴ $$F = kx$$

In equation (1.8) f_x = force in Newton

K = Stiffness constant (N/m)

x = Displacement in m.

Now consider the spring connected between the two moving elements having masses M_1 and M_2 as shown in Fig. 1.35 below

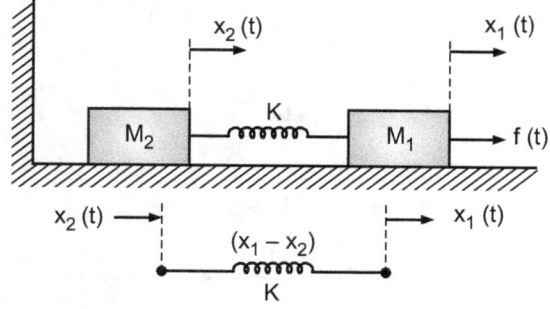

Fig. 1.35 : A spring with displacement at both ends

Mass M_1 will get displaced by $x_1(t)$ but mass M_2 will get displaced by $x_2(t)$ as spring of constant k will store some potential energy and will be the cause for change in displacement.

From Newton's law,

$$F = f_k$$

∴ $$F = k(x_1 - x_2)$$

or $\qquad$ $F_{spring} = k\,[x_1(t) - x_2(t)]$

or $\qquad$ $F_{spring} = k\,[x_1(s) - x_2(s)]$

Keynote :

Friction : Force resisting the relative motion of solid surfaces and materials sliding against each other.

The spring between the moving points causes a displacement from one point to another.

3. **Damper / Friction / Dashpot :** Dash-pot is an energy absorbing element. Whenever there is a motion, there exists a friction. Friction may be between moving element and fixed support or between two moving surfaces.

The friction is generally shown by a dash-pot or a damper, as in Fig. 1.36 below

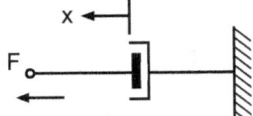

Fig. 1.36 : A damper (one end fixed)

The force of friction is opposite to direction of motion.

Consider a mass M as shown in the Fig. 1.37 below having friction with a support with a constant 'B' represented by a damper.

Friction will oppose the motion of mass M and opposing force is proportional to velocity of mass M.

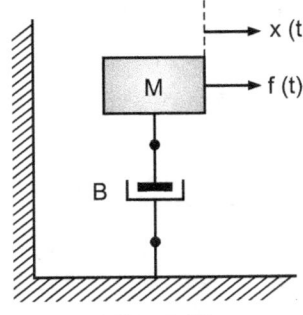

Fig. 1.37

Keynote :

In mass it was applied force F = ma. In spring it was a restoring force $F = f_k$.

In friction it is opposing force $F = f_b$ proportional to the velocity.

$\qquad$ $F_{frictional} = f_b$

$\qquad$ $F_{frictional} = \dfrac{B \cdot dx\,(t)}{dt}$

Taking laplace and neglecting initial conditions,

$\qquad$ $F_{frictional} = Bs\,x(s)$

Similarly, if friction is between two moving surfaces, it is shown in following Fig. 1.38.

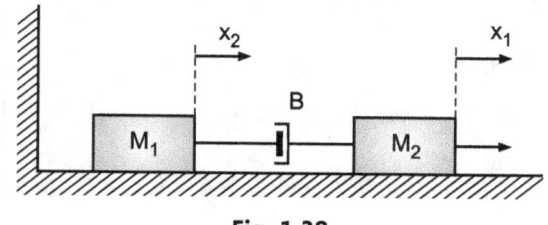

Fig. 1.38

In such case, opposing force is given by,

$$F_{frictional} = B\left[\frac{dx_1(t)}{dt} - \frac{dx_2(t)}{dt}\right]$$

Taking laplace,

$$F_{frictional}(s) = BS[x_1(s) - x_2(s)]$$

Keynote :

The friction between two moving points, cause a change in displacement from one point to another.

1.6.1.2 Rotational Motion

This is the motion about a fixed axis. In such systems, the force gets replaced by a moment about the fixed axis; i.e. (force × distance from fixed axis) which is called torque.

Hence, mechanical rotational systems are similar to translational system except that torque equations are written in place of force equations and the displacement, velocity and acceleration terms are in angular quantity.

Moment of Inertia (J) of mass, rotational friction coefficient of dash-pot (B) and stiffness constant (k) of the spring are the fundamental elements in a rotational system.

1. Mass

The property of a system which stores kinetic energy in rotational system is called Inertia and is denoted by 'J' i.e. moment of inertia.

Keynote :
Rotational motion → spins around an internal axis in a continuous way.

When a torque 'T' is applied to the body as shown in Fig. 1.39 below, it produces an angular acceleration. The reaction torque T_j is equal to product of J and acceleration. That is,

$$T_j = J\frac{d^2\theta}{dt^2} = J\frac{dw}{dt}$$

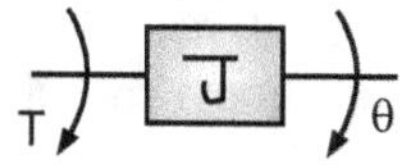

Fig. 1.39 Rotational system

where, $\alpha = \dfrac{d^2\theta}{dt^2}$ = angular acceleration, rad/sec^2

                    J = Moment of Inertia, kg-m^2/rad

                    Q = Angular displacement

                    $w = \dfrac{d\theta}{dt}$ = Angular velocity, rad/sec

                    T_j = Reaction torque, N-m

According to Newton's second law,

                    $T = T_j$

$\therefore$ $T = J\dfrac{d^2\theta}{dt^2}$

Taking Laplace,

                    $T_{due\ to\ inertia} = Js^2\theta(s)$

Keynote :

Torque : A force that tends to cause rotation.

---

2. **Spring :** The elastic deformation of the body can be represented by a spring constant.

When a torque 'T' is applied to a spring as shown in Fig. 1.40 below, it is twisted by an angle θ. The spring will produce an opposing torque 'T_k' which is proportional to angular displacement.

                    $T_k \, \alpha \, \theta$

                    $T_k = k\theta$

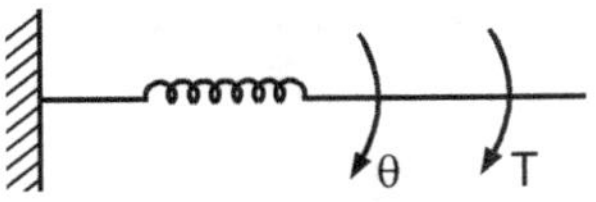

Fig. 1.40 : A spring (fixed at one end)

By Newton's law, $T = T_k$

$\therefore$ $T = K\theta$

For displacement at both ends.

                    $T = K\,(\theta_1 - \theta_2)$

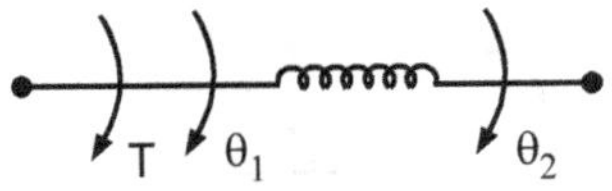

A spring (both ends free)

Fig. 1.41 : A spring (both ends free)

---

3. Damper / Dashpot / Friction : Damper occurs whenever a body moves through a fluid. The damping is represented by a dash-pot with a viscous friction coefficient B.

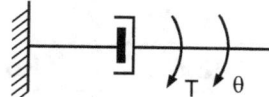

Fig. 1.42 : A dash pot (one end fixed)

$$T_b \; \alpha \; w$$
$$T_b \; = \; Bw$$
$$T \; = \; T_b$$

$\therefore$ $$T \; = \; B \cdot \frac{d\theta}{dt}$$

For both ends free $$T_b \; = \; B \, (w_1 - w_2) \; = \; B\left[\frac{d\theta_1}{dt} - \frac{d\theta_2}{dt}\right]$$

$\therefore$ $$T \; = \; B\left[\frac{d\theta_1}{dt} - \frac{d\theta_2}{dt}\right]$$

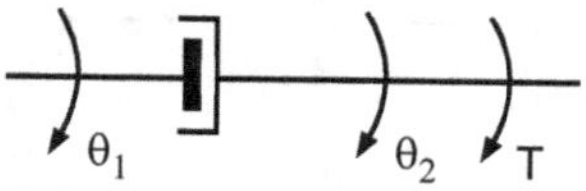

Fig. 1.43 : A dashpot (both ends free)

Variables and parameters of mechanical rotational system.

Table 1.1

Symbol	Quantity	Units
T	Torque	N-m
θ	Angular displacement	radians
ω	Angular velocity	rad/sec
α	Angular acceleration	rad/sec^2
J	Moment of Inertia	kg-m
K	Stiffness constant	N-m/rad
B	Damping Torque	N-m/rad/sec

Various mathematical modeling systems

- Electrical
- Mechanical
- Thermal
- Fluid
- Pneumatic systems
- Hydraulic system

The following Table 1.2 shows the difference between rotational and translational motions of electric and mechanical systems.

Table 1.2

Sr. No.	Translation Motion	Rotational Motion
1.	Mass (M)	Inertia (J)
2.	Friction (B)	Frictional (B)
3.	Spring (k)	Spring (k)
4.	Force (F)	Torque (T)
5.	Displacement (x)	Angular displacement (θ)
6.	Velocity $V = \left(\dfrac{dx}{dt}\right)$	Angular velocity $\left(w = \dfrac{d\theta}{dt}\right)$
7.	Acceleration $= \left(\dfrac{d^2x}{dt^2}\right)$	Angular acceleration $\left(\alpha = \dfrac{d^2\theta}{dt^2}\right)$

Consider a simple mechanical system,

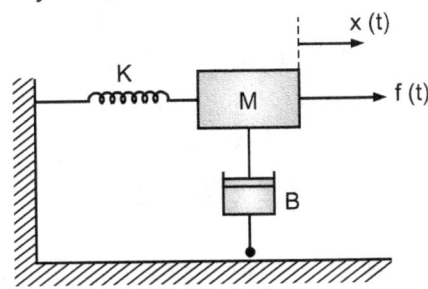

Fig. 1.44

Due to applied force, mass M will displaced by an amount x(t) in the direction of the force f(t) as shown in Fig. 1.44.

According to Newton's law of motion, applied force will cause displacement x(t) in spring, acceleration to mass M against frictional force B.

$\therefore$ $$f(t) = M_a + B_v + Kx(t)$$

$\therefore$ $$f(t) = M \cdot \frac{d^2x(t)}{dt} + B \cdot \frac{dx\,(t)}{dt} + kx\,(t)$$

Taking laplace of above equation

$$F(s) = MS^2x(s) + BS\,x(s) + Kx(s)$$

This is equilibrium equation for the system.

1.6.2 Freebody Diagram

The first step in obtaining mathematical model of a mechanical system is to draw a free body diagram indicating the various forces acting on it. In a free body diagram, each mass is isolated from the rest of the system and the forces acting on the mass that cause displacement, forces opposing the displacement are represented pictorically.

Procedure to Draw Free Body Diagram :

- Assume the direction of displacement of the mass as positive direction.
- Find all the forces with direction acting on the mass.

Example : Force applied in the direction of displacement and opposing forces due to spring, dash-pot and mass are opposite to the direction of displacement.

- Using Newton's laws of motion, express all the forces in terms of displacement or velocity of the mass.

Once the free body diagram is obtained, we can easily write the differential equation by equating the sum of applied forces to the sum of opposing forces.

For example : Consider a mechanical translation system; as shown in Fig. 1.45 below

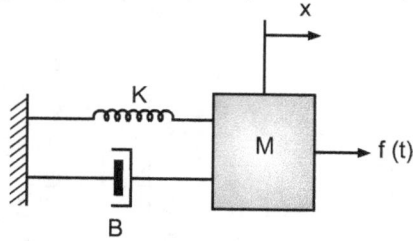

Fig. 1.45

To draw the free body diagram using above steps, we use following procedure .

Step 1 : Consider mass alone from Fig. 1.46.

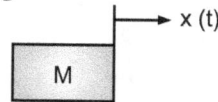

Fig. 1.46 : Free body diagram

Step 2 : The applied force f(t) is in positive direction and the forces due to spring, dash-pot and mass opposes the displacement.

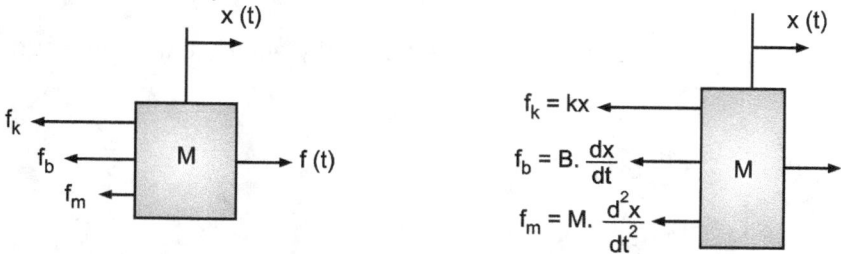

Fig. 1.47 : Free body with forces   **Fig. 1.48 : Forces are function of displacement**

Step 3 : Represent all the forces in terms of displacement as shown in Fig. 1.48.

Using Newton's Law of Motion :

The sum of applied forces, must be equal to the sum of the reactive forces for translational motions.

$$f(t) = M \cdot \frac{d^2x}{dt^2} + B\frac{dx}{dt} + kx \qquad \qquad ...(1.9)$$

The above equation represents the dynamics of the given mechanical system and is called mechanical model of the system.

Taking Laplace transform of equation (1)

$$F(s) = MS^2 x(s) + BS x(s) + K.X (s)$$

This is standard force equilibrium equation for the given system.

1.6.3 Translation Systems

Let us now consider the mechanical system as shown in Fig. 1.49 It is simply a mass M attached to a spring (stiffness k) and a dashpot (viscous friction coefficient f) on which the force F acts.

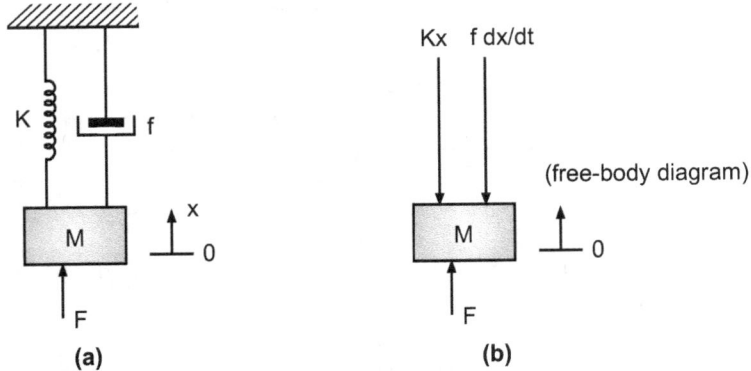

Fig. 1.49

Displacement x is positive in the direction shown. The zero position is taken to be at the point where the spring and mass are in static equilibrium.

The systematic way of analyzing such a system is to draw a free body diagram as shown in Fig. 1.49 (b).

Then by applying Newton's law of motion to the free-body diagram, the force equation can be written as,

$$F - f \cdot \frac{dx}{dt} - kx = M \cdot \frac{d^2x}{dt^2}$$

$$F = M \cdot \frac{d^2x}{dt^2} + f\frac{dx}{dt} + kx$$

Here f is taken as frictional constant instead of B, hence it is $f\frac{dx}{dt}$ instead of $B\frac{dx}{dt}$.

1.6.4 Analogous Systems

The systems for which differential equations have similar form are known as analogous systems.

The basis for applying the principle of analogy is that two different systems represented by equation of the similar form are called analogous.
Hence the dynamic characteristics of analogous systems are identical.

The corresponding variables and parameters in the two systems represented by equations of the similar form are called analogous.

If the mathematical models of two systems are identical, they are said to be analogous.

Example : $F \leftrightarrow V$

$\quad\quad M \leftrightarrow L$

$\quad\quad F \leftrightarrow R$

Using this method of analogy, complex mechanical (or hydraulic) systems can be represented by equivalent circuit diagram for which KCL and KVL can be used to obtain mathematical model of a system.

Steps to Solve Problems on Analogous System :

- Identity all the displacement due to the applied force. The elements spring and friction between two moving surfaces cause change in displacement.

- Draw the equivalent mechanical system based on node basis. The elements under same displacement will get connected in parallel under that node. Element causing change in displacement (either friction or spring) is always connected between the two nodes.

- Write the equilibrium equations. At each node algebraic sum of all the forces acting at the node is zero.

- In F-V analogy, use following replacements and rewrite the equations , $F \to V$, $M \to L$, $B \to R$, $K \to 1/C$, $x \to q$, $\dot{x} \to i$, $x \to \int i\, dt$.

- Simulate the equations using loop method. Number of displacements equal to number of loop currents.

- In F-I analogy, use following replacements $F \to I$, $M \to C$, $B \to 1/R$, $K \to 1/L$, $x \to \phi$, $\dot{x} = e$ (e.m.f.), $x \to \int e\, dt$.

- Simulate the equations using node basic. Number of displacements equal to number of node voltage. Infact the system will be exactly same as equivalent mechanical system obtained in step 2 with appropriate replacements.

Table 1.3 : Tabluar Form of F-V and F-I

Sr. No.	Force-Voltage		Force-Current	
1.	Force	Voltage V	Force	Current I
2.	Mass M	Inductance L	Mass M	C
3.	Frictional constant B	Resistance R	Frictional constant B	1/R
4.	Spring constant k	Recipe of cap 1/c	Spring constant k	1/L
5.	Displacement 'x'	Charge q	Displacement 'x'	$\phi = \int V\, dt$
6.	Velocity $\dot{V} = \dfrac{dx}{dt}$	Current $i = \dfrac{dq}{dt}$	Velocity $\dot{X} = \dfrac{dx}{dt}$	$'e' = \dfrac{d\phi}{dt}$

There are two methods of obtaining electrical analogous networks, namely

1. Force-voltage analogy i.e. Direct Analogy

2. Force-Current Analogy i.e. Inverse Analogy

1.6.4.1 Force Voltage Analogy (Loop Analysis)

In this method, to force in mechanical system, voltage is assumed to be analogous one.

Accordingly other analogous terms can be derived as;

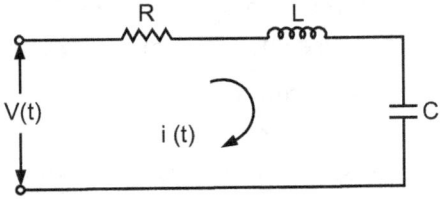

Fig. 1.50

Consider the above electrical network, applying Kirchoff's law, we can write equation as

$$v(t) = R \cdot i(t) + L \cdot \frac{di(t)}{dt} + \frac{1}{c} \int i(t)\, dt \qquad \qquad ...(1.10)$$

Taking laplace,

$$V(s) = I(s) \cdot R + L.S.I(s) + \frac{1}{CS} \cdot I(s) \qquad \qquad ...(1.11)$$

But we cannot compare force and voltage unless we bring them in a same form.

For this we will use current as rate of flow of charge.

$$\therefore \qquad i(t) = \frac{dq}{dt}$$

i.e. $\qquad I(s) = S.Q(s)$ ... Taking Laplace Transform

or $\qquad Q(s) = \dfrac{I(s)}{s}$

Replacing in above equation (2)

$$V(s) = LS^2Q(s) + RSQ(s) + \frac{1}{C}Q(s)$$

Comparing equations for F(s) and V(s); it is clear that

(i) Inductance 'L' is analogous to Mass M.

(ii) Resistance 'R' is analogous to friction B.

(iii) Reciprocal of capacitor i.e. 1/C is analogous to spring of constant k.

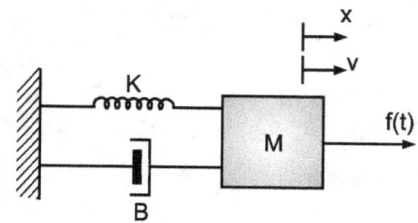

Fig. 1.51 : Analogous mechanical system

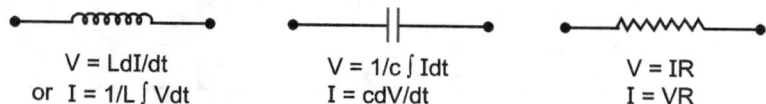

| V = LdI/dt | V = 1/c ∫ Idt | V = IR |
| or I = 1/L ∫ Vdt | I = cdV/dt | I = VR |

1.6.4.2 Force Current Analogy (Node Analysis)

In this system, current is treated as analogous quantity to force in the mechanical system. So, force is replaced by a current source in a system.

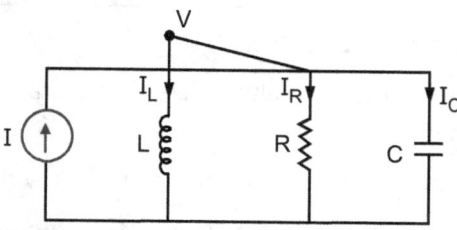

Fig. 1.52

The equation according to kirchoff's current law for the above system is,

$$I = I_L + I_R + I_C$$

Let node voltage be V

$\therefore \qquad\qquad I = \dfrac{1}{L}\int V\,dt + \dfrac{V}{R} + C\dfrac{dv}{dt}$ $\qquad\qquad\qquad$ ...(1.12)

Taking lapalce,

$$\therefore \qquad I(s) = \frac{V(s)}{SL} + \frac{V(s)}{R} + SC.V(s) \qquad\qquad ...(1.13)$$

But to get this equation in similar form as that of F(s), we will use

$$v(t) = \frac{d\phi}{dt}; \phi = \text{flux}.$$

$$\therefore \qquad V(s) = S.\phi(s)$$

$$\therefore \text{ i.e.} \qquad \phi(s) = \frac{V(s)}{S}$$

$$I(s) = CS^2\phi(s) + \frac{1}{R}S\cdot\phi(s) + \frac{1}{L}\phi(s)$$

Comparing equations for F(s) and I(s)

$$F(s) = MS^2 x(s) + BS x(s) + Kx(s)$$

(i)   Capacitor C is analogous to mass M

(ii) Reciprocal of resistance $\frac{1}{R}$ is analogous to frictional constant B.

(iii) $\frac{1}{L}$ is analogous to spring constant K.

Keynote :

The elements which are in series in F-V, analog, get connected in parallel in F-I analogous network and which are in parallel in F-V analogy, get connected in series in F-I analogous network.

Equivalent Mechanical Systems (Node Basis) :

While drawing analogous networks, it is always better to draw the equivalent mechanical system from the given mechanical system.

To draw such systems from the given mechanical system follow the steps below

Step 1 : Due to applied force, identify the displacements in the mechanical system.

Step 2 : Identify the elements which are under the different displacement.

Step 3 : Represent each displacement by a separate node, using Nodal analysis.

Step 4 : Show all the elements in parallel under the respective nodes which are under the influence of respective displacements.

Step 5 : Elements causing same change in displacement will get connected in parallel in between the respective nodes.

Important Remarks on Nodal Method :

(a) The terms for an element connected to a node 'x' and stationary surface (reference) is,

For mass $\rightarrow M \dfrac{d^2x}{dt^2}$

For spring $\rightarrow kx$

For friction $\rightarrow B \dfrac{dx}{dt}$

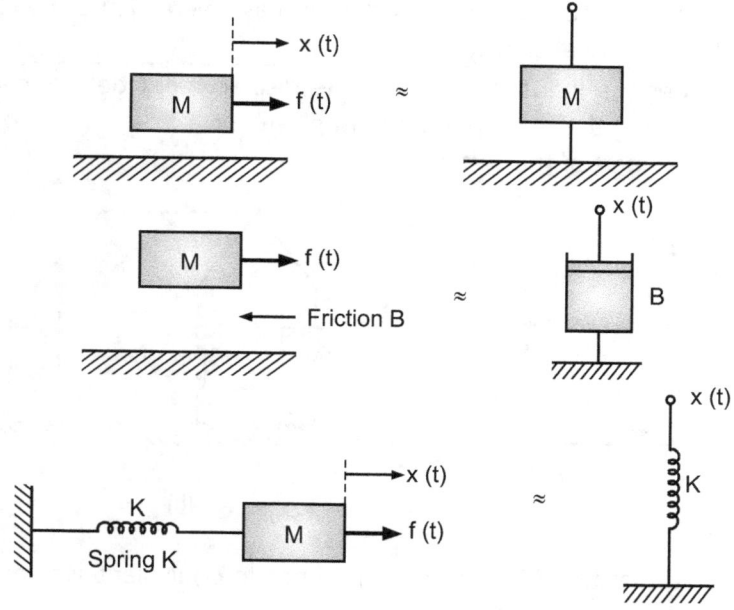

Fig. 1.53

(b) The term for an element connected between the two nodes 'x_1;' and 'x_2' i.e. between two moving surfaces is,

For friction $\rightarrow B \left[\dfrac{dx_1}{dt} - \dfrac{dx_2}{dt}\right]$

For spring $\rightarrow K [x_1 - x_2]$

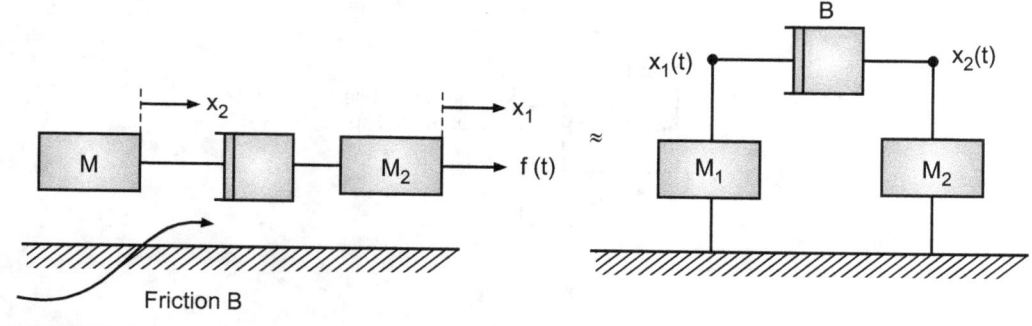

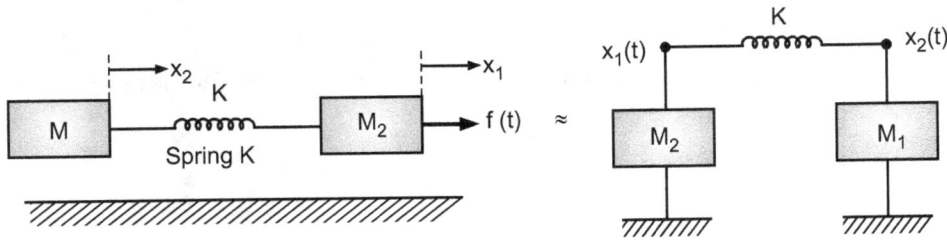

Fig. 1.54

Keynote :
No mass can be between the two nodes as due to mass there cannot be change in force as mass cannot store potential energy.

All the elements under the influence of the same displacement get connected in parallel under that node indicating the corresponding disaplcement.

Example : Consider the part of the system.

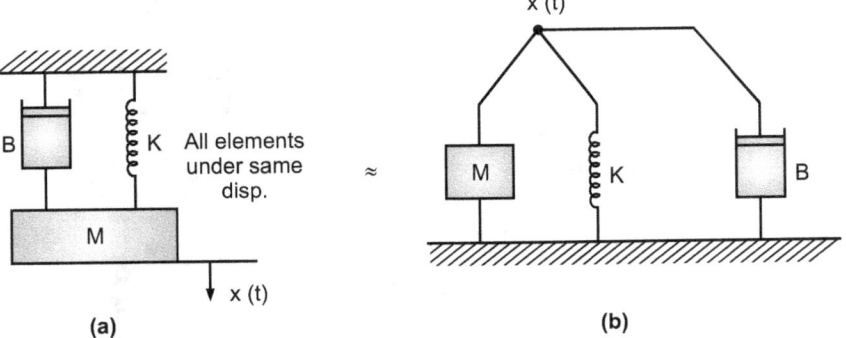

Fig. 1.55

Here M, K, B are all under the influence of $x(t)$. Hence in equivalent system all of them will get connected in parallel, under node x.

Consider another example, Fig. 1.56 below

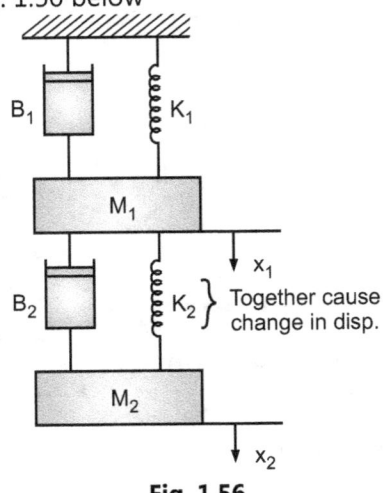

Fig. 1.56

In this system M_1, B_1,K_1 all are under the influence of displacement x_1. This is because all are connected to rigid support.

While there is a change from x_1 to x_2 due to simultaneous effect of B_1 and K_2. So B_2 and K_2 are under the influence of $(x_1 - x_2)$.

But mass M_2 is under the influence of x_2 alone. So the equivalent system can be shown below;

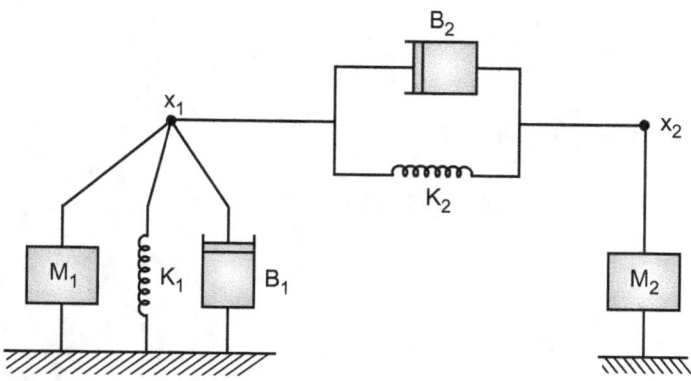

Fig. 1.57

1.6.5 Electrical Systems

The bahaviour of electrical systems is governed by Ohm's law. The dominant elements of an electrical system are,

(i) Resistor (ii) Inductor (iii) Capacitor

(i) Resistor : Resistance carrying current 'I' as shown, then the voltage drop across it can be written as,

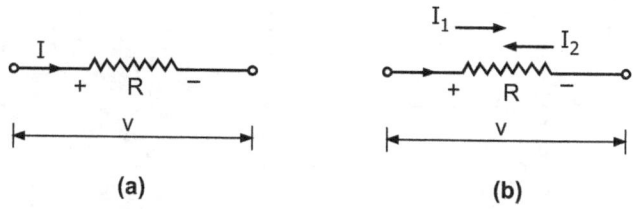

(a)   (b)

Fig. 1.58

Suppose that is carries a current $(I_1 - I_2)$ then for the polarity of the voltage drop shown its equation is,

$$V = (I_1 - I_2) R$$

(ii) Inductor : Consider a inductor carrying a current 'I' then voltage drop across it;

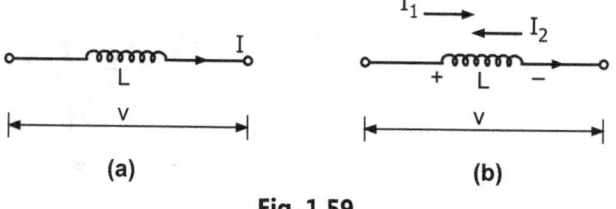

(a)   (b)

Fig. 1.59

$$V = L\frac{dI}{dt} \text{ or}$$

$$I = \frac{1}{L}\int V dt$$

For current $(I_1 - I_2)$ then,

$$V = L\frac{d(I_1 - I_2)}{dt}$$

or $\qquad (I_1 - I_2) = \frac{1}{L}\int V\, dt$

(iii) Capacitor : Voltage drop across a capacitor.

$$V = \frac{1}{C}\int I\, dt$$

$$I = C\frac{dv}{dt}$$

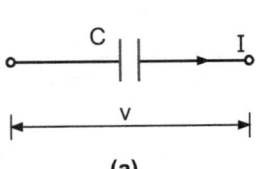   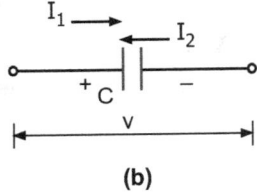

(a)   (b)

Fig. 1.60

For current $(I_1 - I_2)$ then

$$V = \frac{1}{C}\int (I_1 - I_2)\, dt$$

or $\qquad (I_1 - I_2) = C\frac{dv}{dt}$

Modelling of Electrical Systems :

Consider the electrical system as shown in Fig. 1.61 Let the current through the circuit is i.

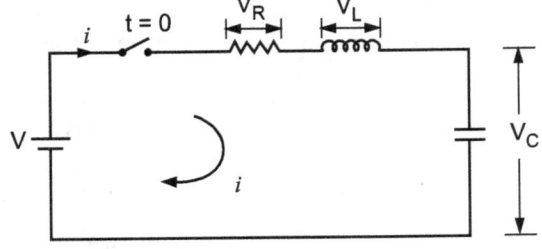

Fig. 1.61

Applying KVL, $V = V_R + V_L + V_C$

$$= R_i + L\frac{di}{dt} + \frac{1}{C}\int i \, dt \qquad\qquad ...(1.14)$$

Equation (1.14) is the mathematical model of electrical system. Taking laplace on both sides,

$$V(s) = R.I(s) + L.SI\,(s) + \frac{1}{CS}I(s)$$

$\therefore$ $$\frac{V_C(s)}{V(s)} = \frac{1}{L^2CS^2 + SCR + 1}$$

Example 1.6 : Obtain the differential equation of mechanical system. Draw the electrical analogous circuit based on force current analogy.

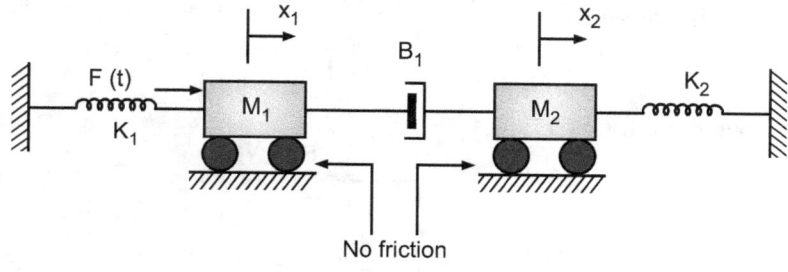

Fig. 1.62

Solution : The free body diagram of mass M_1 from above diagram.

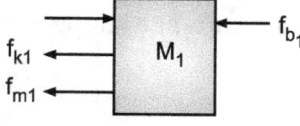

Fig. 1.63

where $f_{k1} = k_1 x_1$

$$f_{m1} = M_1\frac{d^2x}{dt^2}$$

$$f_{b1} = B_1\left[\frac{dx_1}{dt} - \frac{dx_2}{dt}\right]$$

The force balance equation for mass M_1 is,

$$F(t) = f_{k1} + f_{m1} + f_{b1}$$

$$= k_1 x_1 + M_1\frac{d^2x_1}{dt^2} + B_1\left[\frac{dx_1}{dt} - \frac{dx_2}{dt}\right] \qquad ...(1.15)$$

Now the free body diagram for mass M_2, the force balance equation for mass M_2

$$M_2\frac{d^2x_2}{dt^2} + B_1\left[\frac{dx_2}{dt} - \frac{dx_1}{dt}\right] + k_2 x_2 = 0 \qquad ...(1.16)$$

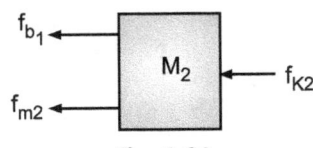

Fig. 1.64

In force-current analogy

$$F(t) \to i(t) \qquad x \to \phi = \int V \, dt$$

$$k \to \frac{1}{L} \qquad\qquad \frac{dx}{dt} \to V$$

$$M \to C$$

$$B \to 1/R \qquad\qquad \frac{d^2x}{dt} \to \frac{dv}{dt}$$

Equation (1.15) can be written as

$$i(t) = c_1 \frac{dv_1}{dt} + \frac{1}{R_1}[V_1 - V_2] + \frac{1}{L_1}\int V_1 \, dt \qquad\qquad\qquad ...(1.17)$$

The circuit for above equation (1.17) is,

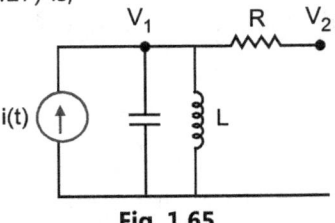

Fig. 1.65

Equation (1.16) can be written in force-current analogy as follow,

$$C_2 \frac{dv_2}{dt} + \frac{1}{R_1}[V_2 - V_1] + \frac{1}{L_2}\int V_2 \, dt = 0 \qquad\qquad\qquad ...(1.18)$$

The circuit for above equation is

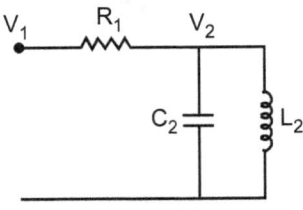

Fig. 1.66

Hence the complete circuit diagram; i.e. electrical network which is analogous to the given mechanical system is shown as;

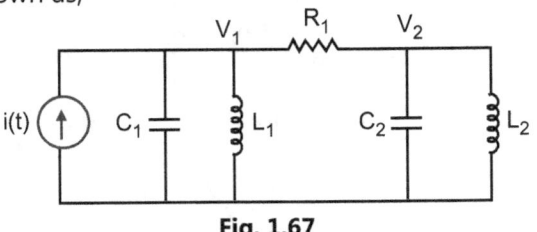

Fig. 1.67

1.7 BLOCK DIAGRAM ALGEBRA

- Complicated control systems are very difficult to analyze it as a whole. To make it easier to analyze; transfer function approach is used, which helps to find out transfer function of each and every complicated system. Hence, by showing connection between the elements, complete system can be splitted into different blocks and can be analyzed conveniently. This is the basic concept of block representation. Basically block diagram is a pictorial representation of the given system.
- A system consists of number of components. The function of each component is represented by a block. All the blocks are interconnected by lines with arrows indicating the flow of signals from output of one block to the input of another. Such block diagram gives an overall ideal of the interrelationships that exist among various components. It explains the cause and effect relationship existing between input and output of the system through the blocks.
- It means that, the block explains mathematical operation on the input by the element to produce the corresponding output. The actual mathematical function is indicated by inserting corresponding transfer function of the element inside the block. Let us consider transfer function G(s) of a system. This system can be represented by a block as shown below

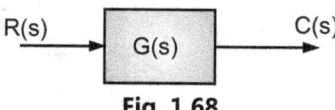

Fig. 1.68

The input signal into the block is R(s) which is the laplace transform of input signal r(t) and the output is C(s) which is laplace transform of C(t).

The flow of signal is unidirectional from the input to the output. The output C(s) is equal to the product of the input signal and the transfer function G(s).

$$\therefore \qquad C(s) = R(s) \cdot G(s)$$

1.7.1 Application

Illustrating concept of block diagram representation.

Example : Liquid level control system.

Consider liquid level system as shown in Fig. 1.69 below,

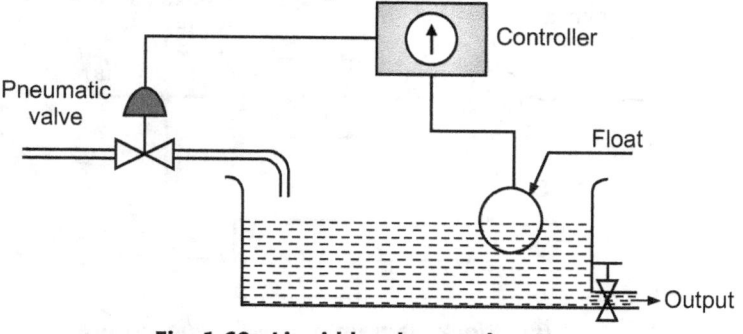

Fig. 1.69 : Liquid level control system

So to represent this by block diagram, identify the elements which are

- Controller
- Pneumatic valve
- Tank
- Float

In this system, float is used as the sensing element, which is used to sense the level of water.

Hence, the float acts as the feedback.

According, the float position with respect to desired level of water, the controller operates the pneumatic valve controlling the flow of water in the tank. When the required level is reached, controller operates the pneumatic valve in such a way that the flow of water in the tank stops.

If the output from the tank is taken, i.e. the water from the tank is drained then the float position changes from the desired position and accordingly the controller operates the pneumatic valve to start the flow of water in the tank.

Hence, indicating all elements by blocks, the block diagram of the system can be developed as,

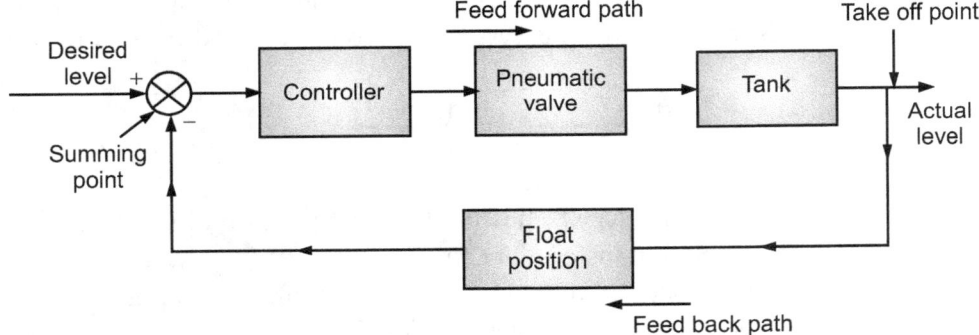

Fig. 1.70 : Block diagram of liquid level control

1.7.2 Representation of a Closed Loop System using Block Diagram

Following Fig. 1.71 (a) shows block diagram of a negative feedback system. With reference to this Fig. 1.71 (a) the terminology used in block diagram of control system is given below

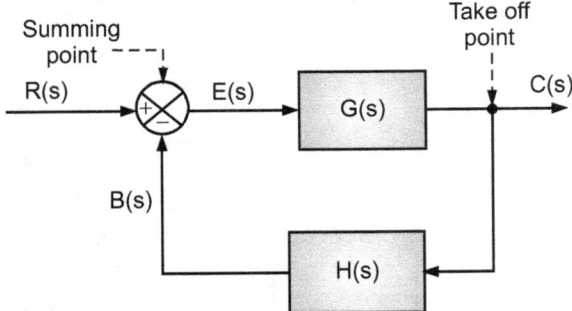

Fig. 1.71 (a) : Block diagram of closed loop system

$$R(s) \ = \ \text{Reference input}$$
$$C(s) \ = \ \text{Output signal or Controlled variable}$$
$$B(s) \ = \ \text{Feedback signal}$$
$$E(s) \ = \ \text{Actuating signal}$$
$$G(s) \ = \ C(s)/E(s) \rightarrow \text{Forward path transfer function}$$
$$H(s) \ = \ \text{Transfer function of feedback elements}$$
$$G(s) \cdot H(s) \ = \ B(s) / E(s) = \text{Loop transfer function}$$
$$T(s) \ = \ C(s)/R(s) = \text{Closed – loop transfer function}$$

From Fig. 1.71 (a); we have

$$C(s) \ = \ G(s) \cdot E(s) \qquad\qquad\qquad \dots(1.19)$$
$$E(s) \ = \ R(s) - B(s)$$
$$= \ R(s) \cdot H(s) \cdot C(s) \qquad\qquad \dots(1.20)$$
$$C(s) \ = \ G(s) \cdot R(s) - G(s) \cdot H(s) \cdot C(s)$$

or
$$\frac{C(s)}{R(s)} \ = \ T(s) = \frac{G(s)}{1 + G(s) \cdot H(s)} \qquad \dots(1.21)$$

Therefore a system shown in Fig. 1.71 (a) can be reduced to a single block as shown in Fig. 1.71 (b) below

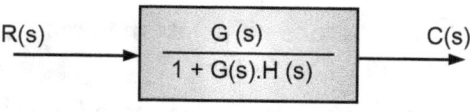

Fig. 1.71 (b)

Keynote :
Rule : use + sign for negative feedback
and use – sign for positive feedback.

Transfer function approach can be used as a standard result to eliminate such simple loops in a complicated system reduction procedure.

1.7.3 Basic Elements Associated with Block Diagram Representation

1. Blocks

2. Transfer function of each element shown inside the blocks

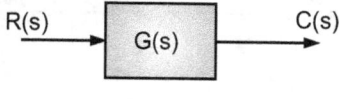

Fig. 1.72

Represents transfer function between the input R(s) and the output C(s).

3.   Summing Point : The output of a summing is the algebraic sum of the signals entering into it. This has a symbol as shown below

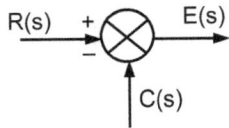

Fig. 1.73

Next to each input is a plus or minus symbol indicating the sign associated with the variable.

The output of given summing point is,

$$E(s) = R(s) - C(s)$$

Keynote :

For a closed loop system, the function comparing different signals is indicated by the summing point.

---

4.   Take Off Point : A take off point on a branch is a physical point in the system where the desired signal is tapped off to utilize elsewhere.

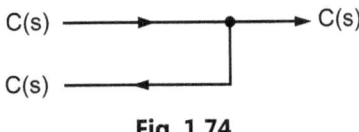

Fig. 1.74

All these summing points, blocks and take off points then must be connected exactly as per actual elements connected in the practical system.

The connection between the blocks is shown by lines called branches of block diagram.

The signal can travel along the direction of arrow only.

Keynote :

A point from which signal is taken for the feedback purpose is indicated by take off point in block diagrams.

1.7.4 Rules for Block Diagram Reduction

Any complicated system can be brought into a simple form. To bring it into simple form it is necessary to reduce the block diagram but using proper logic such that output of that system and the value of any feedback signal should not get disturbed.

Rule 1 : Associative Law

Consider two summing points as shown in the Fig. 1.75.

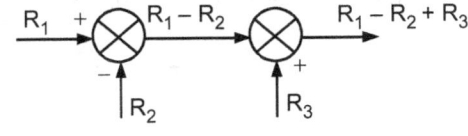

Fig. 1.75

Now change the position of two summing points output remains same.

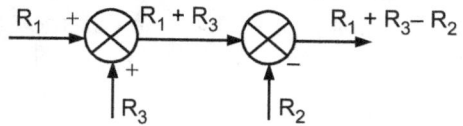

Fig. 1.76

Associative law holds good for summing points which are directly connected to each other. i.e. there is no intermediate block or take off point in between the summing point.

Rule 2 : Cascade Connection of Blocks (or Blocks in Series)

Following Fig. 1.77 shows a cascade connection of two blocks in which the output of block 1 is connected to the input of block 2.

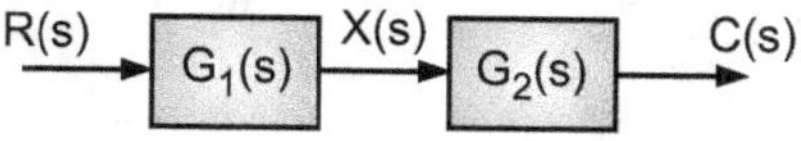

$$R(s) \rightarrow \boxed{G_1(s)} \xrightarrow{X(s)} \boxed{G_2(s)} \rightarrow C(s)$$

Fig. 1.77

We know that the output of a block is equal to the product of input signal and the transfer function of the block.

∴   The output of block 1 is,

$$X(s) = R(s) \cdot G_1(s) \qquad \qquad \ldots(1.22)$$

and the output of block 2 is;

$$C(s) = X(s) \cdot G_2(s)$$
$$= R(s) \cdot G_1(s) \cdot G_2(s) \qquad \qquad \ldots(1.23)$$

where $G_1(s)$ and $G_2(s)$ are the transfer function of each block.

We can find that the cascade connection of two blocks can be replaced by a single block whose transfer function is equal to the product of transfer function of individual block.

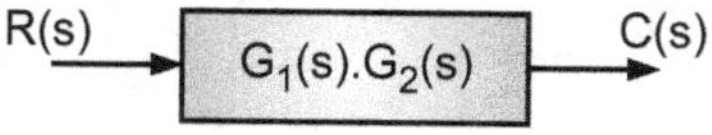

$$R(s) \rightarrow \boxed{G_1(s) . G_2(s)} \rightarrow C(s)$$

Fig. 1.78

Rule 3 : Cascade block transfer function can be replaced by a single block with transfer function equal to the product of transfer functions of individual blocks.

Example :

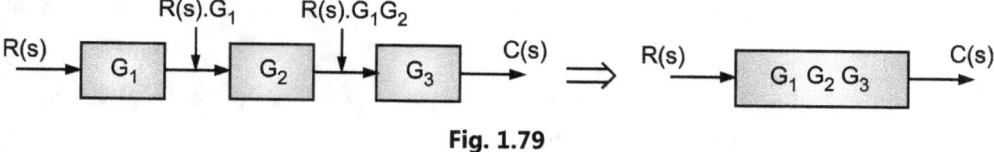

Fig. 1.79

Rule 4 : Parallel connection of blocks

Two systems are said to be in parallel when they have common input and their outputs are combined by a summer. Following Fig. 1.80 shows the blocks that are in parallel.

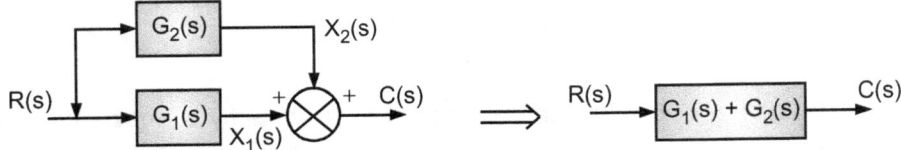

Fig. 1.80

The transfer function of the blocks which are connected in parallel get added algebrically (considering the sign).

From the Fig. 1.80 the output C(s) is sum of the two signals $X_1(s)$ and $X_2(s)$.

$\therefore$ $\qquad\qquad C(s) = X_1(s) + X_2(s)$ $\qquad\qquad$ ...(1.24)

But, $\qquad\qquad X_1(s) = R(s) - G_1(s)$ $\qquad\qquad$ ...(1.25)

and $\qquad\qquad X_2(s) = R(s) \cdot G_2(s)$ $\qquad\qquad$ ...(1.26)

Now, $\qquad\qquad C(s) = R(s) \cdot G_1(s) + R(s) \cdot G_2(s)$

$\qquad\qquad\qquad = R(s) [G_1(s) + G_2(s)]$ $\qquad\qquad$ ...(1.27)

Equation (1.27) shows that the two blocks connected in parallel are represented by a single block whose transfer function is equal to the sum of individual blocks.

Rule 5 : Parallel blocks with transfer function $G_1(s)$ and $G_2(s)$ can be replaced by a single block with a transfer function equal to the sum of transfer functions of individual blocks.

Example :

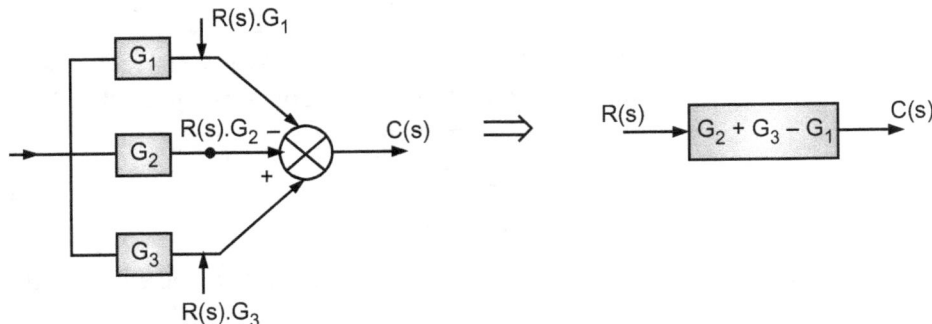

Fig. 1.81

Note : For a parallel combination the direction of signals through the blocks in parallel must be same.

Rule 6 : Moving a takeoff point to the left moving a take off point behind the block (or in the direction opposite of signal flow) of the block.

Consider the combination shown in Fig. 1.82.

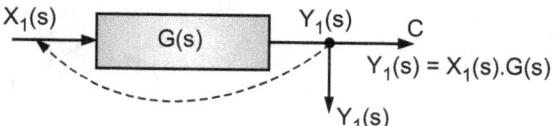

Fig. 1.82

To shift the take off point behind the block, value of signal taking off must remain same.

- Though shifting of take of point without any change doe not affect output directly, the value of feedback signal which is changed affects the output in directly which must be kept same.

- Now moving a take off point from 2 to 1 is equal to avoiding the signal from passing G(S).

- To compensate for this change, multiply the take off signal by G(s).

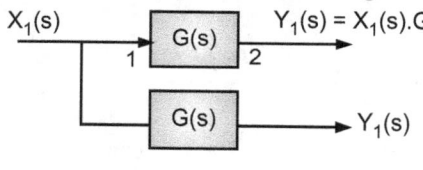

Fig. 1.83

Example :

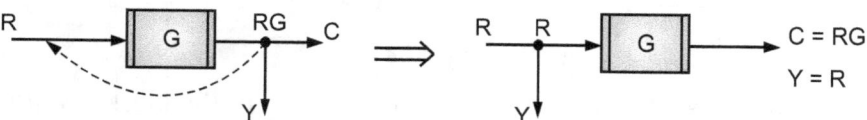

Fig. 1.84

Though output is not affected; but the change in value of feedback signal can affect the output indirectly without any change it is R, it must be RG. So a add block having transfer function same as that off point is to be shifted.

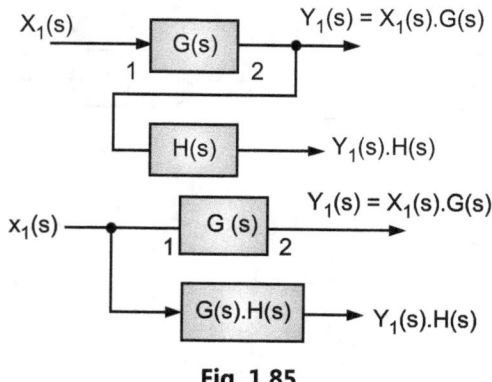

Fig. 1.85

Rule 7 : Moving take off point to the right (beyond) (in the direction of flow of signal.)

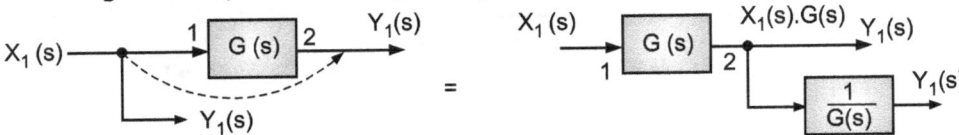

Fig. 1.86

Moving a take off point from 1 to 2 is equal to multiplying the signal $x_1(s)$ by $G(s)$, so to compensate for this change, divide the take off signal by $G(s)$ after moving the takeoff point.

Example :

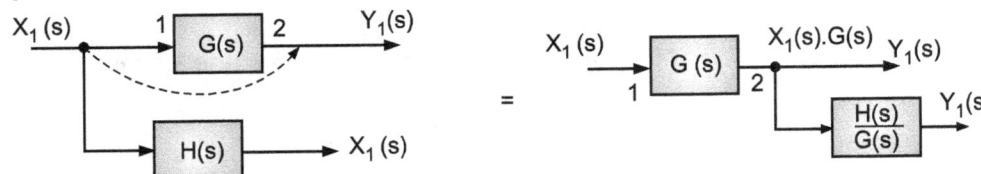

Fig. 1.87

Keynote :

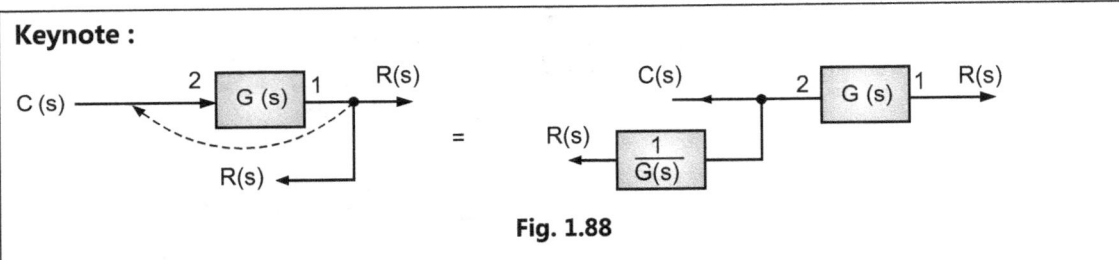

Fig. 1.88

Here it appears that the take off point is moved to the left of the block. But it is not true. See the direction of signal flow.

Rule 8 : Moving summing point to the right of the block

Following is the Fig. 1.89 which shows the summing point is to be moved to the right of the block.

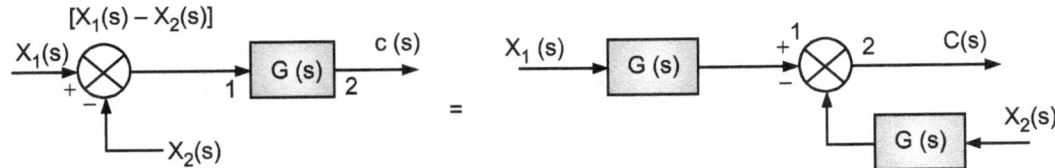

Fig. 1.89

$$C(s) = G(s) \cdot [(X_1(s) - X_2(s)]$$

$$= G(s) \cdot X_1(s) - G(s) \cdot X_2(s)$$

$$C(s) = X_1(s) \cdot G(s) - X_2(s) \cdot G(s)$$

Example : Consider the combination

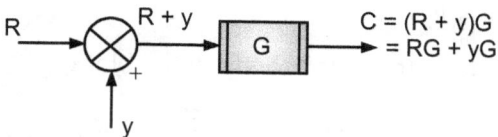

Fig. 1.90

Now, to shift the summing point after the block keeping output same, consider the shifted summing point without any change.

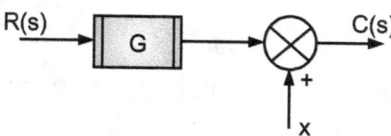

Fig. 1.91

$\therefore$ $\qquad$ RG + x = RG + yG

$\therefore$ $\qquad\qquad$ x = yG

$\qquad$ C(s) = RG + y $\qquad\qquad\qquad\qquad\qquad\qquad$ ...(1.28)

Now we have to shift summing point behind (left) of the block.

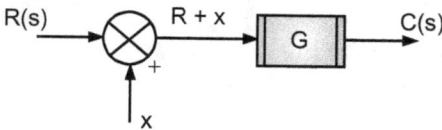

Fig. 1.92

$\qquad$ C(s) = (R + x) $\cdot$ G

$\qquad\qquad$ = RG + xG $\qquad\qquad\qquad\qquad\qquad\qquad$ ...(1.29)

Comparing (1.28) and (1.29)

$\qquad\qquad$ y = xG

$\therefore$ $\qquad\qquad$ x = y/G

So signal y must be multiplied with $\dfrac{1}{G}$ to keep output same.

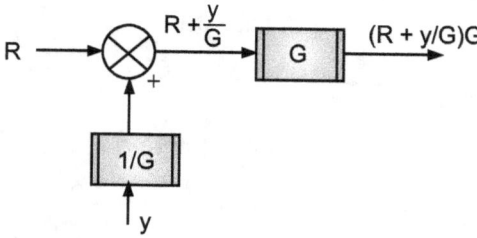

Fig. 1.93

$\qquad$ C(s) = RG + y

That is signal y must be multiplied with the transfer function of the block beyond which summing point is to be shifted.

Rule 9 : Shifting summing point to the left (behind) the block

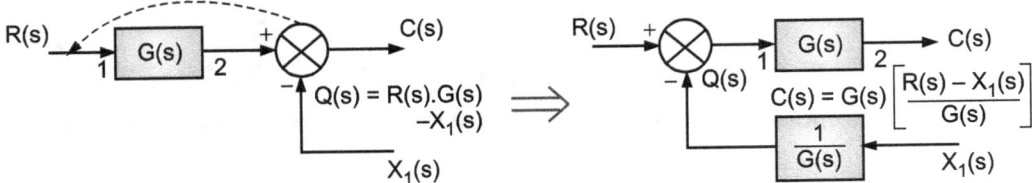

Fig. 1.94

Fig. 1.94 shows a system in which summing point is to be moved to the left of a block G(s). The output C(s) before the summing point is moved from 2 to 1.

$$C(s) = R(s) \cdot G(s) - X_1(s) \qquad \qquad \dots(1.30)$$

The output C(s) after moving summing point moved from 2 to 1.

$$C(s) = [R(s) - Q(s)] \cdot G(s)$$

$$C(s) = R(s) \cdot G(s) - Q(s) \cdot G(s) \qquad \qquad \dots(1.31)$$

Comparing equation (1.30) and (1.31) we have,

$$X_1(s) = Q(s) \cdot G(s)$$

∴ $$Q(s) = \frac{X_1(s)}{G(s)}$$

When the summing point is moved to the left of the block, then the signal $X_1(s)$ must be divided with G(s).

Rule 10 : Eliminating feed back loop

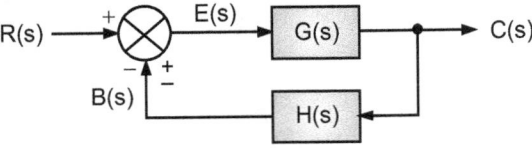

Fig. 1.95

A feedback control system whose open loop transfer function G(s) and feedback transfer function H(s) can be replaced by a single block with

$$\text{Transfer Function} = \frac{G(s)}{1 + G(s) \cdot H(s)}$$

Rule 11 : Any two summing points may be interchanged

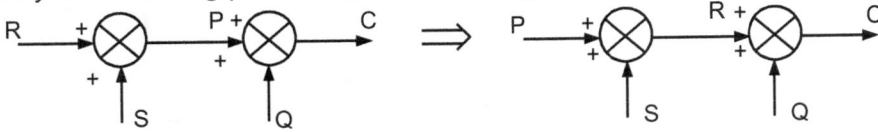

Fig. 1.96

Rule 12 : Any summing points having more than two inputs may be bifurcated into two summing points.

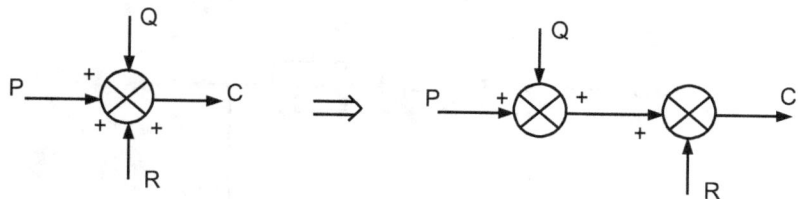

Fig. 1.97

Rule 13 : Similarly any two summing points can be combined.

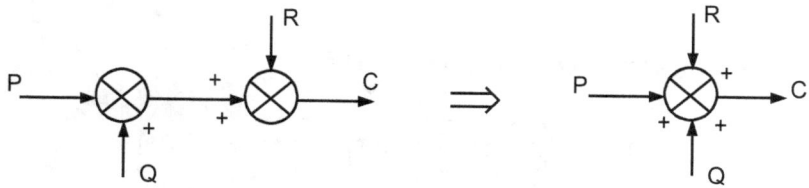

Fig. 1.98

Points to be Remembered while doing Block Diagram Reduction :

- If a block diagram consists of many feedback loops, then find the innermost feedback loop.

- If it does not contain any take off and or summing points inside the loop, simplify the innermost feedback loop to a single block using rule 9.

- If it consists of any take off point and / or summing point inside the innermost loop, then simplify them by using rule 3 to rule 8. After eliminating such points, simplify the innermost rule using Rule 9.

- If any path consists of cascaded blocks then combine them using rule 2.

- Repeat the above steps according the requirement until you left with one block with input R(s) and output C(s).

- If there is any parallel path then use rule 3 simplify it.

Procedure to Solve Block Diagram Reduction Problem :

Step 1 : Reduce the blocks connected in series

Step 2 : Reduce the blocks connected in parallel

Step 3 : Reduce the mirror feedback loops

Step 4 : Try to shift take off points towards right and summing points towards left.

Step 5 : Repeat steps 1 to 4 till simple form is obtained.

Step 6 : Obtain the transfer function of overall system.

Block Diagram Reduction Problems :

Example 1.7 : Reduce each diagram to a single block, determining the resulting equivalent transfer function.

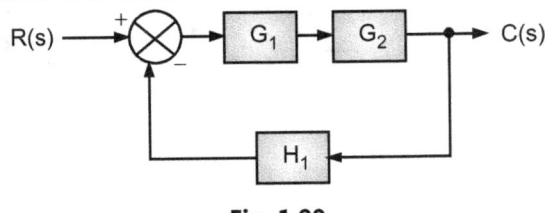

Fig. 1.99

Solution :

Step 1 : Using rule 2 of cascade connection of blocks.

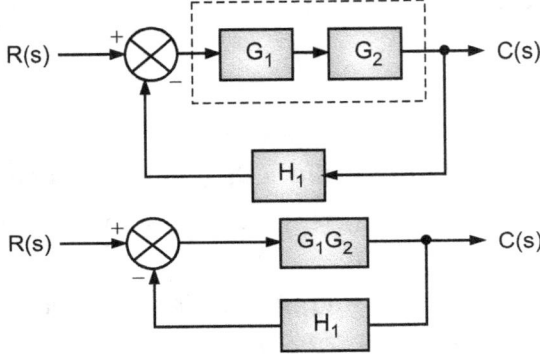

Fig. 1.100

$$\text{Transfer Function} = \frac{G_1G_2}{1 + H_1G_1G_2}$$

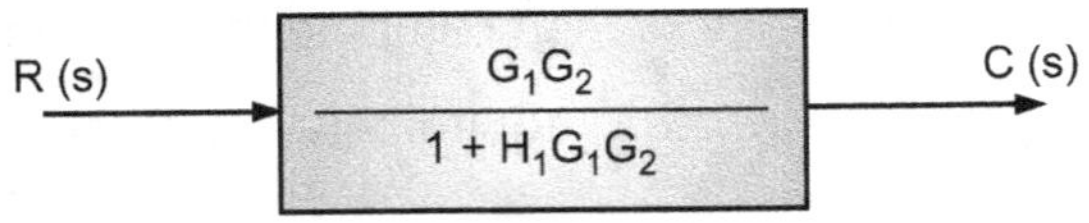

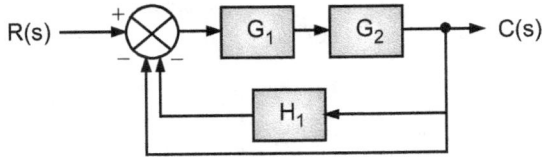

Fig. 1.101

Example 1.8 : Determine the closed loop transfer function of following block diagram.

Fig. 1.102

Solution :

Step 1 : Use the rule of cascade connection

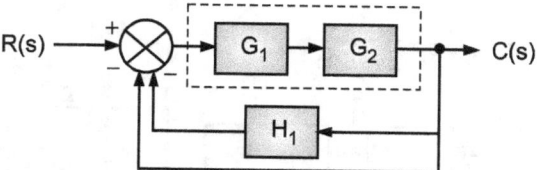

Fig. 1.103

Combine the cascade connection of blocks.

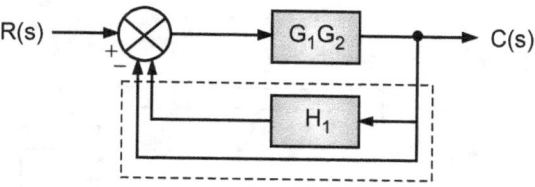

Fig. 1.104

Step 2 : Combining the two feedback paths (parallel paths)

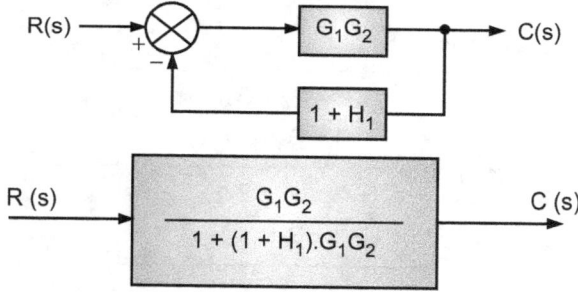

Fig. 1.105

$$\therefore \qquad \frac{C(s)}{R(s)} = \frac{G_1 G_2}{1 + G_1 G_2 + G_1 G_2 H_1}$$

Example 1.9 : Reduce the following Fig. 1.106 using Block diagram reduction technique.

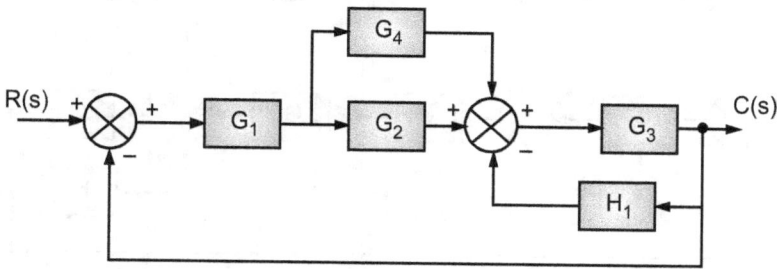

Fig. 1.106

Solution :

Step 1 : Combining parallel blocks G_4 and G_2.

Step 2 : Eliminating feedback loop $\dfrac{G_3}{1+G_3H_1}$.

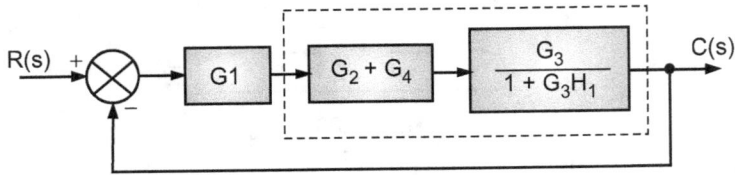

Fig. 1.107

Step 3 : Combining all cascading blocks.

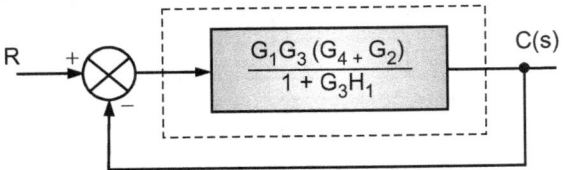

Fig. 1.108

Step 4 : Eliminating feedback loop

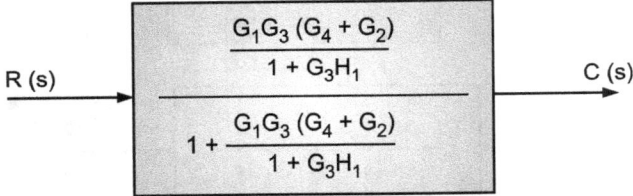

Fig. 1.109

$$\therefore \quad \frac{C}{R} = \frac{G_1G_3G_4 + G_1G_2G_3}{1+G_3H_1 + G_1G_3G_4 + G_1G_2G_3}$$

Example 1.10 : Using block diagram techniques, find the closed loop transfer functions of the following system.

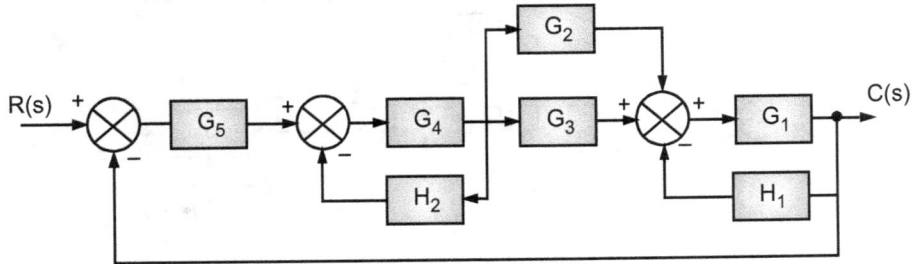

Fig. 1.110

Solution :

Step 1 : According to the rule, split the summing point.

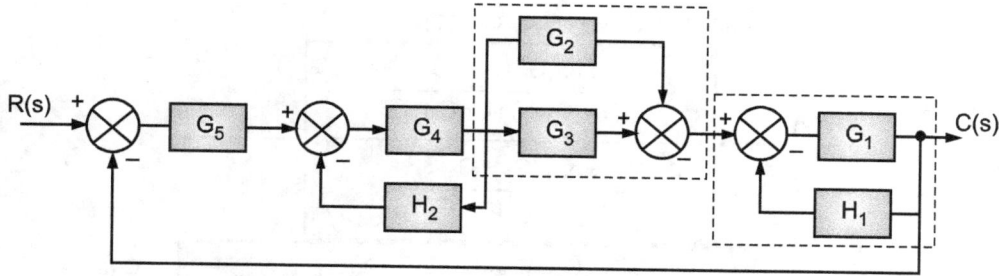

Fig. 1.111

Step 2 : Combining the parallel blocks G_3 and G_2, eliminating feedback loop having G_1 and H_1 blocks yields.

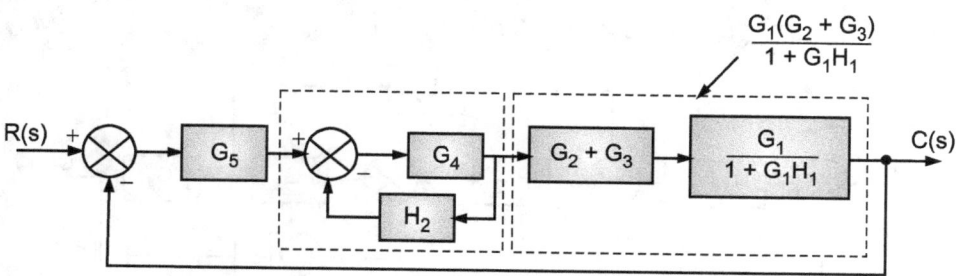

Fig. 1.112

Step 3 : Combine cascade block and eliminating feedback loop.

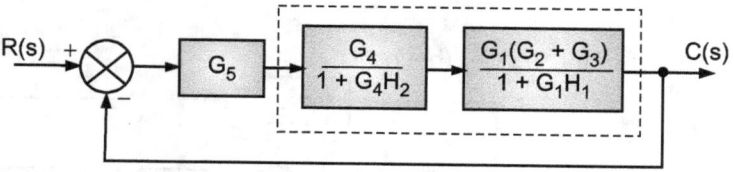

Fig. 1.113

Step 4 : Combine cascaded blocks together.

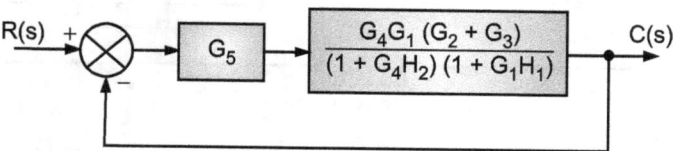

Fig. 1.114

Step 5 : Combine cascade blocks

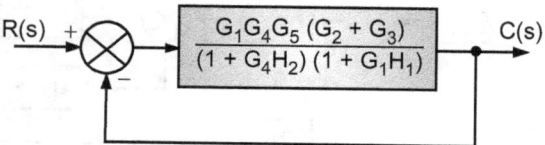

Fig. 1.115

Step 6 : Using the rule to eliminate the feedback loop.

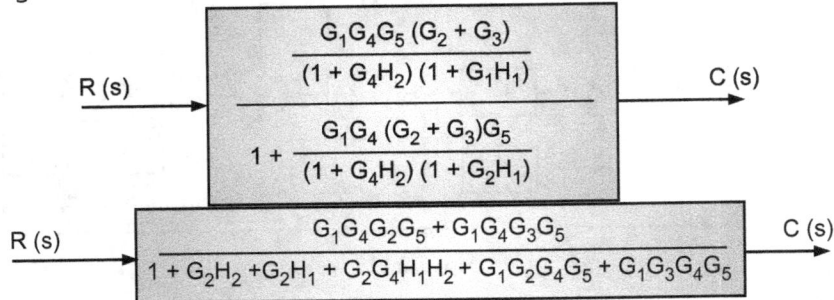

Fig. 1.116

Example 1.11 : Find $\dfrac{C(s)}{R(s)}$ for the following Block diagram.   **(May 2016)**

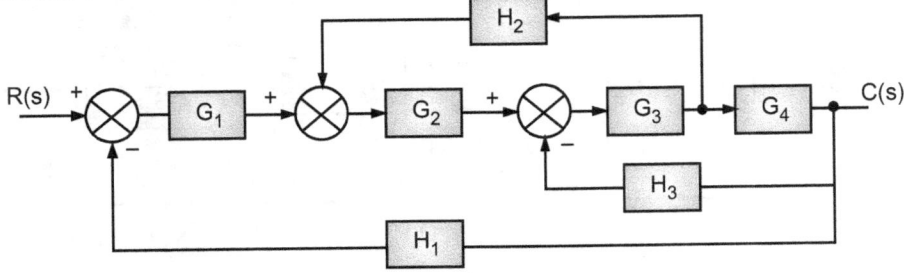

Fig. 1.117

Solution :

Step 1 : Shifting take off point to right (beyond G_4)

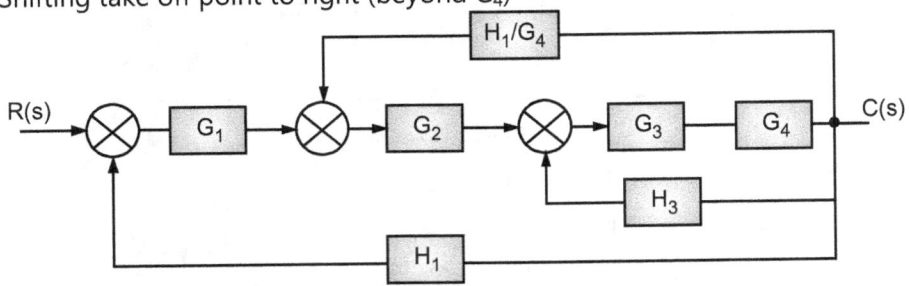

Fig. 1.118

Step 2 : Cascading block G_3 and G_4

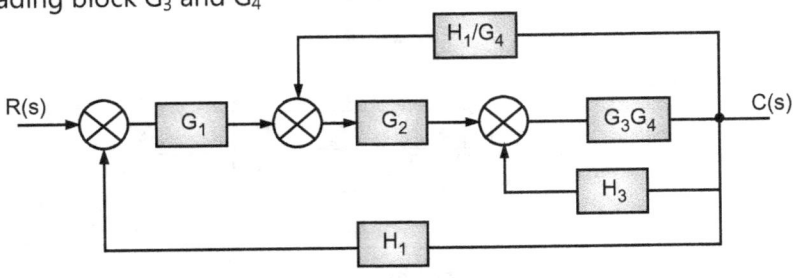

Fig. 1.119

Step 3 : G_3G_4 and H_3 in feedback loop.

$$\frac{G_3G_4}{1 - G_3G_4H_3}$$

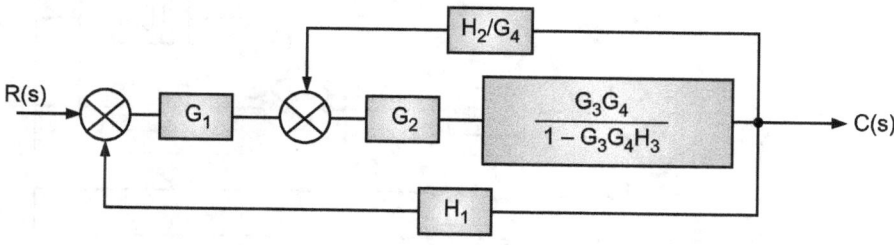

Fig. 1.120

Step 4 : G_2 in cascade with $\dfrac{G_3G_4}{1 - G_3G_4H_3}$

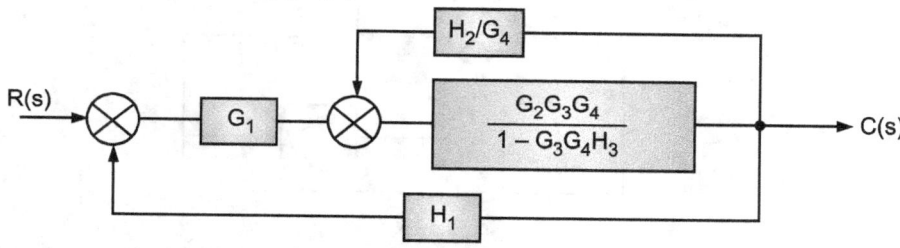

Fig. 1.121

Step 5 : Feedback loop of H_2/G_4 with the block $\dfrac{G_2G_3G_4}{1 - G_3G_4H_3}$ and cascade with G_1.

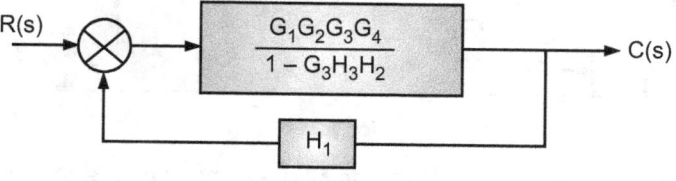

Fig. 1.122

$\therefore$ $\qquad\dfrac{C(s)}{R(s)} = \dfrac{G_1G_2G_3G_4}{1 - G_3H_3H_2H_1}$

Example 1.12 : Using block diagram reduction technique, find the closed loop transfer function

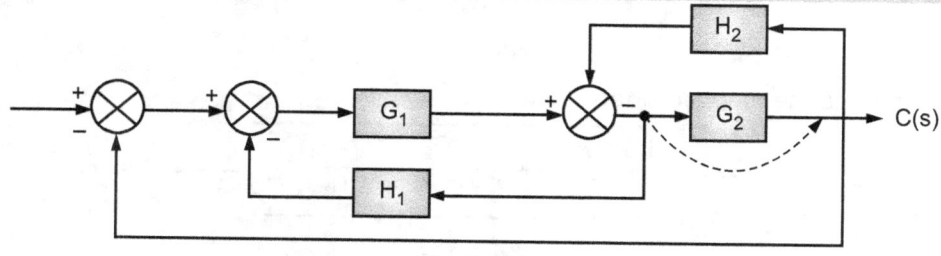

Fig. 1.123

Solution :

Step 1 : Moving take-off point to the right i.e. after G_2.

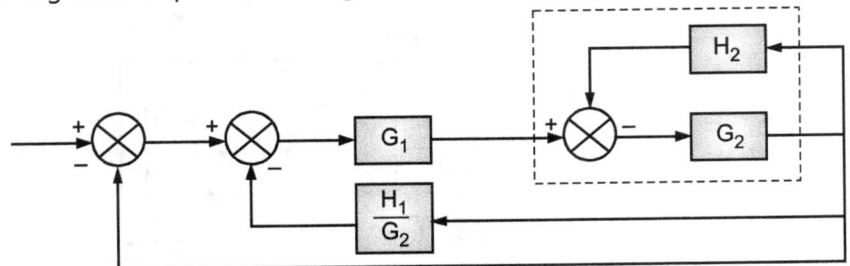

Fig. 1.124

Step 2 : Eliminate the feedback loop and combine the resultant block.

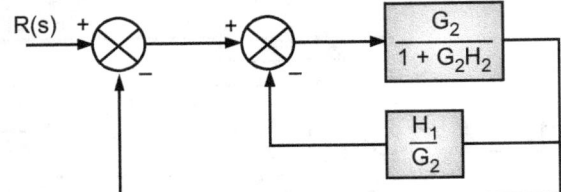

Fig. 1.125

Rule for above Step 2.

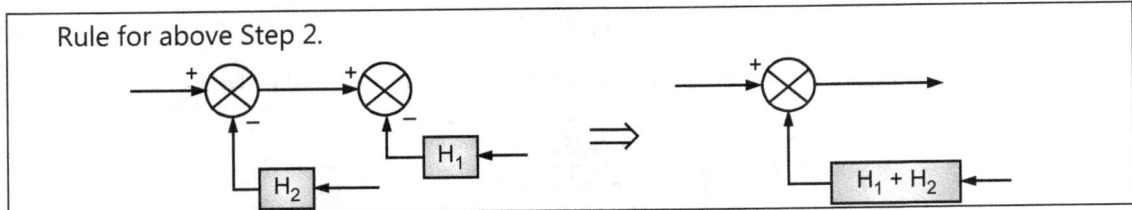

Fig. 1.126

Step 3 : Combine the summing points and add two feedback elements together.

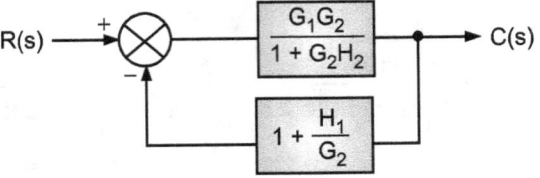

Fig. 1.127

Step 4 : Eliminate the feedback loop.

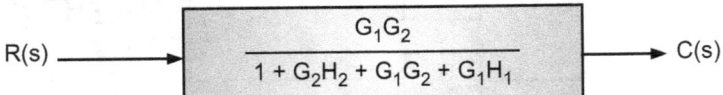

Fig. 1.128

Block Diagram Reduction Rules :

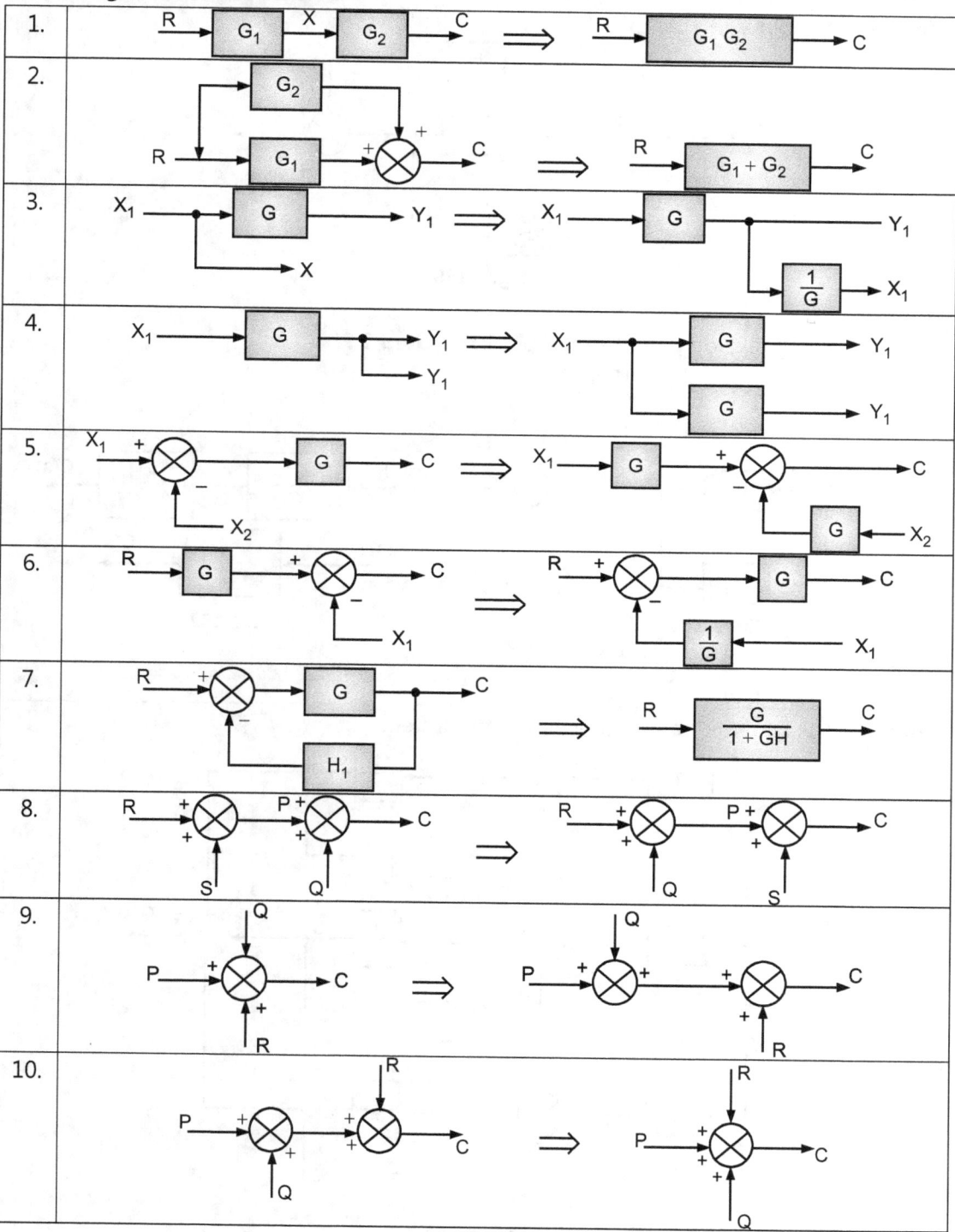

Fig. 1.129

Example 1.13 : Calculate the transfer function of the Fig. 1.130 below with block diagram reduction technique.

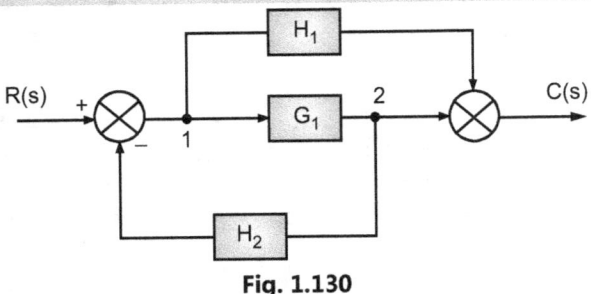

Fig. 1.130

Solution :

Step 1 : Shifting take off point beyond block G.   **Step 2 :**

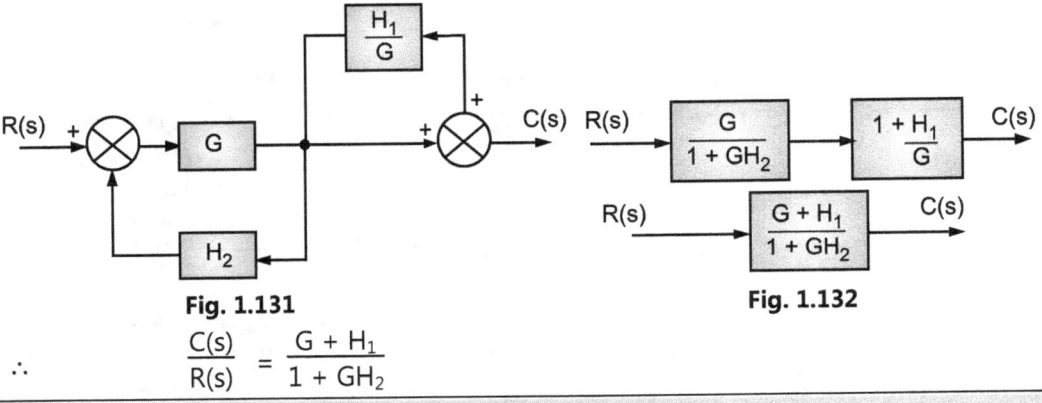

Fig. 1.131   **Fig. 1.132**

$$\therefore \qquad \frac{C(s)}{R(s)} = \frac{G + H_1}{1 + GH_2}$$

Example 1.14 : Find the transfer function of the system

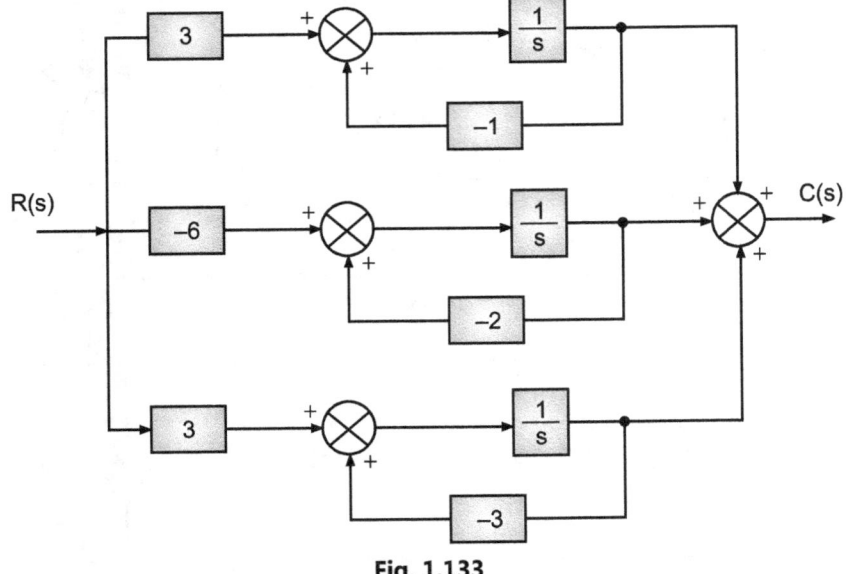

Fig. 1.133

Solution :

  Step 1 :

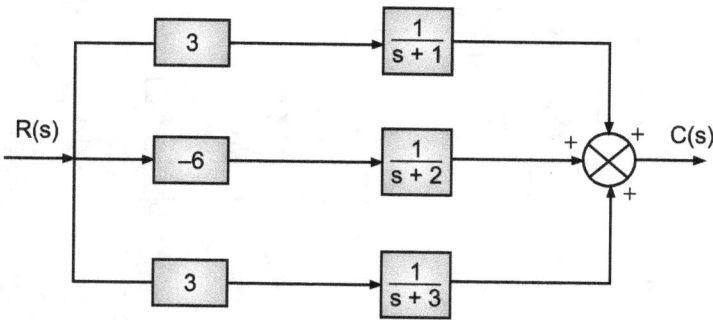

Fig. 1.134

  Step 2 :

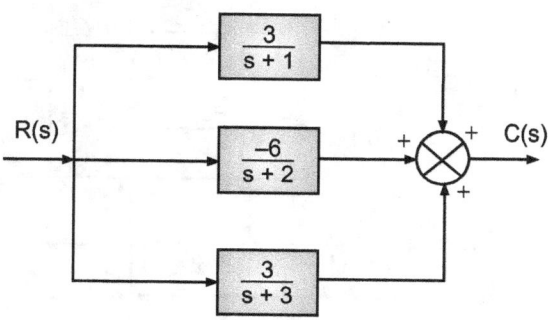

Fig. 1.135

  Step 3 :

$$\frac{C(s)}{R(s)} = \frac{3}{s+1} + \frac{-6}{s+2} + \frac{3}{s+3}$$

$$\frac{(CS)}{R(s)} = \frac{8}{s^3 + 6s^2 + 11s + 6}$$

Example 1.15 : Solve using Block diagram reduction technique.

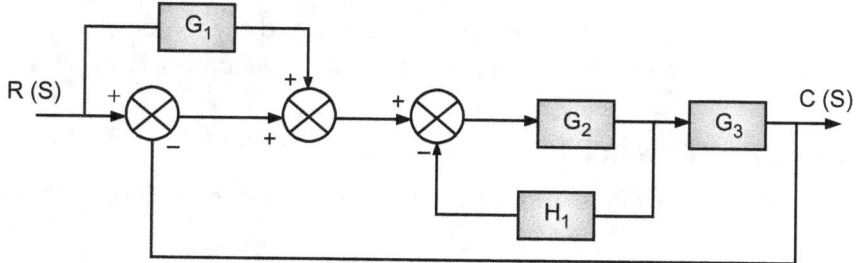

Fig. 1.136

Solution : G_1 and H_1 are in feedback that combination in cascuade with G_3

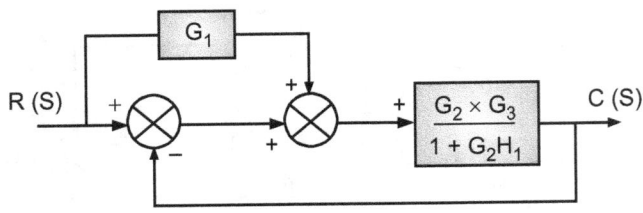

Fig. 1.137

Changing summer position

  (i) Feedback of $\dfrac{G_2G_3}{1 + G_2H_1}$ With 1 and G_1 with 1.

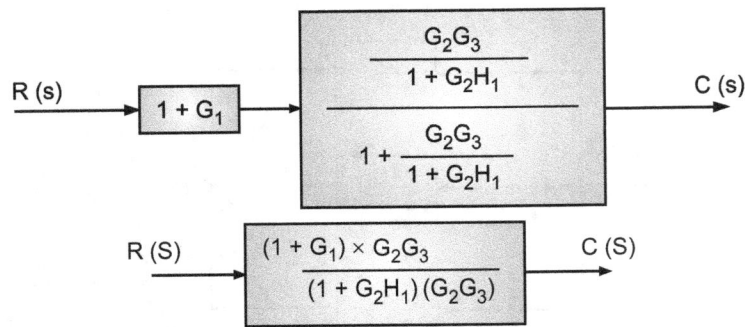

Fig. 1.138

1.8 SIGNAL FLOW GRAPH

Signal flow graph is a graphical representation of the relationship between the variables of a set of linear algebraic equations describing a system.

The Block diagram reduction technique is complex as every stage needs to redraw a modified Block diagram. Hence it is also time consuming. A simple method was developed by S.J. Mason which is known as signal flow graph. This method is very simple and does not require any reduction technique, signal flow graph is applicable to linear systems.

A signal flow graph is composed of nodes (Junctions) and these nodes are connected by directed line called branches. Every branch of signal flow graph is applicable to linear systems.

Components of Signal Flow Graph

1. **Node :** It represents a variable of the system which is sum of all incoming signals at the Node.

2. **Branch :** The line joining 2 nodes is a branch.

3. **Arrow :** It indicates the flow of signal.

According to the direction of arrow, the next node is the effect of the node prior to it.

The branches are always associated with a transfer function. Hence the first node when operated by transfer function gives value of variable at the second node.

1.8.1 Terminology Used in Signal Flow Graph

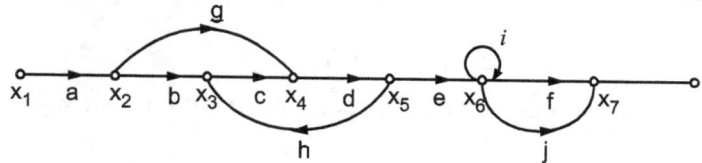

Fig. 1.139

- **Input Node or Source Node :** x_1 Node with only out going branches.
- **Output Node or Sink Node :** It is a node with only incoming branches. If this condition is not met = 8 an addition as branch with unity gain can be introduced.
- **Chain Node :** x_2, x_3, x_4, x_5, x_6. It is node with both incomings and outgoings.
- **Forward Path :** It starts from source node and goes towards since node.

    1st forward path $\Rightarrow x_1$ to x_7

    2nd path $\Rightarrow x_1 - x_2 - x_4 - x_5 - x_6 - x_7$.

- **Feedback loop :** $x_3 - x_4 - x_5 - x_3$. It is the path which originates and terminates at the same node.
- **Self loop :** x_6 It consists of only one single node.
- **Non-Touching Loops :** They have no common loop
- **Forward Path Gain :** It is the product of branch gains while traversing in a forward path.
- **Loop Gain :** Product of branch gains traversing in a loop.

1.8.2 Properties of Signal Flow Graph

- Signal flow graph is applicable to linear time invariant system only.
- The signal flows along the branches and in the direction of arrow.
- The signal gets multiplied by the branch gain during travel.
- The algebraic sum of all signals entering a node = the variable itself at the node.

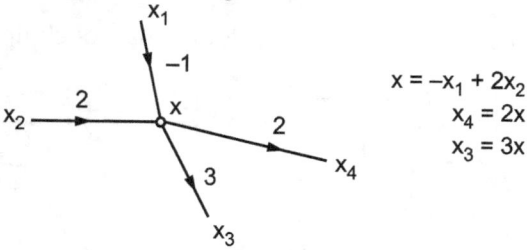

$$x = -x_1 + 2x_2$$
$$x_4 = 2x$$
$$x_3 = 3x$$

Fig. 1.140

$$x = -x_1 + 2x_2$$
$$x_4 = 2x$$
$$x_3 = 3x$$

- The value of the variable represented by a node is transmitted through all the branches leaving the node

  i.e. $x_4 = 2x$, and $x_3 = 3x$

- Parallel Branches can be replaced by a single branch with a gain = algebric sum of their individual gains.

- Series branches can be replaced by a single branch with a gain = product of their individual gains.

- Signal flow graph is not unique for the system.

1.8.3 Mason's Gain Formula

The relationship between an input variable and an output variable of an signal flow graph is given by the net gain between input and output node and is given by the overall gain of the system.

The overall gain (Transfer function) is,

$$\frac{C(s)}{R(s)} = \sum_{i=1}^{p} \frac{P_i \Delta p}{\Delta}$$

Where
$$p = \frac{\text{No. of forward paths}}{P_1, P_2, P_3, P_4 \text{ gains of different forward paths}}$$

Δ = system determinant

$\Delta = 1 - [\Sigma$ loop gain of all individual loop] + [Σ Gain products of possible combination of two non-touching loops – Σ Gain products of all possible combinations of three non-touching loops] + [------]

Δ_i = The value of Δ for the part of graph for non-touching the ith forward path.

It is the value of Δ evaluated after eliminating all loops that touch first forward path.

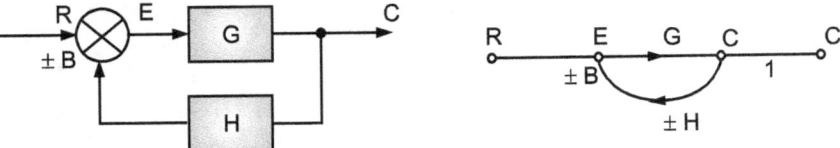

Fig. 1.141

Example 1.16 : Determine C/R for each system using SFG.

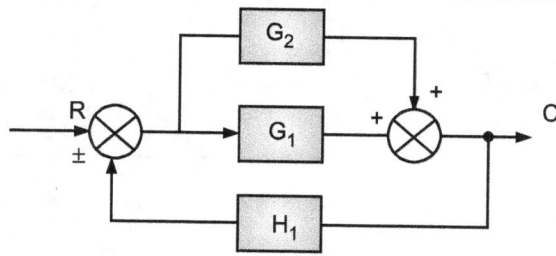

Fig. 1.142

Solution :

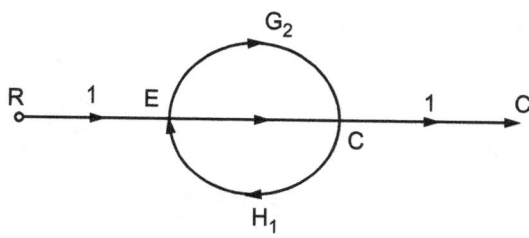

Fig. 1.143

(i)   Forward path gain : $P_1 = G_1,$ $P_2 = G_2$

(ii)   Loop gain $L_{11} = G_1H_1,$ $L_{21} = G_2H_1$

(iii) No Non-touching loops

(iv) $\Delta = 1 - (G_1 H_1 + G_2 H_1)$

     $\Delta_1 = 1, \Delta_2 = 1$

(v)   Overall transfer function :

$$\frac{C(s)}{R(s)} = \frac{P_1\Delta_1 + P_2\Delta_2}{\Delta} = \frac{G_1 + G_2}{1 - G_1H_1 - G_2H_1}$$

Example 1.17 : Determine $\frac{C(s)}{R(s)}$ for the following system using SFG.

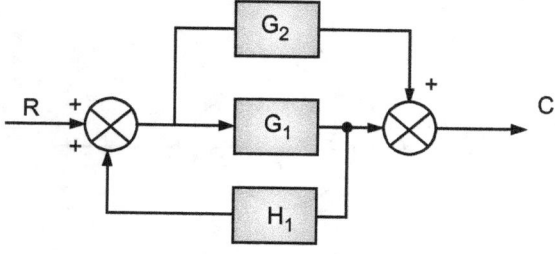

Fig. 1.144

Solution :

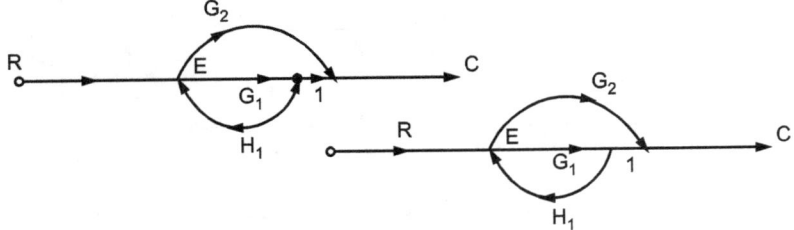

Fig. 1.145

(i)   Forward path :

   $P_1 = G_1, P_2 = G_2$

(ii) Loop gain :

   $L_{11} = G_1 H_1$

(iii) No Non-touching loops

(iv) $\Delta = 1 - G_1 H_1$

   $\Delta_1 = 1, \ \Delta_2 = 1$

(v)   Overall transfer function :

$$\therefore \quad \frac{C(s)}{R(s)} = \frac{G_1 + G_2}{1 - G_1 H_1}$$

Example 1.18 : Determine $\dfrac{C(s)}{R(s)}$ for the following system using SFG.

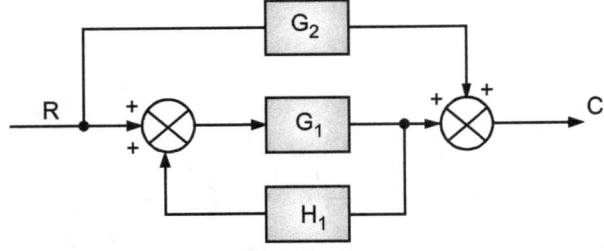

Fig. 1.146

Solution :

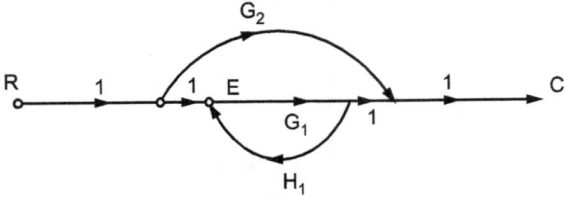

Fig. 1.147

(i)   Forward path gain :

$$P_1 = G_1, \qquad P_2 = G_2$$

(ii)   Loop gain :

$$L_{11} = G_1 H_1$$

(iii) No Non-touching loops

(iv) $$\Delta = 1 - G_1 H_1$$

$$\Delta_1 = 1, \ \Delta_2 = 1 - G_1 H_1$$

(v) $$\frac{C(s)}{R(s)} = \frac{P_1 \Delta_1 + P_2 \Delta_2}{\Delta} = \frac{G_1 + G_2(1 - G_1 H_1)}{1 - G_1 H_1}$$

Example 1.19 : Convert the given block diagram to SFG and evaluate its overall transfer function also check your ans. by block diagram reduction method.

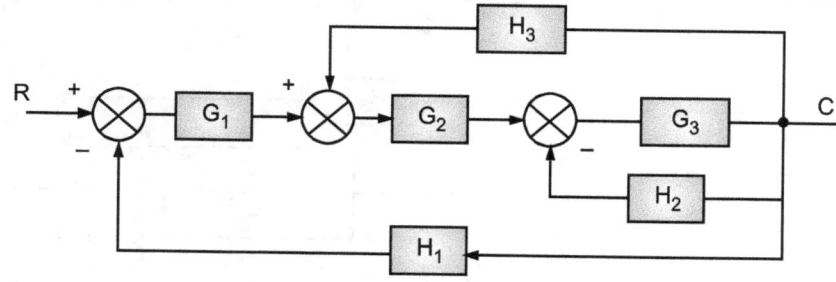

Fig. 1.148

Solution : Using SFG :

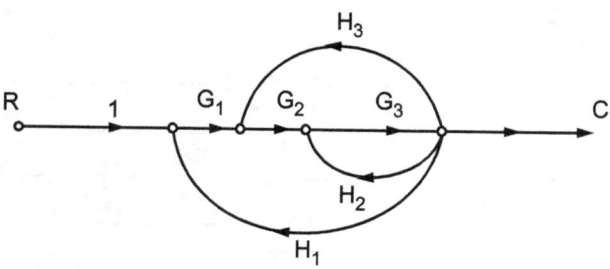

Fig. 1.149

(i)   Forward path gain :

$$P_1 = G_1 G_2 G_3, \qquad P_2 = 0$$

(ii) Loop gains : $$L_{11} = G_1 G_2 G_3 H_1$$

$$L_{21} = G_2 G_3 H_3$$

$$L_{12} = -G_3 H_2$$

(iii) $$\Delta = 1 - (-G_1 G_2 G_3 H_2 + G_2 G_3 H_3 - G_3 H_2)$$

$$\Delta 1 = 1, \qquad\qquad \Delta_2 = 1$$

(iv) No non-touching loops

(v) Overall transfer function :

$$\frac{C(s)}{R(s)} = P_1\Delta_1 + \frac{P_2\Delta_2}{\Delta} = \frac{G_1G_2G_3}{1 + (G_1G_2G_3H_1 - G_2G_3H_3 + G_3H_2)}$$

Using Block Diagram Reduction Method :

1. Solving feedback loop

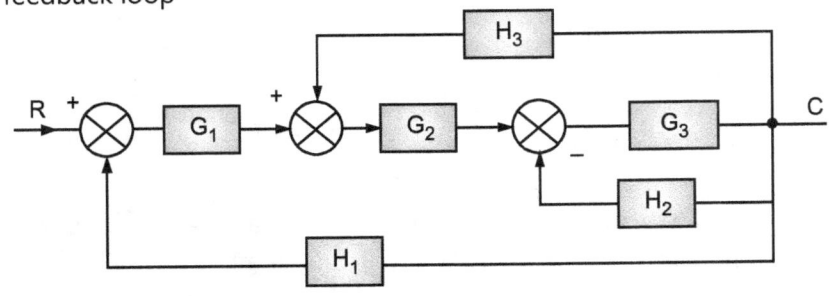

Fig. 1.150

2.

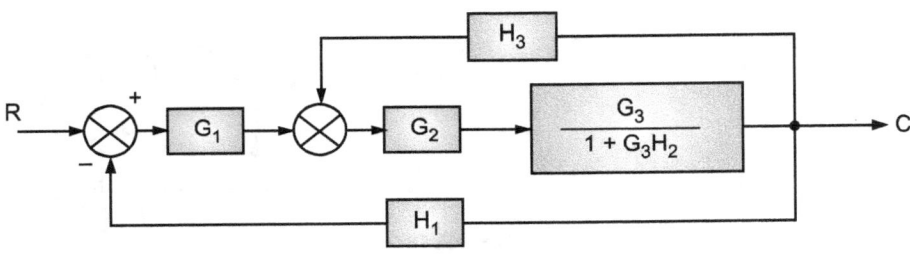

Fig. 1.151

3. G_2 in series with $\dfrac{G_3}{1 + G_3H_2}$

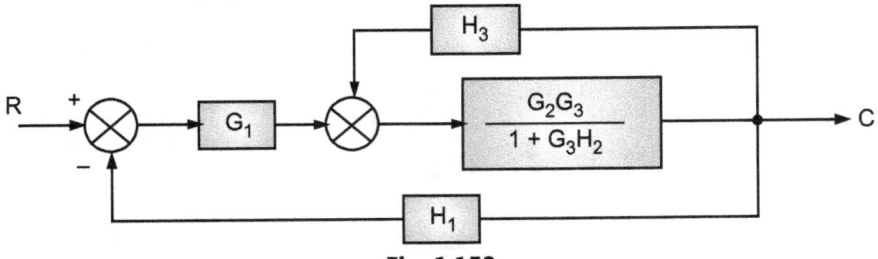

Fig. 1.152

4. Solving the feedback loop (2)

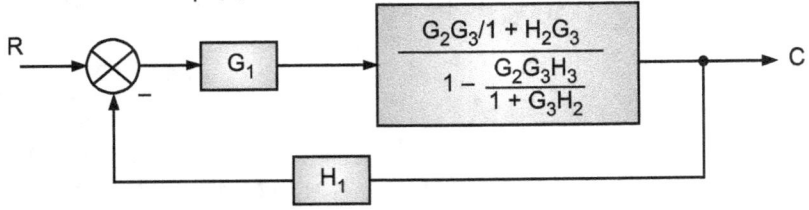

Fig. 1.153

5.

Fig. 1.154

$$\frac{\dfrac{G_1G_2G_3}{1 + G_3H_2 - G_2G_3H_3}}{1 + G_3H_2 - G_2G_3H_3} = \frac{G_1G_2G_3}{1 + G_3H_2 - G_2H_3G_3 + G_1\,G_2G_3\,H_1}$$

Example 1.20 : Determine C/R ratio for the following block diagram using SFG.

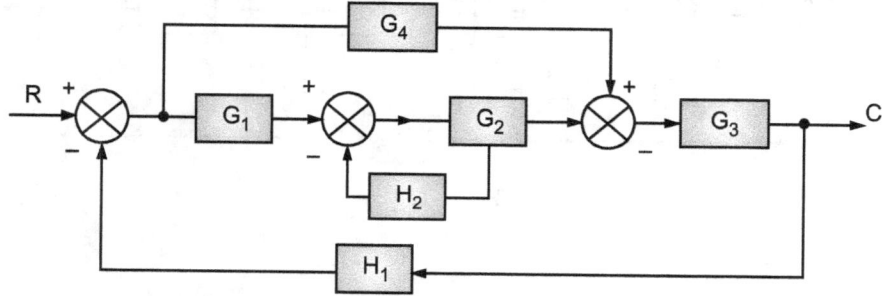

Fig. 1.155

Solution :

    SFG for above BD is

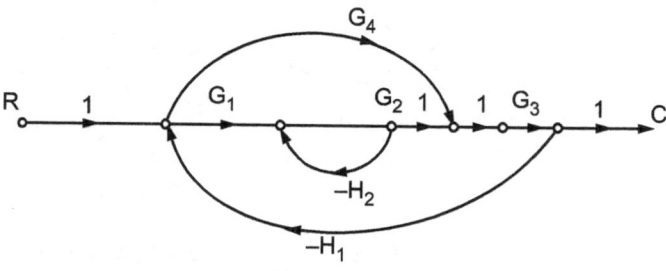

Fig. 1.156

(i) Forward path gain : $P_1 = G_1G_2G_3$ $P_2 = G_4G_3$

(ii) Loop gain : $L_{11} = -G_2H_2$

                            $L_{21} = -G_1G_2G_3H_1$

                            $L_{12} = -G_3G_4H_1$

(iii) One pair of non-touching loops)

                   $L_{12} = L_{11}.\,L_{31} - (G_2H_2)\,(-G_3G_4H_1) = G_2G_3G_4H_1H_2$

(iv) $\Delta = 1 - (-G_2H_2 - G_1\,G_2\,G_3\,H_1 - G_3G_4H_1) + G_3G_2\,G_4\,H_1H_2$

    $\Delta = 1,\, \Delta_2 = 1 + G_2H_2$

$$\text{Transfer function} = \frac{C(s)}{R(s)} = \frac{P_1\Delta_1 + P_2\Delta_2}{\Delta}$$

$$= \frac{G_1G_2G_3 + G_3G_4 (1 + G_2H_2)}{1 + G_2H_2 + G_1 G_3G_2 H_1 + G_3G_4H_1 + G_3G_2G_4H_1H_2}$$

Example 1.21 : Determine C/R ratio for the feedback control system shown below in Fig. 1.157.

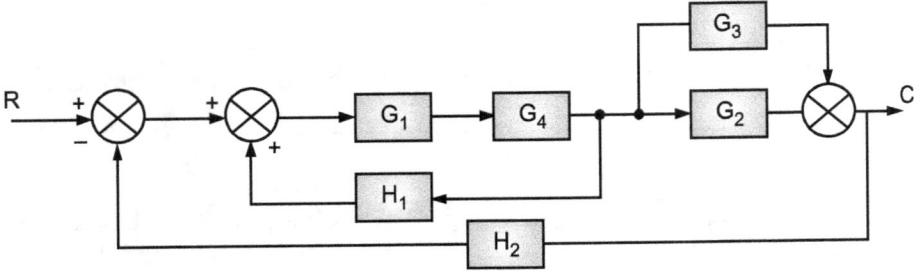

Fig. 1.157

Solution :

SFG for BD is

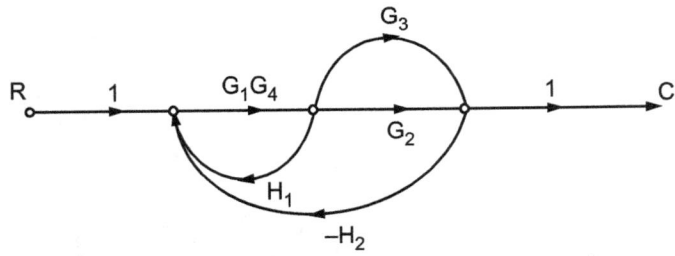

Fig. 1.158

(i) Forward loop gain :

$$P_1 = G_1G_4G_2 \qquad\qquad P_2 = G_1G_4G_3$$

(ii) Loop gain :

$$L_{11} = -G1G_4H_1$$

$$L_{21} = -G_1G_4G_2H_1$$

$$L_{31} = -G_1G_4G_3H_2$$

All are touching loops

(iii) $\Delta = 1 - G_1G_4H_1 + G_1G_4G_2H_2 + G_1G_4G_3H_2$

(iv) $\Delta_1 = 1, \Delta_2 = 1$

(v) $\dfrac{C(s)}{R(s)} = \dfrac{G_1G_4G_2 + G_1 G_4G_3}{1 - G_1G_4H_1 + G_1G_4G_2H_2 + G_1G_4G_3H_2}$

1.8.4 Construction of Signal Flow Graph

- Write a set of simultaneous equations describing the system
- Consider one node for each variable and arrange them from left to right.
- Connect them by appropriate branches.
- If the desired output node has outgoing branches add a dummy node and a unity gain branch.
- Rearrange the loops and/or nodes in graph to achieve maximum pictorial clarity.

Example 1.22 : Find out overall transfer function of given circuit using SFG.

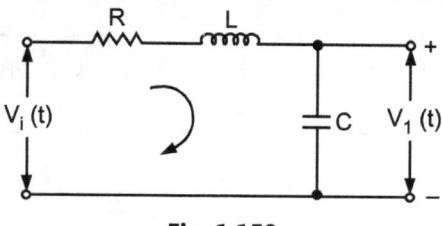

Fig. 1.159

Solution :

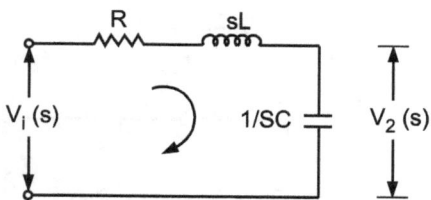

Fig. 1.160

$$I(s) = \frac{V_1(s) - V_2(s)}{R + sL}$$

$$= \frac{1}{(R + sL)} V_1(s) - \frac{1}{R + sL} V_2(s)$$

$$V_2 = \frac{1}{sC} I(s)$$

The SFG Can be

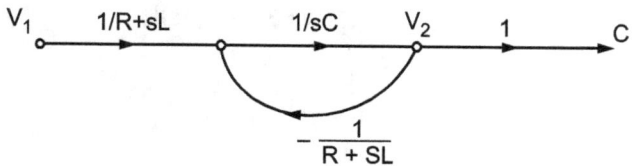

Fig. 1.161

(i) Forward loop path : $P_1 = \dfrac{1}{sC(R + sL)}$, $P_2 = 0$

(ii) Loop gain : $L_{11} = \dfrac{-1}{sC(R + sL)}$

(iii) $\Delta = 1 + \dfrac{1}{sC(r + sL)}$

(iv)   Transfer function $= \dfrac{\dfrac{1}{sC(R + sL)}}{1 + \dfrac{1}{sC(R + sL)}} = \dfrac{1}{s^2LC + sRC + 1}$

Example 1.23 : Find out the overall transfer function of given circuit using SFG.

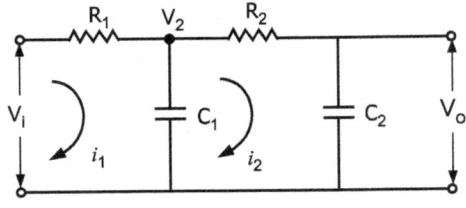

Fig. 1.162

Solution :

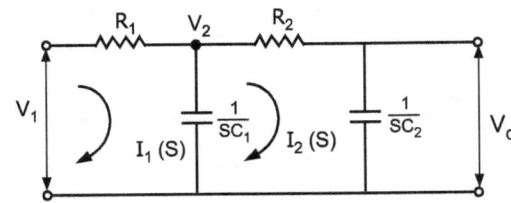

Fig. 1.163

$$I_1(s) = \frac{1}{R_1} [V_1(s) - V_2(s)]$$

$$V_2(s) = \frac{1}{sC_1} [I_1(s) - I_2(s)]$$

$$= \frac{1}{sC_1} I_1(s) - \frac{1}{sC_2} I_2(s)$$

$\therefore$

$$I_2(s) = \frac{1}{R_2} [V_2(s) - V_o(s)]$$

$$= \frac{1}{R_2} V_2(s) - \frac{1}{R_2} V_o(s)$$

$$V_o(s) = \frac{1}{sC_2} I_2(s)$$

Now to draw SFG :

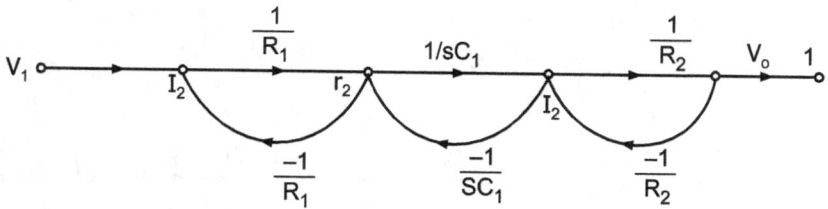

Fig. 1.164

(i) Forward loop path : $P_1 = \dfrac{1}{s_2 R_1 R_2 C_1 C_2}$

(ii) Loop gain : $L_{11} = -\dfrac{1}{sR_1C_1}$ $L_{21} = \dfrac{-1}{sR_2C_1}$

$\qquad\qquad L_{31} = \dfrac{-1}{sR_2C_2}$

$\qquad\qquad L_{12} = L_{11}$ $L_{31} = \dfrac{1}{s^2 R_1 R_2 C_1 C_2}$

(iii) $\Delta_1 = 1,$

(iv) Transfer function $= \dfrac{V_o(s)}{V_1(s)} = \dfrac{P_1 \Delta_1}{\Delta} = \dfrac{\dfrac{1}{s^2 R_1 R_2 C_1 C_2}}{1 - \left(\dfrac{-1}{sR_1C_1}\dfrac{-1}{sRC_1}\dfrac{-1}{sR_2C_2}\right) + \dfrac{1}{s^2 R_1 R_2 C_1 C_2}}$

$\qquad\qquad = \dfrac{1}{s^2\, R_1 R_2 C_1 C_2 + s\,(R_2 C_2 + R_1 C_2 R_1\, C_2 + R_1 C_1) + 1}$

Example 1.24 : Find out the overall transfer gain using SFG.

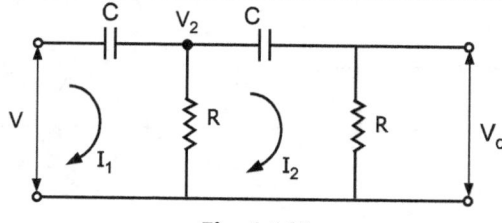

Fig. 1.165

Solution :

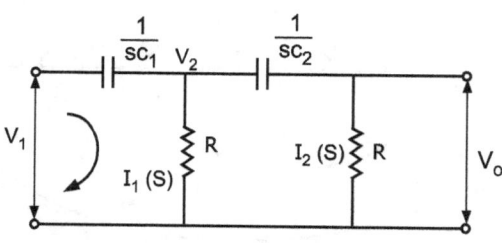

Fig. 1.166

$$I_1 = sCV_1 - sc\ V_2$$
$$V_2 = R\ [I_1\ (s) - I_2\ (s)]$$
$$I_2 = sC\ [V_2(s) - V\ (s)]$$
$$V_o = R\ I_2\ (s)$$

SFG is as follows :

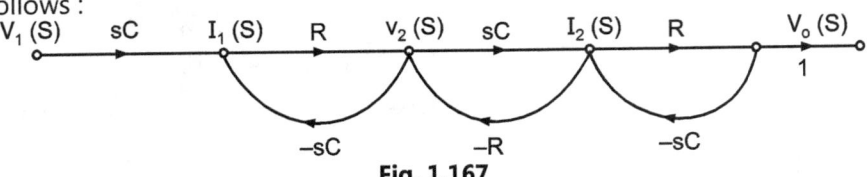

Fig. 1.167

(i)   Forward loop path :
$$P_1 = sc \times R \times sc \times R = s^2R^2C^2$$

(ii) Loop gain $L_{11} = -sRC,$ $L_{21} = -sRC,$ $L_{31} = -sRC$

(iii) Non-touching loops
$$L_4 = (-sRC) \times (-sRC) = s^2R^2C^2$$
$$\Delta_1 = 1$$
$$\Delta = (1 + 3sRC + s^2R^2\ (2)$$

(iv)   Transfer function $= \dfrac{P_1\Delta_1}{1} = \dfrac{s^2R^2C^2}{1 + 3sRC + s^2R^2C^2}$

Example 1.25 : Determine the over all Transfer function of the system shown in the Fig. 1.168 by using SFG

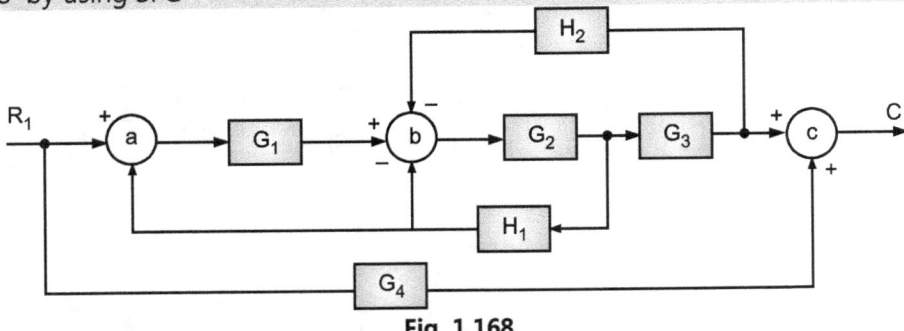

Fig. 1.168

Solution :

SFG is as follows :

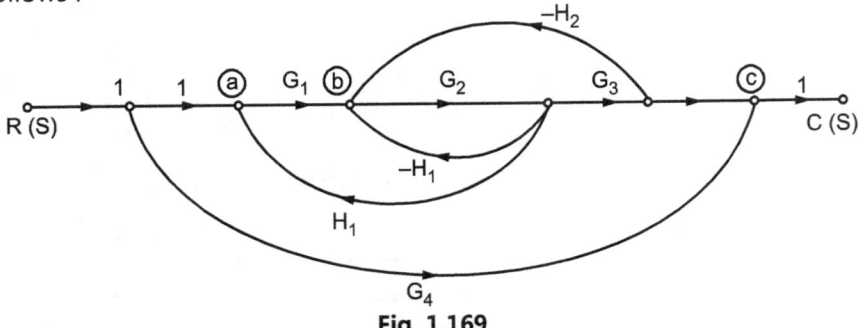

Fig. 1.169

(i)   Forward loop path :

$$P_1 = G_1G_2G_3, \qquad\qquad\qquad P_2 = G_4$$

(ii) Loop gains : $L_{11} = -G_2H_1,$ $\qquad\qquad\qquad L_{21} = -G_2G_3H_2$

$$L_{31} = G_1G_2H_1$$

(iii) No Non-touching loops

(iv) $\Delta_1 = 1$ $\qquad\qquad\qquad\qquad \Delta_2 = \Delta$

(v)   Transfer function$= \dfrac{P_1\Delta_1 + P_2\Delta_2}{\Delta}$

$$= \frac{G_1G_2G_3 + G_4\,(1 + G_2H_1 + G_3G_2H_2 - G_1G_2H_1)}{1 + G_2H_1 + G_2G_3H_2 - G_1G_2H_1}$$

Example 1.26 : Determine the transfer function $\dfrac{C(s)}{R(s)}$ for the block diagram as shown in Fig. 1.170 by first drawing its signal flow graph and then using the Mason's gain formula.

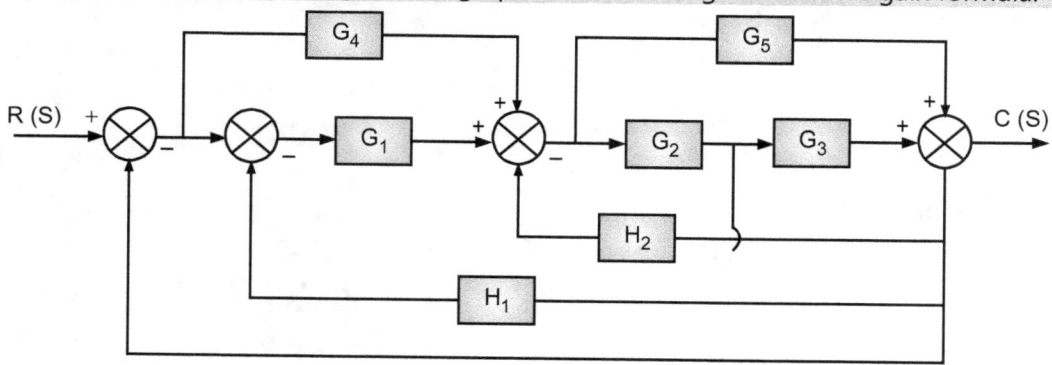

Fig. 1.170

Solution :

Signal flow graph of the Block diagram :

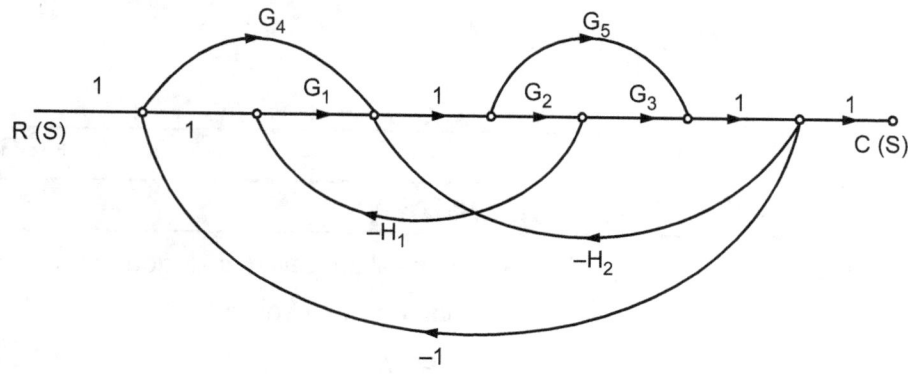

Fig. 1.171

Mason's gain formula,

Overall system gain is given by

$$T = \frac{1}{D} \Sigma P_K \Delta K$$

P_K – gain of kth forward path

Δ = det of the graph

= 1 – (Sum of loop gains of all individual loops) + (Sum of gain products of all possible combinations of two non- touching loops) – (Sum of gain products of all possible combinations of three non touching loops) + ...

Δ_k = the value of Δ for the that part of the graph not touching the Kth forward path.

There are four path gains,

$$P_1 = G_1G_2H_1$$
$$P_2 = G_4G_2H_3$$
$$P_3 = G_1G_5$$
$$P_4 = G_4G_2H_5$$

Individual loop gains are,

$$P_{11} = -G_1G_2H_1 \qquad\qquad P_{51} = -G_1G_2G_3$$
$$P_{21} = G_5H_2 \qquad\qquad\quad P_{61} = -G_4G_2G_3$$
$$P_{31} = G_2G_3 H_2 \qquad\qquad P_{71} = -G_1G_5$$
$$P_{41} = G_45_s$$

There are no non-touching loops

$$\Delta = 1 - (-G_1G_2H_1 - G_5H_2 - G_2 G_3H_2 - G_4G_5 - G_1G_2G_3 - G_4G_2G_3 - G_1G_5)$$

$$T = \frac{P_1\Delta_1 + P_2 \Delta_2 + P_3 \Delta_3 + P_4 \Delta_4}{\Delta}$$

$$= \frac{G_1G_2G_3 + G_4G_2G_3 + G_1G_5 + G_4G_5}{1+ G_1G_2H_1 + G_5 H_2 + G_2G_3 H_2 + G_4 G_5 + G_1G_2 G_3 + G_4 G_2G_3 + G_1G_5}$$

SUMMARY

- Systems whose differential equations are identical are called analogous systems.
- The transfer is defined only when initial conditions are neglected.
- Spring is an element that stores potential energy.
- The force of sliding friction between dry surfaces is called coulomb friction force.

- The force required to initiate motion between two contacting surfaces is called Stiction.
- For proper transfer function, the order of the numerator.
- The friction force acts in a direction opposite to that of motion.
- Mason's gain formula is especially useful in reducing large and complex system diagrams in one step, without requiring step-by-step reductions.
- Non-touching loops are loops which do not possess any common node.
- Block diagrams can be used to represent both linear and non-linear systems.
- Open loop system consumes less power; whereas closed loop system consumes more power.
- Open loop control systems are generally stable; whereas major efforts are needed to make it stable system.

EXERCISE

1. Write the differential equations governing the mechanical system shown in Fig. 1.172 and determine the transfer function.

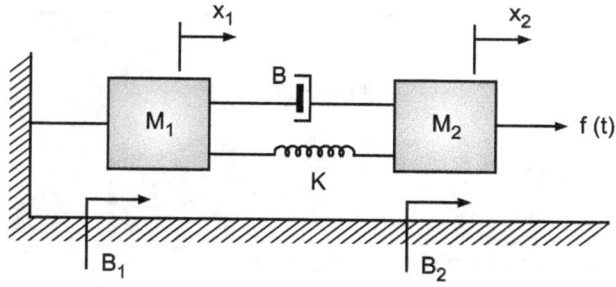

Fig. 1.172

2. Find the overall gain of the system whose signal flow graph is shown in Fig. 1.173.

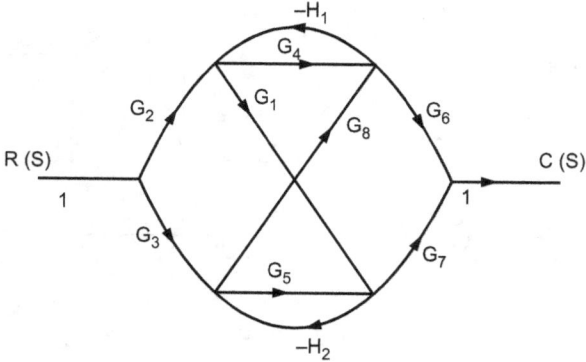

Fig. 1.173

3. Find the output of the given system is

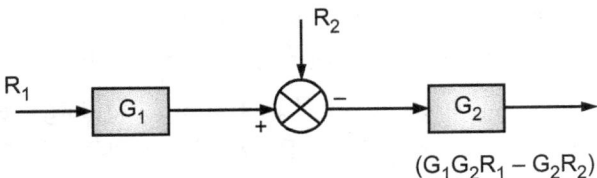

$$(G_1G_2R_1 - G_2R_2)$$

Fig. 1.174

4. Calculate the transfer function using Block diagram reduction techniques.

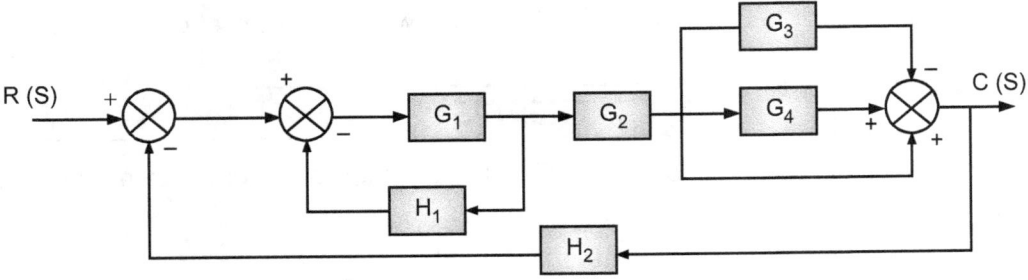

Fig. 1.175

Ans. $$\frac{C(s)}{R(s)} = \frac{G_1\,G_2\,(1 + G_4 - G_3)}{1 + G_1H_1 + [G_1\,G_2\,(1 + G_4 - G_3)]\,H_2}$$

5. Find the transfer function using signal flow graph

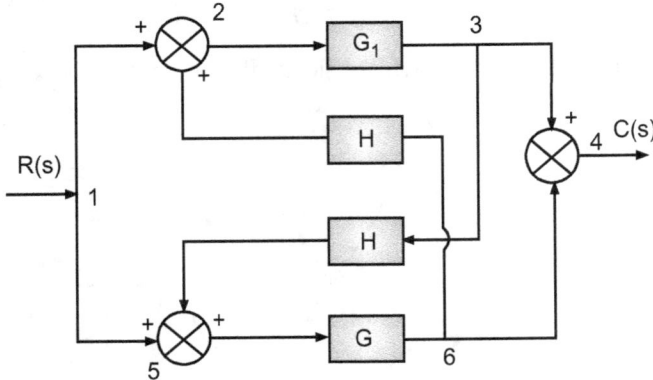

Fig. 1.176

Ans. : Transfer function $= \dfrac{2G}{1 - GH}$

6. Find the transfer function $\dfrac{C(s)}{R(s)}$ for the SFG shown below.

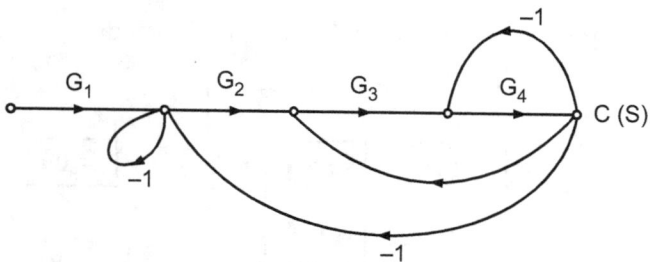

Fig. 1.177

Ans. : $\dfrac{G_1G_2G_3G_4}{1 + G_2\,G_3\,G_4 + 2\,G_3G_4 + 2G_4}$

7. Determine $\dfrac{C(s)}{R(s)}$ for the block diagram shown.

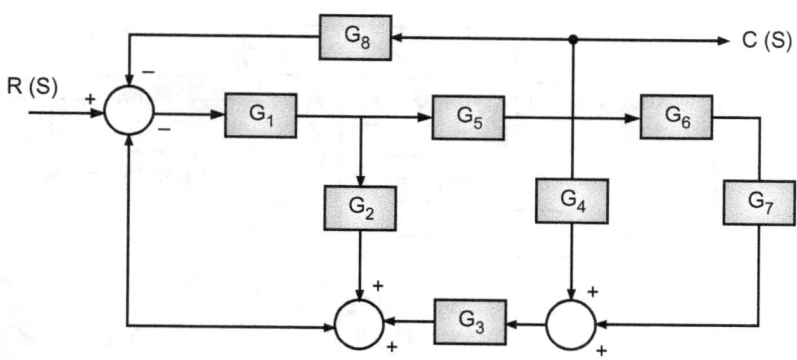

Fig. 1.178

Ans. : $\dfrac{G_1G_5}{1+ G_1\,(G_5G_8 + G_3G_4G_5 + G_2 + G_3G_5\,G_6\,G_7)}$

8. Find the transfer function $\dfrac{V_o(s)}{V_i(s)}$ for the network

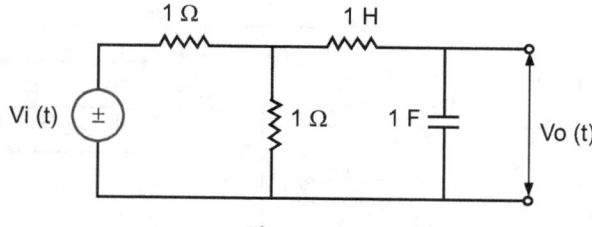

Fig. 1.179

Ans. : $\dfrac{1}{2s^2 + s +2}$

SOLVED UNIVERSITY PROBLEMS

Example 1.1 : Find $\dfrac{C(s)}{R(s)}$ for the system in Fig. 1.180 using block diagram rules.   **[Dec. 2015]**

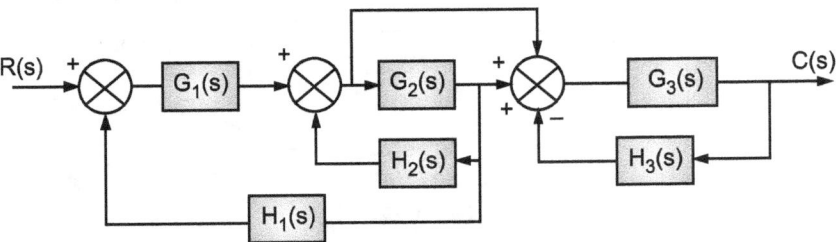

Fig. 1.180

Solution : Indicate summing points and take off points with numbers to solve easy as follows.

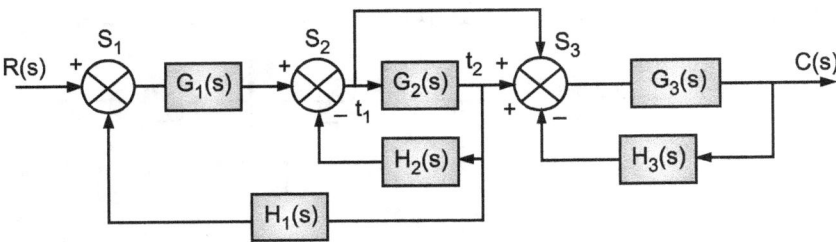

Fig. 1.181

Now apply Block Diagram Reduction rules to find $\dfrac{C(s)}{R(s)}$

Step 1 : Apply feedback rule to $G_3(s)$ and $H_3(s)$

By applying feedback rule $\dfrac{G_3(s)}{1 + G_3(s).\,H_3(s)}$

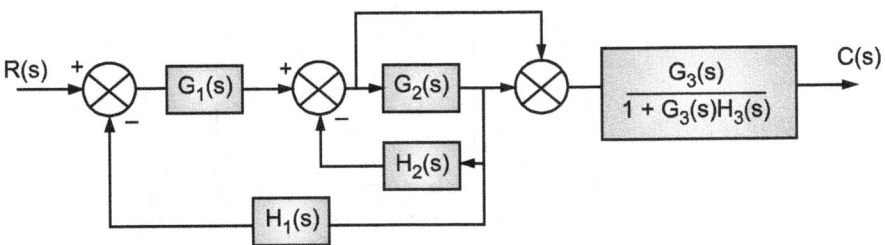

Fig. 1.182

Step 2 : Apply Moving take off point after the block to remove t_1

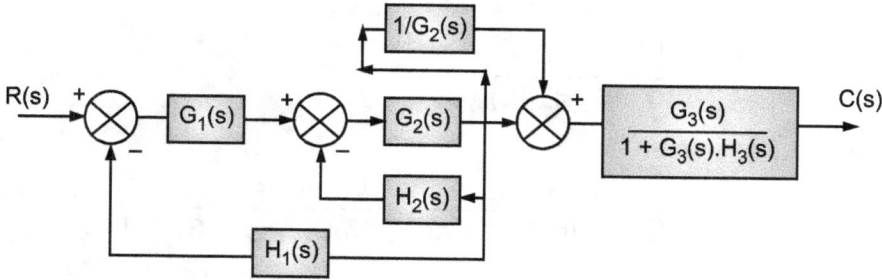

Fig. 1.183

We can interchange t_1 and t_2 no block existed between t_1 and t_2

Step 3 : Apply parallel block rule to 1 and $1/G_2(s)$

$$\frac{1}{G_2(s)} + 1 = \frac{1 + G_2(s)}{G_2(s)}$$

Step 4 : Apply feedback rule to $G_2(s)$ and $H_2(s)$

$$\frac{G_2(s)}{1 + G_2(s).\,H_2(s)}$$

Hence, the reduced block diagram is :

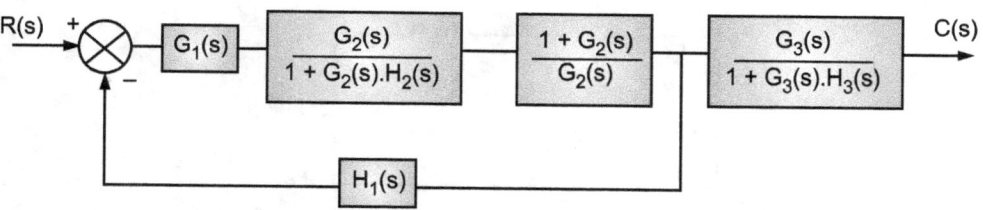

Fig. 1.184

Step 5 : Applying series/cascaded block rule : $\dfrac{G_1(s).\,G_2(s)}{1 + G_2(s).\,H_2(s)}$

Step 6 : Apply feedback rule :

$$= \frac{\dfrac{G_1(s).G_2(s)}{1 + G_2(s).H_2(s)}}{1 + \dfrac{G_1(s).G_2(s)}{1 + G_2(s).H_2(s)}H_1(s)} = \frac{G_1(s).G_2(s)}{1 + G_2(s)\,H_2(s) + G_1(s)\,G_2(s).\,H_1(s)}$$

Step 7 : Apply series block rule to all series blocks

For block 1 : $= \dfrac{G_1(s).G_2(s)}{1 + G_2(s)\,H_2(s) + G_1(s)\,G_2(s).\,H_1(s)}$

For Block 2 : $= \dfrac{1+ G_2(s)}{G_2(s)}$

For Block 3 : $= \dfrac{G_3(s)}{1 + G_3(s).H_3(s)}$

Now multiple all three blocks

$$\left(\dfrac{G_1(s).\ G_2(s)}{1 + G_2(s)H_2(s) + G_1(s)\ G_2(s)H_1(s)}\right)\left(\dfrac{1 + G_2(s)}{G_2(s)}\right)\left(\dfrac{G_3(s)}{1 + G_3(s)\ H_3(s)}\right)$$

Final transform function is

$$\dfrac{C(s)}{R(s)} = \dfrac{(G_1(s)\ G_2(s))(1 + G_2\ (s))\ (G_3(s)\ (s))}{(1 + G_2(s)\ H_2(s) + G_1(s)\ G_2(s)\ H_1(s))\ (G_2(s))\ (1 + G_3(s)\ H_3(s))}$$

$$\dfrac{C(s)}{R(s)} = \dfrac{G_1 G_2 G_3(1 + G_2)}{(1 + G_2 H_2 + G_1 G_2\ H_1)\ (G_2 + G_2 G_3 H_3)}$$

Example 1.2 : Consider the R-L-C network shown in Fig. 1.185.

(i) Obtain transfer function if v_i and v_o are input and output voltage resp.

(ii) Find the location of poles in terms of R, L and C.

(iii) If R = 1 MΩ, C = 1μF, L = 1mH. Is the location of poles of transfer function given in (i) are real ? If yes, find the location.   **[Dec. 2015]**

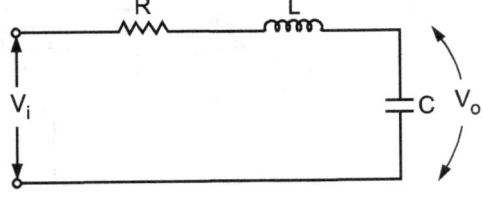

Fig. 1.185

Solution :

To get the transfer function. Apply KVL to get input equations an output equations.

Input equation :

$$Vi(t) = Ri(t) + L\dfrac{di(t)}{dt} + \dfrac{1}{C}\int i(t)\ d_t$$

Apply laplace $$V_I(s) = RI(s) + LSI\ (s) + \dfrac{1}{sC}\ I(s)$$

$$V_I(s) = RI(s) + LSI\ (s) + \dfrac{1}{sC}\ I(s)$$

$$V_I s = \left(R + LS + \dfrac{1}{sC}\right)\ I(s) \qquad\qquad ... (1)$$

Output equation

$$V_o(t) = \frac{1}{sC} \int i(t)\, dt$$

Apply laplace
$$V_o(s) = \frac{1}{C} I(s) \qquad\qquad \dots (2)$$

Transfer function
$$\frac{V_o(s)}{V_I(s)} = \frac{\left(\dfrac{1}{sC}\right) I(s)}{\left(R + Ls + \dfrac{1}{sC}\right) I(s)}$$

$$\frac{V_o(s)}{V_I(s)} = \frac{1}{LCs^2 + RCs + 1}$$

(ii) Poles with respect to R, L, C
   Using this formula,

$$x = \frac{-b \pm \sqrt{b^2 - 4ac}}{2a}$$

Where,   a = LC, b = RC, C = 1

$$S_1, S_2 = \frac{-RC \pm \sqrt{(RC)^2 - 4LC}}{2LC}$$

(iii) If R = 1 M, L = 1mH, and C = 1 mF

$$\frac{V_o(s)}{V_I(s)} = \frac{1}{LCs^2 + RCs + 1}$$

Substitute values we get,

$$\frac{V_o(s)}{V_I(s)} = \frac{1}{(10^{-9}) s^2 + 1s + 1}$$

Poles :

$$S_1 = -1.0001$$
$$S_2 = 999999999 = 1000 \times 10^6$$

Poles are real with given values.

Example 1.3 : Give the various terminology of electrical system and it's analogous quantities based force current analogy.   **[May 2015] [6]**

Solution : Consider the Fig. 1.186.

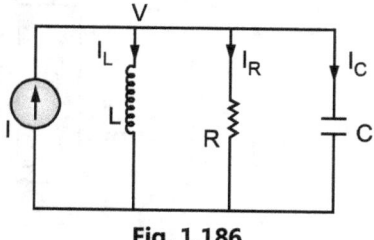

Fig. 1.186

Apply KCL to the circuit,

$$I = I_L + I_R + I_C$$

$\therefore$ Node voltage is v

$$I = \frac{1}{L} \int V \, dt + \frac{v}{R} + C \frac{dv}{dt}$$

$\therefore$ Taking Laplace transform,

$$I(s) = \frac{V(s)}{sL} + \frac{V(s)}{R} + sC\,V(s)$$

But $$V(t) = \frac{d\phi}{dt}$$

$$Vs = s\,\phi(s)$$

i.e. $$\phi(s) = \frac{V(s)}{s}$$ $\because \phi = $ Flux

Put in the equation of I_s

$$Is = Cs^2\,\phi(s) + \frac{1}{R}\,s\,\phi(s) + \frac{1}{L}\,\phi(s)$$

The analogous quantities based on F-I analogy are :

- **Translation :** Force (F), Mass (M), Friction (B), Spring (k), Displace (X), $\dot{X}$ velocity $= \dfrac{dx}{dt}$.

- **Rational :** T, J, B, k, θ, $\dot{\theta} = \dfrac{d\theta}{dt} = \omega$.

- **Electrical :** Current (I), Capacitor (C), Reciprocal of resistance $\left(\dfrac{1}{R}\right)$, Reciprocal of inductance $\left(\dfrac{1}{L}\right)$, ϕ, Voltage 'e' $= \dfrac{d\phi}{dt}$.

Example 1.4 : Write the differential equations of system shown in Fig. 1.187. Also find $\dfrac{X_1(s)}{F(s)}$.

[May 2015] [6]

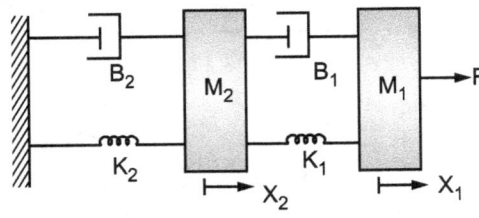

Fig. 1.187

Solution : M_1 is under the influence of x_1. K_1 and B_1 are between x_1 and x_2. Mass M_2, K_2 and B_2 are under the influence of x_2. Fig. 1.188. Shows the equivalent mechanical system.

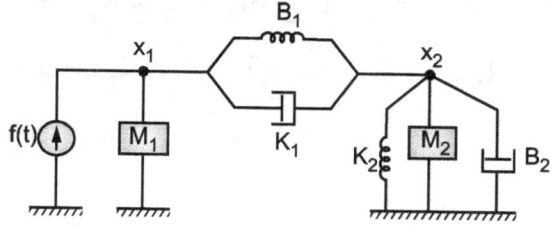

Fig. 1.188

The differential equations are as follows :

$$f(t) = M_1 \frac{d^2 x_1}{dt^2} + B_1 \frac{d(x_1 - x_2)}{dt} + K_1 (x_1 - x_2) \qquad \dots (1)$$

$$0 = B_1 d \frac{(x_2 - x_1)}{dt} + K_1 (x_2 - x_1)$$

$$+ M_2 \frac{d^2 x_2}{dt^2} + B_2 \frac{dx_2}{dt} + K_2 x_2 \qquad \dots (2)$$

Taking Laplace transform of equation (1) and (2),

$$F(s) = M_1 s^2 X_1(s) + B_1 s [X_1(s) - X_2(s)] + K_1[X_1(s) - X_2(s)]$$
$$F(s) = X_1(s) [M_1 s^2 + sB_1 + K_1] - X_2(s) [B_1 s + K_1] \qquad \dots (3)$$
$$0 = B_1 s[X_2(s) - X_1(s)] + K_1[X_2(s) - X_1(s)] + M_2 s^2 X_2(s)$$
$$+ B_2 s X_2(s) + K_2 X_2(s)$$
$$0 = X_2(s) [s^2 M_2 + s(B_1 + B_2) + (K_1 + K_2)]$$
$$- X_1(s) [sB_1 + K_1] \qquad \dots (4)$$

$$\therefore \qquad X_2(s) = \frac{X_1(s) [sB_1 + K_1]}{[s^2 M_2 + s(B_1 + B_2) + (K_1 + K_2)]}$$

and use in equation (3).

$$\therefore \qquad F(s) = x_1(s)$$
$$\left\{ (M_1 s^2 + sB_1 + K_1) - \frac{(B_1 s + K_1)(B_1 s + K_1)}{[s^2 M_2 + s(B_1 + B_2) + (K_1 + K_2)]} \right\}$$

$$\therefore \qquad \frac{X_1(s)}{F(s)} = \frac{s^2 M_2 + s(B_1 + B_2) + (K_1 + K_2)}{\{[M_2 s^2 + s(B_1 + B_2) + (K_1 + K_2)]}$$
$$(M_1 s^2 + sB_1 + K_1) - (B_1 s + K_1)^2\}$$

Example 1.5 : Obtain transfer function of the system shown in Fig. 1.189.   **[May 2015] [6]**

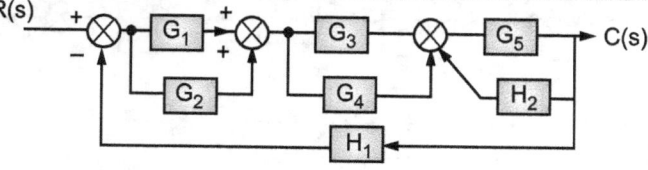

Fig. 1.189

Solution :

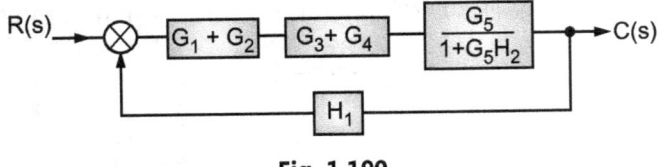

Fig. 1.190

G_1, G_2 are in parallel.

G_4 in parallel given $G_3 + G_4$.

G_5 and H_2 forms minor feedback loop $\dfrac{G_5}{1 + G_5H_2}$

$$\frac{C(s)}{R(s)} = \frac{(G_1 + G_2)(G_3 + G_4)\left(\dfrac{G_5}{1 + G_5H_2}\right)}{1 + (G_1 + G_2)(G_3 + G_4)\left(\dfrac{G_5}{1 + G_5H_2}\right)H_1}$$

$$\frac{C(s)}{R(s)} = \frac{G_1G_3G_5 + G_1G_4G_5 + G_2G_3G_5 + G_2G_4G_5}{1 + G_5H_2 + G_1G_3G_5H_1 + G_1G_4G_5H_1 + G_2G_3G_5H_1 + G_2G_4G_5H_1}$$

Example 1.6 : Find the closed loop transfer function $\dfrac{C(s)}{R(s)}$ of system shown in Fig. 1.191 using block reduction techniques.   **[May 2014] [6]**

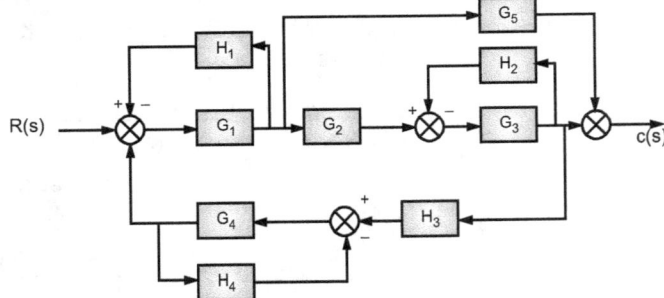

Fig. 1.191

Solution : Reduce the loops of (G_1, H_1), (G_3, H_2) and (G_4, H_4).

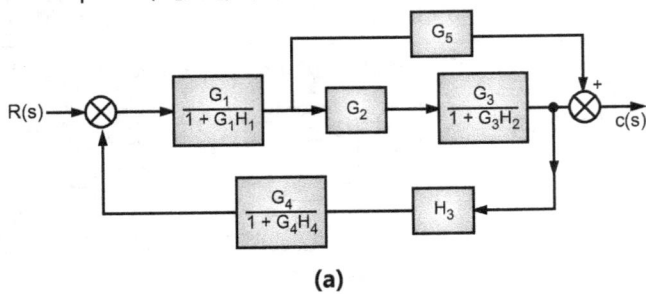

(a)

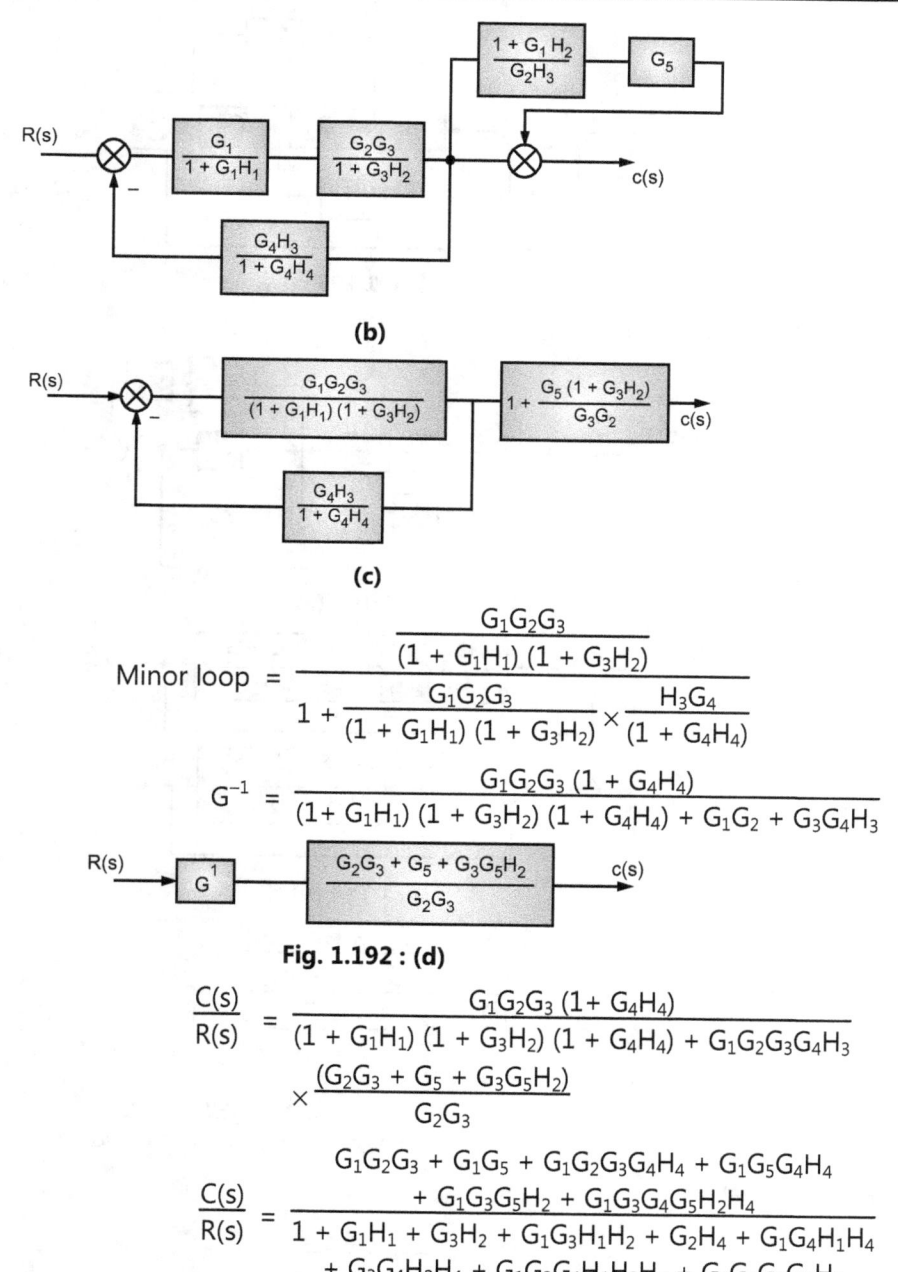

(b)

(c)

$$\text{Minor loop} = \cfrac{\cfrac{G_1 G_2 G_3}{(1 + G_1 H_1)(1 + G_3 H_2)}}{1 + \cfrac{G_1 G_2 G_3}{(1 + G_1 H_1)(1 + G_3 H_2)} \times \cfrac{H_3 G_4}{(1 + G_4 H_4)}}$$

$$G^{-1} = \frac{G_1 G_2 G_3 (1 + G_4 H_4)}{(1 + G_1 H_1)(1 + G_3 H_2)(1 + G_4 H_4) + G_1 G_2 + G_3 G_4 H_3}$$

Fig. 1.192 : (d)

$$\therefore \quad \frac{C(s)}{R(s)} = \frac{G_1 G_2 G_3 (1 + G_4 H_4)}{(1 + G_1 H_1)(1 + G_3 H_2)(1 + G_4 H_4) + G_1 G_2 G_3 G_4 H_3}$$
$$\times \frac{(G_2 G_3 + G_5 + G_3 G_5 H_2)}{G_2 G_3}$$

$$\therefore \quad \frac{C(s)}{R(s)} = \frac{\begin{array}{c} G_1 G_2 G_3 + G_1 G_5 + G_1 G_2 G_3 G_4 H_4 + G_1 G_5 G_4 H_4 \\ + G_1 G_3 G_5 H_2 + G_1 G_3 G_4 G_5 H_2 H_4 \end{array}}{\begin{array}{c} 1 + G_1 H_1 + G_3 H_2 + G_1 G_3 H_1 H_2 + G_2 H_4 + G_1 G_4 H_1 H_4 \\ + G_3 G_4 H_2 H_4 + G_1 G_3 G_4 H_1 H_2 H_4 + G_1 G_2 G_3 G_4 H_3 \end{array}}$$

Example 1.7 : Find closed loop transfer function $\dfrac{Y(s)}{X(s)}$ if

$$G' = G_2 = \frac{1}{s + 1} \text{ and } G_3 = G_4 = s + 1, \ H_1 = 1.$$

Shown in Fig. 1.193 using block diagram.   **[Dec. 2014] [6]**

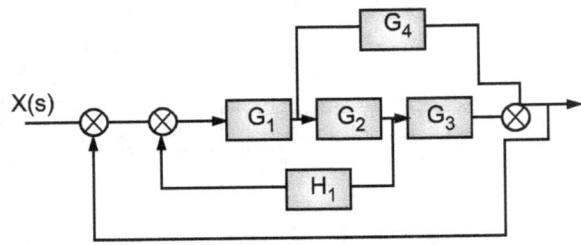

Fig. 1.193

Solution : Shift point G_4 after G_2.

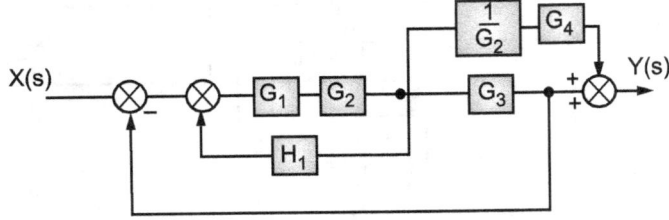

Fig. 1.194 (a)

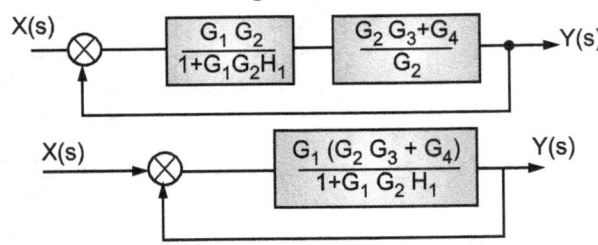

Fig. 1.194 (b)

$$\therefore \quad \frac{Y(s)}{X(s)} = \frac{\dfrac{G_1 (G_2G_3 + G_4)}{1 + G_1G_2H_1}}{1 + \dfrac{G_1(G_2G_3 + G_4)}{1 + G_1G_2H_1}}$$

$$= \frac{G_1G_2G_3 + G_1G_4}{1 + G_1G_2H_1 + G_1G_2G_3 + G_1G_4}$$

Put given values,

$$\frac{Y(s)}{X(s)} = \frac{s^2 + 3s + 2}{2s^2 + 5s + 4}$$

TIME RESPONSE ANALYSIS

2.1 INTRODUCTION

Most of the control systems, use time as its independent variable, so it is important to analyse the response given by the system for the applied excitation which is function of time. Analysis of response means to see the variation of output with respect to time. The evaluation of system is based on analysis of such response.

The complete base of stability analysis lies in the time response analysis.

Definition : The time response of a control system means how output behaves with respect to time. It can also be defined as analysis of response of systems in time domain, when subjected to various types of inputs.

In a practical system, the type of the input signal is not known ahead of time. However, for the purpose of analysis, systems are tested for different types of standard known input signals. These signals are known as test signals. Some of them are the impulse input, step input, ramp input, and parabolic input signals.

Examples :

• **Systems are Like Human Beings :** On hearing the same information, all people do not react in the same way. Some people respond quickly to the information, other take much longer time to react. Some people are over excited while others do not show any interest.

Similarly, if we inject the same type and equal amplitude input signal to different systems, some respond quickly, some respond slowly, some become over excited and bounce around while others sluggishly respond.

This behaviour of the systems is referred to as the dynamics of the systems.

• **Ammeter as a System :** A simple ammeter is connected in a system so as to measure current of magnitude 5A. Ammeter pointer hence must defect to show us 5A reading on it. so 5A is its ideal value that it must show. Now pointer will take some finite time to stabilise to indicate some reading and after stabilising also, it depends on various factors like friction, pointer, inertial, etc. whether it will show accurate 5A or not.

Based on this example, we can classify the total time response into two parts.

(i) Transient response.

(ii) Steady state response.

Total time response = transient response + steady state response.

$$C(t) \ = \ C_{tr}(t) + C_{ss}(t)$$

2.2 TRANSIENT RESPONSE

The transient response implies the manner in which output goes from the initial state to the final state.

- The time required to achieve final value is called transient period.

- Transient response of the systems is the portion of the total time response during which the output changes from one state to another state. In short, it is the response before the output reaching the steady state value.

- Transient vanishes after some time to get the final value closer to the desired value.

- Systems in which transient response dies out after some time are called stable systems.

Mathematically for stable operating systems,

$$\underset{t \to \infty}{\text{Lim}} \; C_t \, (t) = 0)$$

2.2.1 From the Transient Response We Can Get Following Information About the Systems

- When the system has stated showing its response to the applied excitation.

- What is the rate of rise of output ? From this, parameters of system can be designed which can withstand such rate of rise, it also gives indication about speed of the systems.

- Whether output is increasing exponentially or it is oscillating.

- If output is oscillating, whether it is over shooting its final value.

- When it is setting down to its final value.

All this information matters how much the time of designing the system.

Highlights

Transient response of a control system occurs mainly after two conditions.

(i) Just after switching 'on' the system that means at the time of application of an input signal to the system.

(ii) Just after any abnormal conditions. Abnormal conditions may include sudden change in the load, short circuiting etc.

2.3 STEADY STATE RESPONSE

It is that part of the time response which remains after transient response vanishes from the system output.

The Steady-state response means the manner in which the system output behaves as it approaches infinity.

- Steady state response of the system is the response of the system for a given input very long time. In steady state output settles to final steady state value or steady oscillations.

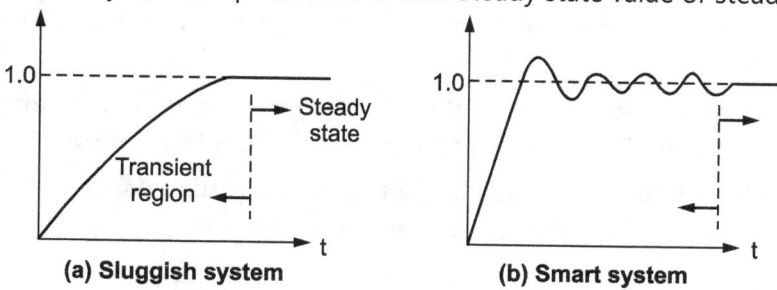

(a) Sluggish system   (b) Smart system

Fig. 2.1

2.3.1 From Steady State Response We Can Get Following Information About The System

- How far away the system output is from its desired value which indicates error.
- Whether this error is constant or varying with time. So the entire information about system performance can be obtained from transient and steady state response.
- The difference between desired output and the actual output of the system is called steady state error which is denoted as e_{ss}. This error indicates the accuracy and plays an important role in designing the systems.

Highlights

- Steady state occurs after the system becomes settled and at the steady state system starts working normally.
- Steady state response is function of i/p signal and it is also called as forced response.
- Steady state response of a control system depends only on the time constant 'T' and it is decaying in nature.

Keynote :
- Transient response may be exponential or oscillatory in nature.
- Steady state response is closely related to accuracy of the systems.
- Transient response shows how system goes from initial to final state.

2.4 TRANSFER FUNCTION

It is defined as ratio of laplace transform of output (Response function) to the laplace transform of input (Reference function) under the assumption all initial conditions are zero.

It is represented as G(s)

$$G(s) = \frac{N(s)}{D(s)} = \frac{a_0(s)^m + a_1(s)^{m-1} + \dots a_m}{b_0(s)^n + b_1(s)^{n-1} + \dots b_n}$$

$$G(s) = K(s - z_0)L(s - Z_1)\dots(s - Z_m)$$

- **Poles :** The value of S which makes the Transfer Function infinite after substituting in the denominator of the Transfer Function are called as poles of Transfer Function. This poles are nothing but roots of equation obtained by equating denominator of the Transfer Function to the zero.

- **Zero :** The value of x which makes the Transfer Function zero after substituting in the numerator of Transfer Function are called as zeros' of the Transfer Function.

- **Characteristic Equation :** The equation obtained by equating denominator to the zero is called as characteristic equation of the Transfer Function.

$$F(s) = b_0 s^n + b_1 s^n + \ldots b_n$$

$$F(s) = 1 + G(s) \cdot H(s) = 0$$

- **Order of the System :** The highest power of S in characteristic equation of Transfer Function is called as order of the system.

  The order of the system : Number of poles in systems.

  So the order of the system is also given by the number of poles of the Transfer Function.

- **Type of System :** The number poles at origin in the Transfer Function of the system is called as type 0 system.

  It indicates the number of open-loop poles present at origin. It decides the steady error.

- **Distinguish between Type and Order of A Control System**

The type number indicates the number of open-loop poles present at origin of the s-plane. It indicates the number of integrators present in the system whereas the order of a system indicates the number of poles present in the system Transfer Function. The type number is specified based on the number of open loop poles at origin of S-plane but order can be specified for open-loop systems as well as the closed-loop systems.

The effect of adding or removing a pole (or zero) at origin in a system affects the type of the system.

2.5 STANDARD TEST INPUT

The input to many practical control systems are not exactly known before time. The actual input may vary in random fashion with respect to time.

This is a challenging task for the designer, because it is difficult to design a control system which perform a satisfactorily to all possible forms of input signals.

In practice many signals are available which are function of time and can be used as reference input for various control system. These signals are step, ramp, sawtooth, square, triangular, etc. However, it is highly impossible to consider each one of it as a input to a system and examine its response. Hence from analysis point of view, those signals which are most commonly used as a reference inputs are defined as standard test input.

Evaluation of the system can be done on the basis of the response given by the system to the standard test inputs. Once the system behaves satisfactorily to the test input, its time response to actual input is assumed to be up to the mark.

By selecting these basic test signal properly, the mathematical treatment of the problems is systematized. The performance criterion may be specified with respect to these test signals so that the system may be designed to meet criteria.

The typical input signals to be used for analyzing system characteristics may be determined by the form of the i/p that the system will be subjected to most frequently under normal operation.

If the inputs to a control system are gradually changing functions of time, then a ramp function of time may be a appropriate input test signal. Similarly, if a system is subjected to a sudden disturbances, a step function may be good as input to a system. The use of such test signals enables one to compare the performance of all systems on the same basis.

2.5.1 Unit Impulse Response

For unit impulse input R(s) = 1

It is the input applied instantaneously of very high amplitude and short duration. Impulse response is the pulse whose width tends to zero and magnitude is infinite.

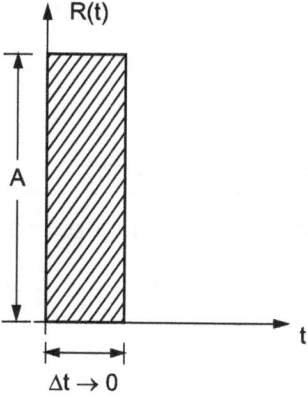

Fig. 2.2

Mathematically defined as,

$$R(t) = A \text{ for } t = 0$$
$$= 0 \text{ for } t \neq 0$$

Also represented as $\delta(t)$

If A = 1; then it is called unit impulse function

$L[\delta(t)] = 1$ for entire S-Plane.

2.5.2 Unit Step Input (Position Function)

Step function is the sudden application of the input at a specified time.

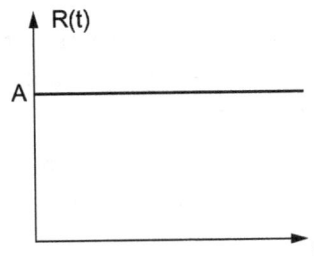

Fig. 2.3

Mathematically defined as ;

$$R(t) = A \text{ for } t \geq 0$$
$$= 0 \text{ for } t < 0$$

If A = 1; then it is called as unit step function and denoted by u(t)

The laplace transform of such input is $\dfrac{1}{s}$

$$u(t) = 1 \qquad \text{for } t \geq 0$$
$$= 0 \qquad \text{for } t < 0$$

∴ $$L[u(t)] = \dfrac{1}{s}$$

2.5.3 Ramp Function (Velocity function)

Ramp function is the constant rate of change in input i.e. gradual application of input. The magnitude of ramp is treated as slope.

Mathematically it is described as :

$$R(t) = At \qquad \text{for } t \geq 0$$
$$= 0 \qquad \text{for } t < 0$$

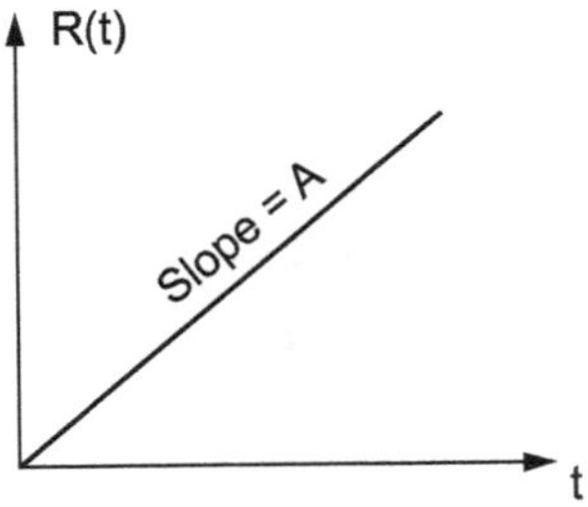

R(t)

Slope = A

Fig. 2.4

If A = 1 then it is called as unit ramp function

The laplace transform of ramp input is $\dfrac{1}{s^2}$

$$u(t) = t \qquad\qquad \text{for } t \geq 0$$

∴
$$L[u(t)] = \dfrac{1}{s^2}$$

2.5.4 Parabolic Input (Acceleration Function)

Parabolic inputs are one degree faster than a ramp type of input.

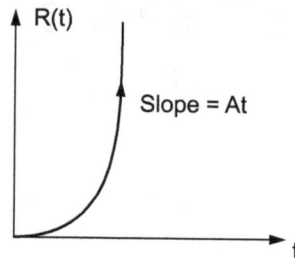

R(t)

Slope = At

t

Fig. 2.5

Mathematically, it is defined as;

$$R(t) = \dfrac{At^2}{2} \qquad\qquad \text{for } t \geq 0$$

$$= 0 \qquad\qquad \text{for } t < 0$$

It A = 1; then it is called unit parabolic function.

The laplace transform of such input is.

∴
$$L[R(t)] = \dfrac{A}{2} \times \dfrac{2!}{s^2+1} = \dfrac{A}{s^3}$$

2.6 TIME RESPONSE ANALYSIS OF FIRST ORDER SYSTEM

Transient Response Analysis

1st order system,

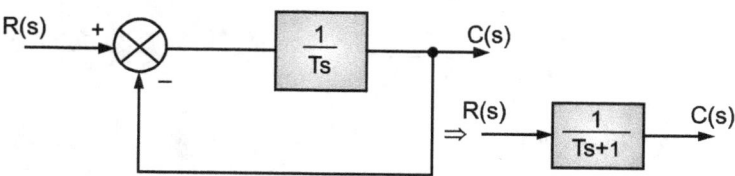

Fig. 2.6

The transient response may be exponential or oscillatory in nature.

First order system generally represented as;

$$\frac{C(s)}{R(s)} = \frac{1}{1 + Ts}$$

Time constant form ... (2.1)

2.6.1 Response to Impulse Input

Unit impulse function $r(t) = 1$, $t = 0$

$\therefore$ $R(s) = 1$

Substituting R(s) in equation (2.1)

$\therefore$

$$C(s) = \frac{1}{1 + Ts} \text{ or } \frac{1}{Ts + 1} = \frac{1/T}{s + 1/T}$$

Therefore, ILT

$$C(t) = L^{-1} \frac{1}{s + a} = e^{-at}$$

$\therefore$

$$C(s) = \frac{1/T}{s + 1/T}$$

$\therefore$

$$C(t) = \frac{1}{T} \cdot e^{-\frac{1}{T} \cdot t} \quad t \geq 0$$

The output c(t) is negative exponential. The response starts from 1/T and finally it becomes to zero.

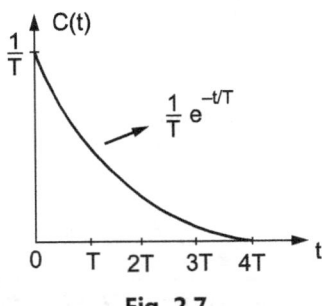

Fig. 2.7

2.6.2 Response to Step Input

A general first order system is represented by

$$\frac{C(s)}{R(s)} = \frac{1}{Ts + 1}$$

... (2.2)

As the input is a unit-step function,

$$r(t) = 1 \quad \text{for } t \geq 0$$

$\therefore$

$$R(s) = \frac{1}{s}$$

Substituting R(s) in equation (2.2)

$$C(s) = \frac{R(s)}{1 + Ts} = \frac{1/s}{1 + Ts}$$

$$C(s) = \frac{1}{s(Ts + 1)}$$

Expanding C(s) into partial fraction gives

$$C(s) = \frac{a}{s} + \frac{b}{Ts + 1}$$

$$a = \left. \frac{1}{Ts + 1} \right|_{s = 0} = 1$$

$$b = \left. \frac{1}{s} \right|_{s = -1/T} = -T$$

∴ $a = 1, b = -t$

∴ $C(s) = \frac{1}{s} - \frac{T}{Ts + 1}$

$$C(t) = \frac{1}{s} - \frac{1}{s + 1/T}$$

Therefore, $C(t) = 1 - e^{-t/T}$ for $t \geq 0$ ... (2.3)

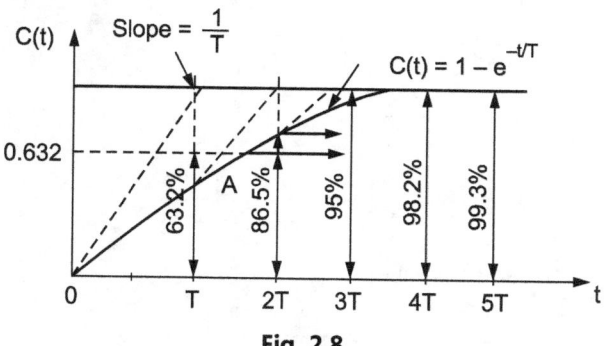

Fig. 2.8

The output C(t) is exponentially. The response is initially zero and finally it becomes unit as shown in Fig. 2.8.

An important characteristic of such an exponential response curve C(t) is that at t = T, the value of C(t) is 0.632, or the response C(t) has reached 63.2% of the final value, i.e.

$$C(T) = 1 - e^{-1} = 0.632$$

The time at which, response reaches 63.2% of its final value is called as time constant is (τ) of the system.

- Smaller the time constant (τ), faster is the system response.

The variation of o/p w.r.t time constant is tabulated in table 2.1

Table 2.1

Time	Output (%)	Error(%)
T	63.2	36.8
2T	86.5	13.5
3T	95	5
4T	98.2	1.8
5T	99.3	0.7

Thus, for t $\geq$ 4T, the response remains within 2% of final value.

2.6.3 Response to Ramp Input

A general first order system is represented by

$$\frac{C(s)}{R(s)} = \frac{1}{Ts + 1} \qquad \qquad \text{... (2.4)}$$

As the input is a unit-ramp function,

$$r(t) = t \quad \text{for } t \geq 0$$

$$\therefore \qquad R(s) = \frac{1}{s^2}$$

Substituting R(s) in equation (2.4)

$$C(s) = \frac{R(s)}{Ts + 1}$$

$$C(s) = \frac{1/s^2}{Ts + 1} = C(s) = \frac{1}{s^2(Ts + 1)}$$

Expanding C(s) into partial fractions gives,

$$C(s) = \frac{a}{s^2} + \frac{b}{s} + \frac{c}{T_{s + 1}} \qquad \qquad \text{... (2.5)}$$

$$a = \left. \frac{1}{Ts + 1} \right|_{s = 0} = 1$$

$$b = \left. \frac{d}{ds} \frac{1}{Ts + 1} \right|_{s = 0} = \frac{d}{ds} (Ts + 1)^{-1}$$

$$= \left. -1 (Ts + 1)^{-2} \, T \right|_{s = 0}$$

$\therefore$ $\qquad\qquad b = -T$

$$C = \left.\frac{1}{s^2}\right|_{s = -1/T}$$

$$C = T^2$$

$\therefore$ $\qquad\qquad a = 1; b = -T, C = T^2$

Substituting these values in equation (2.5)

$$C(s) = \frac{1}{s^2} - \frac{T}{s} + \frac{T^2}{Ts + 1}$$

$$C(s) = \frac{1}{s^2} - \frac{T}{s} + \frac{T}{s + 1/T} \qquad\qquad \text{... (2.6)}$$

Therefore taking ILT of equation (2.6)

$$C(t) = t - T + T.e^{-t/T} \qquad \text{for } t \geq 0 \qquad\qquad \text{... (2.7)}$$

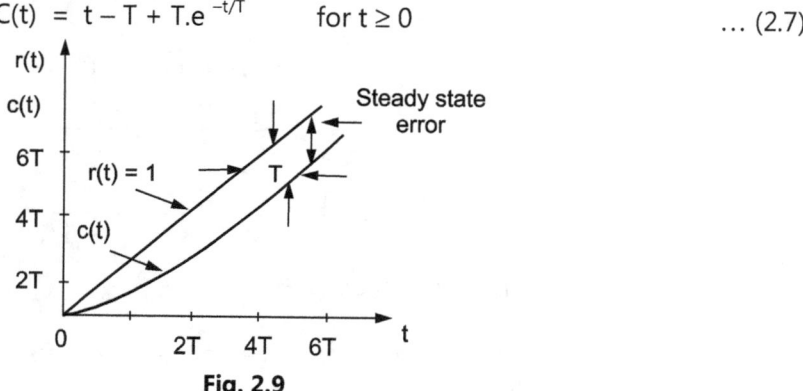

Fig. 2.9

The response is initially zero, and tracs the ramp signal.

2.6.4 Response to Parabolic Input

For first order system :

$$\frac{C(s)}{R(s)} = \frac{1}{Ts + 1} \qquad\qquad \text{... (2.8)}$$

For parabolic i/p $\qquad\qquad R(s) = \frac{1}{s^3}$

$\therefore$ From equation (2.8)

$$C(s) = \frac{1}{s^3 (Ts + 1)} = \frac{1}{s^3} \frac{1/T}{(s + 1/T)}$$

Expanding C(s) into partial fractions gives,

$$C(s) = \frac{A}{s^3} + \frac{B}{s^2} + \frac{C}{s} + \frac{D}{(Ts + 1)}$$

$$= \frac{A}{s^3} + \frac{B}{s^2} + \frac{C}{s} + \frac{D}{(s + 1/T)}$$

$$A = s^3 \left. \frac{1/T}{s^3(s + 1/T)} \right|_{s = 0} = \frac{1/T}{1/T} = 1$$

$$B = \left\{ \frac{d}{ds} \left[\frac{s^3 \, 1/T}{s^3 \, (s + 1/T)} \right] \right\}_{S = 0}$$

$$B = \left\{ \frac{d}{ds} \left[\frac{1/T}{s + 1/T} \right] \right\}_{s = 0} = \left\{ \frac{1}{T} \cdot \frac{-1}{(s + 1/T)^2} \right\}_{s = 0}$$

$$B = \frac{1}{T} \frac{-1}{(1/T)^2} = \frac{1}{T} \frac{-1}{1/T^2} = \frac{1}{T} \times \frac{-T^2}{1}$$

$$B = -T$$

For C and D values on next page

$$a = 1, b = T, c = T^2, d = T^3$$

∴

$$C(s) = \frac{1}{s^3} - \frac{T}{s^2} + \frac{2T^2}{s} - \frac{T^3}{Ts + 1}$$

$$C(s) = \frac{1}{s^3} - \frac{T}{s^2} + \frac{2T^2}{s} - \frac{T^2}{s + 1/T} \qquad \ldots (2.9)$$

Therefore taking ILT of above equation (2.9)

$$C(t) = \frac{t^2}{2} - T_t + T^2 T^2 - T^2, e^{-t/T} \text{ for } t \geq 0$$

In most cases, it is desirable that the transient response be sufficiently fast and be sufficiently damped. Thus, for a desirable transient response, the damping ratio must be between 0.4 and 0.8. For large values of (ξ > 0.8) the systems responds sluggishly.

$$C = \left[\frac{d^2}{ds^2} \left\{ \frac{1/T}{(s + 1/T)} \right\} \right]_{s = 0}$$

$$C = \left[\frac{d}{ds} \left(\frac{d}{ds} \left(\frac{1/T}{(s + 1/T)} \right) \right) \right]_{s = 0}$$

$$C = \left[\frac{d}{ds} \left(\frac{-1/T}{(s + 1/T)^2} \right) \right]_{s = 0}$$

$$C = \frac{-1}{T} \left\{ \frac{d}{ds} \left(\frac{-1}{(s + 1/T)^2} \right) \right\}_{s = 0}$$

$$C = \frac{-1}{T} \left\{ \frac{-1}{((s+1/T)^2)^2} \cdot \frac{d}{ds} \left(s + \frac{1}{T} \right)^2 \right\}_{s = 0}$$

$$C = \frac{-1}{T} \left\{ \frac{-1}{((s + 1/T)^{4)}} \cdot 2 \left(s + \frac{1}{T}\right)^2 \right\}_{s = 0}$$

$$C = \frac{-1}{T} \left\{ \frac{-2}{(s + 1/T)^3} \right\}_{s = 0}$$

$$C = \frac{2}{T} \frac{1}{(1/T^3)}$$

$$C = \frac{2}{1} \frac{T^3}{1} = 2T^2$$

$\therefore$ $$C = 2T^2$$

$$D = (s + 1/T) \left. \frac{1/T}{s^3 \left(s + \frac{1}{T}\right)} \right|_{s = -1/T}$$

$$D = \frac{1/T}{(-1/T)^3} = \frac{1/T}{-1/T^3} = \frac{1}{T} \times \frac{-T^3}{1}$$

$\therefore$ $$D = -T^2$$

2.7 TIME RESPONSE ANALYSIS OF SECOND ORDER SYSTEM

A second order system can be generically represented as,

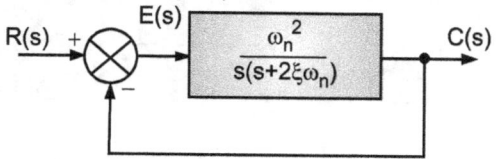

Fig. 2.10

Where, ω_n is the natural frequency of oscillations and ξ is the damping factor.

The closed loop transfer function of the systems is,

$$\frac{C(s)}{R(s)} = \frac{\dfrac{\omega_n^2}{s(s + 2\xi\omega_n)}}{1 + \dfrac{\omega_n^2}{s(s + 2\xi\omega_n)}}$$

$$\frac{C(s)}{R(s)} = \frac{\dfrac{\omega_n^2}{s(s + 2\xi\omega_n)}}{\dfrac{s(s + 2\xi\omega_n) + \omega_n^2}{s(s + 2\xi\omega_n)}}$$

$$\therefore \quad \frac{C(s)}{R(s)} = \frac{\omega_n^2}{s(s + 2\xi\omega_n)} \times \frac{s.(s + 2\xi\omega_n)}{s(s + 2\xi\omega_n) + \omega_n^2}$$

The time response of any system is characterized by the roots of the denominator polynomial q(s) which poles of T.F.

$$\therefore \quad \frac{C(s)}{R(s)} = \frac{\omega_n^2}{s^2 + 2\xi\omega_n s + \omega_n^2}$$

This equation is called the standard form of the second-order system.
The roots of characteristic equation (poles of the system are)

$$F(s) = s^2 + 2\xi\omega_n s + \omega_n^2$$

Using the formula,

$$S_{1,2} = \frac{-b \pm \sqrt{b^2 - 4ac}}{2a}$$

$a = 1, c = 1, \omega_n^2, b = 2\xi\omega_n$

$$\therefore \quad S_{1,2} = \frac{-2\xi\omega_n \pm \sqrt{(2\xi\omega_n)^2 - 4 \times 1 \times \omega_n^2}}{2.1}$$

$$S_{1,2} = \frac{-2\xi\omega_n \pm \sqrt{(4\xi^2\omega_n)^2 - 4\,\omega_n^2}}{2}$$

$$= \frac{-2\xi\omega_n \pm \sqrt{4\omega_n^2(\xi^2 - 1)}}{2} = \frac{-2\xi\omega_n \pm 2\omega_n\sqrt{\xi^2 - 1}}{2}$$

$$S_{1,2} = -\xi\omega_n \pm \omega_n\sqrt{\xi^2 - 1}$$

$\omega_n \rightarrow$ undamped natural frequency
The system breaks into continuous oscillations for $\xi = 0$
Above equation explains the generic roots for second order system.
The dynamic behaviour of second order system can be described in terms of ξ and w_n
The system are classified as;

1. Undamped system ($\xi = 0$)	
2. Underdamped systems ($0 < \xi < 1$)	
3. Critically damped system ($\xi = 1$) Eg. Robotic missile	
4. Overdamped system ($\xi > 1$)	

Another Method for Finding Roots :

$$s^2 + 2\,\xi\omega_n + \omega_n^2 \;=\; 0$$

The roots of this equation are given by,

$$(s^2 + 2\xi\omega_n + \omega_n^2) \;=\; (s - s_1)\,(s - s_2)$$

For $\xi > 1$

$$S_1, S_2 \;=\; -\xi\,\omega_n \pm j\omega_n\sqrt{(1 - \xi^2)}$$
$$\;=\; -\xi\omega_n \pm j\omega_d$$

Where, $\omega_d \;=\; \omega_n\sqrt{1 - \xi^2}$ is damped natural frequency

Most control systems with the exception of robotic control systems are designed with damping factor $\xi < 1$ to achieve high speed.

- As ξ is increased, the response becomes progressively less oscillatory till it becomes critically damped (Just non-oscillatory).

Example : Robotic control systems cannot be allowed to have oscillatory response; otherwise the end effector would strike against the object that the robot is meant to manipulate.

Highest possible speed of response and yet non-oscillating response dictates that a robotic control system shall be designed to have damping facter of $\xi = 1$ (or close to it but not less then unity).

2.7.1 Unit Step Response of Underdamped Second-Order System

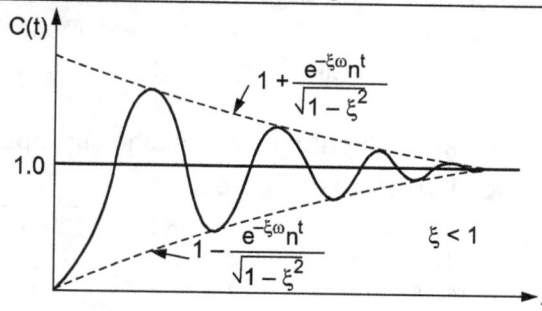

Fig. 2.11

The time response of underdamped sinusoid is ploted based on :

$$C(t) \;=\; 1 - \frac{e^{-\xi}}{\sqrt{1 - \xi^2}}\,\sin\!\left[w_n\sqrt{(1 - \xi^2)}\,t + \tan^{-1}\sqrt{\frac{(1 - \xi^2)}{\xi}}\right]$$

- It is damped sinusoid
- The response reaches a steady state value of $C_{ss} = 1$.
- The steady – state error of this system approaches zero.
- The system breaks into continuous oscillations for $\xi = 0$.

Poles Location of Second Order System

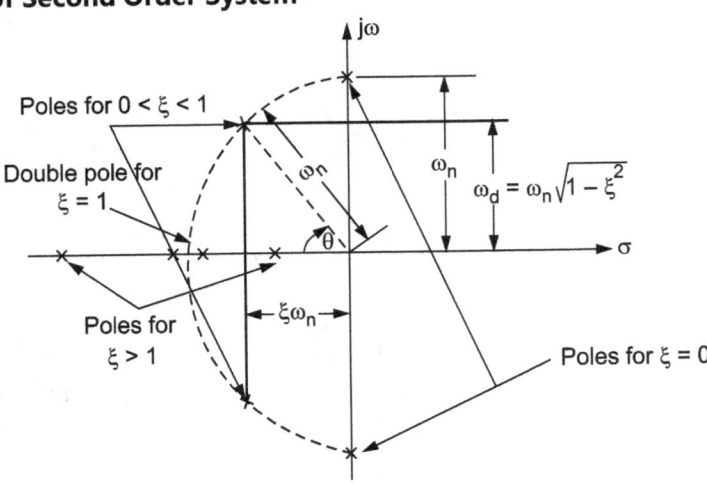

Fig. 2.12 :Pole locations for second-order systems

Above Fig. 2.12 Shows poles location (Locus of poles) of the second order system with ω_n held constant and ξ varying from 0 to ∞.

- As ξ increases the poles move away from the imaginary axis along a circular path of radius w_n meeting at the point $r = -\omega_n$ and then separating and travelling along the real axis, one towards zero and the other towards infinity.
- For $0 < \xi < 1$, the poles are complex conjugate pair and making an angle of $\theta = \cos^{-1} \xi$ with the negative real axis.
- It is observed that, an underdamped system with ξ between 0.5 and 0.8 gets close to the final value more rapidly than a critically damped or overdamped system.
- Among the systems responding oscillations, a critically damped system exhibits the fastest response.
- An overdamped system is always sluggish in responding any inputs.

2.7.2 Damped and Undamped Oscillation

Damped Oscillations : Damped oscillations is shown in Fig. 2.13 below :

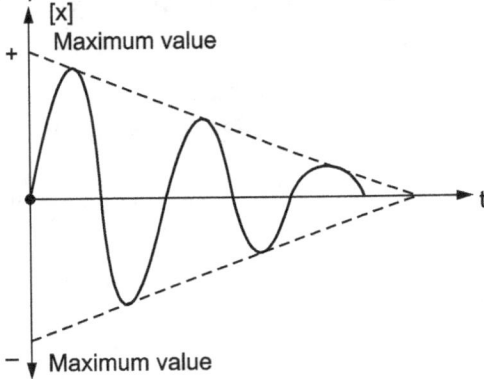

Fig. 2.13

In such a case, during each oscillation, some energy is lost due to electrical losses (I^2R). The amplitude of the oscillation will be reduced to zero as no compensating arrangement for electrical losses is provided. The only parameters that will remain unchanged are the frequency or time period. They will change only according to circuit parameters.

- **Undamped Oscillations :** As shown in Fig. 2.14 undamped oscillations have constant amplitude oscillation.

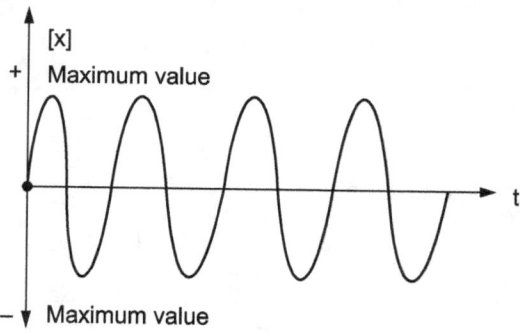

Fig. 2.14

1. When $\xi = 0$, the poles on the Imaginary axis which are not repeated, the system is marginally stable and system response is constant amplitude and frequency of oscillations, which are called undamped oscillations.

2. In the harmonic oscillation equation, the exponential factor $e^{-Rt/2L}$ must become unity. i.e. the value of dissipation component in the circuit, R should be zero. It it's value is negative the amplitude goes on increasing with time t. It its value is positive, the amplitude decrease with time t.

Damping :

Damping is the inherent ability of the system to oppose the oscillatory nature of the system's transient response.

- More damping has effect of less percent overshoot and slower setting time.
- Larger value of damping coefficient or damping factor produces transient response with lesser oscillator nature.

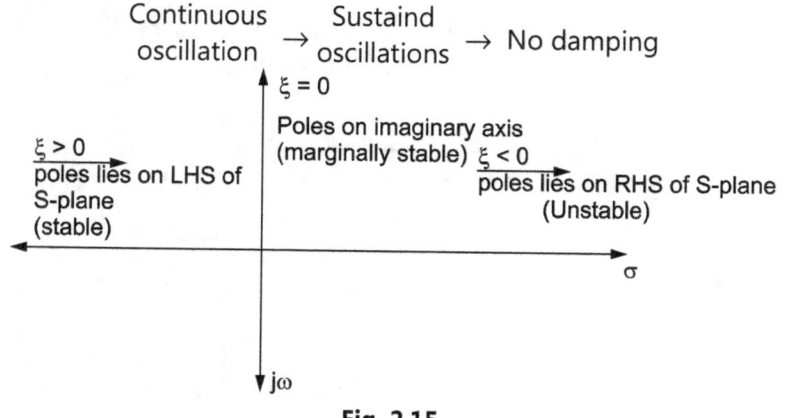

Fig. 2.15

2.7.3 Response of a Second Order System to Step Input

$$\frac{C(s)}{R(s)} = \frac{\omega_n^2}{s^2 + 2\xi \omega_n s + \omega_n^2}$$

is the Transfer function of a second order system and its roots of characteristic equation are

$$S_{1,2} = -\xi \omega_n \pm \omega_n \sqrt{\xi^2 - 1}$$

1. **Undamped System $\xi = 0$**

    The damping ratio is $\xi = 0$

∴ The roots of characteristic equation are

$$S_{1,2} = -\xi \omega_n \pm \omega_n \sqrt{\xi^2 - 1}$$
$$= 0 \pm \omega_n \sqrt{0 - 1}$$
$$= \pm \omega_n \sqrt{-1}$$
$$S_{1,2} = \pm j\omega_n \qquad \qquad \text{Poles are imaginary and lie on } j\omega \text{ axis}$$

∴
$$\frac{C(s)}{R(s)} = \frac{\omega_n^2}{(s + j\omega_n)(s - j\omega_n)}$$

As the input is a unit step function

$$r(t) = u(t) \quad \text{for } t \geq 0$$

∴
$$R(s) = \frac{1}{s}$$

∴
$$C(s) = \frac{\omega_n^2}{(s + j\omega_n)(s - j\omega_n)} R(s)$$

$$C(s) = \frac{\omega_n^2}{(s + j\omega_n)(s - j\omega_n)} \frac{1}{s}$$

$$C(s) = \frac{\omega_n^2}{s(s + j\omega_n)(s - j\omega_n)}$$

∴
$$C(s) = \frac{A}{s} + \frac{B}{(s + j\omega_n)} + \frac{C}{(s - j\omega_n)}$$

$$A = s \left. \frac{\omega_n^2}{s(s + j\omega_n)(s - j\omega_n)} \right|_{s = 0}$$

$$A = \frac{\omega_n^2}{(j\omega_n)(-j\omega_n)} = \frac{\omega_n^2}{-j^2\omega_n^2}$$

∴

$$A = \frac{\omega_n^2}{-(-1)\omega_n^2} = 1$$

$$A = 1$$

$$B = \left. \frac{\omega_n^2 (s + j\omega_n)}{s(s + j\omega_n)(s - j\omega_n)} \right|_{s = -j\omega n}$$

$$B = \left. \frac{\omega_n^2}{s(s - j\omega_n)} \right|_{s = -j\omega n}$$

∴

$$B = \frac{\omega_n^2}{(-j\omega_n - j\omega_n)(-j\omega_n)}$$

$$B = \frac{\omega_n^2}{-j\omega_n(-2j\omega_n)} = \frac{\omega_n^2}{2j^2\omega_n^2}$$

$$B = \frac{-1}{2} = -0.5$$

$$C = \left. (s - j\omega_n) \cdot \frac{\omega_n^2}{s(s + j\omega_n)(s - j\omega_n)} \right|_{s = j\omega n}$$

$$C = \left. \frac{\omega_n^2}{j\omega_n(j\omega_n + j\omega_n)} \right|$$

$$C = \frac{\omega_n^2}{j\omega_n \cdot 2j\omega_n} = \left(\frac{\omega_n^2}{2j^2\omega_n^2} \right)$$

$$C = \frac{1}{2(-1)} = -0.5$$

$$C(s) = \frac{A}{s} - \frac{0.5}{(s + j\omega_n)} - \frac{0.5}{(s - j\omega_n)}$$

Therefore,

$$C(t) = [u(t) - 0.5.e^{-j\omega nt} - 0.5\ e^{j\omega nt}]$$

$$C(t) = [1 - 0.5\ e^{-j\omega nt} - 0.5\ e^{j\omega nt}] \qquad \text{for } t \geq 0$$

$$C(t) = 1 - 0.5\left[\frac{e^{-j\omega nt} + e^{j\omega nt}}{2}\right].2$$

$$C(t) = 1 - \cos \omega_n t \qquad\qquad \text{for } t \geq 0$$

Where $\omega_n \rightarrow$ natural frequency of the system.

The response is undamped and oscillations continue indefinitely. The transient response does not dies out.

2. Underdamped Systems $(0 < \xi < 1)$

The system which produces damped oscillations are called underdamped system.

The damping ratio is $0 < \xi < 1$

The roots of characteristic equation are,

$$S_{1,2} = -\xi\omega_n \pm \omega_n \sqrt{\xi^2 - 1}$$

$$= -\xi\omega_n \pm \omega_n - 1\sqrt{(1-\xi^2)}$$

$$= -\xi\omega_n \pm j\omega_n \sqrt{1-\xi^2}$$

$$= -\alpha \pm j\omega_d \rightarrow \text{Poles are complex conjugate and lie in left s-phase.}$$

where
$$\alpha = \xi\,\omega_n\ ;\ \omega_d = \omega_n\sqrt{1-\xi^2}$$

$$= -\xi\,\omega_n \pm j\omega_n\sqrt{1-\xi^2}$$

A second order system given for the roots for $0 < \xi < 1$ is represented as,

$$\frac{C(s)}{R(s)} = \frac{\omega_n^2}{s^2 + 2\,\omega_n s + \omega_n^2}$$

$$= \frac{\omega_n^2}{(s + \xi\omega_n + j\omega_n\sqrt{1-\xi^2}\,)(s + \xi\omega_n - j\omega_n)\sqrt{1-\xi^2}\,)}$$

$$= \frac{\omega_n^2}{(s + \alpha + j\omega_d)(s + \alpha - j\omega_d)}$$

As the input is unit step function $r(t) = 1$ for $t \geq 0$

∴
$$R(s) = \frac{1}{s} \quad \text{for } t \geq 0$$

∴
$$C(s) = \frac{\omega_n^2}{s(s + \alpha + j\omega_d)(s + \alpha - j\omega_d)}$$

$$C(s) = \frac{\omega_n^2}{s[(s+\alpha)^2 - j^2\omega_d^2]}$$

$$C(s) = \frac{\omega_n^2}{s(s^2 + 2\alpha s + \alpha^2 + \omega_d^2)}$$

Where, $\alpha = \xi\omega_n$, $\omega_d = \omega_n\sqrt{1-\xi^2}$

$\qquad\quad \alpha^2 = \xi^2\omega_n^2$ $\omega_d^2 = \omega_n^2(1-\xi^2)$

$\therefore$ $\alpha^2 + \omega_d^2 = \xi^2\omega_n^2 + \omega_n^2 - \xi^2\omega_n^2$

$\therefore$ $\alpha^2 + \omega_d^2 = \omega_n^2$

Apply partial fraction

$$C(s) = \frac{A}{s} + \frac{Bs + C}{(s^2 + 2\alpha s + \omega_n^2)}$$

$$A = s\frac{\omega_n^2}{s(s^2 + 2\alpha s + \omega_n^2)}\bigg|_{s=0} = \frac{\omega_n^2}{\omega_n^2}$$

$\therefore$
$$\frac{\omega_n^2}{s(s^2 + 2\alpha s + \omega_n^2)} = \frac{1}{s} + \frac{Bs + C}{s^2 + 2\alpha s + \omega_n^2}$$

$$\frac{\omega_n^2}{s(s^2 + 2\alpha s + \omega_n^2)} = \frac{s^2 + 2\alpha s + \omega_n^2 + Bs^2 + C}{s(s^2 + 2\alpha s + \omega_n^2)}$$

$\therefore$ $\omega_n^2 = s^2 + 2\alpha s + \omega_n^2 + Bs^2 + Cs$

$\qquad\qquad 0 = (1 + B)s^2 + (2\alpha + c)s$

$\therefore$ $1 + B = 0,\qquad 2\alpha + C = 0$

$\therefore$ $B = -1, C = -2\alpha$

$\therefore$
$$C(s) = \frac{1}{s} + \frac{-s - 2\alpha}{(s^2 + 2\alpha s + \omega_n^2)}$$

$\therefore$
$$C(s) = \frac{1}{s} - \frac{(s + 2\alpha)}{(s^2 + 2\alpha s + \omega_n^2)}$$

Consider, $s^2 + 2\alpha s + \omega_n^2$ and equate with $e^{-at}\cos\omega t\, u(t)$ or $e^{-at}\sin\omega t\, u(t)$ formula.

$$e^{-at} \cos \omega t \, u(t) \;=\; \frac{(s+a)}{(s+a)^2 + \omega^2} \qquad \text{Laplace transform}$$

$$e^{-at} \sin \omega t \, u(t) \;=\; \frac{\omega}{(s+a)^2 + \omega^2}$$

$$\therefore \quad s^2 + 2\alpha s + \omega_n^2 \;=\; (s+a)^2 + \omega^2$$

$$s^2 + 2\alpha s + \omega_n^2 \;=\; s^2 + 2as + a^2 + \omega^2$$

Comparing equations

$$2\alpha \;=\; 2a \qquad\qquad \omega_n^2 \;=\; a^2 + \omega^2$$

$$\alpha \;=\; a \qquad\qquad \omega^2 \;=\; \omega_n^2 - a^2$$

$$\omega^2 \;=\; \alpha^2 + \omega_d^2 - \alpha^2$$

$$\omega^2 \;=\; \omega_d^2 \quad \Rightarrow \omega = \omega_d$$

$$\therefore \quad C(s) \;=\; \frac{1}{s} - \left\{ \frac{(s+\alpha) + \alpha}{(s+\alpha)^2 + \omega_d^2} \right\}$$

$$C(s) \;=\; \frac{1}{s}\left\{ \frac{(s+\alpha)}{(s+\alpha)^2 + \omega \text{ eq }_d^2} + \frac{\frac{1}{\omega_d}\,\alpha\,\omega_d}{(s+\alpha)^2 + \omega_d^2} \right\}$$

$$C(s) \;=\; \frac{1}{s} - \left\{ \frac{(s+\alpha)}{(s+\alpha)^2 + \omega_d^2} + \frac{\alpha}{\omega_d}\cdot\frac{\omega_d}{(s+\alpha)^2 + \omega_d^2} \right\}$$

Taking inverse laplace transform,

$$C(t) \;=\; u(t) - \left\{ e^{-\alpha t} \cos \omega_d t \cdot u(t) + \frac{\alpha}{\omega_d} e^{-\alpha t} \sin \omega_d t \, u(t) \right\}$$

$$C(t) \;=\; u(t)\, e^{-\xi \omega_n t} \cos \omega_d t \, u(t) - \frac{\alpha}{\omega_d} e^{-\xi \omega_n t} \sin \omega_d t \, u(t)$$

$$\alpha \;=\; \xi \omega_n \quad \omega_d = \omega_n \sqrt{1 - \xi^2}$$

$$\therefore \quad C(t) \;=\; \left[1 - e^{-\xi \omega_n t} \cos \omega_d t - \frac{\xi \omega_n}{\omega_n \sqrt{1 - \xi^2}} \cdot e^{-\xi \omega_n t} \sin \omega_d t \right] \text{ for } t \geq 0$$

$$C(t) \;=\; [-e^{-j\omega_n t} \cos \omega_d t - \frac{\xi}{\sqrt{1 - \xi^2}} e^{-\xi \omega_n t} \sin \omega_n t]$$

$$C(t) \;=\; 1 - \frac{e^{-\xi \omega_n t}}{\sqrt{1 - \xi^2}} \left[\sqrt{1 - \xi^2} \cos \omega_d t + \xi \sin \omega_d t \right]$$

Let
$$\sin\theta = \sqrt{1-\xi^2} \ ; \cos\theta = \xi$$
$$\sqrt{1-\xi^2} = \cos\omega_d t + j\sin\omega_d t$$
$$= \sin\theta\cos\omega_d t + \cos\theta\sin\omega_d t$$
$$= \sin(\omega_d t + \theta)$$

$\therefore$
$$C(t) = 1 - \frac{e^{-\xi\omega_n t}}{\sqrt{1-\xi^2}}\sin(\omega_d t + \theta)$$

And
$$\tan\theta = \frac{\sqrt{1-\xi^2}}{\xi}$$

$$\theta = \tan^{-1}\left(\frac{\sqrt{1-\xi^2}}{\xi}\right) \text{ radians}$$

$\therefore$ Response of underdamped system is given as;

$$C(t) = 1 - \frac{e^{-\xi\omega_n t}}{\sqrt{1-\xi^2}}\sin(\omega_d t + \theta)$$

Where,
$$\omega_d = \omega_n\sqrt{1-\xi^2}$$

3. Critically Damped System ($\xi = 1$)

The damping ratio is
$$\xi = 1$$

The roots of characteristic equation are

$$S_{1,2} = -\xi\omega_n \pm \omega_n\sqrt{\xi^2-1}$$

Where, $\xi = 1$ for critically damped

$\therefore$
$$S_{1,2} = -\omega_n \pm \omega_n\sqrt{1-1}$$
$$= -\omega_n, -\omega_n$$

- The closed loop poles are real, equal and negative on the left half of s-plane
- Rises slowly and reaches final value.

A generic second-order system given by

$$\frac{C(s)}{R(s)} = \frac{\omega_n^2}{\xi^2 + 2\xi_n s + \omega_n^2}$$

$$= \frac{\omega_n^2}{(s + \omega_n)(s + \omega_n)}$$

As the input is a unit step function $r(t) = 1$ for $t \geq 0$

Therefore
$$R(s) = \frac{1}{s}$$

$$C(s) = \frac{\omega_n^2}{s(s + \omega_n)(s + \omega_n)} = \frac{\omega_n^2}{s(s + \omega_n)^2}$$

Expanding $C(s)$ into partial fraction

$$C(s) = \frac{A}{s} + \frac{B}{(s + \omega_n)} + \frac{C}{(s + \omega_n^2)}$$

$$A = s. \left.\frac{\omega_n^2}{s(s + \omega n)^2}\right|_{s = 0} = \frac{\omega_n^2}{\omega_n^2} = 1$$

$$B = \frac{d}{ds}\left\{(s + \omega_n)^2.\frac{\omega_n^2}{(s + \omega_n)^2}\right\}_{s = -\omega_n}$$

$$B = \left\{\frac{d}{ds}\frac{\omega_n^2}{s}\right\}_{s = -\omega n}$$

$$B = \omega_n^2\left\{\frac{d}{ds}(1/s)\right\}_{s = -\omega_n}$$

$$= \omega_n^2\left(\frac{-1}{s^2}\right)_{s = -\omega n}$$

$$B = \frac{\omega_n^2}{(-\omega_n)^2} = \frac{-\omega_n^2}{\omega_n^2} = -1$$

$$C = \left\{(s + \omega_n)^2\frac{\omega_n^2}{s(s + \omega_n)^2}\right\}_{s = -\omega_n}$$

$$C = \frac{\omega_n^2}{-\omega_n} = -\omega_n$$

$$C(s) = \frac{1}{s} - \frac{\omega_n}{(s + \omega_n)^2} - \frac{-1}{(s + \omega_n)}$$

$$C(t) = u(t) - \omega_n + e^{-\omega_n t}u(t)e^{-\omega_n t}u(t)$$

$$C(t) = (1 - \omega_n t\, e^{-\omega n t} - e^{\omega n t})u(t)$$

$$C(t) = 1 - e^{-\omega_n t}(1 + \omega_n t) \qquad\qquad \text{for } t \geq 0$$

The response is exponential and there are no oscillations in the output.

When $\xi = 1$; The pole on the negative real axis at the same location the system is stable, the response is critically damped because it generates critically or hardly one damped oscillations.

4. Overdamped System ($\xi > 1$)

The damping ratio is $\xi > 1$

The roots of characteristic equation are

$$S_{1,2} = -\xi\omega_n \pm \omega_n \sqrt{\xi^2 - 1}$$

The closed loop poles are real, unequal and negative on left half of s-plane.

The generic second order system is given by

$$\frac{C(s)}{R(s)} = \frac{\omega_n^2}{s^2 + 2\xi\omega_n s + \omega_n^2}$$

$$= \frac{\omega_n^2}{(s + \xi\omega_n + \omega_n\sqrt{\xi^2 - 1})(s + \xi\omega_n - \omega_n\sqrt{\omega^2 - 1})}$$

As the input is unit step function, $r(t) = 1$ for $t \geq 0$

$$\therefore \qquad R(s) = \frac{1}{s}$$

$$C(s) = \frac{\omega_n^2}{s(s + \xi\omega_n + \omega_n\sqrt{\xi^2 - 1})(s + \xi\omega_n - \omega_n\sqrt{\xi^2 - 1})}$$

Apply input as unit-step function $r(t) = u(t)$

$$R(s) = \frac{1}{s}$$

$$C(s) = \frac{A}{s} + \frac{B}{(s + \xi\omega_n + \omega_n\sqrt{\xi^2-1})} + \frac{C}{(s + \xi\omega_n - \omega_n\sqrt{\xi^2-1})}$$

$$A = s.\frac{\omega_n^2}{(s + \xi\omega_n + \omega_n\sqrt{\xi^2-1})(s + \xi\omega_n - \omega_n\sqrt{\xi^2-1})}\bigg|_{s=0}$$

$$A = \frac{\omega_n^2}{(s + \xi\omega_n + \omega_n\sqrt{\xi^2-1})(s + \xi\omega_n - \omega_n\sqrt{\xi^2-1})}$$

$$A = \frac{\omega_n^2}{\xi^2\omega_n^2 - \omega_n^2(\xi^2 - 1)}$$

$$A = \frac{\omega_n^2}{\xi^2\omega_n^2 - \xi^2\omega_n^2 + \omega_n^2}$$

$$A = \frac{\omega_n^2}{\omega_n^2} = 1 \qquad \therefore \qquad A = 1$$

$$B = \frac{\omega_n^2}{(-\xi\omega_n + \omega_n\sqrt{\xi^2-1})(-\xi\omega_n - \omega_n\sqrt{\xi^2-1} + \xi\omega_n - \omega_n\sqrt{\xi^2-1})}$$

$$B = \frac{\omega_n^2}{(-\xi\omega_n - \omega_n\sqrt{\xi^2-1})(-2\omega_n\sqrt{\xi^2-1})}$$

$$B = \frac{\omega_n^2}{2\omega_2^n \xi\sqrt{\xi^2-1} + 2\omega_n^2(\xi^2-1)}$$

$$B = \frac{\omega_n^2}{2\omega_n^2(\xi\sqrt{\xi^2-1} + (\xi^2-1))}$$

$$B = \frac{1}{2\sqrt{\xi^2-1}(\xi + \sqrt{\xi^2-1})}$$

Similarly

$$C = \frac{(s + \xi\omega_n - \omega_n\sqrt{\xi^2-1})\omega_n^2}{s(s + \xi\omega_n + \omega_n\sqrt{\xi^2-1})(s + \xi\omega_n - \omega_n\sqrt{\xi^2-1})}$$

At

$$s = -\xi\omega_n + \omega_n\sqrt{\xi^2-1}$$

$$C = \frac{\omega_n^2}{(-\xi\omega_n + \omega_n\sqrt{\xi^2-1})(s + \xi\omega_n + \omega_n\sqrt{\xi^2-1})}$$

$$C = \frac{\omega_n^2}{(-\xi\omega_n + \omega_n\sqrt{\xi^2-1})(-\xi\omega_n + \omega_n\sqrt{\xi^2-1} + \xi\omega_n + \omega_n\sqrt{\xi^2-1})}$$

$$C = \frac{\omega_n^2}{(-\xi\omega_n + \omega_n\sqrt{\xi^2-1})(2\omega_n\sqrt{\xi^2-1})}$$

$$C = \frac{\omega_n^2}{(-2\xi\omega_n\sqrt{\xi^2-1}) + (2\omega_n\sqrt{\xi^2-1})}$$

$$C = \frac{\omega_n^2}{\omega_n(-\xi\omega_n\sqrt{\xi^2-1}) + (2\omega_n\sqrt{\xi^2-1})}$$

$$C = \frac{\omega_2^n}{-2\omega_2^n[\sqrt{\xi^2-1}\, 2\omega_n^2 + (\xi^2-1)]}$$

$$C = \frac{\omega_n^2}{2\omega_n^2[-\xi\sqrt{\xi^2-1} + (\xi^2-1)]}$$

$$C = \frac{1}{2\sqrt{\xi^2-1}(-\xi + \sqrt{\xi^2-1})}$$

$$C = \frac{1}{2\sqrt{\xi^2-1}\,(-\xi+\sqrt{\xi^2-1})}$$

$$C = \frac{-1}{2\sqrt{\xi^2-1}\,(-\sqrt{\xi^2-1})}$$

$$C(s) = \frac{1}{s} + \frac{1}{2\sqrt{\xi^2-1}\,(\xi+\sqrt{\xi^2-1})}\;\frac{1}{(s+\xi\omega_n+\omega_n\sqrt{\xi^2-1})}$$

$$= -\frac{1}{(2\sqrt{\xi^2-1})(\xi-\sqrt{\xi^2-1})}\;\frac{1}{(s+\xi\omega_n-\omega_n\sqrt{\xi^2-1})}$$

$$C(t) = u(t) + \frac{1}{2\sqrt{\xi^2-1}\,(\xi+\sqrt{\xi^2-1})}\;e^{-(\xi\omega_n+\omega_n\sqrt{\xi^2-1})\,t}\cdot u(t)$$

$$-\frac{1}{2\sqrt{\xi^2-1}\,(\xi-\sqrt{\xi^2-1})}\cdot e^{-(\xi u_n-\omega_n\sqrt{\xi^2-1})\,t}\cdot u(t)$$

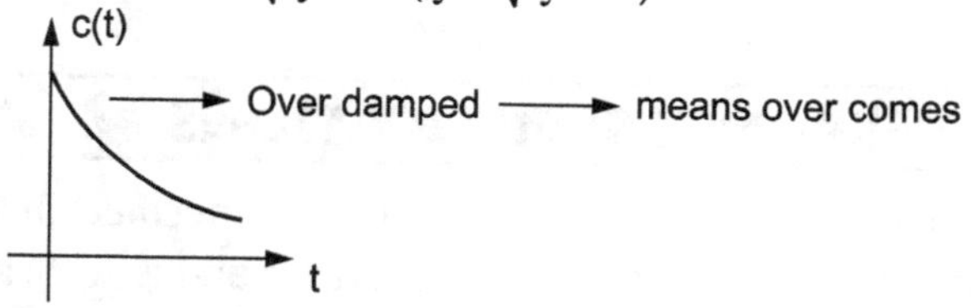

c(t)

Over damped ⟶ means over comes

t

Fig. 2.16

When $\xi > 1$ the poles on the negative real axis are at different locations. The system is stable, and the system response is over damped because the system response eliminates or over comes the damped oscillations.

- The ξ increase from 0 to 1, the poles moves towards left half of S-plane and nearer to the real axis. Hence the system time constant and frequency of oscillations are decreased.

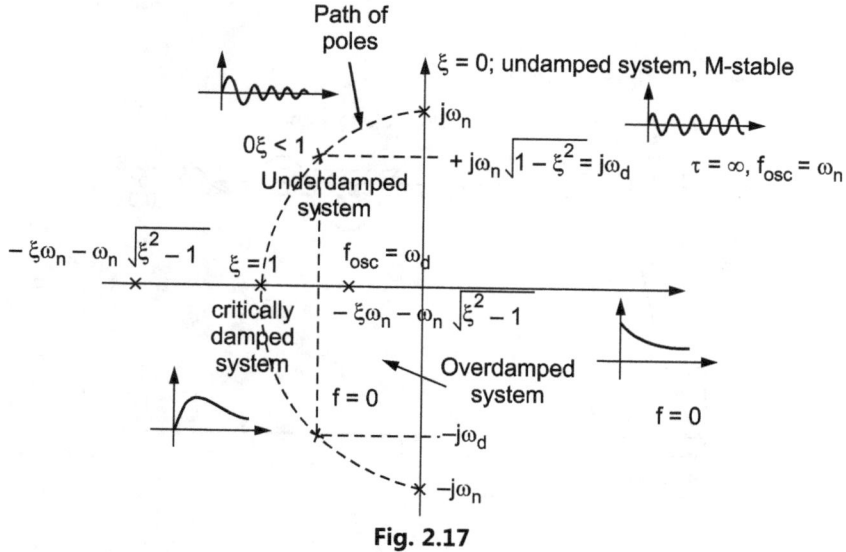

Fig. 2.17

- When $\xi \geq 1$ and increase the frequency of oscillations becomes zero because the poles lies on the real axis only.

- When $\xi > 1$ and increases the system τ increase because one pole moves towards the origin of the real axis.

Order of Time Constant :

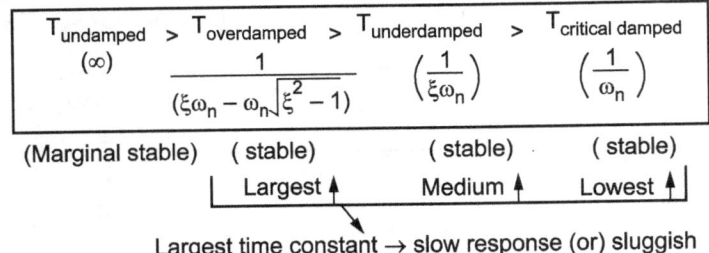

$T_{undamped}$	$>$	$T_{overdamped}$	$>$	$T_{underdamped}$	$>$	$T_{critical\ damped}$
(∞)		$\dfrac{1}{(\xi\omega_n - \omega_n\sqrt{\xi^2 - 1})}$		$\left(\dfrac{1}{\xi\omega_n}\right)$		$\left(\dfrac{1}{\omega_n}\right)$
(Marginal stable)		(stable)		(stable)		(stable)
		Largest		Medium		Lowest

Largest time constant $\rightarrow$ slow response (or) sluggish

Fig. 2.18

2.8 TRANSIENT RESPONSE SPECIFICATIONS

The performance characteristics of a control system are specified in terms of the transient response to a unit-step input, since it is easy to generates and is sufficiently drastic.

(If the response to a step input is known it is mathematically possible to compute the response to any input).

- As pointed out earlier, control systems are generally designed with damping less than one, oscillatory step response. High order control systems usually have a pair of complex conjugate poles with damping less than one which dominate over other poles.

The time response of a second order underdamped system to a unit step input is shown in Fig. 2.19 below.

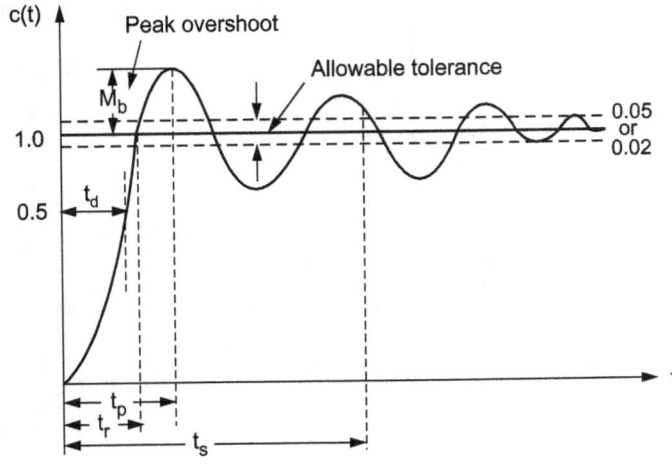

Fig. 2.19

The output response is given as,

$$C(t) = 1 - \frac{e^{-\xi \omega_n t}}{\sqrt{1-\xi^2}} \sin(\omega_{dt} + \theta)$$

Where,

$$\omega_d = \omega_n \sqrt{1-\xi^2}$$

$$\theta = \tan^{-1}\left(\frac{\sqrt{1-\xi^2}}{\xi}\right) \text{ radians}$$

ξ is damping ratio and ω_n is the natural frequency of oscillation.

- **Delay Time (t_d)** : It is the time required for the response to reach 50% of the final value in first attempt.

Complex deviation,
$$t_d = \frac{1 + 0.7\xi}{\omega_n}$$

- **Rise Time (t_r)** : The time required for the response to rise from 10% to 90%, 5% to 95% or 0% to 100% of its final value.

  For underdamped second order systems, the 0% to 100% rise time is normally used.

  For overdamped systems, the 10% to 90% rise time is commonly used.

$$t_r = \frac{\pi - \theta}{\omega_d} = \frac{\pi - \theta}{\omega_n\sqrt{1 - \xi^2}}$$

- **Peak Over Shoot (M_p)** : It is the maximum peak value of response curve measured from unity.

$$M_p = \exp\left(\frac{-\pi\xi}{\sqrt{1-\xi^2}}\right) \times 100\%$$

The amount of maximum percent overshoot directly indicates the relative stability of the system.

- **Setting Time (t_s)** : It is required for the response to reach and stay within a specified range of final value (usually 2% or 5%)

The setting time is related to the largest time constant of the control system.

The % error criterion to use may be determined from the objectives of the system design in question.

$$t_s = \frac{4}{\xi\omega_n} \quad \begin{array}{l} 4T = 2\% \\ 5T = 1\% \end{array}$$

From the Fig. 2.19 of the time response specifications it has been observed that the step response has a number of overshoots and undershoots with respect to final steady value.

Since, the overshoots and undershoots decays exponentially, the peak overshoot is the first overshoots which is decay exponentially, and is the same as peak of complete time response.

- **Steady State Error (e_{ss})** : It indicates the error between the actual output and the desired output as t tends to infinity i.e.

$$e_{ss} = \lim_{t \to \infty} [\, r(t) - c(t)]$$

In most cases, it is desirable that the transient response be sufficiently fast and be sufficiently damped. Thus, for a desirable transient response, the damping ratio must be between 0.4 and 0.8. For large values of ξ ($\xi > 0.8$) the system responds sluggishly.

2.8.1 Problems on Transient Response Analysis :

(Time Domain Specification)

Steps to be Followed for Solving Problems

1. Determine the closed loop Transfer function of a system

2. Compare with standard Transfer function.

3. Get ξ, ω_n

4. Substitute, and get time domain specifications.

- We need closed loop Transfer function for solving problems on transient response.

Keynote : For solving numerical an transient response, use closed loop transfer function. And for steady state analysis use open loop transfer function.

SOLVED EXAMPLES

Example 2.1 : A unity feedback has G(s) = $\dfrac{200}{s(s + 12)}$. Find time domain specifications for a unit step input.

Solution : As stated that, the given system is unity feedback.

$\therefore$ $\qquad\qquad\qquad\qquad$ H(s) = 1

The closed loop transfer is given as;

$$\frac{C(s)}{R(s)} = \frac{G(s)}{1 + G(s)\,H(s)} = \frac{\dfrac{200}{s(s + 12)}}{1 + \dfrac{200}{s(s + 12)}}$$

$$\frac{C(s)}{R(s)} = \frac{\dfrac{200}{s(s + 12)}}{\dfrac{s(s + 12) + 200}{s(s + 12)}} = \frac{200}{s^2 + 12s + 200}$$

$$\frac{C(s)}{R(s)} = \frac{200}{s^2 + 12s + 200}$$

The standard Transfer function of 2nd order system is given as;

$$\frac{C(s)}{R(s)} = \frac{\omega_n^2}{s^2 + 2\xi\omega_n s + \omega_n^2}$$

Comparing Transfer function of given systems with the standard transfer function.

$$\omega_n^2 = 200, \qquad \omega_n = \sqrt{200} = 14.44 \text{ rad/s}$$

$$2\xi\omega_n = 12, \qquad \xi = \frac{12}{2 \times 14.14} = \frac{6}{\omega_n}$$

$$\therefore \qquad \xi = 0.424$$

- Natural frequency $\omega_n = 14.14$
- Damping factor $\xi = 0.424$
- Damping frequency ω_d

$$\omega_d = \omega_n \sqrt{1 - \xi^2}$$
$$= 14.14 \sqrt{1 - (0.424)^2}$$
$$\therefore \qquad \omega_d = 12.806 \text{ rad/s}$$

(4) Angle θ

$$\theta = \tan^{-1}\left(\frac{\sqrt{1-\xi^2}}{\xi}\right) = \tan^{-1}\left(\frac{\sqrt{1-(0.424)^2}}{(0.424)}\right)$$

$$\theta = 1.133 \text{ rad}$$

(5) The time domain specifications are calculated as :

(a) Delay time (t_d)

$$t_d = \frac{1 + 0.7\xi}{\omega_n} = \frac{1 + 0.7 \times 0.424}{14.14} = 0.0917 \text{ sec}$$

$$\therefore \qquad t_d = 0.917 \text{sec}$$

(b) Rise time (t_r)

$$t_r = \frac{\pi - \theta}{\omega_d} = \frac{\pi - 1.133}{12.806} = 0.1568 \text{ sec}$$

$$\therefore \qquad t_r = 0.1568 \text{ sec}$$

(c) Peak time (t_p) $\qquad t_p = \frac{\pi}{\omega_d} = \frac{\pi}{12.806} = 0.245 \text{ sec}$

$$\therefore \qquad t_p = 0.245 \text{ sec}$$

(d) Peak overshoot (M_p)

$$M_p = \exp\left(\frac{-\pi\xi}{\sqrt{1-\xi^2}}\right) \times 100$$

$$M_p = \exp\left(\frac{-0.424 \times \pi}{\sqrt{1-(0.424)^2}}\right) \times 100$$

$$M_p = 22.96\%$$

(e) Setting time (t_s) $$t_s = \frac{4}{\xi\omega_n} = \frac{4}{0.424 \times 14.14}$$

∴ $$t_s = 0.672 \text{ sec}$$

Example 2.2 : A control system is shown in Fig. 2.20 below.

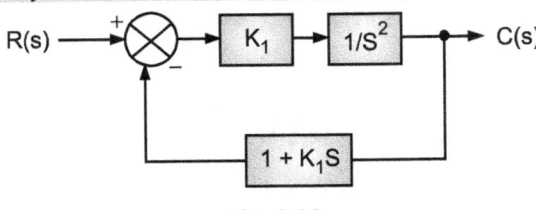

Fig. 2.20

Find the values of K_1 and K_2. so that M_p = 25% and T_p = 4sec. Assume unit step input.

Solution : For the given system,

$$G(s) = \frac{K_1}{s^2} \quad \text{and } H(s) = (1 + K_2 s)$$

The closed-loop transfer function is given as;

$$\frac{C(s)}{R(s)} = \frac{G(s)}{1 + G(s) \, H(s)}$$

$$= \frac{K_1/s_2}{1 + \frac{K_1}{s_2}(1 + K_2 s)}$$

$$= \frac{K_1}{s^2 + K_1 K_2 s + K_1}$$

The standard transfer function of a 2nd order system is given as;

$$\frac{C(s)}{R(s)} = \frac{\omega_n^2}{s^2 + 2\xi\omega_n s + \omega_n^2}$$

Compare transfer functions of given systems with standard transfer function.

$$\omega_n^2 = K_1; \qquad\qquad 2\xi\omega_n = K_1 K_2$$

$$\omega_n = \sqrt{K_1} \qquad\qquad \xi = \frac{K_1 K_2}{2\xi\omega_n}$$

$$\xi = \frac{K_1 K_2}{2\sqrt{K_1}} = \frac{1}{2}\sqrt{K_1 . K_2}$$

The peak overshoot (M_p) is given as 25%

$$\therefore \qquad M_p = \exp\left(\frac{-\pi\xi}{\sqrt{1-\xi^2}}\right) \times 100 = 25$$

$$\exp = \left(\frac{-\pi\xi}{\sqrt{1-\xi^2}}\right) = \frac{25}{100} = \frac{1}{4} = 0.25$$

$$= \frac{-\pi\xi}{\sqrt{-1-\xi^2}} = 1.3862$$

$$= l_n(0.25)$$

$$\xi = 0.4036$$

The peak time T_p is given as 4sec.

$$\therefore \qquad t_p = \frac{\pi}{\omega_d} = \frac{\pi}{\omega_n\sqrt{1-\xi^2}} = 4$$

$$\therefore \qquad \omega_n = \frac{\pi}{4\sqrt{1-\xi^2}} = 0.8584$$

$$\therefore \qquad \omega_n = 0.8584$$

$$\omega_n = \sqrt{K_1} = 0.8584$$

$$\therefore \qquad K_1 = 0.7369$$

$$\xi = \frac{1}{2}\sqrt{K_1 . K_2}$$

$$K_2 = \frac{\xi_1 \times 2}{\sqrt{K_1}} = \frac{0.492 \times 2}{1.03622}$$

$$\therefore \qquad K_2 = 0.9405$$

Example 2.3 : The open loop transfer function of a unity feedback system is,

$$G(s) = \frac{K}{s(1 + T_s)}$$

Where K and T are constant.

Determine the factor by which gain K should be multiplied so that overshoot of unit step response be reduced from 75% to 25%.

Solution : As the given, system is unity feedback H(s) = 1

$$\therefore \qquad \frac{C(s)}{R(s)} = \frac{G(s)}{1 + G(s)\, H(s)} = \frac{\dfrac{K}{s(1 + Ts)}}{1 + \dfrac{K}{s(1 + Ts)}}$$

$$\therefore \qquad \frac{C(s)}{R(s)} = \frac{\dfrac{K}{s(1 + Ts)}}{\dfrac{s(1 + Ts) + K}{s(1 + T_s)}} = \frac{K}{s(1 + T_s) + K}$$

$$\frac{C(s)}{R(s)} = \frac{K}{s + Ts^2 + K} = \frac{K/T}{s^2 + \dfrac{1}{T}s + \dfrac{K}{T}}$$

The standard transfer functions of a 2nd order system is given as;

$$\frac{C(s)}{R(s)} = \frac{\omega_n^2}{s^2 + 2\,\omega_n s + \omega_n^2}$$

Compare transfer function of given system with standard transfer function.

$$\omega_n^2 = \frac{K}{T} \qquad\qquad 2\xi\omega_n = \frac{1}{T}$$

$$\omega_n = \sqrt{\frac{K}{T}} \qquad\qquad \xi = \frac{1}{2\omega_n t}$$

$$\xi = \frac{1}{2\sqrt{\dfrac{K}{T}\cdot T}} = \frac{1}{2\sqrt{Kt}}$$

The peak overshoot (M_p) is reduced from 75% to 25%,

Therefore, $\qquad M_{p_1} = \exp\left(\dfrac{-\pi\xi_1}{\sqrt{1 - \xi_1^2}}\right) \times 100 = 75$

$$M_{p_2} = \exp\left(\dfrac{-\pi\xi_2}{\sqrt{1 - \xi_2^2}}\right) \times 100 = 25$$

$$\therefore \qquad\qquad \xi_1 = 0.0911$$

$$\xi_2 = 0.4037$$

i.e. ξ must be changed from 0.0911 to 0.4037 to reduce the peak overshoot from 75% to 25%.

Value of ξ is dependent on K and T. However as only the gain K is to changed T is assumed constant.

$$\therefore \qquad \xi_1 = \frac{1}{2\sqrt{K_1 T}} = 0.0911$$

$$\xi_2 = \frac{1}{2\sqrt{K_2 T}} = 0.4037$$

$$\frac{\xi_1}{\xi_2} = \frac{\dfrac{1}{2\sqrt{K_1 T}}}{\dfrac{1}{2\sqrt{K_2 T}}} = \frac{0.0911}{0.4037}$$

$$\sqrt{\frac{K_2}{K_1}} = 0.22566$$

$$\frac{K_2}{K_1} = 0.05092$$

Thus, the gain K must be multiplied by 0.05092 to reduce the peak overshoot from 75% to 25%.

Example 2.4 : $G(s) = \dfrac{K}{s(1 + Ts)}$ The open loop transfer function of unity feedback system is overshoot reduces from 0.6 to 0.2 due to change in K.

Solution :
$$\frac{C(s)}{R(s)} = \frac{G(s)}{1 + G(s)\,H(s)} = \frac{\dfrac{K}{s(sT + 1)}}{1 + \dfrac{K}{(sT + 1)}}$$

$$\frac{\dfrac{K}{s(sT + 1)}}{\dfrac{s(sT + 1) + K}{s(sT + 1)}} = \frac{K}{s(sT + 1)\,K} = \frac{K}{s + sT + sT^2}$$

$$\frac{C(s)}{R(s)} = \frac{(K/T)}{s^2 + \dfrac{s}{T} + \dfrac{K}{T}}$$

Compare above equation, with standard transfer function equation.

$$\frac{C(s)}{R(s)} = \frac{\omega_n^2}{s^2 + 2\xi\omega_n s + \omega_n^2}$$

$$= s^2 + \frac{s}{T} + \frac{K}{T}$$

$$\omega_n^2 = \frac{K}{T} \qquad\qquad 2\xi\omega_n = \frac{1}{T}$$

$$\omega_n = \sqrt{\frac{K}{T}} \qquad \xi = \frac{1}{2\sqrt{KT}}$$

Overshoot reduces from 0.6 to 0.2.

$$\xi_1 = 0.6; \qquad\qquad\qquad \xi_2 = 0.2$$

$$\xi_1 = 0.6 = \frac{1}{2\sqrt{K_1 T_1}}; \qquad \xi_2 = 0.2 = \frac{1}{2\sqrt{K_2 T_2}}$$

$$\frac{0.6}{0.2} = \frac{\sqrt{K_1 T_2}}{\sqrt{K_2 T_1}};$$

$\therefore \qquad\qquad K_2 = 0.11 K_1$

$\therefore$ K must be reduced by factor 0.11

$$\frac{\xi_1}{\xi_2} = \frac{0.6}{0.2} = \frac{\sqrt{K_1}}{\sqrt{K_2}}$$

$$\frac{0.36}{0.04} = \frac{K_1}{K_2}$$

$$\frac{K_2}{K_1} = \frac{0.04}{0.36}$$

2.9 STEADY STATE ANALYSIS

Steady state is a part of time response which remains after complete transient response vanishes from the system output.

- The steady state response is the final value achieved by the system output.
- This response indicates accuracy of the system by means of measuring the actual output with reference to the desired value.

$$C_{ss} = \lim_{t \to \infty} C(t)$$

- Mainly steady state response has following properties.

1. Settling Time : How much time system takes to reach its steady state. It is related to transient response also because same time will be required by transients to die out completely from the system output.

2. Steady State Error : How far the actual output is reached from its desired value which is called steady state error (e_{ss}).

Out of these two, steady state error specification is most important as it is related to only the steady state.

Points to be studied about steady state error.

- On which factors it depends.
- How to calculate it.
- How to reduce it.

2.9.1 Steady State Error (e_{ss})

Steady-state errors constitute an extremely important aspect of system performance, for it would be meaningless to design for dynamic accuracy if the steady output differed substantially from the desired value for one reason or another.
The steady state error is measure of system accuracy.

These errors arise from the nature of inputs, type of system, and from nonlinearities of system components such as static friction, backlash, etc.

The steady state performance of a stable control system is generally judged by its steddy state error to step, ramp, and parabolic inputs.

Consider a closed-loop system as shown in Fig. 2.21.

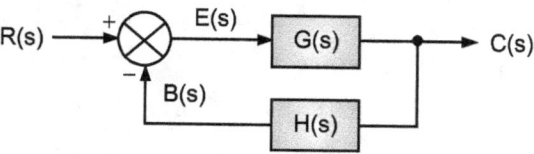

Fig. 2.21

The closed loop transfer function as,

$$\frac{C(s)}{R(s)} = \frac{G(s)}{1 + G(s)\, H(s)}$$

Now,

$$C(s) = G(s)\,.\,E(s)$$

Therefore,

$$\frac{G(s).E(s)}{R(s)} = \frac{G(s)}{1+ G(s).H(s)}$$

This gives,

$$E(s) = \frac{R(s)}{1 + G(s).H(s)}$$

Using final value theorem in Laplace Transform,

$$\lim_{t \to \infty} f(t) = \lim_{s \to 0} s\,.\,F(s)$$

Therefore,

$$e_{ss} = \lim_{s \to 0} e(t) = \lim_{s \to 0} s\,.E(s)$$

The steady state error is given as ;

$$e_{ss} = \lim_{s \to 0} \frac{s.R(s)}{1+ G(s).\,H(s)} \qquad \dots (2.10)$$

From the above equation it is easily verified that the steady state error is dependent on;

* R(s) reference i/p (type and magnitude)
* G(s).H(s) open loop Transfer function

2.9.2 Effect on Steady State Error

Effect of change in input and output, product G(s).H(s) on the value of steady state error.

The steady state error, e_{ss} is given as

$$e_{ss} = \lim_{s \to \infty} \frac{s.R(s)}{1+ G(s).H(s)} \tag{2.11}$$

1. Reference Input = Step Function of Magnitude A

$$r(t) = A$$

$$R(s) = A/s$$

We have,

$$e_{ss} = \lim_{s \to 0} \frac{s.R(s)}{1+ G(s).H(s)}$$

Substitute value of R(s) in above equation,

$$= \lim_{s \to 0} \frac{s.A/s}{1+G(s).H(s)}$$

$$= \lim_{s \to 0} \frac{A}{1+ G(s).H(s)}$$

$$= \frac{A}{1 + \lim\limits_{s \to 0} G(s).H(s)}$$

$$\therefore \quad e_{ss} = \frac{A}{1 + K_p}$$

Where, $K_p = \lim\limits_{s \to 0} G(s). H(s)$ is the position error constant.

Therefore, when step input is selected as the reference input, the error in the system is controlled by velocity error coefficient Kv and the magnitude of input applied.

2. Reference Input = Ramp Function of Magnitude A

$$Y(t) = At$$

$$R(s) = \frac{A}{s^2}$$

We have,

$$e_{ss} = \lim_{s \to 0} \frac{s.R(s)}{1+G(s).H(s)} = \lim_{s \to 0} \frac{s.A/s^2}{1+G(s).H(s)}$$

$$= \lim_{s \to 0} \frac{A}{s(1 + G(s).H(s))} = \lim_{s \to 0} \frac{A}{s + s.G(s).H(s)}$$

$$= \frac{A}{s + \lim\limits_{s \to 0} s.G(s).H(s)}$$

$\therefore$ $e_{ss} = \dfrac{A}{K_v}$

Where, $K_v = \underset{s \to 0}{\lim}\ s.G(s).H(s)$ is the velocity error constant.

Therefore ramp input is selected as a reference input, the error in the system is controlled by velocity error coefficient K_v and the magnitude of input applied.

3. **Reference Input = Parabolic Function of Magnitude A**

$$r(t) = \dfrac{At^2}{2}$$

$$R(s) = \dfrac{A}{s^3}$$

We have $e_{ss} = \underset{s \to 0}{\lim}\ \dfrac{s.R(s)}{1+G(s).\,H(s)}$

$$= \underset{s \to 0}{\lim}\ \dfrac{s.A/s^3}{1+G(s).\,H(s)} = \dfrac{A}{s^2\,(1+G(s).\,H(s))}$$

$$= \underset{s \to 0}{\lim}\ \dfrac{A}{s^2 + s^2\,G(s).\,H(s)}$$

$\therefore$ $e_{ss} = \dfrac{A}{K_a}$

Where, $K_a = \underset{s \to 0}{\lim}\ s^2.\,G(s).H(s)$ is the acceleration error constant.

Therefore, when parabolic input is selected as a reference input, the error in the system is controlled by acceleration error coefficient K_a, and the magnitude of input applied.

Example 2.5 : A unity feedback system has open loop T.F.

$$G(s) = \dfrac{K(s + 2)}{S(s^3 + 7s^2) + 125}$$

Find :

(a) type of the system

(b) error coefficients

(c) Steady state error when i/p to the system is $\dfrac{R}{2}t^2$

Solution :

As the given systems is unity feedback

$$H(s) = 1$$

Open loop transfer function = G(s). H (s)

$$G(s).H(s) = \frac{K(s+2)}{s(s^3 + 7s^2 + 12s)}$$

Convert the open loop transfer function into time constraint form

$$G(s)H.(s) = \frac{2K(1 + s/2)}{s.s. (s^2 + 7s + 12)} = \frac{2K (1 + s/2)}{s^2(s + 4) (s + 3)}$$

$$= \frac{2K (s + s/2)}{s^2. 4\left(1 + \frac{s}{4}\right)^3 \left(1 + \frac{s}{3}\right)}$$

$$= \frac{2K/12 (1 + s/2)}{s^2 (1 + s/4) (1 + s/3)}$$

(a) There are 2 poles at origin Hence Type of system is 2

(b) The error coefficients are :

- $$K_p = \frac{\lim}{s \to 0} G(s).H(s) = \frac{\lim}{s \to 0} \frac{K/6 (1 + s/2)}{s^2. 1\left(1 + \frac{s}{4}\right)\left(1 + \frac{s}{3}\right)}$$

$$= \infty$$

- $$K_v = \frac{\lim}{s \to 0} s.G(s). H(s)$$

$$= \frac{\lim}{s \to 0} \frac{s.K/6 (1 + s/2)}{s^2\left(1 + \frac{s}{4}\right)\left(1+ \frac{s}{3}\right)}$$

$$\frac{\lim}{s \to 0} = \frac{K/6 (1 + S/2)}{s (1 + s/4) (1 + s/3)}$$

$$K_v = \infty$$

- $$K_a = \frac{Lim}{s \to 0} s^2 G(s). H(s)$$

$$\frac{\lim}{s \to 0} = \frac{s^2 K/6 (1 + s/2)}{s^2 (1 + s/4) (1 + s/3)}$$

$$\frac{\lim}{s \to 0} = \frac{K/6 (1 + s/2)}{(1 + s/4) (1 + s/3)}$$

$$K_a = K/6$$

(c) Steady state error is gives as,

$$e_{ss} = \frac{\lim}{s \to 0} \frac{s.R.(s)}{1 + G(s) H(s)}$$

$$r(t) = R. \frac{t^2}{2}$$

$$\therefore \quad R(s) = \frac{R}{s^3}$$

$$e_{ss} = \lim_{s \to 0} \frac{s.R/s^3}{1 + \dfrac{K/6(1 + s/2)}{s^2(1 + s/4)(1 + s/3)}}$$

$$= \lim_{s \to 0} \frac{R/s^2}{1 + \dfrac{K/6(1 + s/2)}{s^2(1 + s/4)(1 + s/3)}}$$

$$= \lim_{s \to 0} \frac{R}{s^2 + \dfrac{K/6(1 + s/2)}{(1 + s/4)(1 + s/3)}} = \frac{R}{K/6}$$

$$e_{ss} = \frac{6R}{K}$$

Example 2.6 : A unity feedback system has a open-loop transfer function as;

$$G(s) = \frac{K}{s(s + 1)}$$

Determine the range of K such that $e_{ss} \leq 0.005$; for an i/p r(t) = 0.1t

Solution : Open loop transfer function is given as;

$$G(s) \, H(s) = \frac{K}{s(s + 1)}$$

As the input is r(t) = 0.1t

$$\therefore \quad R(s) = \frac{0.1}{s^2}$$

$$\therefore \quad e_{ss} = \lim_{s \to 0} \frac{s.R(s)}{1 + G(s).H(s)}$$

$$\therefore \quad e_{ss} = \lim_{s \to 0} \frac{s.0.1}{s^2}{1 + \dfrac{K}{s(s + 1)}}$$

$$e_{ss} = \lim_{s \to 0} \frac{0.1/s}{1 + \dfrac{K}{s.(s + 1)}}$$

$$e_{ss} = \lim_{s \to 0} \frac{0.1}{s + \dfrac{K}{(s + 1)}}$$

$\therefore$

$$e_{ss} = \frac{0.1}{K}$$

Maximum allowable error = 0.005 = e_{ss}

Minimum value of error should be = 0 = e_{ss}

$$K = \frac{0.1}{e_{ss}} = \frac{0.1}{0}$$

$$K = \infty \text{ for minimum } e_{ss}$$

$$K = \frac{0.1}{0.005} = 20 \text{ for maximum } e_{ss}$$

$\therefore$ Range of K is $20 \le K \le \infty$

Example 2.7 : The block diagram shown in Fig. 2.22, determine steady state temperature represents a heat treating oven. The set point (Desired temperature is 1000°C)

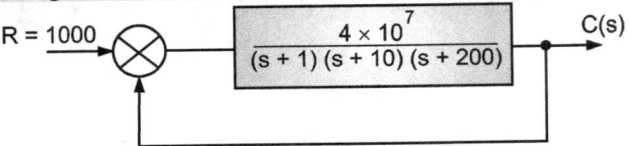

R = 1000 $\dfrac{4 \times 10^{7}}{(s + 1)\,(s + 10)\,(s + 200)}$ C(s)

Fig. 2.22

Solution : Given H(s) = 1 $G(s) = \dfrac{4 \times 10^{7}}{(s + 1)\,(s + 10)\,(s + 200)}$

Input is step of magnitude 1000

$$R(s) = \frac{1000}{s}$$

$$e_{ss} = \lim_{s \to 0} \frac{s.R(s)}{1 + G(s).\,H(s)}$$

$$= \lim_{s \to 0} \frac{s.(1000)/s}{1 + \dfrac{4 \times 10^{7}}{(s + 1)\,(s + 10)\,(s + 200)}}$$

$$e_{ss} = \frac{1000}{1 + \dfrac{4 \times 10^{7}}{(1)\,(10)\,(200)}}$$

$$e_{ss} = \frac{1000}{1 + 20000}$$

$$e_{ss} = 0.04999$$

The steady state error (e_{ss}) is the difference between desired o/p and steady state o/p

$$e_{ss} = e_{desired} - e_{ss}$$

$$= 1000 - 0.04999 = 999.95$$

Steady state temperature is 999.95°C.

SUMMARY

Standard Test Inputs

Input	Function	Description	Sketch	Use
Impulse	$\delta(t)$	$\delta(t) = \infty$ for $0- < t < 0+$ $= 0$ elsewhere $\int_{0-}^{0+} \delta(t)dt = 1$		Transient response Modeling
Step	$u(t)$	$u(t) = 1$ for $t > 0$ $= 0$ for $t < 0$		Transient response Steady-state error
Ramp	$tu(t)$	$tu(t) = t$ for $t \geq 0$ $= 0$ elsewhere		Steady-state error
Parabola	$\frac{1}{2}t^2 u(t)$	$\frac{1}{2}t^2 u(t) = \frac{1}{2}t^2$ for $t \geq 0$ $= 0$ elsewhere		Steady-state error
Sinusoid	$\sin \omega t$			Transient response Modeling Steady-state error

Second Order Systems

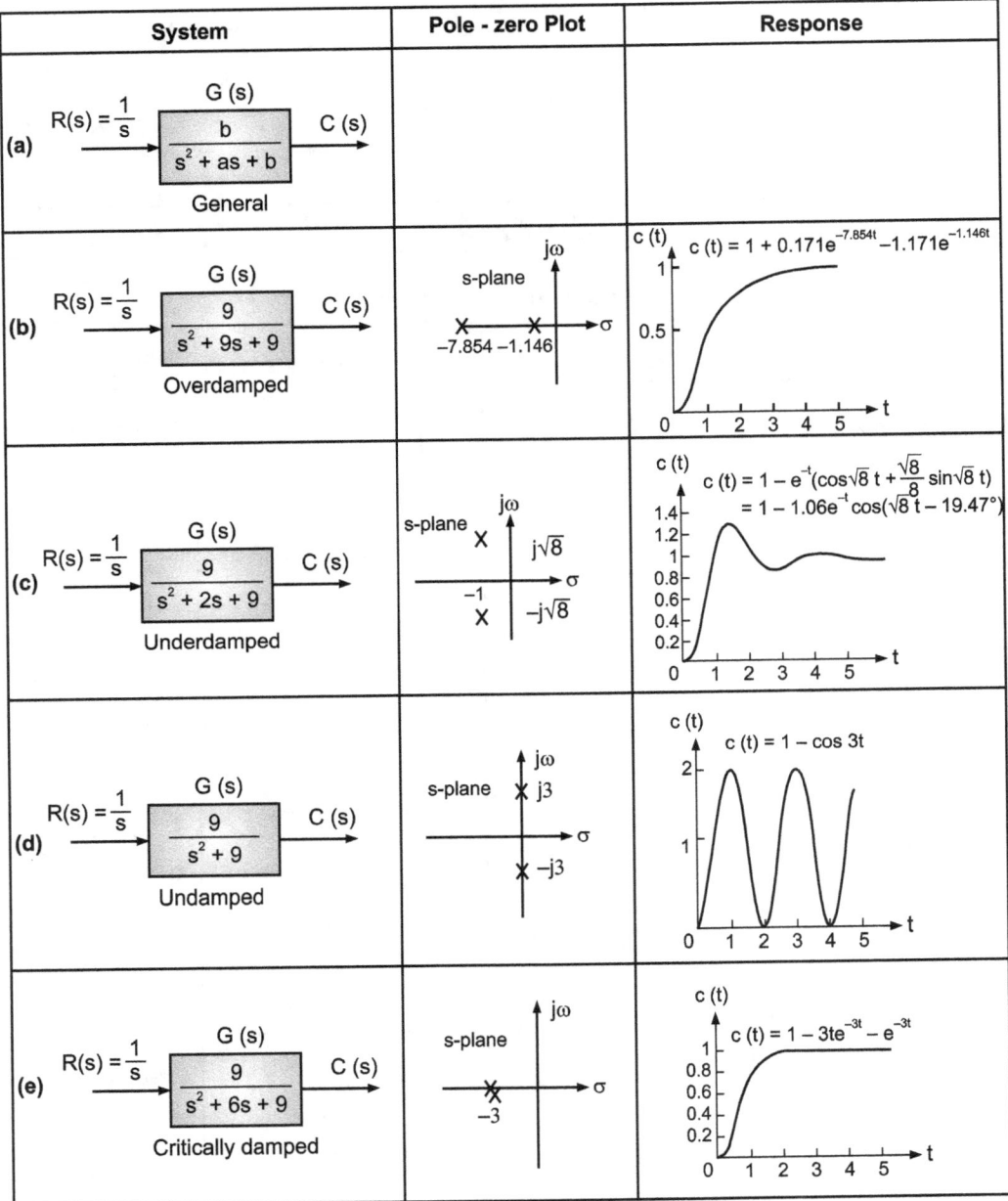

System	Pole - zero Plot	Response
(a) $R(s) = \dfrac{1}{s}$ → $G(s)$: $\dfrac{b}{s^2 + as + b}$ → $C(s)$ General		
(b) $R(s) = \dfrac{1}{s}$ → $G(s)$: $\dfrac{9}{s^2 + 9s + 9}$ → $C(s)$ Overdamped	s-plane, poles at -7.854, -1.146	$c(t) = 1 + 0.171e^{-7.854t} - 1.171e^{-1.146t}$
(c) $R(s) = \dfrac{1}{s}$ → $G(s)$: $\dfrac{9}{s^2 + 2s + 9}$ → $C(s)$ Underdamped	s-plane, poles at $-1 \pm j\sqrt{8}$	$c(t) = 1 - e^{-t}\left(\cos\sqrt{8}\,t + \dfrac{\sqrt{8}}{8}\sin\sqrt{8}\,t\right)$ $= 1 - 1.06e^{-t}\cos(\sqrt{8}\,t - 19.47°)$
(d) $R(s) = \dfrac{1}{s}$ → $G(s)$: $\dfrac{9}{s^2 + 9}$ → $C(s)$ Undamped	s-plane, poles at $\pm j3$	$c(t) = 1 - \cos 3t$
(e) $R(s) = \dfrac{1}{s}$ → $G(s)$: $\dfrac{9}{s^2 + 6s + 9}$ → $C(s)$ Critically damped	s-plane, double pole at -3	$c(t) = 1 - 3te^{-3t} - e^{-3t}$

Test Signals

Input	r(t)	R(s)
Step Input	A	A/s
Ramp Input	At	A/s^2
Parabolic Input	$At^2 / 2$	A/s

Second Order System Responses Damping Cases :

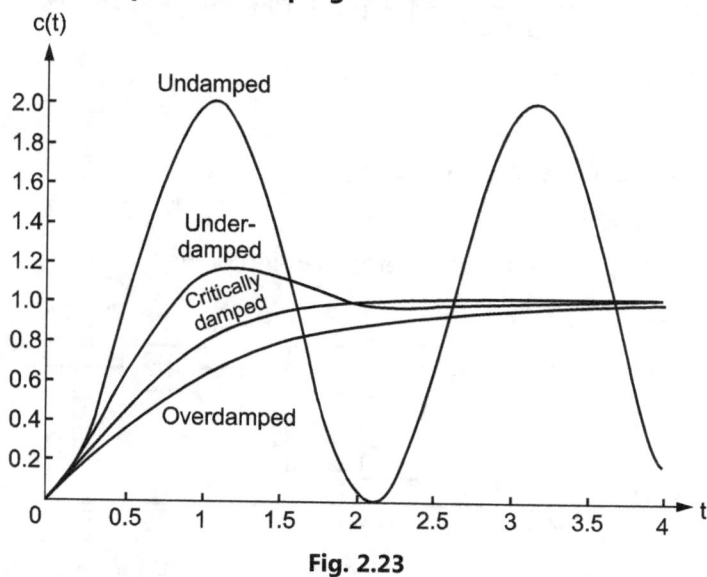

Fig. 2.23

EXERCISE

1. A unit step input is applied to the unity feedback system for which open- loop transfer function is $G(s) = \dfrac{16}{s(s + 8)}$ Find

   (a) The closed loop transfer function

   (b) Natural frequency of oscillation ω_n

   (c) Damping ration ξ

   (d) Damped frequency of oscillation ω_d

   (e) Output response

2. A system is given by differential equation

   $$\frac{d^2y}{dt^2} + 4\frac{dy}{dt} + 8y = 8x \text{ where } y = \text{output and } x = \text{input}$$

   Determine all the time domain specifications for unit step input

3. A system has the following transfer function,

   $$\frac{C(s)}{R(s)} = \frac{20}{(s + 10)}$$

   Determine unit impulse, step and ramp response with zero initial condition and sketch the response.

4. A system has $G(s) = \dfrac{15}{(s + 1)(s + 3)}$ and $H(s) = 1$. Determine,

    (a) Characteristic equation

    (b) ω_n and ξ

    (c) Time at which first undershoot occurs

    (d) Time period of oscillation

    (e) No. of cycles, output will perform before settling down

5. For a system shown,

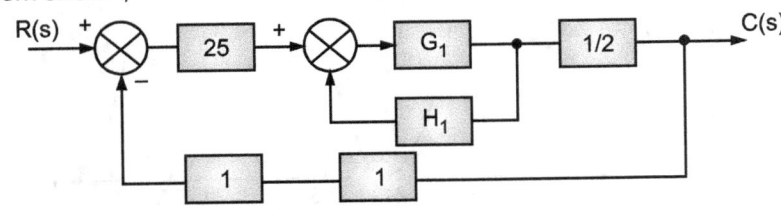

Fig. 2.24

$G_1 = \dfrac{20}{(s + 4)(s + 10)}$ and $H_1 = 10s$

Determine type of system, error coefficients and error for following inputs

    (a) $r(t) = 10$

    (b) $r(t) = 5t$

    (c) $r(t) = 10 + 5t + \dfrac{6}{2}t^2$

6. A unity feedback system has open-loop transfer function as,

    $G(s) = \dfrac{20}{s(1 + 4s)(1 + s)}$

    (a) Determine static error coefficients – K_p, K_v, K_a

    (b) Eetermine steady state error $-e_{ss}$ if $r(t) = \left(2 + 4t + \dfrac{t^2}{2}\right)$

7. A unity feedback system has open-loop transfer function as,

    $G(s) = \dfrac{K(s + 2s)}{s(1 + s)(1 + 0.4s)^2}$

    Determine the value of K to limit steady error to 10% when input to the system is t

8. The closed-loop transfer function of a unity-feedback control system is,

    $\dfrac{C(s)}{R(s)} = \dfrac{Ks + b}{s^2 + as + b}$

    Determine the open loop transfer function G(s)

SOLVED UNIVERSITY PROBLEMS

Example 2.1 : If $G(s) = \dfrac{K}{s(s + 64)}$ with H(s) = 1, determine value of K so that damping factor is 0.5. for this value of K. determine

   (i)   Rise time and

   (ii) Setting time

Assume unit step input.   **[Dec. 2016] [6]**

Solution :

Given
$$G(s) = \frac{K}{s(s + 64)}, H(s) = 1$$

Damping factor
$$\xi = 0.5$$

We have closed loop transfer function i.e.

$$T(s) = \frac{C(s)}{R(s)} = \frac{G(s)}{1 + G(s).H(s)}$$

Substitute in G(s) and h(s) in T(s); then will get

$$T(s) = \frac{\dfrac{K}{s(s + 64)}}{1 + \dfrac{K}{s(s + 64)}}$$

By simplification T(s); We get.

$$T(s) = \frac{K}{s(s + 64) + K}$$

$$= \frac{K}{s^2 + 64s + K} \tag{1}$$

We have second order transfer function i.e T(s)

$$T(s) = \frac{\omega_n^2}{s^2 + 2\xi_n s + \omega_n^2} \tag{2}$$

Now compare denominator of (1) and (2) we get

$$\omega_n^2 = K \text{ and } 2\xi\omega_n = 64$$

Given $\xi = 0.5$, therefore
$$2(0.5)\,\omega_n = 64$$

$$\omega_n = 64$$

$$\omega_n^2 = K = (64)^2$$

Now by taking K value out

$$T(s) = \frac{(64)^2}{S^2 + 2(0.5)(64)s + (64)^2}$$

$$= \frac{(64)^2}{s^2 + 64s + (64)^2}$$

Now we know, $\xi = 0.5$ and $\omega_n = 64$

(i) Rise time $T_r = \dfrac{\pi - \theta}{\omega_d}$, where $\omega_d = \omega_n \sqrt{(1 - \xi^2)}$

And $\theta = \dfrac{\tan^{-1}\sqrt{(1 - \xi^2)}}{\xi}$

Substitute $\xi = 0.5$ and $\omega_n = 64$ in ω_d and θ

We get, $T_r = \dfrac{3.141 - 1.047}{55.425}$

                                $T_r = 0.03778$ sec

(ii) Setting Time : $T_s = \dfrac{4}{\xi\omega_n}$ for 2% tolerance band

By substituting $\xi = 0.5$ and $\omega_n = 64$

                                $T_s = \dfrac{4}{(0.5)(64)}$

                                $T_s = 0.125$ sec for 2% tolerance band

∴ $T_r = 0.03778$ sec $T_s = 0.125$ sec

Example : 2.2 : A unity feedback system has open loop transfer function :

$$G(s) = \frac{K}{s(s + 10)}$$

Determine 'K' so that damping factor is 0.5 for this value of 'K' determine.
1. Location of closed loop poles
2. Peak overshoot and
3. Peak time Assume input is unit step.   **[Dec. 14] [6]**

Solution : $G(s) = \dfrac{K}{s(s + 10)}$

To obtain the transient domain specifications. We work with the closed loop transfer function.

∴ $\dfrac{C(s)}{R(s)} = \dfrac{G(s)}{1 + G(s).H(s)} = \dfrac{\dfrac{K}{s(s + 10)}}{1 + \dfrac{K}{s(s + 10)}}$

$$= \frac{K}{s(s + 10) + K} = \frac{K}{s^2 + 10s + K} \tag{1}$$

Comparing equation (1) with the standard closed loop transfer function.

$$\frac{C(s)}{R(s)} = \frac{\omega_n^2}{s^2 + 2\xi\omega_n s + \omega_n^2}$$

$$\therefore \ \omega_n^2 = K \quad \text{i.e.} \quad \omega_n = \sqrt{K}$$

$$2\xi\omega_n = 10 \ \therefore \quad \xi = \frac{10}{2\xi\omega_n} = \frac{5}{\sqrt{K}}$$

Given damping ratio $\xi = 0.5$

$$\therefore \quad 0.5 = \frac{5}{\sqrt{K}} \ \therefore \ \sqrt{K} = 10 \ \therefore \ K = 100$$

The value of the gain K is 100

$$\omega_n = \sqrt{K} = 10 \text{ rad/sec}$$

$$\omega_d = \omega_n \sqrt{1 - \xi^2} = 10\sqrt{1 - 0.5^2} = 8.66 \text{ rad/sec.}$$

1. Location of closed loop poles

The position of the poles depend on the value of ξ

2. Peak time $\qquad T_p = \dfrac{\pi}{\omega_d} = 0.3627$ sec.

Example 2.3 : If open loop transfer function is

$$G(s) = \frac{1}{s + 1}$$

Obtain unit step response. Also find output at time t = 0, 1, 2, 3, 4, 5. Assume unity feedback and G(s) is in closed loop. **[Dec. 2014] [6]**

Solution :

Given $\qquad G(s) = \dfrac{1}{s+1}, \ H(s) = 1$

Closed loop system is

$$\frac{G(s)}{R(s)} = \frac{G(s)}{1 + G(s).H(s)} = \frac{\dfrac{1}{s+1}}{1 + \dfrac{1}{s+1}} = \frac{1}{s + 2}$$

Input is unit step r(t) =1

i.e. $R(s) = \dfrac{1}{s}$

$$C(s) = R(s).\dfrac{1}{s+2}$$

$$C(s) = \dfrac{1}{s}\,\dfrac{1}{s+2}$$

As $\xi < 1$, $\sqrt{\xi^2 - 1}$ becomes complex and hence is written as $j\sqrt{1-\xi^2}$

$\therefore$ $S_1, S_2 = -\xi\omega_n \pm j\omega_n \sqrt{1-\xi^2}$

$$S_1 = -\xi\omega_n + j\omega_n\sqrt{1-\xi^2}$$

And $S_2 = -\xi\,\omega_n - j\omega_n\sqrt{1-\zeta^2}$

Location of poles :

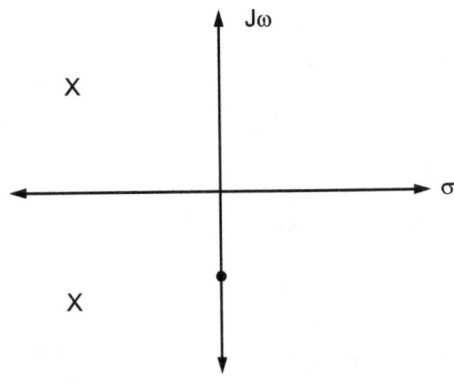

Fig. 2.25

From the Fig. 2.25 it is seen that the poles are complex conjugates of each other.

(2) Peak overshoot

Peak overshoot is given by % $M_p = e^{\dfrac{-\xi\pi}{\sqrt{1-\xi^2}}} \times 100$

$\%\ M_p = 16.30\ \%$

By applying partial fractions we get,

$$C(s) = \dfrac{A}{s} + \dfrac{B}{S+2}$$

$\therefore$ $\dfrac{1}{s(s+2)} = \dfrac{0.5}{s} + \dfrac{-0.5}{s+2}$

Apply inverse laplace we get

$$C(t) = 0.5 - 0.5e^{-2t} \tag{1}$$

at	$t = 0$;	$C(t) = 0$
at	$t = 1$;	$C(t) = 0.43$
at	$t = 2$	$C(t) = 0.49$
at	$t = 3$;	$C(t) = 0.498$
at	$t = 4$,	$C(t) = 0.499$
at	$t = 5$;	$C(t) = 0.4999$

Example 2.4 : The open-loop transfer function of unity feedback system is $G(s) = \dfrac{K}{s(Ts + 1)}$, K, C > o with a given value of K, the peak overshoot was found to be 80%. Suppose peak overshoot is decreased to 20% by decreasing gain K. Find the new value of K (say K_2) in terms of the old value.   **[May 15] [6]**

Solution :

Given
$$G(s) = \frac{K}{s(1 + s)}, \quad H(s) = 1$$

$$\frac{C(s)}{R(s)} = \frac{G(s)}{1 + G(s).H(s)} = \frac{\dfrac{K}{s(1 + s\tau)}}{1 + \dfrac{K}{s(1 + s\tau)}}$$

$$\frac{C(s)}{R(s)} = \frac{K}{\tau s^2 + s + K} = \frac{K/c}{s^2 + \dfrac{1}{\tau} + \dfrac{K}{\tau}}$$

Comparing denominator with $s^2 + 2\xi\omega_n s + \omega_n^2$.

$$\omega_n^2 = \frac{K}{T}$$

$$\omega_n = \sqrt{\left(\frac{K}{T}\right)} \tag{1}$$

$$2\xi\omega_n = \frac{1}{T}$$

$$\xi = \frac{1}{2\sqrt{(KT)}} \tag{2}$$

For 80% M_p,   let $\xi = \xi_1$

$$0.8 = e^{\dfrac{-\pi\xi_1}{\sqrt{(1-\xi_2^1)}}}$$

$$l_n(0.8) = \dfrac{-\pi\xi_1}{\sqrt{(1-\xi_2^1)}}$$

$$\xi_1 = \dfrac{(l_n(0.8)^2)}{\pi^2 + (l_n(0.8))^2}$$

∴ $\xi_1 = 0.07085$

For 20% Mp,   let $\xi = \xi_2$

$$0.2 = e^{\dfrac{-H\xi_2}{\sqrt{(1-\xi_2^2)}}}$$

$$l_n(0.2) = \dfrac{-\pi\xi_2}{\sqrt{(1-\xi^2)}}$$

$$(\xi_2) = \sqrt{\dfrac{(ln(0.2))^2}{\pi^2 + (l\,n\,(0.2)^2)}}$$

∴ $\xi_2 = 0.4559$

For changing ξ_1 to ξ_2 let K is to be changed from K_1 to K_2 with t constant. Hence using equation (2).

$$0.07089 = \dfrac{1}{2\sqrt{(K_1T)}} \quad \text{and} \quad 0.4559 = \dfrac{1}{2\sqrt{(K_1T)}}$$

$$\dfrac{0.07085}{0.4559} = \sqrt{\dfrac{(K_2)}{(K_1)}}$$

$$0.02415 = \dfrac{K_2}{K_1}$$

∴ $K_2 = 0.02415K_1$

STABILITY ANALYSIS

3.1 INTRODUCTION

In designing a control system, the main objective of a control system engineer is that the designed system must be stable when it is subjected to command signals, extraneous inputs anywhere in a loop and change in parameters of the feedback loop.

Stability is a Very Important Characteristic of any System :

Stability in a system implies that small changes in the systems input, in initial conditions or in system parameters do not result in large changes in a system output.

A linear time invariant system is said to be stable if it satisfies the following conditions.

1. If the system is excited by a bounded input, the output must be bounded.

2. If the input to system is zero, the output must be zero irrespective of all the initial conditions.

The second notion of stability generally concerns a free space relative to its transient behaviors.

The first notion concerns a system under influence of an input clearly, if a system is subjected to an unbounded input and produces an unbounded response, nothing can be said about stability.

But, if it is subjected to a bounded input produces an unbounded response, it is by definition unstable.

Actually the output of a unstable system may increase to a certain extent and then the system may break down or become non-linear after output exceeds a certain magnitude, so that linear mathematical model no longer applies.

Above two notions of stability are essentially equivalent in linear-time invariant systems.

Simple and powerful tools are available to determine stability of such systems.

For non-linear systems because of possible existence of multiple equilibrium states and other anomolies the concept of stability is difficult to define, so that there is no clear cut correspondence between two nations of stability defined above.

For a free stable non-linear system, there is no guarantee that output will be bounded whenever input is bounded.

Also, if output is bounded for a particular bounded input, it may not be bounded for other bounded input.

Many of the important results obtained thus for concern of stability of non-linear systems in the sense of second notion above.

The stability are classified into various ways based on different operating conditions :

1. **Absolutely Stable System :**

   Here the system is stable for all values of parameters. Like K from θ to ∞.

2. **Conditional Stable System :**

   Here the system is stable for certain range of parameters like K from 0 to 100.

3. **Marginal/Critical/Limitedly Stable System :**

   A LTI system is said to be marginal stable if for the bounded input, the output maintains the constant amplitude. The non-repeated poles on imaginary axis gives the response of constant amplitude and frequency of oscillations the system is marginally stable.

3.2 PHYSICAL IMPLICATION OF TWO NOTIONS OF STABILITY

By considering single input-single output system with T.F.

$$\frac{C(S)}{R(S)} = G(S) = \frac{b_0 s^m + b_i s^{n-1} + \ldots \ldots b_m}{a_0 s^n + a_1 s^{n-1} + \ldots \ldots a_n} \; ; m < n \qquad \ldots (1)$$

With the initial conditions assumed to be zero the output of system is given by,

$$C(S) = G(S) \cdot R(S)$$

∴ Taking Laplace inverse,

$$C(t) = L^{-1} [G(S) \cdot R(S)]$$

Applying correlation property of Laplace transform

$$C(t) = \int_0^\infty g(\tau) \, r(t - \tau) \, d\tau$$

Where, $g(t) = L^{-1} (G(S))$ is the impulse response of the system.

$$|C(t)| = \left| \int_0^\infty g(\tau) \cdot r(t - \tau) \, d\tau \right| \qquad \ldots (2)$$

Since, the absolute value of the integral is not greater than the integral of absolute value of the integral.

$$|C(t)| \le \int_0^\infty |g(\tau) \cdot r(t - \tau)| \, d\tau$$

$$\le \int_0^\infty |g(\tau)| \cdot |r(t - \tau)| \, d\tau$$

The first notion of stability is for every bounded input

$$|r(t)| \leq M_1 < \infty$$

The output is also bounded.

$$|C(t)| \leq M_2 < \infty$$

We have for bounded input, bounded output condition as,

$$|C(t)| \leq M_1 \int_0^\infty |g(\tau)| \, d\tau \leq M_2$$

Thus the first notion of stability is satisfied if the g(t) impulse response is absolutely integrable; i.e.

$$\int_0^\infty g(\tau) \, d\tau \text{ is finite}$$

(i.e. area under absolute value of impulse response g(t) evaluated from t = 0 to t = ∞ must be finite)

The nature of g(t) is dependent on poles of transfer function G(S) which are roots of the characteristics equation.

Thus for bounded input, bounded output stability,

- If all roots of characteristics equation has negative real part, i.e. they lie in left half of s-plane, then the system is stable (BIBO) and the impulse response to be bounded which finally becomes zero i.e.

$$\int_0^\infty |g(\tau)| \, d\tau \text{ is finite}$$

- If any root of given characteristics equation has positive real part, i.e. they lies in the right half of s-plane, the impulse response bounded and is therefore infinite, this makes system unstable.

$$\int_0^\infty |g(\tau)| \, d\tau \text{ is infinite.}$$

➤ **Stable System :**

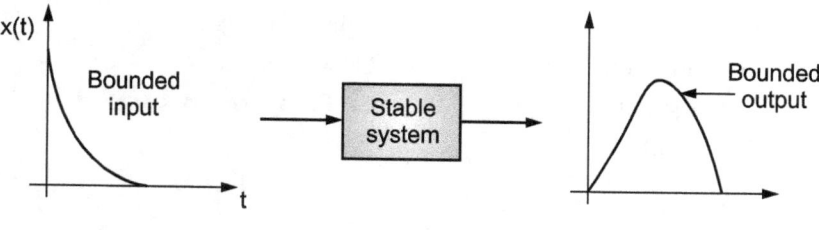

Fig. 3.1

> **Unstable System :**

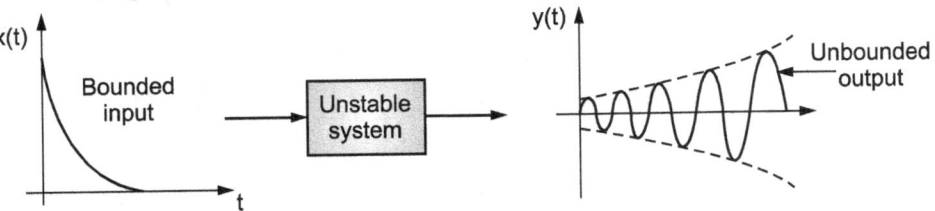

Fig. 3.2

- If there are repeated roots on imaginary axis, the impulse response g(t) is unbounded axis, and infinite, and the system is unstable.

- If one or more non-repeated roots of the characteristics equation on imaginary axis then the impulse response g(t) is bounded but $\int\limits_0^\infty |g(\tau)|\, d\tau$ is infinite, which makes the system unstable.

3.3 DOMINANT POLES AND ZEROS

Theory :

The variable 's' is a complex variable defined by

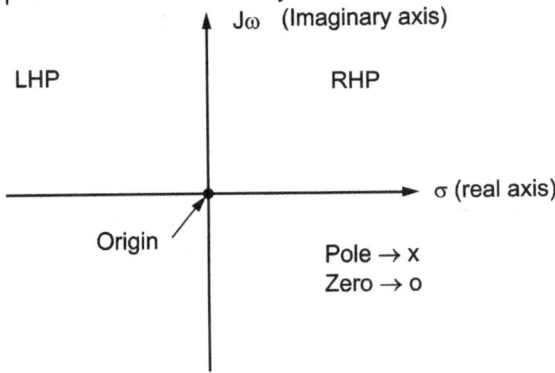

Fig. 3.3

Where r is real part of 's' and 'w' is imaginary part of s.

> Horizontal axis → Real axis
> (w = 0 and s = σ)
> Vertical axis → Imaginary axis
> (σ = 0 and s = jω)

Origin → 0 + j_0
R.H.P. → 0 < σ < ∞
L.H.P. → − σ < σ < 0

Equation of T.F in S-domain

$$\frac{C(S)}{R(S)} = G(S)$$

∴ $C(S) = R(S) \cdot G(S)$

From above equation, the denominator polynomial of G(S) in partial form can be written as,

$$G(S) = \frac{A_1}{s - s_1} + \frac{A_2}{s - s_2} + \ldots \ldots \frac{A_n}{s - s_n}$$

The poles of transfer function G(S) can be either real, imaginary or complex and the poles may lie in left half of s-plane or right half of s-plane or on $j\omega$ axis also.

> **Keynote :**
>
> Depending upon the location of poles on the s-plane, the system has different types of impulse responses.

Real Poles :

The partial fraction form of the transfer function is;

$$G(S) = \frac{A_K}{s + s_K} = \frac{A_K}{s + a}$$

- If a is −ve, $s_K = a$, $s = -a$ and is located in left half of s-plane and the corresponding impulse response is $A_K.e^{-at} u(t)$.

∴   After sometime the impulse response dies out to zero.

- If a is +ve, $s_K = -a$, and $s = a$, 'a' is positive and is located in right-half of the s-plane and the impulse response is $A_K.e^{at} u(t)$.

∴   The response increase without any bound as 't' tends to ∞.

Thus for a stable system G(S) must have poles in the left half of the s-plane.

If the pole is at origin, the response is a constant value for t > 0. (∵ s = 0).

Similarly, for complex poles and repeated poles are discussed in the below.

3.3.1 Relation between Location of Poles and Response

- **Real Poles :**

Poles on negative real-axis.	Impulse response is exponentially decaying.
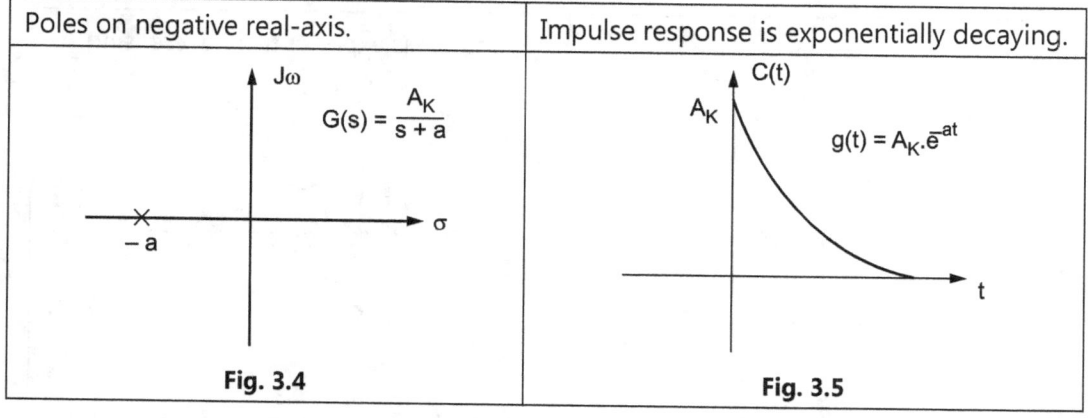	
Fig. 3.4	Fig. 3.5

contd...

Poles on positive real axis.	Response is exponentially increasing.
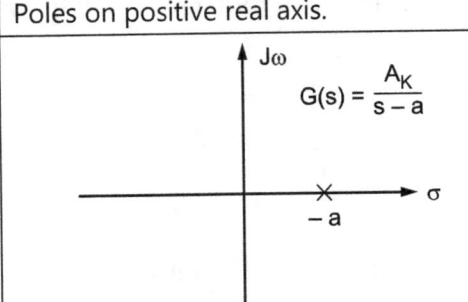 $G(s) = \dfrac{A_K}{s - a}$ **Fig. 3.6**	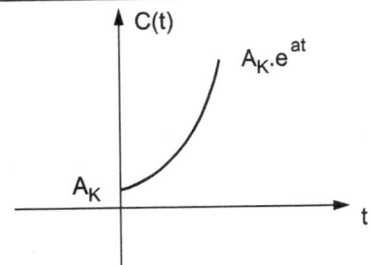 $A_K \cdot e^{at}$ **Fig. 3.7**
Pole at origin :	Response is constant :
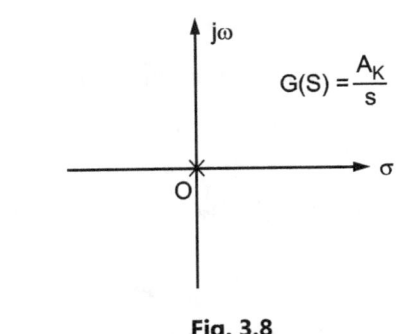 $G(S) = \dfrac{A_K}{s}$ **Fig. 3.8**	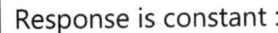 $C(t) = A_K$ **Fig. 3.9**

- **Complex Poles :**

Complex poles on left half of s-plane; $$G(S) = \dfrac{A_1}{s + (a + Jb)} + \dfrac{A_1{}^*}{s + (a - Jb)}$$	$g(t) = A_1 e^{-(a+Jb)t} + A_1 e^{-(a-Jb)t}$ $\quad = 2\,A_1 e^{-at} \cos bt$ $\quad = 2\,A_1 e^{-at} \sin(bt + 90°)$
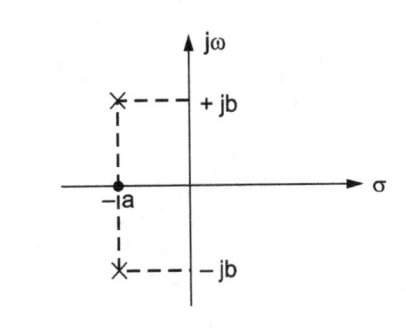 **Fig. 3.10**	Response is exponentially decreasing. 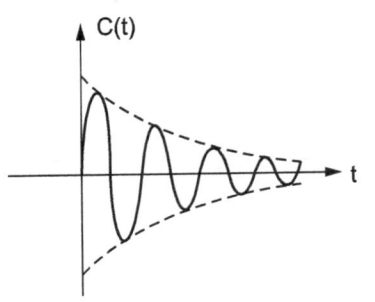 **Fig. 3.11**

Contd...

• Complex poles on the right half of the s-plane $G(S) = \dfrac{A_1}{s-(a+Jb)} + \dfrac{A_1{}^*}{s-(a-Jb)}$	$g(t) = A_1.e^{-(-a+Jb)t} + A_1.e^{-(a-Jb)-t}$ $\quad = 2A_1e^{at}\cos bt$ $\quad = 2A_1e^{at}\sin(bt+90°)$
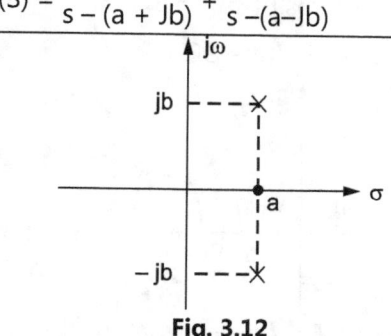 **Fig. 3.12**	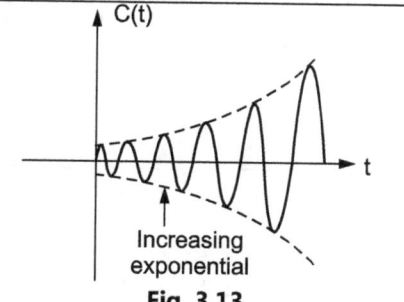 Increasing exponential **Fig. 3.13**

• **Poles on Imaginary Axis :**

$G(S) = \dfrac{A_1}{s+jb} + \dfrac{A_1{}^*}{s-jb}$ $(\because a = 0)$	$g(t) = A_1e^{-jb} + A_1e^{+jb}$ $\quad = 2A_1\cos bt$ $\quad = 2A\sin(bt+90°)$ Response is oscillatory (continues oscillations)
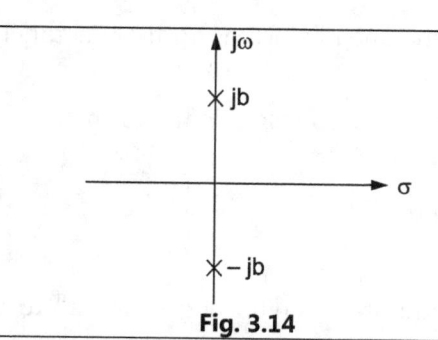 **Fig. 3.14**	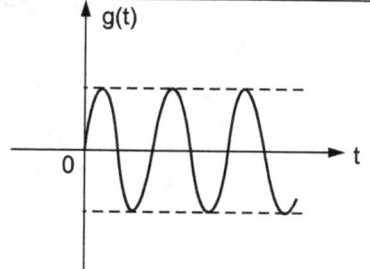 **Fig. 3.15**

• **Repeated Poles :**

1.	Repeated poles at origin $G(S) = \dfrac{A_K}{s^2}$	$g(t) = A_Kt$ Response is linearly increases with time
	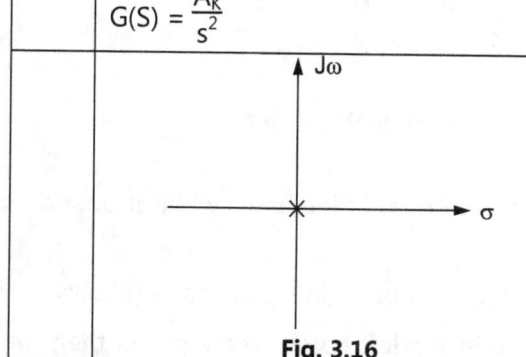 **Fig. 3.16**	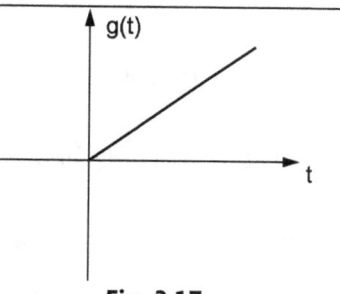 **Fig. 3.17**

Contd...

2.	Repeated poles on imaginary axis	Response is linearly increasing sinusoidal.
	$$G(S) = \dfrac{A_1}{(s + jb)^2} + \dfrac{A_1^*}{(s - jb)^2}$$ **Fig. 3.18**	$g(t) = A_1 t.e^{-Jb} + A_1 t e^{Jb}$ $= 2A_1 t \cos bt$ $= 2A_1 t \sin (bt + 90°)$ **Fig. 3.19**

Highlights :

- Repeated real poles in the left half of the s-plane, impulse response is of the form

$$C(t) = (A_1 + A_2 t) . e^{-at}$$

The exponential time function decreases faster than the linearly increasing time factor. The response ultimately dies out.

- If the repeated poles in the right half of the s-plane, the response is in the form of

$$C(t) = (A_1 + A_2 t).e^{at}$$

∴ The response increases exponentially without bound.

Conclusions :

- All the roots which have non-zero real parts contribute a multiplying factor e^{at} to the response.

  ➢ It $a < 0$, the response e^{at} vanishes as $t \to \infty$, $\displaystyle\int_0^\infty |g(\tau)| \, d(\tau)|$ is finite.

  ➢ If $a > 0$, the response e^{at} increases as $t \to \infty$, $\displaystyle\int_0^\infty |g(\tau) \, d(\tau)|$ is infinite.

Also, the repeated poles on Jω-axis contribute the term e^{at} that increases without bound as $t \to \infty$.

So, the stability of the system depending on the location of poles in s-plane is as follows :

- If all the roots of the characteristic equation lie in the left half of the s-plane, then the system is stable.

- If any one of the roots of characteristic equation lie in the right half of the s-plane, then the system is unstable.

- For the presence of one or more non-repeated roots on the imaginary axis or simple root at origin in the s-plane, then the system is marginally stable.

- If the characteristic equation has repeated roots on the $j\omega$-axis or repeated roots at origin, then the system is unstable.

Keynote :

- The stability or instability is a property of a system itself, i.e. closed loop poles of the system and does not depend on input or driving function.

- The poles of input do not affect stability of system, they affect only on steady state output.

3.4 CONDITIONALLY STABLE SYSTEM

A linear time invariant system is said to be conditionally stable if for a certain condition of a particular parameter of the system; its output is bounded one otherwise if that condition is violated output becomes unbounded and the system becomes unstable, i.e. stability of system depends on condition of parameters of the system. Such system is called conditionally stable system.

So s-plane can be divided into three distinct zones from stability point of view as shown in Fig. 3.20.

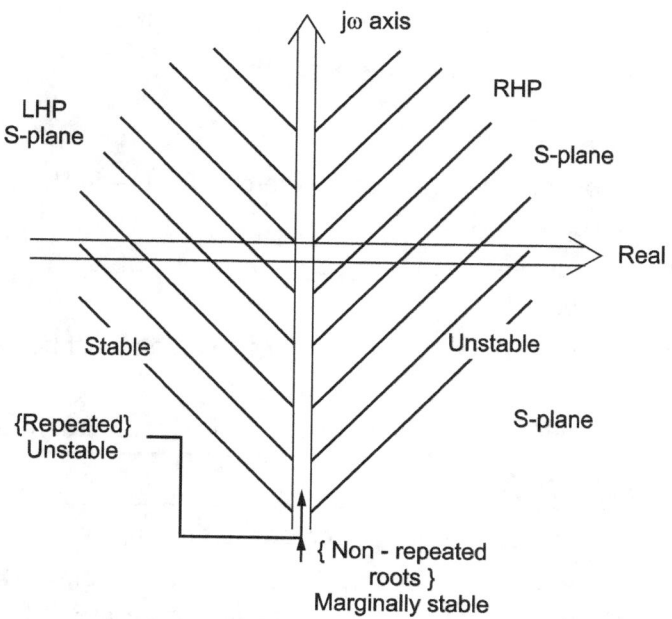

Fig. 3.20 : Division of s-plan for stability aspect

> **Keynote :**
>
> Stable - Left half of s-plane
>
> Unstable - Right half of s-plane
>
> Unstable - Imaginary axis repeated roots
>
> Marginally Stable - Non-repeated roots on imaginary axis

- **Zero Input and Asymptotic Stability :**

Consider RC circuit with capacitor initially charged to some voltage. This initial voltage is sufficient to operate the system without any external input. This initial voltage drives the current till capacitor gets fully discharge.

The stability related to such a system which is under zero input conditions but operated under initial conditions is called zero input stability of the system.

The current through RC circuit reduces to zero as capacitor gets fully discharged.

The current in such a case is called zero input response of the system, which is only due to the initial conditions.

If zero input response of the system is subjected to finite initial conditions reaches to zero as time 't' approaches infinity; the system is said to be zero input stable otherwise, it is called zero input unstable.

Asymptotic Stability :

Mathematically if C(t) is the zero input response of the system then for zero input stability there exists a positive number M which depends on set of finite initial conditions such that

$$|C(t)| \leq M < \infty \text{ for all } t \geq t_0.$$

and
$$\lim_{t \to \infty} |C(t)| = 0$$

- As magnitude of zero input response reaches zero as $\lim t \to \infty$, the zero input stability is called as the asymptotic stability.
- Asymptotic stability depends on closed-loop poles of system i.e. roots of the characteristic equation.
- For asymptotic stability all roots of characteristics equation must be located in left half of s-plane.
- If a system is stable – BIBO stable, then it must be zero input or asymptotically stable.

3.5 RELATIVE STABILITY

- The relative stability concept applied for only stable system.
- It is not sufficient to known that system is stable but a stable system must meet the specifications of relative stability which is quantitative measure of how fast transient die out of the system. (Settling time).

- Relative stability may be measured by relative settling times of each root or pair of roots.
- The settling time is inversely proportional to real part of the dominant roots, the relative stability can be specified by requiring that all roots of characteristics equation be more negative than a certain value, i.e. all roots must lie to the left of lines $s = -s_1$ ($s_1 > 0$).

The characteristics equation of the system under study is the modified by shifting the origin of the s-plane to $s = -\sigma_1$ i.e. by substitution.

The main purpose of relative stability concept is to find system time constant, settling time, time required to reach steady state, (tss).

$$s = Z - s_1$$

As illustrated in Fig. 3.21 If new characteristics equation in 'z' satisfies the route criterion, it implies that all the roots of the original characteristics equation are more negative.

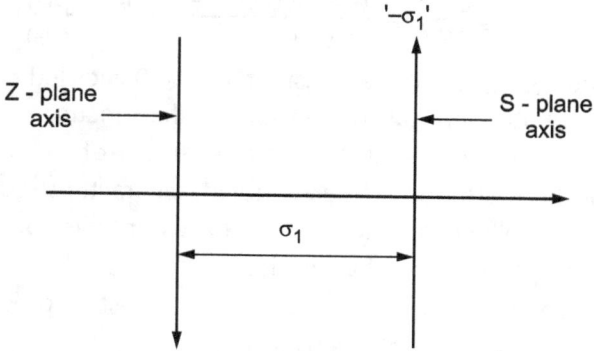

Fig. 3.21

- A system is said to be relatively more stable or unstable on the basis of settling time. System is said to be relatively more stable if settling time for that system is less than that of the other system.
- Relative stability of the system improves, as the closed loop poles move away from the imaginary axis in left half of s-plane.

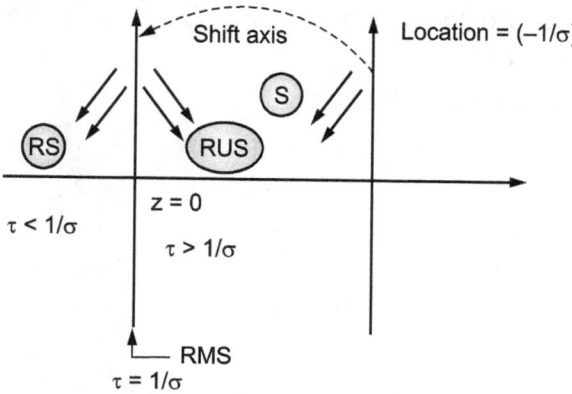

S- Stable, RS : Relatively stable

RUS : Relative unstable, RMS : Relative marginally stable

Fig. 3.22

3.6 ROUTH-HURWITZ CRITERION

- A Hurwitz and E. J. Routh independently published the method of investing the sufficient conditions of stability of a system.
- The Hurwitz criterion is in terms of determinants and Routh criterion is in terms of array formulation.
- We know that, system is stable if all the roots of characteristics equation lie on left side of s-plane.
- A Routh-Hurwitz criterion is the method of determining poles of transfer functions (roots of characteristics equation) without actually solving the equation.

Consider the T.F. of linear control system,

$$\text{T.F.} = \frac{C(S)}{R(S)} = \frac{b_0 s^m + b_1 s^{m-1} + \dots b_m}{a_0 s^n + a_1 s^{n-1} + \dots a_n} = \frac{p(s)}{q(s)}$$

Where, $a_0, a_1, \dots, a_n$ and $b_0, b_1, \dots, b_n$ are constant. $q(s) = 0$ is called characteristic equation. Roots of characteristic equation are called poles of transfer function.

- For stable systems, all these poles must lie on the left half-of s-plane.
- To check whether the system is stable or not its characteristic equation must satisfy certain conditions. The following conditions are necessary but not sufficient too;

1. All the co-efficient of $q(s)$ must be of same sign.
2. None of the coefficient vanish i.e. all the powers of 's' must be present from 'n to 0'.

These two conditions can be easily checked by inspection.

3.6.1 Hurwitz's Criterion

The sufficient condition for having all roots of characteristic equation in left half of s-plane is given by Hurwitz. It is referred as Hurwitz's criterion. It states that,

Definition :

The necessary and sufficient condition to have all roots of characteristic equation in left half of s-plane is that the sub-determination. D_K K = 1, 2, ..., n obtained from Hurwitz's determinant 'H' must all be positive.

Method of forming Hurwitz's Determinant :

$$H = \begin{vmatrix} a_1 & a_3 & a_5 & \dots & a_{2n-1} \\ a_0 & a_2 & a_4 & \dots & a_{2n-2} \\ 0 & a_1 & a_3 & \dots & a_{2n-3} \\ 0 & a_0 & a_2 & \dots & a_{2n-4} \\ 0 & 0 & a_1 & \dots & a_{2n-5} \\ . & . & . & . & . \\ . & . & . & . & . \\ . & . & . & . & . \\ 0 & . & . & . & a_n \end{vmatrix}$$

The order is $n \times n$ where,

$$n = \text{order of characteristic equation.}$$

In Hurwitz's determinant, all coefficients with suffices greater than 'n' or negative suffices must all be replaced by zeros.

From Hurwitz's determinant sub-determinants D_K, $K = 1, 2, ..., n$ must be formed as follows :

$$D_1 = |a_1|, \quad D_2 = \begin{vmatrix} a_1 & a_3 \\ a_0 & a_2 \end{vmatrix}, \quad D_3 = \begin{vmatrix} a_1 & a_3 & a_5 \\ a_0 & a_2 & a_4 \\ 0 & a_1 & a_3 \end{vmatrix}$$

$$D_K = |H|$$

For the system to be stable, all the above determinates must be positive.

SOLVED EXAMPLES

Example 3.1 : Determine the stability of the given characteristic equation by Hurwitz's method. $F(s) = s^3 + s^2 + s^1 + 4 = 0$ is a characteristic equation.

Solution : $a_0 = 1$, $a_1 = 1$, $a_2 = 1$, $a_3 = 4$, $n = 3$.

$$H = \begin{vmatrix} a_1 & a_3 & a_5 \\ a_0 & a_2 & a_4 \\ 0 & a_1 & a_3 \end{vmatrix} = \begin{vmatrix} 1 & 4 & 0 \\ 1 & 1 & 0 \\ 0 & 1 & 4 \end{vmatrix}$$

$$D_1 = |1| = 1$$

$$D_2 = \begin{vmatrix} 1 & 4 \\ 1 & 1 \end{vmatrix} = -3$$

$$D_3 = \begin{vmatrix} 1 & 4 & 0 \\ 1 & 1 & 0 \\ 0 & 1 & 4 \end{vmatrix} = -12$$

As D_2 and D_3 are negative, given system is unstable.

3.6.2 Disadvantages of Hurwitz's Method

- For higher order systems, to solve the determinants of higher order is very complicated and time consuming.

- Number of roots located in right-half of s-plane for unstable system cannot be judged by this method.

- Difficult to predict marginal stability of the system.

Due to these limitations, a new method is suggested by the scientist Routh called Routh's method. It is also called Routh – Hurwitz's method.

3.6.3 Routh's Stability Criterion

The Routh stability criterion is based on ordering the coefficients of coefficients of the characteristic equation, into a schedule called the Routh array as shown below;

$$F(s) = a_0s^n + a_1s^{n-1} + a_2s^{n-2} + \dots a_{n-1}s + a_n = 0$$

Where $a_0 > 0$

Method of Forming Array :

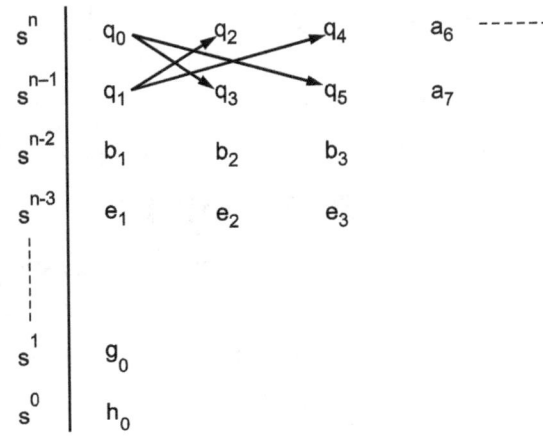

Fig. 3.23

Coefficients of first two rows can be written directly from the characteristic equation. From these two rows, next rows can be obtained as follows :

$$b_1 = \frac{a_1a_2 - a_0a_3}{a_1}, \qquad b_2 = \frac{a_1a_4 - a_0a_5}{a_1}$$

$$b_3 = b_3 = \frac{a_1a_6 - a_0a_7}{a_1}$$

From 2nd and 3rd row, 4th row can be obtained.

$$c_1 = \frac{b_1a_3 - a_1b_2}{b_1}, \qquad c_2 = \frac{b_1a_5 - a_1b_3}{b_1}$$

continued process till s_0.

3.6.4 Special Cases of Routh's Criterion

Occasionally, in applying the Routh stability criterion certain difficulties arise causing the breakdown of Routh's test. The difficulties encountered are generally of following types.

1. Difficulty 1 (Special Case 1) :

When the first term in any row of Routh array is zero while rest of the row has atleast one non-zero term.

Because of this zero term, the terms in the next row become infinite and Routh test breaks down.

- **Methods to Overcome this Difficulty :**

Method 1 : Substitute a small positive number ϵ for the zero and proceed to evaluate the rest of the Routh array.

Then examine the signs of first column of Routh array by letting $\epsilon \rightarrow 0$.

Method 2 : Modify the original characteristic equation by replacing s by "$1/z$". Apply the routh test on modified equation in terms of "z". The number of z roots with positive real parts are the same as number of s-roots with positive real parts. This method works in most but not in all cases.

Example 3.2 : Consider the characteristic equation :

$s^5 + s^4 + 2s^3 + 2s^2 + 3s + 5 = 0$ Examine stability.

Solution : The Routh array is

$a_0 = 1, a_1 = 1, a_2 = 2, a_3 = 2, a_4 = 3, a_5 = 5$

s^5	1	2	3	0
s^4	1	2	5	
s^3	0	$\dfrac{(1 \times 3) - (5)}{1} = -2$	0	
s^4	∞			

Hence, replace 0 by positive constant ϵ to avoid failure of Routh array

s^5	1	2	3	0
s^4	1	2	5	
s^3	ϵ	-2	0	
s^2	$\dfrac{2\epsilon + 2}{\epsilon}$	$5\epsilon /\epsilon$		
		$= 5$		
s^1	$\dfrac{-4\epsilon - 4 - 5\epsilon^2}{2\epsilon + 2}$	0		
	$= -2$			
s^0	5			

- From Routh array it is seen that first element in the third row is '0'. This is replaced by ϵ.

- The first element in the 4th row is now $\left(\dfrac{2\epsilon + 2}{\epsilon}\right)$ which has positive sign as $\epsilon \rightarrow 0$.

- The first terms on 4th row is $(-4\epsilon - 4 - 5\epsilon^2)/(2\epsilon + 2)$; which has a limiting value of -2 as $\epsilon \rightarrow 0$.

- Examine the terms in first column of the Routh array, it is found that there are two changes in sign and hence system is unstable having two poles in right half of s-plane.

- In the Routh's stability criterion, we are interested only in signs of the terms in the first column and not in their magnitude.

Keynote :

In the Routh's stability criterion, we are interested only in signs of the terms in the first column and not in their magnitudes.

Example 3.3 : Consider the characteristic equation :

$s^5 + s^4 + 2s^3 + 2s^2 + 3s + 15 = 0.$ Examine stability using Routh's method.

Solution : The Routh array is

$a_0 = 1, a_1 = 1, a_2 = 2, a_3 = 2, a_4 = 3, a_5 = 15$

s^5	1	2	3
s^4	1	2	15
s^3	0	−12	0

Replace 0 by small positive number $\in$.

s^5	1	2	3	0
s^4	1	2	15	
s^3	$\in$	−12	0	
s^2	$\dfrac{2\in + 12}{\in}$	$15\in/\in$ $= 15$	0	
s^1	$\dfrac{\left(\dfrac{2\in + 12}{\in}\right)(-12) - 15\in}{\dfrac{2\in + 12}{\in}}$	0	0	
s^0	15			

$$s^2 \to \lim_{\in \to 0} = \frac{2\in + 12}{\in} = \frac{2 + 12}{0} = \infty$$

$$s^1 \to \lim_{\in \to 0} \frac{\left(\dfrac{2\in + 12}{\in}\right)(-12) - 15\in}{\dfrac{(2\in + 12)}{\in}}$$

$$= \lim_{\in \to 0} \frac{-24\in - 144 - 15\in^2}{2\in + 12}$$

$$= \frac{0 - 144 - 0}{0 + 12} = -12$$

$\therefore$

s^5	1	2	3
s^4	1	2	15
s^3	$\in$	-12	0
s^2	$+\infty$	15	0
s^1	-12	0	
s^0	15		

There are two sign changes, so system is unstable and two poles present in right half of s-plane.

Special Case (2) :

All the elements of row in a Routh's array are zero.

Effect : The terms of the next row cannot be determined and Routh's test fails.

s^5	a	b	c
s^4	d	e	f
s^3	o	o	o

Row of zeros, special case 2

This indicates non-availability of coefficient in that row.

- **Procedure to Eliminate this Difficulty :**

1. Form an equation by using the coefficients of a row which is just above the row of zeros. Such an equation is called an Auxiliary equation denoted as A(s). For above case, such an equation is

$$A(s) = ds^4 + es^2 + f$$

- The coefficients of any row are corresponding to alternative powers of 's' starting from the power indicated against it.

  ➢ So, 'd' is coefficient corresponding to s^4, hence first term is ds^4 of A(s).

  ➢ Next coefficient 'e' is corresponding to alternate power of 's' from 4, i.e. s^2, hence the term es^2 and so on.

2. Take derivative of an auxiliary equation with respect to 's'.

i.e. $\dfrac{dA(s)}{ds} = 4ds^3 + 2es$

3. Replace row of zeros by the coefficient of $\dfrac{dA(s)}{ds}$

$\therefore$

s^5	a	b	c
s^4	d	e	f
s^3	4d	2e	0

4. Complete array in terms of these new coefficients.

Importance of an Auxiliary Equation :

Auxiliary equation is always the part of the original characteristic equation. This means **the roots of the auxiliary equation are some of the roots of original characteristic equation.**

- Not only this, the stability can be predicted from the root of $A(s) = 0$ rather than the roots of characteristic equation as the roots of $A(s) = 0$ are the most dominant from the stability point of view.
- The remaining roots of characteristic equation are always in the left half and they do not play any significant role in the stability analysis.

$$A(s) = 2s^4 + 4s^2 + 2 = 0$$

i.e.
$$s^4 + 2s^2 + 1 = 0$$

$$\frac{dA(s)}{ds} = 4s^3 + 4s$$

s^6	1	4	5	2
s^5	3	6	3	0
s^4	2	4	2	0
s^3	4	4	0	0
s^2	2	2	0	0
s^1	0	0	0	0 ← Special case 2

Row of zeros again

$$A'(s) = 2s^2 + 2 = 0$$

$\therefore$

$$\frac{dA'(s)}{ds} = 4s + 0 = 0$$

$\therefore$

Hence, Routh array can be constructed as;

s^6	1	4	5	2
s^5	3	6	3	0
s^4	2	4	2	0
s^3	4	4	0	0
s^2	2	2	0	0
s^1	4	0	0	0
s^0	2	0	0	0

No sign change; hence no root located in R.H.S. of s-plane.

As rows of zeros occur, system may be marginally stable or unstable.

To examine that find the roots of first auxiliary equation.

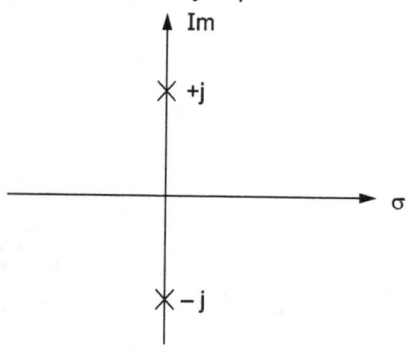

Fig. 3.24

$$A(s) = s^4 + 2s^2 + 1 = 0$$

$$s^2 = \frac{-2 \pm \sqrt{4-4}}{2} = -1$$

$s^2 = -1$, $s^2 = -1$, $s_{1,2} = \pm j$, $s_{3,4} = \pm j$.

The roots of $A'(s) = 0$ are the roots of $A(s) = 0$. So do not solve second auxiliary equation. Predict the stability from the nature of roots of 1st auxiliary equation.

$$\lim_{\epsilon \to 0} \frac{576}{\epsilon} = \infty$$

∴   One sign change and system is stable.

$$A(s) = 3s^4 - 48 = 0$$

Put, $s^2 = y$

∴ $3y^2 = 48$,   ∴ $y^2 = 16$,   ∴ $y = \pm\sqrt{16}$

∴ $s^2 = \pm\sqrt{16} = 4$ $s^2 = -4$

∴ $s = \pm 2$ $s = \pm 2j$

Roots with positive real part → One.

Roots with negative real part → Three.

Roots with zero real part → Two.

Example 3.4 : For a system with characteristic equation;

$$F(s) = s^6 + 3s^5 + 4s^4 + 6s^3 + 5s^2 + 3s + 2 = 0$$

examine stability.

Solution :

$$F(s) = s^6 + 3s^5 + 4s^4 + 6s^3 + 5s^2 + 3s + 2 = 0$$

$a_0 = 1,\ a_1 = 3,\ a_2 = 4,\ a_3 = 6,\ a_4 = 5,\ a_5 = 3,\ a_6 = 2$

s^6	1	4	5	2
s^5	3	6	3	0
s^4	2	4	2	0
s^3	0	0	0	0

$\underbrace{\qquad\qquad\qquad}$ ← Special case 2

Row of zeros again

Example 3.5 : $s^6 + 4s^5 + 3s^4 - 16s^2 - 64s - 48 = 0$. Check the stability of the given characteristic equation using Routh's method.

$$s^6 + 4s^5 + 3s^4 - 16s^2 - 64s - 48 = 0$$

$a_0 = 1,\ a_1 = 4,\ a_2 = 3,\ a_3 = 0,\ a_4 = -16,\ a_5 = -64,\ a_6 = -48.$

s^6	1	4	2	-48
s^5	4	3	-64	0
s^4	3	0	-48	0
s^3	0	0	0	← Special case 2

Create a Auxiliary equation,

$$A(s) = 3s^4 - 48 = 0$$

$$\frac{dA(s)}{ds} = 12s^3$$

s^6	1	3	-16	-48
s^5	4	0	-64	0
s^4	3	0	-48	0
s^3	12	0	0	0
s^2	$0[\in]$	-48	0	0 ← Special case 1
s^1	$\dfrac{576}{0}$	0	0	
s^0	-48			

3.7 ROOT LOCUS

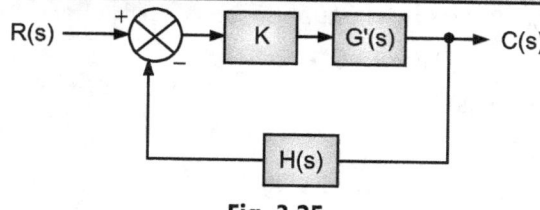

Fig. 3.25

Characteristic equation is given by

$$1 + G(s) H(s) = 0$$
$$1 + KG^1 (s) = 0$$

Closed loop poles i.e. roots of the above equation are now dependent on the values of K.

If gain 'K' is varied from $-\infty$ to ∞ then for each separate value of K, we will get separate set of locations of roots from characteristic equation. If all such locations are joined, the resulting locus is called as root locus.

Root locus is defined as the locus of closed loop poles obtained from system when 'K' (gain) is varied from $-\infty$ to ∞.

Let

$$G(s) = KG'(s) = K/s$$
$$1 + G(s) H(s) = 0; \ H(s) = 1$$
$$1 + \frac{K}{s} = 0$$
$$s + K = 0 \ \therefore s = -K$$

K	s = –K
0	0
1	–1
10	–10
100	–100
$+\infty$	$-\infty$

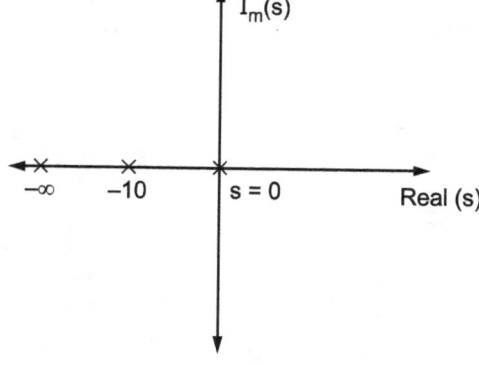

Fig. 3.26

Angle and Magnitude Criterion :

For a closed loop system, characteristic equation is

$$1 + G(s) H(s) = 0$$
$$G(s) H(s) = -1$$

As s-plane is complex $s = \sigma + j\omega$

$$G(s) H(s) = -1 + 0j$$

All s-values can be expressed as $\sigma + j\omega$ ∴ G(s) H(s) term is also complex one. Hence for any value of 's'. if it has to be on root locus, it must satisfy above equation

$$G(s) H(s) = -1 + 0j \text{ is in rectangular form}$$

We can convert both sides into polar form and equate angle and magnitude of both sides. It gives two conditions on root locus called as

(i) Magnitude condition (ii) Angle condition

(i) Magnitude Condition :

$$|G(s) H(s)| = |-1 + j0) = 1$$

At any point in s-plane using magnitude conditions, we can find values of 'K'. Use of magnitude condition totally depends on existence of a point on root locus. Magnitude criterion can be used only when a point in s-plane is confirmed for its existence on root locus by the use of angle condition.

(ii) Angle Condition :

$$G(s) H(s) = -1 + j_0$$
$$\angle G(s) H(s) = \pm (2q + 1) 180°, q = 0, 1, 2, ;$$

Point $-1 + j0$ is a point on negative real axis which can be traced as magnitude 1 at an angle $\pm 180°, \pm 540°, \pm 900° \ldots (2q + 1) 180°$

Example 3.6 :

$G(s) H(s) = \dfrac{K}{s (s + 2) (s + 4)}$ and s = -0.75 is confirmed on root locus. At what value of K, s = -0.75 is one of the root of $1 + G(s) H(s) = 0$.

Solution : Use Magnitude criterion,

$$|G(s) H(s)|_{s = -0.75} = 1$$

$$\frac{|K|}{|s| |(s + 2)| |s + 4|} = 1$$

$$\frac{|K|}{|-0.75| |-0.75 + 2| |0.75 + 4|} = 1$$

$$\frac{|K|}{(0.75) (1.25) (3.25)} = 1$$

∴ $K = 3.0468$

Example 3.7 : $G(s)\,H(s) = \dfrac{K}{s\,(s+2)}$, obtain nature of the root locus.

Solution :
$$1 + G(s)\,H(s) = 1 + \frac{K}{s\,(s+2)} = 0$$

$$s^2 + 2s + K = 0$$

Roots ,
$$s_{1,2} = \frac{-2 \pm \sqrt{4 - 4 \times K}}{2}$$

$$s_{1,2} = -1 \pm \sqrt{1 - K}$$

$$s_1 = -1 + \sqrt{1 - K}$$

$$s_2 = -1 - \sqrt{1 - K}$$

Vary K from 0 to ∞

K	s_1	s_2
0	0	−2
0.2	−0.105	−1.895
0.8	−0.552	−1.448
1	−1	−1
5	−1 + 2j	−1 −2j
∞	−1 + j∞	−1 − j∞

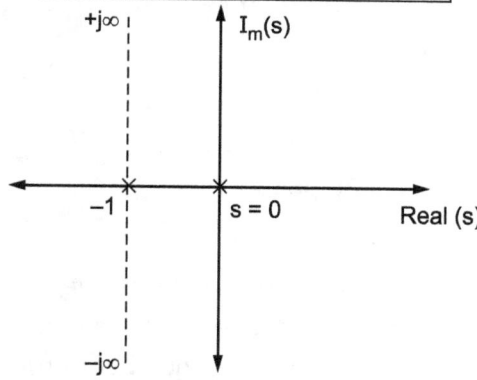

Fig. 3.27

Example 3.8 : Consider a system with $G(s)\,H(s) = \dfrac{K}{s(s+4)\,(s+5)}$, find whether s = −1 is on root locus or not using angle condition.

Solution : The angle condition is

$$\angle\,G(s)\,H(s) = \pm 180\,(2q + 1)$$

$$\angle\,G(s)\,H(s) = \frac{\angle\,(K + 0j)}{\angle(-1 + 0j)\,\angle(-1 + 4 + 0j)\,\angle\,(-1 + 5 + 0j)}$$

$$\angle \ G(s) \ H(s) \ = \ \frac{0°}{180° \ 0° \ 0°} \ = \ -180°$$

Since $\angle \ G(s) \ H(s) \ = \ -180°$ at s = −1, this satisfies the angle condition, hence point s = − 1 is on root locus.

For magnitude condition, find the values of which s = −1 is one of roots of 1 + G(s) H(s) = 0

$$|G(s) \ H(s)| \ = \ +1 \text{ at } s = -1$$

$$\frac{K}{|-1| \ |-1 + 4| \ |-1 + 5|} \ = \ +1$$

$$\frac{K}{1 \cdot 3 \cdot 4} \ = \ +1$$

$$K \ = \ 12$$

For K = 12, one can find that one of the roots is located at s = −1.

Rules for Construction of Root Locus :

Rule 1 : The root locus is symmetrical about real axis.

The roots of the characteristic equation are either real or complex conjugates or combination of both, therefore their locus must be symmetrical about the real axis of the s-plane.

Rule 2 : Let G(s) H(s) = Open loop T.F. of the system

P → No. of open loop poles

Z → No. of open loop zeros

For case P > Z

(a) No. of branches equal to open loop poles

N = P (No. of poles of open loop T.F.)

(b) Branch will start from each of location of open loop pole, out of 'P' number of branches 'Z' number of branches will terminate at locations of open loop zeros. The remaining 'P-Z' branches will approach to infinity. If P = 3, z = 1 number of root locus branches are P = 3, number of branches approaching to ∞ P-Z i.e. 2.

All branches of root locus starts at open loop poles (when K = 0) and ends at either open loop zero or infinity. The number of branches terminating at infinity equal to the difference between number of poles and number of zeros.

Rule 3 : A point on real axis lies on the root locus if the sum of the no. of open loop pole and no. of open loop zeros, on the real axis to the right hand side of this point is odd.

(i) Consider, $G(s) \ H(s) \ = \ \dfrac{K(s + 2) \ (s + 5)}{s(s + 4) \ (s + 6)}$

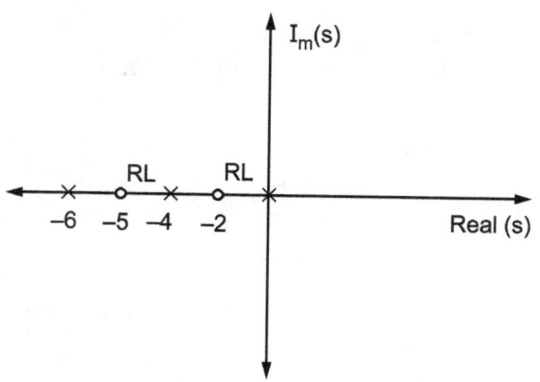

Fig. 3.28

(ii) $$G(s)\,H(s) = \frac{K(s+2)}{s^2\,(s^2+2s+2)\,(s+3)}$$

Poles are at s = 0, 0, –3, – 1 ± j

zeros are at s = – 2

For positive real axis, there is no pole and zero to right hand side so sum is zero and hence there is no root locus.

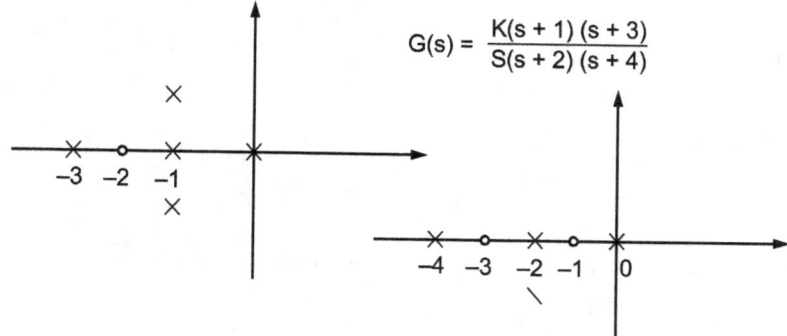

$$G(s) = \frac{K(s+1)\,(s+3)}{S(s+2)\,(s+4)}$$

Fig. 3.29

Step 1 : Number of open loop poles are three. Therefore the number of branches of root locus are three.

Step 2 : The three branches of the root locus start from open loop pole s = 0, –2, –4. Out of these three branches two branches of the root locus terminate at the two open loop zeros and one branch terminate at infinity.

Step 3 : All the points between 0, –1, –2, –3, –4 and –∞ lies on the root locus for which the sum of open loop poles and zeros to the right of test points are 1, 3 and 5 res. (All points having odd no. of poles and zeros to the right).

Rule 4 : Generally number of poles are more than number of zeros and in such case 'P–Z' branches will approach to infinity. This rule gives information about how there branches will approach to infinity.

The branches which are approaching to infinity do so along the straight lines called asymptodes of root locus. Asymptodes are the guide lines for the branches approaching to infinity.

Angles of such asymptodes are given by

$$\theta = \frac{(2q \pm 1)}{(P - Z)} 180°$$

where
$$q = 0, 1, 2 ... (P - Z - 1)$$

Rule 5 : Only angles of asymptodes are not sufficient but also where asymptodes are located in s-plane is also important.

All asymptodes intersects the real axis at a common point known as centroid by '6'. The co-ordinates of centroid can be calculated as

$$\sigma = \frac{\sum \text{real parts of poles G(s) H(s)} - \sum \text{Real parts of zeros}}{(p - z)}$$

Centroid is always real, it may be noted on negative or positive real axis.
It may of may not be part of root locus.

Example : $$G(s) \, H(s) = \frac{K}{(s + 1)(s + 2 + 2j)(s + 2 - 2j)}$$

P = 3, zero = 0, P – Z = 3 – 0 = 3
Braches approaches at N = P = 3.
Poles at s = –1, s = –2 – 2 j, s = – 2 + 2j
Magnitude of asymptodes are given by

$$\theta = \frac{(2q + 1) \, 180°}{(p - z)} \quad q = 0, 1, 2 ... (p - z - 1)$$

Number of aymptodes = No. of branches approaches to infinity

For q = 0, $$\theta_1 = \frac{180}{3} = 60°$$

For q = 1, $$\theta_2 = \frac{3 \times 180}{3} = 180°$$

For q = 2, $$\theta_3 = \frac{5 \times 180}{3} = 5 \times 60 = 300°$$

All these aymptodes are given to interest on real axis called centorid.

$$\sigma = \frac{\sum \text{Real axis of poles} - \sum \text{Real axis of zeros}}{(p - z)}$$

$$\sigma = \frac{(-1 - 2 - 2) - (0)}{3} = -\frac{5}{3} = -1.67$$

Centroid σ = – 1.67

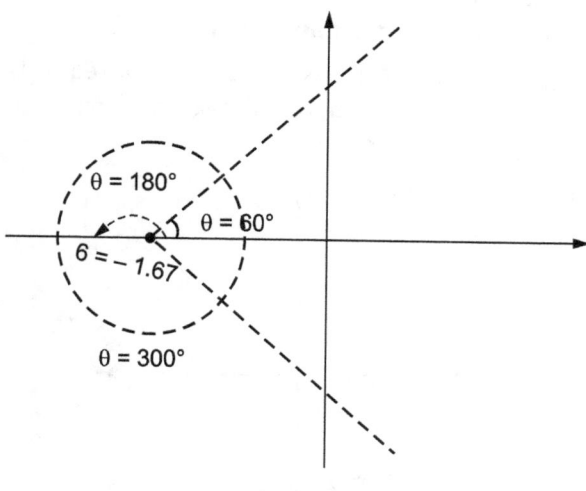

Fig. 3.30

Rule 6 : Break away point

Breakaway point is a point on root locus where multiple root of characteristic equation occurs.

Example : $G(s)\,H(s) = \dfrac{K}{s\,(s+2)}$

$$1 + G(s)\,H(s) = 0, \quad 1 + \frac{K}{s\,(s+2)} = 0$$

$$s^2 + 2s + K = 0$$

$$s_1 = -1 + \sqrt{1-K}\,,\ s_2 = -1 - \sqrt{1-K}$$

K	s_1	s_2
0	0	−2
0.2	−1.05	−1.895
0.8	−0.552	−1.448
1	−1	−1
5	−1 + 2j	−1 −2j
⋮		
∞	−1 + j∞	−1 − j∞

As gain 'K' increases from 0 to ∞ both roots approaches to common value '−1' and then both roots breakaways from s = −1 as pair of complex conjugate roots when 'K' is increases from 0 to ∞.

General Predictions of Existence of Break away Points

1. If there are adjacently placed on real axis and section of real axis in between them is a part of root locus then there exists minimum one breakaway point adjacently placed zeros.

$$G(s)\, H(s) \;=\; \frac{K(s + 2)\,(s + 4)}{s^2\,(s + 6)}$$

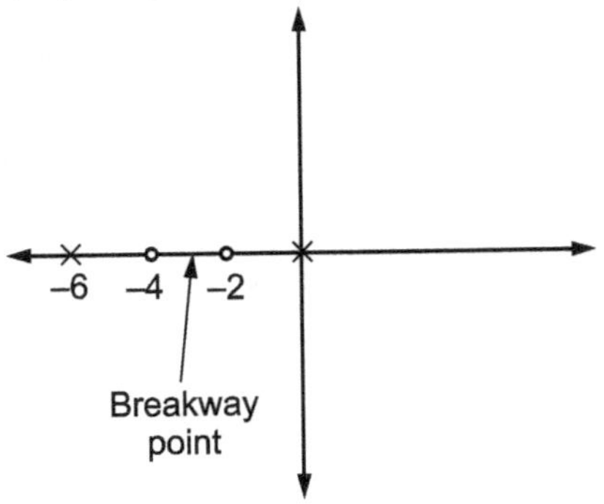

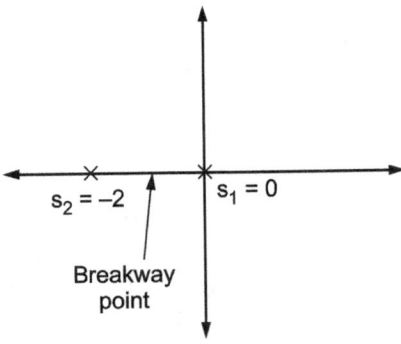

Fig. 3.31

2. If there are adjacently placed poles on real axis and real axis between them is a part of root locus then there exists minimum one breakaway point in between adjacent places poles.

Fig. 3.32

3. If there is zero on real axis and the left of the zero there is no pole or zero existing on real axis and complete real axis to the left of this zero is a part of the root locus, there exists minimum one break away point to the left of that zero.

Steps to determine co-ordinates of breakaway point.

Step 1 : Construct the characteristic equation $1 + G(s)\, H(s) = 0$ of the system.

Step 2 : From this equation, separate the terms involving K and terms of 's', write value of K in terms of s.

Step 3 : Differentiate above equation w.r.t 's' and equate it to zero i.e. $\dfrac{dK}{ds} = 0$.

Step 4 : Roots of the equation $\dfrac{dK}{ds} = 0$ gives us breakaway point of s.

By this method we get all breakaway points applicable for range of 'K' from '$-\infty$' to '$+\infty$'. So to decide valid breakaway points, substitute breakaway point value in the equation 'K' to get value of 'K'. If value of 'K' is positive, the breakaway point is valid in root locus. For breakaway point, if values of 'K' negative, breakaway points are invalid.

Example 3.9 :

For $G(s) H(s) = \dfrac{K}{s \, (s + 1) \, (s + 4)}$, determine the co-ordinates of valid breakaway point.

Solution : Characteristic equation,

$$1 + G(s) H(s) = 0$$

$$1 + \frac{K}{s \, (s + 1) \, (s + 4)} = 0$$

$$s \, (s + 1) \, (s + 4) + K = 0$$

$$s \, (s^2 + 5s + 4) + K = 0$$

$$s^3 + 5s^2 + 4s + K = 0$$

$$K = -s^3 - 5s^2 - 4s$$

$$\frac{dK}{ds} = -3s^2 - 105 - 4 = 0$$

$$3s^2 + 10s + 4 = 0$$

Breakaway points

$$= \frac{-10 \pm \sqrt{100 - 4 \times 4 \times 5}}{2 \times 3} = -0.46, -2.86$$

For s = -0.46,

$$K = -(-0.46)^3 - 5 \, (-0.46)^2 - 4 \, (-0.46)$$

$$K = +0.8793$$

For s = -2.86,

$$K = -(-2.86)^3 - 5 \, (-2.86)^2 - 4 \, (-2.86)$$

$$K = -6.064$$

For s = -0.46, K is positive

s = -0.46 is value breakaway point for root locus

Rule 7 : Find Intersection of root locus on imaginary axis.

$$1 + G(s) H(s) = 0$$

$$s^3 + 5s^2 + 4s + K = 0$$

Apply routh stability criterion

s^3	1	4	0
s^2	5	K	0
s^1	$\dfrac{20 - K}{5}$	0	0
s^0	K	0	0

$$K_{mar} = 20$$

$$A(s) = 5s^2 + K = 0$$

$$5s^2 + 20 = 0$$
$$5s^2 = -20$$
$$s^2 = -\frac{20}{5} = -4$$
$$s = \pm\sqrt{-4} = \pm 2j$$

$s = \pm 2j$ are the points of intersection of root locus with imaginary axis.

If K_{mar} is positive, there is valid intersection of root locus with imaginary axis.

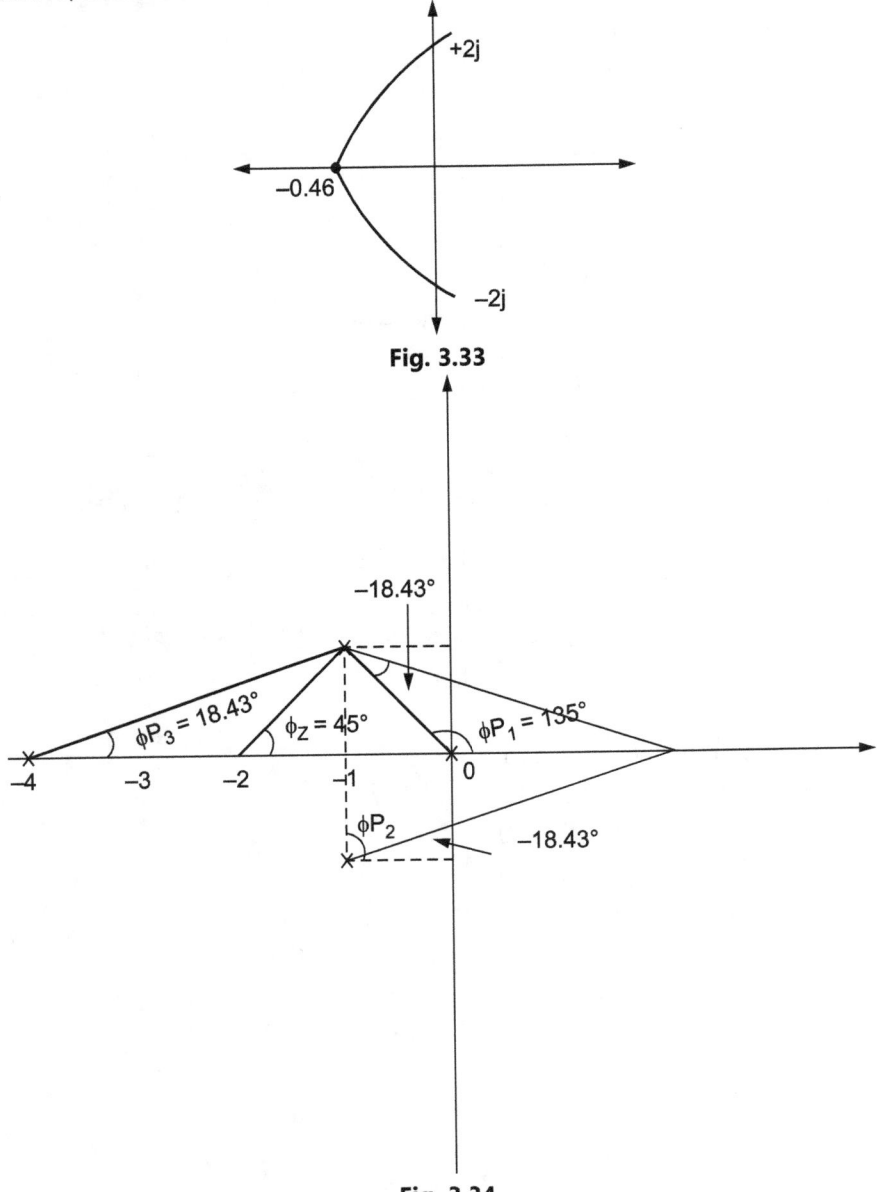

Fig. 3.33

Fig. 3.34

Rule 8 : Angle of departure at complex conjugate pole and angle of arrival at complex zeros.

As branch always leaves from open loop pole it is advantage to know that at what angle it departs from complex conjugate pole. This angle at which it departs from complex pole is called as angle of departure denoted as 'ϕ_d'.

$$\phi_d = 180° - \phi$$

where

$$\phi = \Sigma\,\phi_p - \Sigma\,\phi_z$$

$\Sigma\,\phi_p \rightarrow$ contributions by the angles made by remaining poles at the pole at which ϕ_d is to be calculated

$\Sigma\,\phi_z \rightarrow$ contributions by the angles made by remaining zeros at the pole at which ϕ_d is to be calculated

Let

$$G(s)\,H(s) = \frac{K(s + 2)}{s(s + 4)\,(s^2 + 2s + 2)} \quad \begin{array}{l} s = 0 \\ s = -4 \\ s = -1 \pm j \end{array}$$

Plot on graph paper,

$$\phi_{p1} = 135°,\ \phi_{p2} = 90°,\ \phi_{p3} = 18.43°$$

$$\Sigma\,\phi_p = 135 + 90 + 18.43 = 243.43$$

$$\Sigma\,\phi_z = 45°$$

$$\phi = \Sigma\,\phi_p - \Sigma\,\phi_z$$

$$\phi = 243.43 - 45 = 198.43°$$

$$\phi_d = 180 - \phi = 180 - 198.43°$$

$$\phi_d = -18.43$$

Root locus branch leaving this pole will depart tangentially to the line whose angle is given by

$$\phi_d = -18.43°$$

For second complex conjugate pole sign of ϕ_d will be just opposite as root locus is always symmetrical about real axis. So root locus branch departing from $-1 - j$ will depart tangentially to the line where angle is given by

$$\phi_d = 18.43°$$

Angle of Arrival at Complex Zero

Angle of arrival at a complex zero can be calculated by the same method which is denoted by ϕ_a. The only change to calculate the angle of arrival is

$$\phi_a = 180 + \phi$$

Where,

$$\phi = \Sigma\,\phi_p - \Sigma\,\phi_z$$

Such branches will arrive and terminate at complex zeros sunning tangentially to the lines whose angles are given by ϕ_a

Example 3.10 : Draw a root locus plot for

$$G(s)\, H(s) \;=\; \frac{K}{s\,(s+1)\,(s+3)}$$

Solution :

Rule 1 : There are three open loop poles at s = 0, s = –1, s = –3.

Rule 2 : Hence there are three branches of root locus. There are no finite open loop zeros. So all three zeros are at infinity. Therefore there are three asymptodes.

Rule 3 :

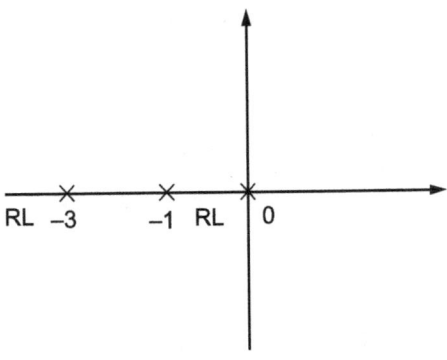

Fig. 3.35

The three branches of the root locus start at the open loop poles at s = 0, s = –1 and s= –3 (K = 0) and terminate at the open-loop zeros at infinity where K = ∞.

Rule 4 : The three branches of the root locus go the zeros at infinity along straight line asymptotes making angle of

$$\theta_q \;=\; \frac{(2q+1)\,180}{(p-z)} \text{ for } q = 0, 1, \dots\, p-z-1.$$

$$\theta_q \;=\; \frac{(2q+1)\,180}{3}\, ; q = 0, 1, 2$$

$$\theta_0 \;=\; 60°$$

$$\theta_1 \;=\; \frac{3\pi}{3} = 180°$$

$$\theta_3 \;=\; \frac{5\pi}{3} = 300°$$

Rule 5 : The point of intersection of asymptotes on the real axis called centroid

$$\sigma \;=\; \frac{\Sigma \text{ sum of poles} - \Sigma \text{ sum of zero}}{p-z}$$

$$=\; \frac{(0-1-3)-(0)}{3-0} = -1.33$$

Rule 6 : Break point

$$G(s)\, H(s)\ =\ \frac{K}{s(s + 1)\, (s + 3)}$$

$$1 + G(s)\, H(s)\ =\ 0$$

$$1 + \frac{K}{s(s + 1)\, (s + 3)}\ =\ 0$$

$$s\,(s + 1)\,(s + 3) + K\ =\ 0$$

$$s\,(s^2 + 4s + 3) + K\ =\ 0$$

$$s^3 + 4s^2 + 3s + K\ =\ 0$$

$$\therefore \qquad K\ =\ -s^3 - 4s^2 - 3s$$

$$\frac{dK}{ds}\ =\ -3s^2 - 8s - 3\ =\ 0$$

$$3s^2 + 8s + 3\ =\ 0$$

$$s\ =\ -0.451,\ -2.28$$

$$s\ =\ -0.451 \text{ is the actual break point}$$

Rule 7 : Apply routh stability criterion

$$s^3 + 4s^2 + 3s + K\ =\ 0$$

s^3	1	3	0
s^2	4	K	0
s^1	$\dfrac{12 - K}{4}$	0	0
s^0	K		

Marginal stability

$$K\ =\ 12$$

$$4s^2 + K\ =\ 0$$

$$4s^2 + 12\ =\ 0$$

$$4s^2\ =\ -12$$

$$s^2\ =\ -3$$

$$s\ =\ \pm\sqrt{-3}$$

$$s\ =\ \pm j\sqrt{3}$$

$$w_0\ =\ \sqrt{3}$$

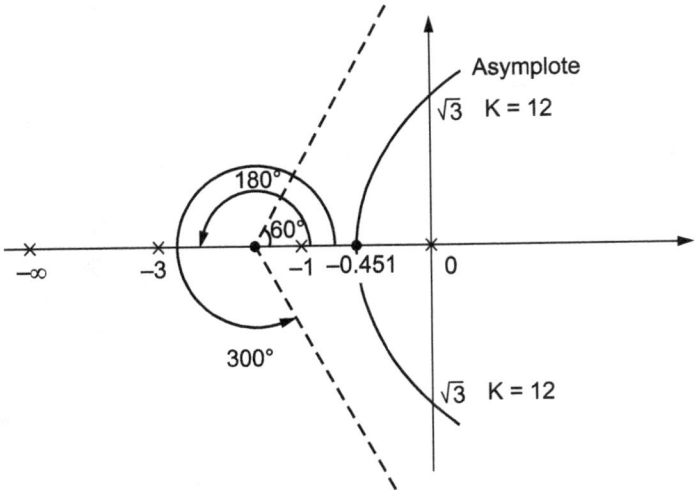

Fig. 3.36

Example 3.11 : For a unity feedback system the open loop transfer is given by

$$G(s) = \frac{K}{s(s + 2)(s^2 + 6s + 25)}$$

Sketch root locus.

Solution :

Rule 1 : Poles are at $0, -2, -3 + 4j, -3 - 4j$

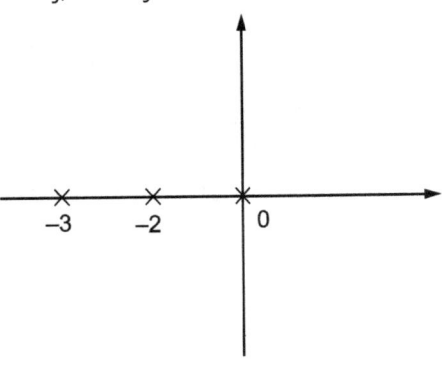

Fig. 3.37

The segment on real axis between $s = 0$ and $s = -2$ is the part of root locus.

Rule 2 :

Number of locus = Number of poles = 4

Rule 3 : Centroid of asymptodes

$$\sigma = \frac{\sum \text{real part of poles} - \sum \text{real part of zeros}}{p - z}$$

$$\sigma = \frac{(0-2-3-3)-(0)}{4-0}$$

$$\sigma = \frac{-8}{4} = -2$$

Rule 4 : Angle of asymptodes

$$\phi = \frac{(2q+1)\times 180°}{(p-z)} , q = 0, 1, p-z-1$$

$$q = 0, \ \phi_1 = 45°$$

$$q = 1, \ \phi_2 = 135°$$

$$q = 2, \ \phi_3 = 225°$$

$$q = 3, \ \phi_4 = 315°$$

Rule 5 : Breakaway point

$$1 + G(s) H(s) = 0$$

$$1 + \frac{K}{s(s+2)(s^2+6s+25)} = 0$$

$$s(s+2)(s^2+6s+25) + K = 0$$

$$s^4 + 8s^3 + 37s^2 + 50s + K = 0$$

$$K = -s^4 - 8s^3 - 37s^2 - 50s$$

$$\frac{dK}{ds} = -4s^3 - 24s^2 - 74s - 50 = 0$$

$$4s^3 + 24s^2 + 74s + 50 = 0$$

By trial method s $= -0.8981$ between '0' and '–z' on root locus.

Rule 6 : jω crossover

$$s^4 + 8s^3 + 37s^2 + 50s + K$$

$$K = 192.18$$

Auxillary equation

$$30.75 s^2 + K = 0$$

$$30.75 s^3 + 192.18 = 0$$

$$s = \pm j\, 2.5$$

Angle of departure (from upper complex pole)

$$\phi_d = 180° - (104 + 90 + 127)$$

$$\phi_d = -141°$$

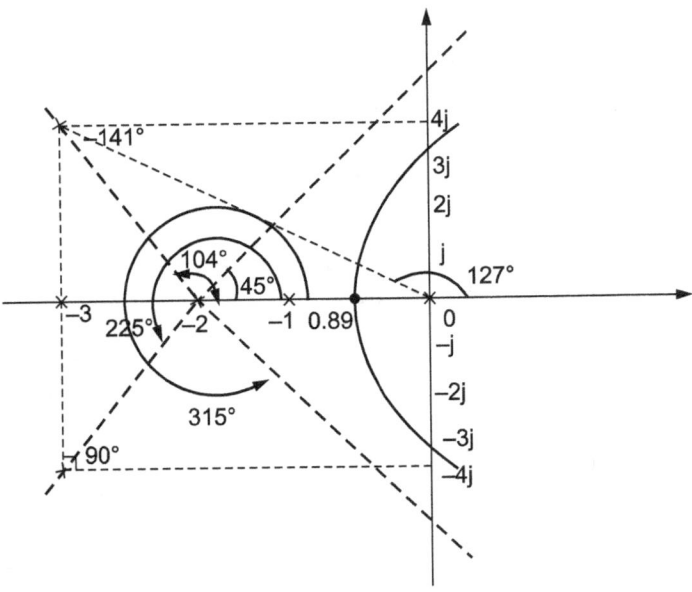

Fig. 3.38

3.8 APPLICATION OF ROOT LOCUS

Root Locus is contributing majorly in determining stability of a system. In Industrial applications, Root Locus plays a major part in determining stability or unstability of a system. While predicting properties of a control system, its mathematical model is designed. From the mathematical model, methods like Root Locus are used to predict how stable the system is to be used in industrial applications.

- Consider an application where Root Locus method can be used to study stability of a motorcycle and rider combination. Analysis of motorcycle/rider system must include a model of the rider in addition to handling characteristics of the motorcycle.

- Similar systems can be designed for Roll attitude-control system for a missile containing attitude and rate gyros.

- The pitch attitude control system for a booster rocket containing attitude and rate gyros, for this Root Locus can be sketched to find maximum value of K that would permit stable operation.

- For satellite navigation system, to predict stability of each module of navigation system.

- In robotic arm or various tracking robots.

- In antennas.

- Also can be used as a simulation software in industries to Predict stability of a complex mechanical structures.

SUMMARY

- **Root Locus :**

  Symmetrical about real axis

  RL branch starts from OL poles and terminates at OL zeroes

  No. of RL branches = No. of poles of OLTF

  Centroid is common intersection point of all the asymptotes on the real axis

  Asymptotes are straight lines which are parallel to RL going to ∞ and meet the RL at ∞

  No. of asymptotes = No. of branches going to ∞

  At Break Away point, the RL breaks from real axis to enter into the complex plane

  At BI point, the RL enters the real axis from the complex plane

EXERCISE

1. Using Routh criterion determine the stability of the system whose characteristics equation is $s^4 + 8s^3 + 18s^2 + 16s + 5 = 0$ **[6]**

2. Sketch the root locus for the open loop transfer function of unity feedback control system given below : $G(s)\,H(s) = \dfrac{K}{s(s + 2)\,(s + 4)}$. **[8]**

3. Sketch the Nyquist plot for a system with the open loop transfer function $G(s)\,H(s) = \dfrac{K\,(1 + 0.5s)\,(1 + s)}{(1 + 10s)\,(s - 1)}$. Determine the range of values of K for which the system is stable. **[8]**

4. State and explain the Nyquist stability criterion. **[5]**

5. When is a control system said to be robust? **[4]**

6. Explain the procedure to be followed when in the Routh's array all the elements of a row corresponding to 4's are zeros. **[4]**

SOLVED UNIVERSITY PROBLEMS

Example 3.1 : Comment on stability using Routh criteria if characteristic equation is :

$Q(s) = s^5 + 2s^4 + 3s^3 + 4s^2 + 5s + 6 = 0$

How many poles lie in right half of s-plane? **[Dec. 14] [4]**

Solution :

Given equation

$Q(s) = s^5 + 2s^4 + 3s^3 + 4s^2 + 5s + 6 = 0$

s^5	1	3	5	0
s^4	2	4	6	0
s^3	1	2	0	0
s^2	$\times$	6	0	0
s^1	$\dfrac{2x - 6}{x}$	0	0	0
s^0	6	0	0	0

Since we have zero in the first column we have replaced 0 with a very small value x as a first element in a row.

- Now we will complete routh array in terms of x and then examine the sign change by taking lim $x \to 0$.

- To examine sign change lim $x \to 0 = \dfrac{2x - 6}{x}$

$$\lim_{n \to o} = \delta - \infty = \infty$$

- Hence, Now Routh array will be;

s^5	1	3	5	0
s^4	2	4	6	0
s^3	1	2	0	0
s^2	×	6	0	0
s^1	$-\infty$	0	0	0
s^0	6	0	0	0

Since there are two sign changes in the first column the system is unstable and there are two roots in the right half of the s-plane.

Example 3.2 : Comment on the stability of a system using Routh's stability criteria whose characteristics equations is $s^4 + 2s^3 + 4s^2 + 6s + 8 = 0$. How many poles of system lie in right half of s-plane.   **[May 14] [4]**

Solution : Here, $a_0 = 1$, $a_1 = 2$, $a_2 = 4$, $a_3 = 6$, $a_4 = 8$.

Arranging the Routh array

s^4	1	4	8
s^3	2	6	0
s^2	1	8	
s^1	−10	0	
s^0	8		

As there are two sign changes, the given system is unstable with two closed loop poles lying on the right half of the s-plane.

Example 3.3 : Open loop transfer function of unity feedback system is

$G(s) = \dfrac{K}{s(s + 3)(s + 5)}$. Sketch the complete root locus and find marginal gain.   **[May 14] [8]**

Solution :

1. To find total number of loci :
   Number of poles = p   = 3
   Number of zeros = z   = 0
   ∴   Number of loci going to infinity = p − z = 3

2. Draw the pole zero plot :

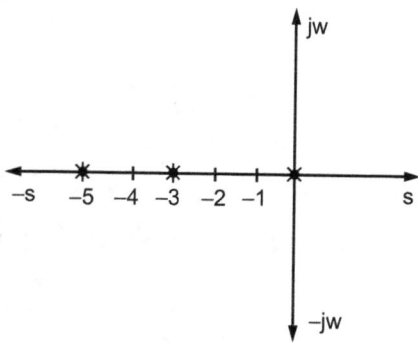

Fig. 3.39

3. Obtain the real axis loci :
  (i) Present between $-3 < s < 0$
  (ii) Present at $s < -5$

4. Obtain angle of asymptotes :

$$\beta_x = \frac{(2x + 1)}{p - z} \times 180$$

$$x = 0, 1, \ldots p - z - 1 \qquad\qquad \therefore x = 0, 1, 2$$

$$\beta_0 = 60°;\ \beta_1 = 180°;\ \beta_2 = 300°$$

5. Centroid :

$$\sigma_c = \frac{\sum \text{Real parts of poles} - \sum \text{Real parts of zeros}}{p - z}$$

$$\sigma_c = \frac{-3 - 5}{3} = -2.66$$

6. Breakaway point :
  For breakaway point, take the characteristics equation,

$$1 + G(s)\,H(s) = 0$$

$$\therefore\ 1 + \frac{K}{s\,(s + 3)\,(s + 5)} = 0$$

$$\therefore\ s\,(s + 3)\,(s + 5) + K = 0$$

$$\therefore\ s^3 + 8s^2 + 15s + K = 0$$

$$\therefore\ \qquad K = -s^3 - 8s^2 - 15s$$

$$\frac{dK}{ds} = 0 = 3s^2\ 16s - 15$$

  i.e. $3s^2 + 16s + 15 = 0$

$$s = -4.11 \qquad \text{and } s = -1.21$$

As the breakaway point has to lie on the root locus, $s = -1.21$ is a valid breakaway point.

7. Angle of Departure : Angle of departure is not required, as there are no complex poles.

8. Intersection with the imaginary axis : Considering the characteristics equation,

$$s^3 + 8s^2 + 15s + K = 0$$

$$
\begin{array}{c|cc}
s^3 & 1 & 15 \\
s^2 & 8 & K \\
s^1 & \dfrac{120-K}{8} & 0 \\
s^0 & K &
\end{array}
$$

To intersect with imaginary axis, there must be a row of zeros

$$
\therefore \qquad \frac{120-K}{8} = 0
$$

$$
\therefore \qquad K_{marginal} = 120
$$

Substituting this value of K in the preceding row auxiliary equation

i.e. $\qquad 8s^2 + K = 0 \qquad \therefore \quad 8s^2 + 120 = 0$

$$
\therefore \qquad s^2 = -15 \quad \therefore \quad s = \pm j\,3.87
$$

Thus, the root locus intersects the imaginary axis at $\pm j\,3.87$.

Fig. 3.40 shows the final root locus,

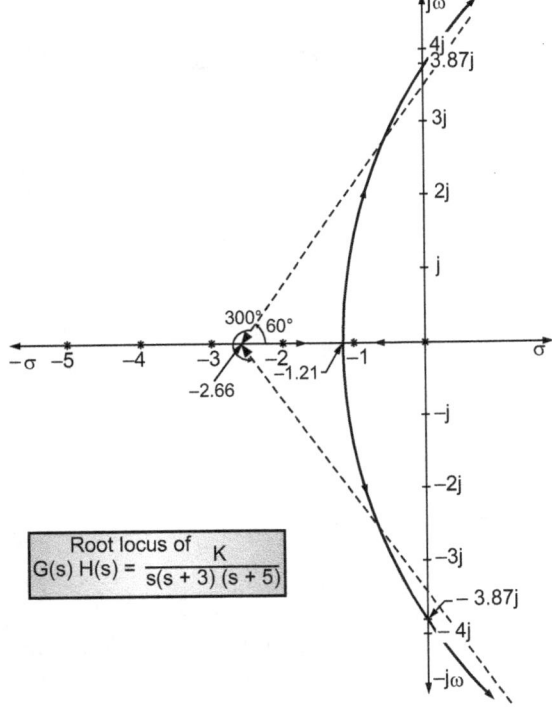

Fig. 3.40

$$T(s) = \frac{C(s)}{R(s)} = \frac{G(s)}{1 + G(s)\,H(s)}$$

$$\therefore \quad T(s) = \frac{\dfrac{21}{s(s+5)}}{1 + \dfrac{21}{s(s+5)} \cdot 1}$$

$$= \frac{\dfrac{21}{s(s+5)}}{\dfrac{s(s+5) + 21}{s(s+5)}}$$

$$\therefore \quad T(s) = \frac{21}{s^2 + 5s + 21}$$

Comparing this with the standard second order system

$$\frac{\omega_n^2}{s^2 + 2\,\xi\,\omega_n s + \omega_n^2}$$

$$\therefore \quad \frac{\omega_n^2}{s^2 + 2\xi\omega_n s + \omega_n^2} = \frac{21}{s^2 + 5s + 21}$$

$$\therefore \quad \omega_n^2 = 21$$

$$\therefore \quad \omega_n = 4.58 \text{ rad/sec.}$$

$$\therefore \quad 2\xi\omega_n = 5 \qquad \therefore 2\xi \times 4.58 = 5$$

$$\therefore \quad \xi = \frac{5}{2 \times 4.58} = 0.5458$$

$$\text{Resonance peak } M_r = \frac{1}{2\xi\sqrt{1 - \xi^2}} = \frac{1}{2 \times 0.5458\sqrt{1 - 0.5458^2}}$$

$$M_r = \frac{1}{1.0916\sqrt{0.7021}} = \frac{1}{1.0916 \times 0.8379}$$

$$M_r = 1.0933$$

Resonance frequency, $\omega_r = \omega_n \sqrt{1 - 2\xi^2}$

$$\omega_r = 4.58\sqrt{1 - 2 \times 0.54582}$$

$$= 4.58\sqrt{1 - 0.5957}$$

$$\therefore \quad \omega_r = 4.58\sqrt{0.4043} = 4.58 \times 0.6358$$

$$\omega_r = 2.911 \text{ rad/sec.}$$

Example 3.4 : If $G(s)\,H(s) = \dfrac{K(s+2)}{s(s+1)(s+3)}$ construct root locus and comment on stability of systems.

Solution : 1. $P = 3, Z = 1,$

$N = P = 3, P - Z = 2$ branches to ∞

starting : $0, -1, -3,$

terminating : $-2, \infty, \infty.$

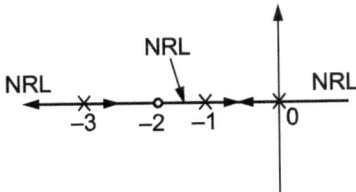

Fig. 3.41

2. Sections of real axis one break away point possible between $s = 0$ and -1.

3. Angles of asymptotes :

$\theta = \dfrac{(2q+1)\,180°}{p-z}$, $\theta_1 = 90°$, $\theta_2 = 270°$ for $q = 0.1$.

4. Centroid $= \dfrac{\sum \text{R.P. of O.L. poles} - \sum \text{R.P. of O.L. zeros}}{P-Z}$

$= \dfrac{0-1-3-(-2)}{2} = -1$

5. Breakaway point

$1 + G(s)\,H(s) = 0$ i.e. $1 + \dfrac{K(s+2)}{s(s+1)(s+3)} = 0$

$s^3 + 4s^2 + 3s + K(s+2) = 0$ i.e. $K = \dfrac{-s^3 - 4s^2 - 3s}{(s+2)}$ ... (1)

$\therefore \dfrac{dK}{ds} = 0$ gives

$(s+2)(-3s^2 - 8s - 3) - (-s^3 - 4s^2 - 3s)(1) = 0$

$\therefore -3s^3 - 8s^2 - 3s + 6s^2 - 16s - 6 + s^3 + 4s^2 + 3s = 0$

$\therefore 2s^3 + 10s^2 + 16s + 6 = 0$

$\therefore s = -0.534, -2.232 \pm j\,0.793$

Thus $s = -0.534$ is valid breakaway point and from equation (1) $K = +0.4186$

6. The characteristic equation is given as

$s^3 + 4s^2 + s(3 + K) + 2K = 0$

s^3	1	3 + K	For K_{mar}, 12 + 2K = 0
s^2	4	2K	$K_{mar} = -6$
s^1	$\dfrac{12 + 2K}{4}$	0	As K_{mar} is negative there is no intersection of root locus with imaginary axis.
s^0	2K		

7. No angle of departure required as no complex poles are present.

8. Fig. 3.42 shows the root locus.

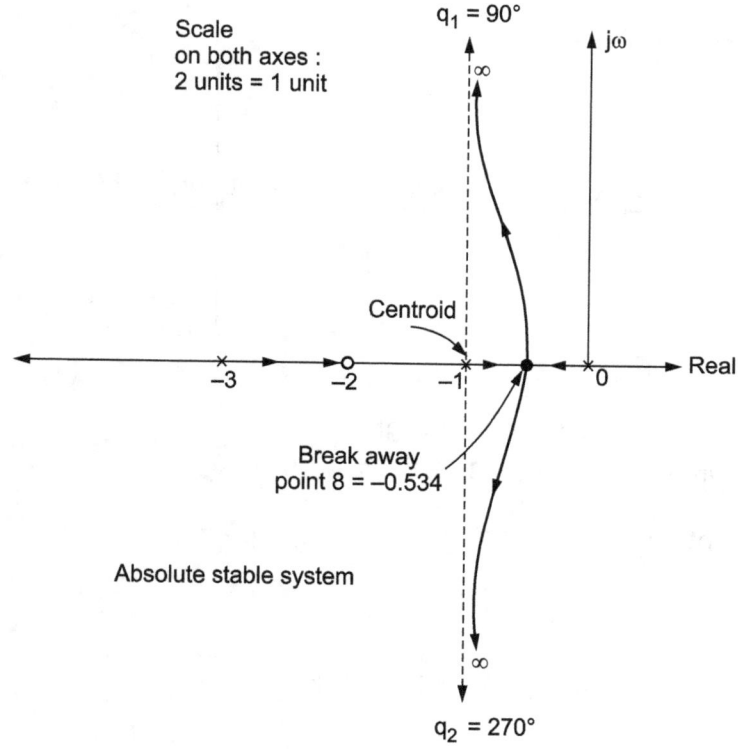

Scale on both axes : 2 units = 1 unit

$q_1 = 90°$

Centroid

Break away point 8 = –0.534

Absolute stable system

$q_2 = 270°$

Fig. 3.42

Example 3.5 : If G(s) H(s) = $\dfrac{K}{s(s + 1)(s + 10)}$, sketch the complete root locus and comment on the stability.

[May 15] [4]

Solution :

1. Obtain number of loci and loci ending at infinity :

Here,   Number of poles=p = 3

Number of zeros=z = 0

∵   p > z, Number of loci = p = 3

and, Number of loci ending at infinity = p – z = 3

Thus, there are three root loci. All proceed to end at infinity.

2. Draw the poles and zeros to suitable scale.

3. To find the real axis loci :

Moving from origin on negative X-axis, root locus is present whenever the total number of poles and zeros to right is odd. Accordingly real axis loci can be given as :

*   Present between $-1 < \sigma < 0$

*   Absent between $-10 < \sigma < -1$

*   Present between $-\infty < \sigma < -10$

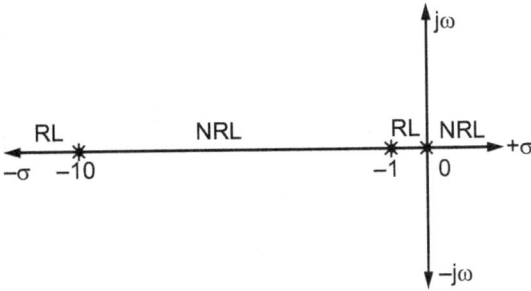

Fig. 3.43

4. Find number of asymptotes and their angles :

*   Number of asymptotes = p – z = **3**

*   Angle of asymptotes = $\beta_x = \dfrac{(2x + 1)\,180}{p - z}$ x = 0, 1, ... p – z – 1

$$\beta_x = (2x + 1)\left(\frac{180}{3}\right); x = 0, 1, 2$$

i.e. $\beta_0 = 60°, \beta_1 = 180°, \beta_2 = 300°$

5. Centroid :

As per centroid formula,

$$\sigma_c = \frac{\sum \text{Real part of poles of OLTF} - \sum \text{Real part of zeros of OLTF}}{p - z}$$

$$\sigma_c = \frac{(0 + (-1) + (-10)) - 0}{3 - 0} = -3.66$$

6. Breakaway points :

Considering the characteristic equation

$$1 + G(s)\,H(s) = 0$$

$$1 + \frac{K}{s(s + 1)(s + 10)} = 0$$

$\therefore \quad s(s + 1)(s + 10) + K = 0$

$s^3 + 11s^2 + 10s + K = 0$

Writting this equation in terms of K

$\therefore \qquad\qquad K = -(s^3 + 11s^2 + 10s)$

Now, $\qquad\qquad \dfrac{dK}{ds} = 0$

$$0 = -(3s^2 + 22s + 10)$$

i.e. $\quad 3s^2 + 22s + 10 = 0$

$\therefore \qquad\qquad s = -0.486 \text{ and } -6.85$

From above two breakaway points (BAP), only s = − 0.486 is valid BAP since it lies on the root locus. So we select s = −0.486 as breakaway point.

7. Not needed, as no complex poles or zeros are present.

8. Intersection of imaginary axis :

To find the intersection with imaginary axis,

$\therefore \qquad s^3 + 11s^2 + 10s + K = 0$

Routh's array can be given as,

$$
\begin{array}{c|cc}
s^3 & 1 & 10 \\
s^2 & 11 & K \\
s^1 & \dfrac{110 - K}{11} & 0 \\
s^0 & K &
\end{array}
$$

For stability, column 1 should be positive, Therefore $K > 0$ and $\dfrac{110 - K}{11} > 0$

i.e. K < 110 $\qquad$ i.e. K_{mar} = 110

Hence, 0 < K < 110 is stable range of K.

At K_{mar} = 110, a row of zero is obtained and hence the preceding row (s^2 row) becomes the auxiliary equation.

$\qquad\qquad 11s^2 + K_{mar} = 0$

i.e. $\qquad\qquad 11s^2 = -K_{mar}$

$\therefore \qquad\qquad 11s^2 = -110$

$\therefore \qquad\qquad s^2 = -10$

$\qquad\qquad s = \pm j\sqrt{10} = \pm j\,3.16 = \pm j\omega_{mar}$

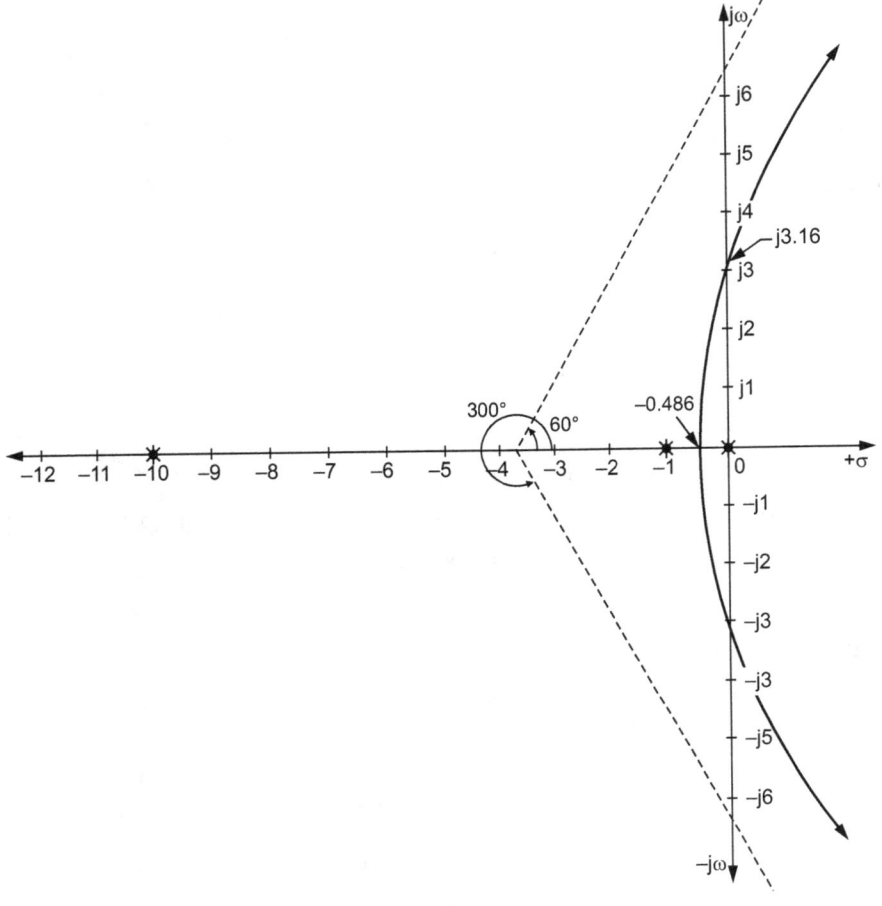

Fig. 3.44

So, the root locus intersects the imaginary axis ±j 3.16.

Fig. 3.44 show the complete root locus.

Example 3.6 : Open loop transfer function of unity feedback system is :

$G(s) = \dfrac{K}{s(s + 2)(s + 10)}$. Sketch the complete root locus and comment on stability of system.

[Dec. 15] [8]

Solution :

1.   P = 3, Z = 0, N = 3

                              P − Z = 3 branches to ∞

                         Starting : s = 0, − 2, − 10

                         Terminating = ∞, ∞, ∞

2.   Fig. 3.45 shows sections of real axis.

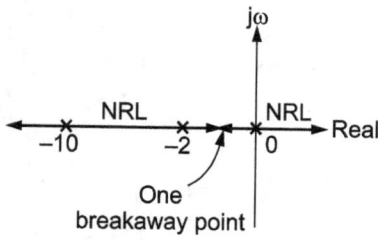

Fig. 3.45

3.   Angles of asymptotes :

$$\theta = \frac{(2q + 1)\,180°}{P - Z}, q = 0, 1, 2$$

$\therefore$ $\theta_1 = 60°, \theta_2 = 180°, \theta_3 = 300°$

4. $\text{Centroid} = \dfrac{\sum \text{R.P. of O.L. poles} - \sum \text{R.P. of O.L. zeros}}{P - Z}$

$$= \frac{0 - 2 - 10}{3} = -4$$

5. Breakaway point, $1 + G(s)\,H(s) = 0$

$\therefore 1 + \dfrac{K}{s(s + 2)\,(s + 10)} = 0$ i.e. $s^3 + 12^2 + 20s + K = 0$ ... (1)

$\therefore$ $K = -s^3 - 12s^2 - 20s$ ... (2)

$\therefore \dfrac{dK}{ds} = 0$ gives $3s^2 + 24s + 20 = 0$ i.e. $s = -0.95, -7.05$

$\therefore$ $s = -0.95$ is valid breakaway point with $K = +5.59$ from equation (2)

6.   Intersection with $j\omega$ axis :

From equation (1)

s^3	1	20
s^2	12	K
s^1	$\dfrac{240 - K}{12}$	0
s^0	K	

$\therefore$ $240 - K = 0$ for $K = K_{mar}$

$\therefore$ $K_{mar} = 240$

$12s^2 + K_{mar} = 0$ is $A(s) = 0$

$\therefore$ $s^2 = -20$ i.e. $s = \pm j\,4.47$

7.   Angles of departure not required as no complex poles.

8. Fig. 3.46 shows the complete root locus.

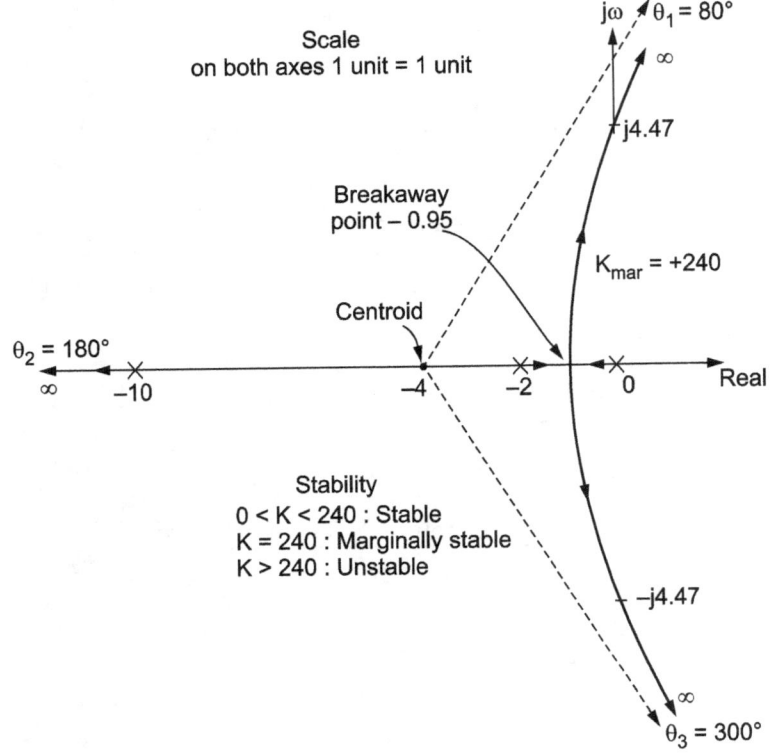

Fig. 3.46

FREQUENCY RESPONSE ANALYSIS

4.1 INTRODUCTION

The frequency response of a system is a frequency dependent function which expresses how a sinusoidal signal of a given frequency on the system input is transferred through the system. Time-varying signals at least periodical signals – which excite systems, as the reference (set point) signal or a disturbance in a control system or measurement signals which are input signals to signal filters, can be regarded as consisting of a sum of frequency components. Each frequency component is a sinusoidal signal having certain amplitude and a certain frequency. (The Fourier series expansion or the Fourier transform can be used to express these frequency components quantitatively.) The frequency response expresses how each of these frequency components is transferred through the system. Some components may be amplified, others may be attenuated, and there will be some phase lag through the system.

The frequency response is an important tool for analysis and design of signal filters (as low pass filters and high pass filters), and for analysis, and to some extent, design of control systems. Both signal filtering and control systems applications are described (briefly) later in this chapter. The definition of the frequency response which will be given in the next section applies only to linear models, but this linear model may very well be the local linear model about some operating point of a non-linear model. The frequency response can found experimentally or from a transfer function model. It can be presented graphically or as a mathematical function.

The Nyquist criterion proves both the absolute and relative stabilities of linear closed loop systems from knowledge of their open-loop frequency response characteristics. An advantage of the frequency response approach is that all the frequency response tests are simple, economical, and can be made accurately by use of readily available sinusoidal signal generators and accurate electronic measurement equipments. Also the transfer functions of the complex systems can be determined experimentally by frequency response tests. In addition, the frequency response analysis has an advantage that system can be designed such that undesired noise effects are negligible and such analysis and design can be extended to certain non-linear control systems.

The correlation between frequency response and transient response is indirect, except for second order systems. In designing a closed loop system, we adjust the frequency response characteristic of the open-loop transfer function by using various design criteria in order to obtain acceptable transient-response characteristics for the system.

- **Time Response Analysis**

The time signals such as impulse, step, ramp etc. are used as input to the system and the output response is obtained for these various inputs. It is called time response analysis or time domain analysis.

- **Frequency Response Analysis**

When the sinusoidal signal of variable frequency is used as input to the system and by varying this input the magnitude and phase of steady state output of the system is obtained, it is called frequency response analysis or frequency domain analysis.

4.2 NEED OF FREQUENCY RESPONSE ANALYSIS

- Extraction of transfer function from time domain is difficult using differential equations.
- Using frequency response, transfer function can be easily obtained from the experimental data.
- A system may be designed, so effects of noise are neligible.
- Analysis and design are extended to certain non-linear control systems.
- The design of controller can be easily done in the frequency domain method, as compared to the time domain method.
- Has ability to obtain the relative stability of feedback control system.
- Lead compensator can be designed conveniently to meet a steady state error requirement and transient response requirement.

4.3 CONCEPT OF FREQUENCY RESPONSE

For the frequency response analysis, a sinusoidal wave is applied at its input.

Let the sinusoidal signal be,

$$x(t) = A \sin(\omega t)$$

The steady state output will be a sinusoidal signal of the same frequency as input, but possibly with different magnitude and phase.

Suppose the output is

$$Y(t) = \beta A \sin(\omega t + \phi)$$

The frequency response analysis can be diagrammatically represented as,

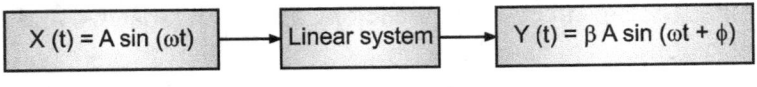

Fig. 4.1

In the output equation, the term β represents the multiplication factor for the magnitude and ϕ represents the relative phase shift between input and the output.

If $\beta > 1 \rightarrow$ system amplifier input.

If $\beta < 1 \rightarrow$ system attenuates the input.

Following Fig. 4.2 shows graphical concept of frequency response.

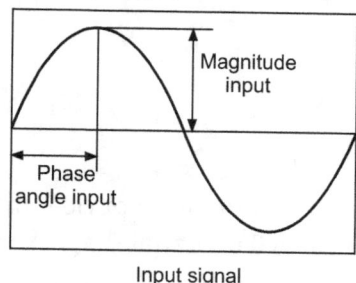
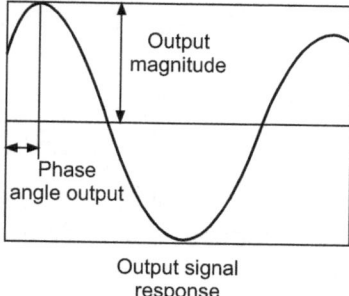

Input signal

Output signal response

Fig. 4.2

4.4 FREQUENCY RESPONSE OF SECOND ORDER SYSTEM

Assume a second order system with the transfer function

$$\frac{C(s)}{R(s)} = \frac{\omega_n^2}{s^2 + 2\xi\omega_n s + \omega_n^2} \qquad \ldots(4.1)$$

For frequency response analysis, s is replaced by $j\omega$

$$\frac{C(j\omega)}{R(j\omega)} = \frac{\omega_n^2}{(j\omega)^2 + 2\xi\omega_n (j\omega) + \omega_n^2}$$

$$= \frac{\omega_n^2}{-\omega^2 + j2\xi\omega_n\omega + \omega_n^2} \quad \ldots \because j_2 = -1 \qquad \ldots(4.2)$$

Dividing the equation (4.2) by ω_n^2

$$\frac{C(j\omega)}{R(j\omega)} = \frac{1}{-\left(\dfrac{\omega}{\omega_n}\right)^2 + j2\,\xi\,\dfrac{\omega}{\omega_n} + 1} \qquad \ldots(4.3)$$

Defining $v = \dfrac{\omega}{\omega_n}$, this is called normalization of the frequency ω, with respect to the natural frequency ω_n.

Hence, equation (4.3) can be written as;

$$\frac{C(j\omega)}{R(j\omega)} = \frac{1}{1 - v^2 + j2\,\xi v} \qquad \ldots(4.4)$$

The magnitude M is

$$M = \frac{1}{\sqrt{(1-v^2)^2 + 4\xi^2 v^2}} \cdots \frac{1}{\sqrt{x^2 + y^2}} \qquad ...(4.5)$$

$$= ((1-v^2)^2 + 4\xi^2 v^2)^{-1/2}$$

and phase ϕ is

$$\phi = -\tan^{-1}\left(\frac{2\xi v}{1-v^2}\right) \cdots -\tan^{-1}\left(\frac{y}{x}\right) \qquad ...(4.6)$$

Magnitude and phase from equation (4.5) and (4.6). From this it is not clear that the value of magnitude response monotonically decreases from 1 to 0 or it attains a maximum value and then decreases to zero.

Table 4.1 shows the magnitude and phase of second order systems for different values of 'v'.

Table 4.1

Valve of V	Magnitude M	Phase ϕ in deg.
0	1	0
1	$1/2\xi$	−90
∞	0	−180

It magnitude M has a maximum value at a particular frequency, then its derivative should be zero.

Derivation of Resonance Frequency ω_r

Taking derivative of both sides of equation (4.5) w.r.t. v,

$$\frac{dM}{dv} = -\left(\frac{1}{2}\right)\frac{2(1-v^2)(-2v) + 8\xi^2 v}{[(1-v^2) + 4\xi^2 v^2]^{3/2}} = 0 \qquad ...(4.7)$$

After simplification,

$$v^3 - v + 2\xi^2 v = 0 \qquad ...(4.8)$$

$$\therefore \quad v[v^2 + 2\xi^2 - 1] = 0$$

$$v = 0 \text{ or } v^2 + 2\xi^2 - 1 = 0$$

$$\therefore \qquad v^2 = 1 - 2\xi^2$$

$$\therefore \qquad v = \sqrt{1 - 2\xi^2}$$

$$\therefore \qquad v = v_r = \frac{\omega_r}{\omega_n} = \sqrt{1 - 2\xi^2} \qquad ...(4.9)$$

where ω_r, is the resonance frequency and given by;

$$\omega_r = \omega_n \sqrt{1 - 2\xi^2} \qquad ...(4.10)$$

The frequency at which system exhibits enhanced vibration, oscillation, response is known as resonance frequency.

Also, it is the frequency where magnitude becomes maximum.

$$\omega_r = \omega_n \sqrt{1 - 2\xi^2}$$

Derivation of M_r Resonance Peak :

It is the maximum value of magnitude, In the range of 1–1.5.

Re-write Magnitude equation (4.5) with ω_r/ω_n form term 'v'.

$$M_r = \frac{1}{\sqrt{(1 - (\omega_r/\omega_n)^2)^2 + 4\xi^2 (\omega_r/\omega_n)^2}} \qquad \ldots(4.11)$$

Put $\qquad \omega_r = \omega_n \sqrt{1 - 2\xi^2}$

$$M_r = \frac{1}{\sqrt{(1 - (\omega_n \sqrt{1 - 2\xi^2}/\omega_n)^2)^2 + 4\xi^2 (\omega_n \sqrt{1 - 2\xi^2}/\omega_n)^2}} \qquad \ldots(4.12)$$

$$M_r = \frac{1}{(4\xi^4) + 4\xi^2 (1 - 2\xi^2)} \qquad \ldots(4.13)$$

or $\qquad M_r = \dfrac{1}{2\xi \sqrt{1 - \xi^2}} \qquad \ldots(4.14)$

Formula of resonance peak is,

$$M_r = \frac{1}{2\xi\sqrt{1 - \xi^2}}$$

Phase Angle of Resonance Frequency:

Re-writing phase equation (4.6) with ω_r/ω_n for term 'v';

$$\phi = -\tan^{-1}\left(\frac{2\xi\omega_r/\omega_n}{1 - (\omega_r/\omega_n)^2}\right) \qquad \ldots(4.15)$$

Put $\qquad \omega_r = \omega_n \sqrt{1 - 2\xi^2}$

$$\phi = -\tan^{-1}\left(\frac{2\xi\sqrt{1 - 2\xi^2}}{2\xi^2}\right) = -\tan^{-1}\left(\frac{\sqrt{1 - 2\xi^2}}{\xi}\right) \qquad \ldots(4.16)$$

Case 1 : $\xi = 0$

The magnitude response goes from 1 to ∞ at $\omega_r = \omega_n$ and phase is –90 deg.

Case 2 : $\xi < 0.707$ (frequency is never negative).

If $\xi > 1/\sqrt{2}$, the resonance frequency becomes imaginary and the magnitude response does not have a peak and the response monotonically decreases from a value 1 at $v = 0$ to zero at $v = \infty$.

Highlights :

- The resonant peak M_r depends only on the damping factor ξ.
- The resonant frequency is a measure of speed of response of the system.
- The setting time in time domain is depend on the damping factor ξ by relation $4/(\xi\omega_n)$.
- The resonant peak and resonance frequency can be used as performance measures for a control system in frequency domain.

4.4.1 Concept of Bandwidth

The control systems are considered as low pass filters when the magnitude M = 1 frequency v = 0 and the frequency at which the magnitude falls to – 3db is known as the Bandwidth of the system.

If ξ < 0.707 and frequency v > v_r, the magnitude decreases monotonically after peak resonant. The frequency where the magnitude becomes $\dfrac{1}{\sqrt{2}}$ is called cut-off frequency. At

cut-off frequency the magnitude in dB is $20 \log \dfrac{1}{\sqrt{2}} = -3\text{dB}$.

Fig. 4.3 shows magnitude response with bandwidth.

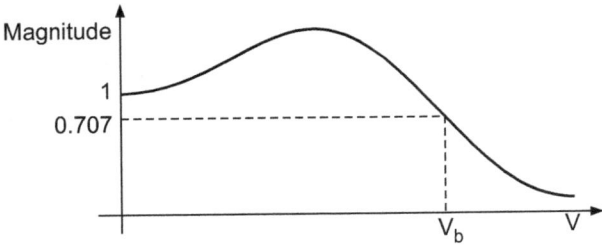

Fig. 4.3 : Magnitude response showing bandwidth

Derivation of Bandwidth: The equation of the magnitude is,

$$M = \frac{1}{(1 - v^2)^2 + 4\xi^2 v^2}$$

Put $M = \dfrac{1}{\sqrt{2}}$ and $v = v_b$ in above equation

$$\frac{1}{\sqrt{2}} = \frac{1}{(1 - v_b^2)^2 + 4\xi^2 v_b^2} \qquad \qquad \dots(4.17)$$

$$(1 - v_b^2)^2 + 4\zeta v_b^2 = 2$$

$$v_b^4 - 2 v_b^2 + 1 + 4\xi^2 v_b^2 = 0 \qquad \qquad \dots(4.18)$$

$$v_b^4 - 2(1 - 2\xi^2) v_b^2 - 1 = 0$$

This equation is similar to $ax^2 + bx + c = 0$, where $x = v_b^2$ and solution is x_1,

$$2 = \frac{-b \pm \sqrt{b^2 - 4ac}}{2a}$$

Therefore, $$v_b = \frac{\sqrt{2(1 - 2\xi^2)} \pm \sqrt{4(1 - 2\xi^2)^2 + 4}}{2}$$

The frequency v_b must be positive and real, therefore consider only positive sign

$$v_b = \sqrt{(1 - 2\xi^2) + \sqrt{2 - 4\xi^2 + 4\xi^4}}$$

Put $v_b = \omega_b/\omega_n$ in above equation. The bandwidth is

$$\omega_b = \omega_n \sqrt{(1 - 2\xi^2) + \sqrt{2 - 4\xi^2 + 4\xi^4}}$$

If damping factor ξ is known, the bandwidth ω_n, is a measure of ω_n and hence the speed of response. The bandwidth is more i.e., the speed of response is high.

4.4.2 Correlation between Time and Frequency Domain

In time domain, important specifications are

Peak Overshoot

$$M_p = e - \frac{\pi\xi}{\sqrt{1 - \xi^2}}$$

Setting Time

$$t_s = \frac{4}{\xi\omega_n}$$

Frequency of Oscillation (Damped)

$$\omega_d = \omega_n \sqrt{1 - \xi^2}$$

In frequency domain, important specifications are

Resonant Peak (for $\xi < 0.707$)

$$M_r = \frac{1}{2\xi\sqrt{1 - \xi^2}}$$

Bandwidth $$\omega_b = \sqrt{\omega_n \sqrt{1 - 2\xi^2} + \sqrt{2 - 4\xi^2 + 4\xi^4}}$$

Frequency of resonance

$$\omega_r = \omega_n \sqrt{1 - 2\xi^2}$$

4.4.3 Correlation between Peak Overshoot and Resonant Peak

- It is important to note that both peak overshoot M_p and resonant peak M_r are dependent on only factor, that the damping factor ξ and hence both are indicative of damping in the system.

- If peak overshoot M_p is known, the resonant peak M_r can be calculated after obtaining damping factor ξ providing that ξ is less than 0.707.

- If resonant peak M_r is known the peak overshoot M_p can be calculated after obtaining damping factor ξ provided that ξ is less than 0.707.

- Thus it can be said that the resonant peak M_r and peak overshoot M_p are well correlated.

- A plot of correction of M_r and M_p with respect to damping factor ξ is given in Fig. 4.4.

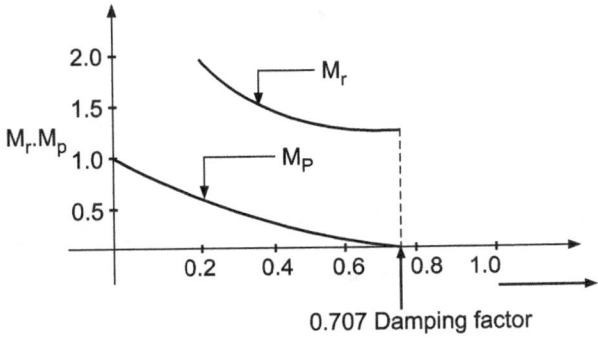

Fig. 4.4

Correlation of M_r and M_p with respect to damping factor ξ.

4.4.4 Correlation between Settling Time and Bandwidth

The speed of response is indicated by settling time in time domain and it is given by $t_s = \dfrac{4}{(\xi \omega_n)}$. The *bandwidth;* a frequency domain concept, is also indicative of speed of response. Thus we can see that there is a perfect correlation between time domain measure given one, the other can be obtained easily.

4.4.5 Correlation between Damped Frequency and Resonance Frequency

There is correlation between the time domain specification of damped natural frequency and the frequency domain specification of resonance frequency.

- For a given damping factor ξ, the ratio of $\dfrac{\omega_r}{\omega_d} = \dfrac{\sqrt{1-2\xi^2}}{\sqrt{1-\xi^2}}$ is fixed.

- For example, if $\xi = 0.5$, the ratio $\dfrac{\omega_r}{\omega_d} = 0.8165$, if $\xi = 0.6$, the ratio $\dfrac{\omega_r}{\omega_d} = 0.6614$ and so on.

- The time domain specification ω_d = 0.8660 with ξ = 0.5 is known, we can calculate resonance frequency using these parameters.

  For ξ = 0.5, $\dfrac{\omega_r}{\omega_d}$ = 0.8165 is fixed. Therefore frequency domain specification ω_r = 0.8165, ω_d = 0.7071.

- The frequency domain specification ω_r = 0.7071 with ξ = 0.5 is known, we can calculate damped natural frequency using: for ξ = 0.5, $\dfrac{\omega_r}{\omega_d}$ = 0.8165 is fixed. Therefore time domain specification ω_d = $\dfrac{\omega_r}{0.8165}$ = 0.8660.

- From above two points, it is clear that whenever the damping factor ξ known, it is easy to calculate frequency domain specification, from corresponding time domain specification and vice versa.

SOLVED EXAMPLES

Example 4.1 : If G(s) of a unity feedback system is $\dfrac{10}{s(s + 10)}$ determine steady state response of the system when the excitation applied is r(t) = 10 sin 8t.

Solution :

$$G(s) = \frac{10}{s(s + 10)} \quad H(s) = 1$$

$$\therefore \quad T(s) = \frac{C(s)}{R(s)} = \frac{G(s)}{1 + G(s) \cdot H(s)}$$

i.e.

$$T(s) = \frac{10}{s^2 + 10s + 10}$$

In the frequency domain, replace s by jω,

$$\therefore \quad T(j\omega) = \frac{10}{(j\omega)^2 + 10j\omega + 10} = \frac{10}{(10 - \omega^2) + j10\omega}$$

$$T(j\omega) = M \angle \phi \text{ where}$$

$$M = \frac{|10|}{|(10 - \omega^2) + j10\omega|} = \frac{10}{\sqrt{(10 - \omega)^2 + 100\ \omega^2}}$$

and

$$\phi = -\tan^{-1}\left(\frac{10\omega}{10 - \omega^2}\right)$$

Now,

$$r(t) = 10 \sin (8t) = A \sin (\omega t)$$

$$r(t) = A \sin (\omega t) \text{ we can write}$$

$$A = \text{Amplitude} = 10 \text{ and } \omega t = 8t$$

$$C(t) = (AM) \sin (\omega t + \phi)$$

Hence, in this case substituting all the values, we get the steady state response as,

$$\therefore \qquad C(t) \; = \; \frac{10 \times 10}{\sqrt{(10 - \omega^2) + 100\,\omega}} \sin\left(8t - \tan^{-1}\left(\frac{10\omega}{10 - \omega}\right)\right)$$

$$= \; \frac{100}{\sqrt{(10 - \omega^2)^2 + 100\,\omega^2}} \sin\left(8t - \tan^{-1}\left(\frac{10\omega}{10 - \omega^2}\right)\right)$$

Example 4.2 : A unit step input is applied to a unity feedback control system having open loop transfer function.

$$G(s) \; = \; \frac{K}{s(1 + sT)}$$

Determine, the values of K and T to have M_p = 20% and resonant frequency ω_r = 6 rad/sec. Calculate the resonant peak M_r.

Solution : The open loop transfer function is

$$G(s) \; = \; \frac{K}{s(1 + sT)} \;\; \text{and} \;\; H(s) = 1$$

$$\therefore \qquad \frac{C(s)}{R(s)} \; = \; \frac{G(s)}{1 + G(s) \cdot H(s)} \; = \; \frac{\dfrac{K}{s(1 + sT)}}{1 + \dfrac{K}{s(1 + sT)}} \; = \; \frac{K}{Ts^2 + s + K} \; = \; \frac{K/T}{s^2 + \dfrac{1}{T}s + \dfrac{K}{T}}$$

Comparing this with standard form,

$$\omega_n \; = \; \sqrt{K/T} \qquad\qquad\qquad \text{...(4.19)}$$

$$\xi \; = \; \frac{1}{2\sqrt{KT}} \qquad\qquad\qquad \text{...(4.20)}$$

Now, M_p = 20% i.e. $0.2 = e^{-\pi\xi/\sqrt{(1 - \xi^2)}}$

Solving $\qquad\qquad \xi \; = \; 0.455$ and ω_r = 6 rad/sec

$$\therefore \qquad\qquad \omega_r \; = \; \omega_n \sqrt{1 - 2\xi^2}$$

$$\therefore \qquad\qquad \sigma \; = \; \omega_n \sqrt{1 - 2 \times (0.455)^2}$$

$$\therefore \qquad\qquad \omega_n \; = \; 7.8382 \text{ rad/sec}$$

Using equation (4.19),

$$7.8382 \; = \; \sqrt{K/T} \;\text{ i.e. } 61.437 = K/T$$

Using equation (4.20),

$$0.455 \; = \; \frac{1}{2\sqrt{KT}} \;\text{ i.e. } 0.8281 = \frac{1}{KT}$$

Substituting from equation (4.19) into equation (4.20),

$$\therefore \qquad\qquad 61.437 \; = \; \frac{1}{0.8281T^2}$$

i.e. $\qquad$ $T^2 = 0.0196$

i.e. $\qquad$ $T = 0.14$

$\therefore$ $\qquad$ $K = 8.6133$

$$M_r = \frac{1}{2\xi\sqrt{1-\xi^2}} = \frac{1}{2 \times 0.455\sqrt{1-(0.455)^2}} = 1.234$$

Example 4.3 : A second order system has a natural frequency of oscillation.

(ω_n) = 2.5 rad/sec , and Undamped frequency of oscialltion

(ω_d) = 2.0 rad/sec.

(i) Calculate its % overshoot, when it is subjected to a step input.

(ii) Calculate the resonant peak, if it is subjected to sinusoidal input.

Solution : ω_n = 2.5 and ω_d = 2

Now, $\qquad$ $\omega_d = \omega_n\sqrt{1-\xi^2}$

$\qquad$ $2 = 2.5\sqrt{1-\xi^2}$

$\therefore$ $\qquad$ $1-\xi^2 = 0.64$

i.e. $\qquad$ $\xi = 0.6$

(i) $\qquad$ $\%\,M_p = e^{\frac{-\pi\xi}{\sqrt{1-\xi^2}}} \times 100$

$\qquad\qquad$ $= e^{\frac{-\pi \times 0.6}{\sqrt{1-0.36}}} \times 100$

$\qquad\qquad$ $= 9.478\,\%$

(ii) $\qquad$ $M_r = \frac{1}{2\xi\sqrt{1-\xi^2}}$

$\qquad\qquad$ $= \frac{1}{2 \times 0.6\sqrt{1-0.36}}$

$\qquad\qquad$ $= 1.0416$

Example 4.4 : If M_r =2 and ω_r = 4 rad/sec, Determine the steady state error for unit ramp input and unity feedback system with a closed loop transfer function of a second order system.

Solution : M_r = 2 and ω_r = 4

Now, $\qquad$ $M_r = \frac{1}{2\xi\sqrt{1-\xi^2}} = 2$

i.e. $\qquad$ $4 = \frac{1}{4\xi^2\,(1-\xi^2)}$

Solving $\qquad \xi^2 = 0.0669$ or 0.933

i.e. $\qquad \xi = 0.2588$ or 0.966

But for $\xi = 0.966$, M_r does not exist, hence $\xi = 0.2588$

Now, $\qquad \omega_r = \omega_n \sqrt{1 - 2\xi^2} = 4$

$$\omega_n = \frac{4}{\sqrt{1 - 2 \times (0.2588)^2}}$$

$$= 4.2961 \text{ rad/sec}$$

The transfer function of 2nd order system is

$$\frac{C(s)}{R(s)} = \frac{\omega_n^2}{s^2 + 2\xi\omega_n s + \omega_n^2} = \frac{18.4564}{s^2 + 2.2236s + 18.4564}$$

$$C(s) = R(s)\left[\frac{18.4564}{s^2 + 2.2236s + 18.4564}\right]$$

and $\qquad R(s) = \dfrac{1}{s^2}$

Now, $\qquad E(s) = R(s) - C(s) = \dfrac{1}{s^2} - \dfrac{1}{s^2}\left[\dfrac{18.4564}{s^2 + 2.2236s + 18.4564}\right]$

$$= \frac{1}{s^2}\left[1 - \frac{18.4564}{s^2 + 2.2236s + 18.4564}\right]$$

$\therefore \qquad e_{ss} = \displaystyle\lim_{s \to 0} sE(s) = \lim_{s \to 0} s \times \frac{1}{s^2}\left[1 - \frac{18.4564}{s^2 + 2.2236s + 18.4564}\right]$

$$= \lim_{s \to 0} \frac{1}{s}\left[\frac{s^2 + 2.2236s + 18.4564 - 18.4564}{s^2 + 2.2236s + 18.4564}\right]$$

$$= \lim_{s \to 0} \frac{1}{s}\left[\frac{s(s + 2.2236)}{s^2 + 2.2236s + 18.4564}\right] = \frac{2.2236}{18.4564}$$

$$= 0.1204 \text{ i.e. } 10.04 \% \text{ ...steady state error.}$$

Example 4.5 : (a) Consider into feedback system shown in Fig. 4.5. Find the value of K and (b) to satisfy the following frequency domain specification. $M_r = 1.1$, $\omega_r = 12$ rad/s (c) For the values of a K and b determined in part (a) calculated setting time and B.W. of system

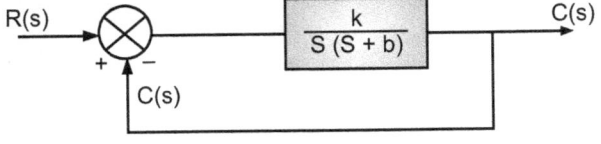

Fig. 4.5

Solution : The closed loop transfer of system is

$$\frac{C(s)}{R(s)} = \frac{K/s(s+6)}{1 + K/s\,(s+6)}$$

$$= \frac{K}{s^2 + 6s + K}$$

Comparing with standard form of closed loop transfer function

$$\frac{K}{s^2 + 6s + K} = \frac{\omega_n^2}{s^2 + 2\xi\,\omega_n s + \omega_n^2}$$

$$\omega_n^2 = K \qquad\qquad \xi^2 = \frac{b^2}{4K}$$

$$\omega_n = \sqrt{K}$$

$$2\xi\,\omega_n = b$$

$$\xi = \frac{b}{\sqrt{K}}$$

We know,
$$M_r = \frac{1}{2\xi\sqrt{1-\xi^2}} = 1.1$$

$$(1.1)^2 = \frac{1}{4\xi^2\,(1-\xi^2)} = \frac{1}{\dfrac{4b^2}{4K}\left(1 - \dfrac{b^2}{4K}\right)}$$

$$= \frac{1}{\dfrac{b^2}{K}\left[1 - \dfrac{b^2}{4K}\right]}$$

$$\omega_r = \omega_n\sqrt{1 - 2\xi^2} = 12$$

$$(12)^2 = \omega_n^2\,(1 - 2\xi^2)\cdot K\left[1 - \frac{2b^2}{4K}\right]$$

$$144 = K - \frac{b^2}{2}$$

$$b^2 = 2K - 288$$

$$1.21 = \frac{1}{\dfrac{b^2}{K}\left(1 - \dfrac{b^2}{4K}\right)} \qquad\qquad\qquad\qquad\qquad \ldots(4.21)$$

$$b^2\,(4K - b^2) - \frac{4K^2}{1.21} = 3.305\,K^2 \qquad\qquad\qquad\qquad \ldots(4.22)$$

Substituting (4.21) in and (4.22) we get

$$(2K - 288)(4K - 2K + 280) = 3.305\,K^2$$

$$4K^2 - 288^2 = 3.305\,K^2$$

$$0.695\,K^2 = 288^2$$

$$K^2 = \frac{288^2}{0.695}$$

$$K = 345.7$$

$$b = \sqrt{2K - 288}$$

$$= \sqrt{2 \times 345.7 - 288}$$

$$= 20.08$$

$$\omega_n = \sqrt{K} = \sqrt{345.7} = 18.593 \text{ rad/s}$$

$$\xi = \frac{b}{2\sqrt{K}} = \frac{20.08}{2 \times 18.593} = 0.54$$

Settling time $\qquad t_s = \dfrac{4}{\xi\omega_n} = \dfrac{4}{0.54 \times 18.593} = \dfrac{4}{10.04}$

$$t_s = 0.398s \;\ldots \text{ for 2\% criterion}$$

For 5% $\qquad t_s = \dfrac{3}{\xi\omega_n} = \dfrac{3}{0.54 \times 18.593} = 0.298 \text{ s}$

The BW, $\qquad \omega_b = \omega_n \left[1 - 2\xi^2 + \sqrt{2 - 4\xi^2 + 4\xi^2}\right]^{1/2}$

$$= 18.593 \left[1 - 2 \times 0.54^2 + \sqrt{2 - 4 \times 0.54^2 + 4 \times 0.54^4}\right]^{1/2}$$

$$\omega_b = 22.068 \text{ rad/s}$$

(a) For $M_r = 1.1$, $\omega_r = 12$ rad/s , $K = 345.7$ and $b = 20.08$

(b) $K = 345.7$, $b = 20.08$, $t_s = 0.398s$ or 0.2955

(c) BW = 22.068 rad/s

Example 4.6 : A unit step response test conducted on 2nd order system yielded peak oversheet $M_p = 0.12$ and $t_p = 0.25$. Obtain corresponding frequency response indices (M_r, ω_r, ω_n) for system.

Solution: $\qquad M_p = e^{\dfrac{-\xi\pi}{\sqrt{1 - \xi^2}}}$

$$ln\,(M_p) = \frac{-\pi\xi}{\sqrt{1 - \xi^2}}$$

$$l_n \, (M_p)^2 = \frac{\pi^2 \xi^2}{1 - \xi^2}$$

$$\therefore \qquad (1 - \xi^2) \, (ln \, M_p)^2 = \pi^2 \xi^2$$

$$\xi^2 \, [\pi^2 + (ln \, M_p)^2] = [ln \, (M_p)^2]$$

$$\xi^2 = \frac{[l_n \, \mu_p]^2}{\pi^2 + (ln \, M_p)^2}$$

$$M_p = 0.12$$

$$\xi = 0.559$$

$$M_r = \frac{1}{2\xi \sqrt{1 - \xi^2}} = \frac{1}{2 \times 0.559 \sqrt{1 - 0.559^2}}$$

$$= 1.079$$

$$t_p = \frac{\pi}{\omega_d} = \frac{\pi}{\omega_n \sqrt{1 - \xi^2}}$$

$$\omega_r = \omega_n \sqrt{1 - 2\xi^2} = 10.88 \text{ rad/s}$$

$$\omega_n = 17.78 \text{ rad/s}$$

$$\omega_n = \omega_n \sqrt{1 - 2\xi^2 + \sqrt{4\xi^4 - 4\xi^2 + 2}}$$

$$\omega_n = 21.36 \text{ rad/s}$$

4.5 BODE PLOT

- Basic of any frequency response is to plot magnitude M and angle ϕ against input frequency ω.

- When ω is varied from 0 to ∞ there is wide range of variations in M and ϕ; hence it becomes difficult to accommodate all such variations with linear scale.

- Bode plots, also called logarithmic plots, are in two parts :

  (a) One is the logarithm of the magnitude of a sinusoidal transfer function $G(j\omega) \cdot H(j\omega)$ expressed in dB versus ω.

  (b) Second one is phase angle in degrees versus ω both plotted on the log scale.

- One advantage of Bode plots is that since logarithmic representation is used, multiplication and division of magnitudes is easier.

- Both high frequency and low frequency portions can be represented on the same graph because a wide range of frequencies can be represented on the same plot.

- Another advantage of bode plots is an approximate plot using straight line asymptotes can be drawn very quickly and easily and corrections can be made later to obtain an accurate plot.

> **Keynote :**
>
> Both absolute stability and relative stability can be determined using Bode plots.

- We observe that the logarithmic scale is non-linear, and we cannot locate the point $\omega = 0$ on the log scale, since $\log 0 = -\infty$.

- In Bode diagrams frequency ratios are expressed in terms of octaves and decades.

Decade :

- The range of frequency from ω to $10\,\omega$ is called a decade.

- 'Decade' is an increase in frequency by ten times so the slope can be measured in decibels / decade.

- If initially, $\omega = 1$ then range of frequency from $\omega = 1$ to $\omega = 10$ is called a decade.

- For a decade frequency range ($\omega = 1$ to $\omega = 10$) the magnitude is changed from 0dB to a -20 dB value.

Octave :

- Another way of measuring slope is decibels per octave.

- The 'Oct' in octave comes from the latin word eight, but it doesn't means that the frequency is increased by a factor of 8.

- Octave is an increase in frequency by a factor of 2.

- When the frequency is doubled the magnitude is decreased by 6 dB. The range of frequencies from $\omega_1 = 1$ to $\omega_2 = 2$ are called octave.

Therefore the slope is -6 dB/octave.

- The line with slope -20dB/dc can be called as line with a slope -6dB/octave.

- So in, general Bode plot consists of two plots are

1. Magnitude expressed in logarithmic values against logarithmic values of frequency called magnitude plot.

To express magnitude of $G(j\omega) \cdot H(j\omega)$ in dB take $20 \log |G(j\omega) \cdot H(j\omega)|$.

2. Phase angle in degrees against logarithmic values of frequency called phase angle plot.

- The experimental determination of the transfer function if easier is frequency response data is presented in the form of the logarithmic plot.

- Bode plot gives us information more clearly than the corresponding linear plot. The information compressed near the origin in a linear plot can be easily visualized in Bode plot since the logarithmic frequency is magnified near origin.

- Bode plots drawn on semi-log sheets using the log scale for frequency and the linear scale for magnitude and phase.

4.5.1 Basic Factors of $G(j\omega) \cdot H(j\omega)$

The basic factors that very frequently occur in an arbitrary transfer function $G(j\omega) \cdot H(j\omega)$ are as follows :

- Gain K

- Poles at origin (integral factor) $1/j\omega$

- Multiple poles at origin $1/(j\omega)^n$

- Zeros at origin (derivative factor) $j\omega$

- Multiple zeros at origin $(j\omega)^n$

- Factors of the form $K/(j\omega)^r$

- First-order pole on the real axis $1/(1 + j\omega T)$

- Multiple poles on the real axis $1/(1 + j\omega T)^n$

- First order zero on the real axis $(1 + j\omega T)$

- Multiple zeros on the real-axis $(1 + j\omega T)^n$

The starting slope of the Bode plot for the function $G(s) \cdot H(s)$ gets decided by number of poles or zeros at origin present in $G(s) \cdot H(s)$.

- Quadratic poles $\dfrac{1}{[1 + 2\xi\,(j\omega/\omega_n) + (j\omega/\omega_n)^2]}$

- Quadratic zeros $[1 + 2\xi\,(j\omega/\omega_n) + (j\omega/\omega_n)^2]$

Once we become familiar with the logarithmic plots of these basic factors, it is possible to utilize them in constructing a composite logarithmic plot for any general form of $G(j\omega) \cdot H(j\omega)$ by sketching the curves for each factor and adding individual curves graphically, because adding the logarithms of gain corresponds to multiplying them together.

Gain K :

Let us consider $G(s) = K$.

The sinusoidal transfer function

$$G(j\omega) = K$$
$$A = \text{magnitude in dB} = 20 \log |G(j\omega)|$$
$$= 20 \log K$$
$$\text{Phase angle } \phi = LG\,(j\omega) = 0°$$

Constant gain K is a positive real number as a result no phase angle is associated with it.

The log magnitude curve for a constant gain K I b Fig. 4.6 is horizontal straight line at the magnitude of 20 log K dB.

The phase angle of the gain K is zero. So the phase plot is a straight line at 0°.

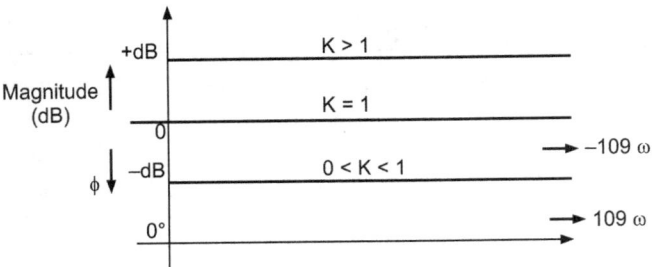

Fig. 4.6 : Bode plot of constant gain K

Poles or zeros at origin

In the T.F. ; $G(j\omega) = \dfrac{K}{j\omega^r}$

If r is + ve → r poles at origin.

If r is − ve → r zeros at origin.

Magnitude in dB

$$20 \log |G(j\omega)| = 20 \log \left|\frac{K}{j\omega^r}\right| = 20 \log K - 20\, r \log (\omega)$$

If there is no pole or zero at origin, the bode plot is 20 log K = constant

For the term 20 log (ω) .

1. Number of pole at origin is zero (r = 0) ; the slope of the line is 0 dB/decade.

2. (r = 1) ; the slope of line is − 20 dB/decade

3. (r = 2); the slope = − 40 dB decade

No. of poles at origin are r; the slope of the line is − 20 r dB/decade.

Similarly for zeros;

1. (r = 0); slope = 0 dB/decade

2. (r = −1) ; slope = 20 dB/decade

3. (r = − 2); slope = − 40 dB/decade

No. of zeros at origin are − r; the slope of the line is + 20 r dB/decade.

In phase plot, the phase given by r poles and zeros at origin is − 90r and + 90r respectively.

- **Pole at Origin (Integral Factor)** $\dfrac{1}{j\omega}$

The logarithmic magnitude 1/jω in dB is

$$20 \log |1/j\omega| = -20 \log \omega \text{ dB}$$

$$G(j\omega) = \frac{1}{j\omega}$$

$$= 0 - \frac{j}{\omega} \text{ (in rectangular for m)}$$

$$= \frac{1}{\omega} \angle 90° \text{ (in polar form)}$$

The magnitude in decibels ;

$$A = 20 \log 1/\omega$$

$$= -20 \log \omega$$

The phase angle,

$$\phi = \angle G(j\omega) = -90°$$

For $\omega = 1$; $|1/j\omega| = -20 \log 1 = 0 \text{ dB}$

For $\omega = 0.1$; $= 20 \log 10 = +20 \text{ dB}$

For $\omega = 10$; $= -20 \log 10 = -20 \text{ dB}$

So, if the magnitude of $-20 \log \omega$ dB is plotted against ω on a logarithmic scale, it is a straight line with a slope of -20 dB/decade passing through the 0 dB line at $\omega = 1$ rad/s.

The phase angle is constant $= -90°$.

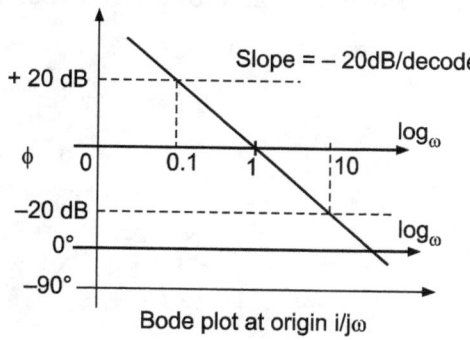

Bode plot at origin i/jω

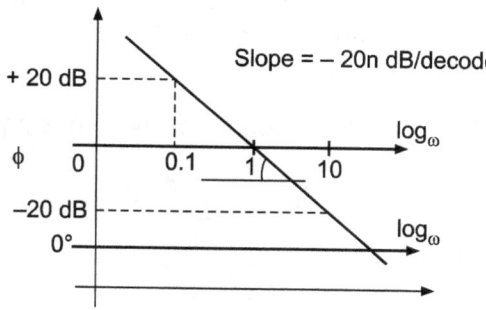

Fig. 4.7

Multiples Poles at Origin $\dfrac{1}{(j\omega)^n}$

$$20 \log |1/(j\omega)^n| = -20 \log \omega_n = -20 n \log \omega$$

So magnitude plot of $\left| \dfrac{1}{(j\omega)^n} \right|$ is a straight line with a slope of -200 dB/decade; passing through 0 dB.

For $\omega = 1$; $|j\omega| = 20 \log 1 = 0 \text{ dB}$

For $\omega = 0.1$; $|j\omega| = 20 \log 0.1 = -20 \text{ dB}$

For $\omega = 10$; $|j\omega| = 20 \log 10 = 20 \text{ dB}$

So the log magnitude curve of $20 \log \omega$ dB is plotted against ω.

Hence the slope at 20 dB/decade and phase angle of $j\omega$ is constant and equal to $+90°$.

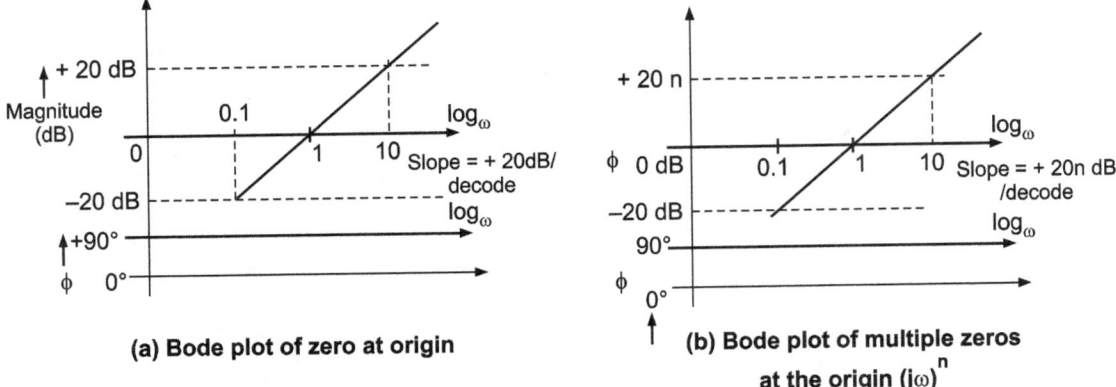

(a) Bode plot of zero at origin   **(b) Bode plot of multiple zeros at the origin $(j\omega)^n$**

Fig. 4.8

- **Multiple zeros at the origin $(j\omega)^n$**

The log magnitude of $(j\omega)^n$ in dB is

$$20 \log |(j\omega)^n| = 20 n \log \omega$$

So the magnitude plot of $(j\omega)^n$ is a straight line with a slope of $+20 n$ dB/decade; passing through the 0 dB line at $\omega = 1$ rad/sec.

Simple Real Poles:

- The transfer function in the time constant form,

$$G(j\omega) = \frac{1}{1 + j\omega T}$$

Magnitude in dB is,

$$20 \log |G(j\omega)| = 20 \log \frac{1}{\sqrt{(1 + \omega^2 T^2)}}$$

$$= -20 \log (1 + \omega^2 T^2)^{1/2}$$

$$= -10 \log [1 + \omega^2 T^2]$$

For low frequencies, for $\omega T_1 << $; the log magnitude can be expressed as;

$$\frac{20}{2} \log [1/(1 + j\omega T)] = 10 \log 1 = 0 \text{ dB}$$

i.e. low frequency asymptote is the zero dB line.

For high frequency, $\omega T >> 1$;

$$20 \log |1/(1 + j\omega T)| = -10 \log \omega^2 T^2$$

$$= 20 \log \left[\frac{1}{\sqrt{1 + \omega^2 T^2}} \right] = -20 \log \omega T = -20 \log \omega - 20 \log T$$

High frequency asymptote is a straight line with -20 dB/dec and it intersects the zero dB frequency asymptote at $\omega T_1 = 1$.

The phase angle is

$$\phi = -\tan^{-1}(\omega T_1)$$

At, $\omega = 1/T$, the log magnitude equals 0 dB.

At $\omega = 10/T$, the log magnitude $= -20$ dB.

Thus, log magnitude curve decreases by 20 dB for every decade of ω.

The log magnitude versus log frequency curve of $\dfrac{1}{(1+j\omega T)}$ can be approximated by the two straight line asymptotes, one a straight line with a slope of 0 dB/decade for the frequency range of $0 < \omega < 1/T$ and the other slope of -20 dB/decade for the frequency range $1/T < \omega < \infty$.

Basics :

Gain : Ratio of output magnitude by input margin.

Gain Margin : As gain 'K' is increased the system stability reduces and for a certain value of K it becomes marginally stable.

Definition : Gain margin is defined as the margin in gain allowable by which gain can be increased till system reaches on the verge of instability.

The positive gain margin means increase in 'K' is possible before system becomes unstable, hence system is stable.

The negative gain margin means K is $> K_{mar}$ and the system becomes unstable.

So K is required to be reduced to make the system stable.

Mathematically defined as,

$$\therefore \qquad G.M. = \frac{1}{|G(j\omega) \cdot H(j\omega)|_{\omega = \omega_{pc}}}$$

In dB $\qquad GM = -20 \log 10 |G(j\omega) \cdot H(j\omega)|_{\omega = \omega pc}$

More +ve GM more stable system.

Phase Crossover : The frequency at which phase angle of $G(j\omega) \cdot H(j\omega)$ is $-180°$ is called phase crossover frequency ω_{pc}.

Gain Crossover : The frequency at which the magnitude of $G(j\omega) \cdot H(j\omega)$ is unity i.e. 1 or 0 dB is called gain crossover frequency.

Phase Margin : Similar to gain, it is possible to introduce phase lag in the system i.e. negative angles without affecting magnitude plot of $G(j\omega) \cdot H(j\omega)$.

Definition : The amount of additional phase lag which can be introduced in the system till system reaches on the verge of instability is called Phase Margin P.M.

The positive phase margin means such negative angle introduction in system is possible before system becomes unstable. Such system is stable.

While negative PM : Present negative phase lag should be changed by adding positive angle hence phase margin is said to be negative and system is unstable.

$$PM = |\angle G(j\omega) \; A\,(j\omega)|_{at \; \omega = \omega_{gc}}$$

$$= -[(-180°)]$$

$$PM = 180° + \angle G(j\omega) \cdot H(j\omega)|_{\omega = \omega_{gc}}$$

Example 4.7 : Draw the Bode plot

$$G(s)\,H(s) = \frac{54\,(s+4)}{s\,(s+1)\,(s^2 + 8s + 36)}$$

Solution : Converting the given transfer function into time constant form.

$$G(s)\,H(s) = \frac{\dfrac{54\,(s+1)\,(4)}{4}}{s\,(s+1)\left(\dfrac{s^2}{36} + \dfrac{8s}{36} + 1\right)36}$$

$$= \frac{6\left(\dfrac{s}{4} + 1\right)}{s\,(s+1)\left(\dfrac{s^2}{36} + \dfrac{1}{20}s + 1\right)}$$

Converting it in frequency domain

$$GH\,(j\omega) = \frac{6\left(\dfrac{j\omega}{4} + 1\right)}{j\omega\,(j\omega + 1)\left(\dfrac{\omega^2}{36} + \dfrac{j\omega}{20} + 1\right)}$$

Comparing the quadratic pole with the standard equation

$$\frac{1}{1 + \dfrac{2j\xi\omega}{\omega_n} - \dfrac{\omega^n}{\omega_n^2}} = \frac{1}{\left(-\dfrac{\omega^2}{36} + \dfrac{j\omega}{20} + 1\right)}$$

$$\therefore \qquad \omega_n^2 = 36$$

$$\omega_n = 6$$

$$\frac{2\xi}{\omega_n} = \frac{1}{20}$$

$$\therefore \qquad \xi = \frac{6}{20 \times 2} = \frac{3}{20} = 0.15$$

Correction factor in magnitude $\omega_n = 6$ is $-20 \log \sqrt{4\rho^2} = 10.4575$ dB

Factor Present in T.F.

Sr. No.	Factor	Magnitude curve	Phase curve
1.	$K = 6$	Straight line of $20 \log K = 15.56$ dB	$\theta = 0°$
2.	$1 + \dfrac{j\omega}{4}$	0 dB/dec for $\omega < 4$ 20 dB/dec for $\omega > 4$	$\theta = \tan^{-1}\left(\dfrac{\omega}{4}\right)$
3.	$\dfrac{1}{j\omega}$	Straight line 20 dB/dec slope and passing through ($\omega = 1$, 0 dB)	$\phi = -90°$
4.	$\dfrac{1}{1 + j\omega}$	0 dB/dec for $\omega < 1$ -20 dB/dec for $\omega > 1$	$\theta = -\tan^{-1}(\omega)$
5.	$\dfrac{1}{1 + \dfrac{j\omega}{20} - \dfrac{\omega^2}{30}}$	0 dB/dec for $\omega < 6$ -40 dB/dec for $\omega > 6$	$\phi = \tan^{-1}\left(\dfrac{\omega/20}{1 - \dfrac{\omega^2}{36}}\right)$

Table for Magnitude Plot:

Table 4.2

Sr. No.	Factor	Resultant Slope	Start Point	End Point
1.	$K = 2$	Straight line of 6.02 dB	0.1	∞
2.	$\dfrac{1}{j\omega}$	-20 dB/dec	0.1	20
3.	$\dfrac{1}{1 + \dfrac{j\omega}{2}}$	$-20 + (-20) = -40$ dB/dec	2	20
4.	$\dfrac{1}{1 + \dfrac{j\omega}{20}}$	$-40 + (-20) = -60$ dB/dec	20	∞

Table for Phase Angle :

$$\phi_{resultant} = -90° - \tan^{-1}\left(\frac{\omega}{2}\right) - \tan^{-1}\left(\frac{\omega}{20}\right)$$

Table 4.3

ω	$\dfrac{1}{j\omega}$	$\tan^{-1}\left(\dfrac{\omega}{2}\right)$	$-\tan^{-1}\left(\dfrac{\omega}{20}\right)$	$\phi_{resultant}$
0.1	− 90°	− 2.862	−0.286	−93.148
0.5	−90°	−14.036	−1.432	−105.468
1	−90°	−26.56	−2.86	−119.42
5	−90°	−68.19	−14.04	−172.23
10	−90°	−78.69	−26.56	−195.25
50	−90°	−87.71	−68.19	−245.9
100	−90°	−88.85	−78.69	−257.54
500	−90°	−89.77	−87.71	−267.48

From the bode plot

$$\omega_{pc} = 6 \text{ rad/sec} \qquad GM = 20 \text{ dB}$$
$$\omega_{gc} = 1.8 \text{ rad/sec} \qquad PM = 48°$$

Since $\omega_{gc} < \omega_{pc}$, system is stable

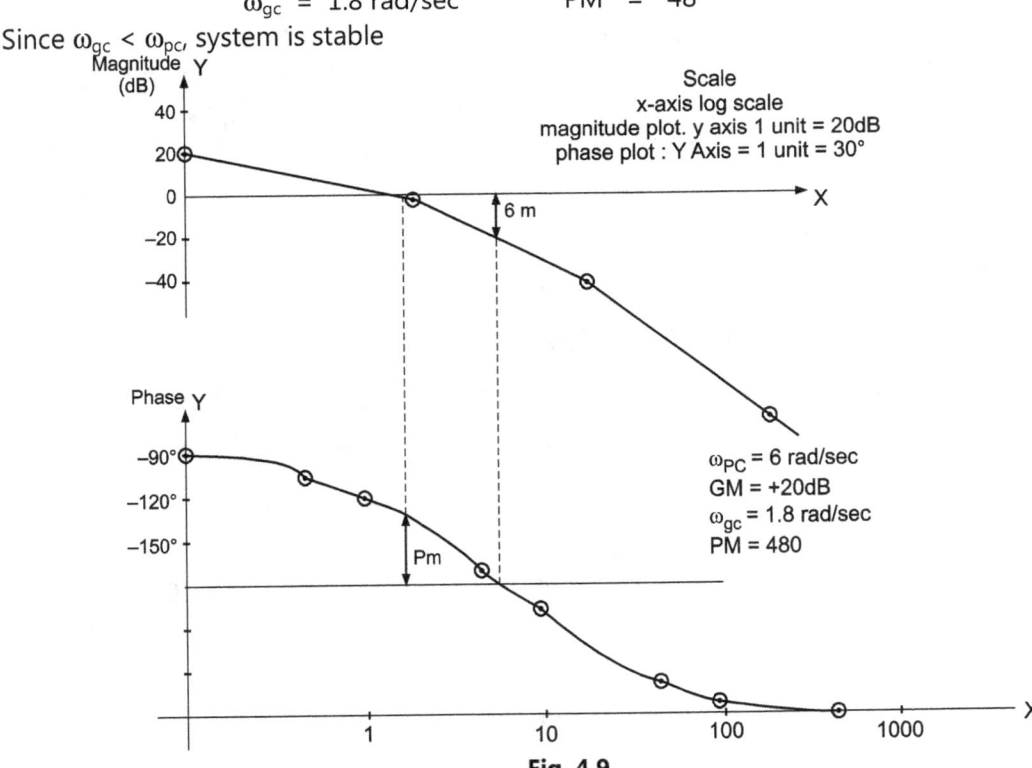

Fig. 4.9

Example 4.8 : Draw the Bode plot

$$G(s)\,H(s)\ =\ \frac{80}{s\,(s+2)\,(s+20)}$$

Solution :

Step 1 : Solving the equation in standard time constant form

$$G(s)\,H(s)\ =\ \frac{80}{s\times2\left[1+\dfrac{s}{2}\right]\times20\left[1+\dfrac{s}{20}\right]}$$

$$=\ \frac{2}{s\left[1+\dfrac{s}{2}\right]\left[1+\dfrac{s}{20}\right]}$$

Step 2 : Obtain frequency domain transfer function (s = jω)

$$G(j\omega)\,H(j\omega)\ =\ \frac{2}{j\omega\left[1+\dfrac{j\omega}{2}\right]\left[1+\dfrac{\omega}{20}\right]}$$

Step 3 : Factors present in the T.F.

(a) Poles at origin $=\dfrac{1}{j\omega}$

(b) First order pole $=\dfrac{1}{\left[1+\dfrac{j\omega}{2}\right]}$

$\therefore\qquad\qquad \omega_0\ =\ 2$

(c) First order pole $=\dfrac{1}{\left[1+\dfrac{j\omega}{20}\right]}$ $\quad\therefore\ \omega_{c2}=20$

(d) Constant K = 2

Step 4 : Table of factor

Table 4.4

Sr. No.	Factor	Magnitude curve	Phase curve
1.	K = 2	Straight line of 20 log 2 = 6.02 dB	$\phi = 0°$
2.	$\dfrac{1}{j\omega}$	Straight line of slope of − 20 dB/dec passing through [ω = 1.0 dB]	$\phi = 90°$ for all value of ω

Contd...

| 3. | $\dfrac{1}{1 + \dfrac{j\omega}{2}}$ | Line slopes are
1. 0 dB/dec for $\omega < 2$
2.   20 dB/dec for $\omega > 2$ | $\phi = \tan^{-1}[\omega/2]$ for all value of ω |
| 4. | $\dfrac{1}{1 + \dfrac{j\omega}{20}}$ | Line slopes are
(i) 0 dB/dec for $\omega < 20$
(ii) -20 dB/dec for $\omega > 20$ | $\phi = \tan^{-1}\left(\dfrac{\omega}{20}\right)$ for all values of ω |

Step 5 : Table for magnitude plot

Table 4.5

Sr. No.	Factor	Resultant Slope	Standard Point	End Point
1.	$K = 6$	Straight line of 15.56 dB	0.1	∞
2.	$\dfrac{1}{j\omega}$	-20 dB/dec	0.1	1
3.	$\dfrac{1}{1 + j\omega}$	$-20 + (-20) =$ -40 dB/dec	1	4
4.	$\dfrac{j\omega}{1 + \dfrac{}{4}}$	$-40 + 20 =$ -20 dB/dec	4	6
5.	$\dfrac{1}{1 + \dfrac{j\omega}{20} - \dfrac{\omega^2}{36}}$	$-20(-40) =$ -60 dB/dec	6 (add error coefficient 10.46 dB)	∞

Step 6 : Table for phase angle

$$\phi_{resultant} = -90° -\tan^{-1}(\omega) - \tan^{-1}\left(\frac{\omega}{4}\right) - \tan^{-1}\left[\frac{\omega/20}{1 - (\omega^2/36)}\right]$$

Table 4.6

ω	$\dfrac{1}{j\omega}$	$-\tan^{-1}(\omega)$	$-\tan^{-1}\left(\dfrac{\omega}{4}\right)$	$-\tan^{-1}\left[\dfrac{\omega/20}{1-(\omega^2/30)}\right]$	ϕ_R
0.1	$-90°$	$-5.71°$	$-1.43°$	$-0.29°$	$-97.43°$
0.5	$-90°$	$-26.56°$	$-7.13°$	$-1.44°$	$-125.13°$
1	$-90°$	$-45°$	$-14°$	$-2.94°$	$-151.94°$
2	$-90°$	$-63.43°$	$-26.56°$	$-6.42°$	$-186.41°$
4	$-90°$	$-75.96°$	$-45°$	-19.79	$-230.75°$
6	$-90°$	$-80.54°$	$-56.31°$	$2°$	$-226.85°$
8	$-90°$	$-82.87°$	$-63.43°$	$27.22°$	$-209.08°$
10	$-90°$	$-84.29°$	$-68.19°$	$15.71°$	$-226.77°$
50	$-90°$	$-88.85°$	$-85.43°$	$2.09°$	$-262.19°$
100	$-90°$	$-89.43°$	$-87.71°$	$1.03°$	$-266.11°$

Step 7 : From the bode plot

$$\omega_{pc} = 1.9 \text{ rad/sec}$$
$$GM = 6 \text{ dB}$$
$$\omega_{gc} = 2.6 \text{ rad/sec}$$
$$PM = -24°$$

Since $\omega_{gc} > \omega_{pc}$, system is unstable.

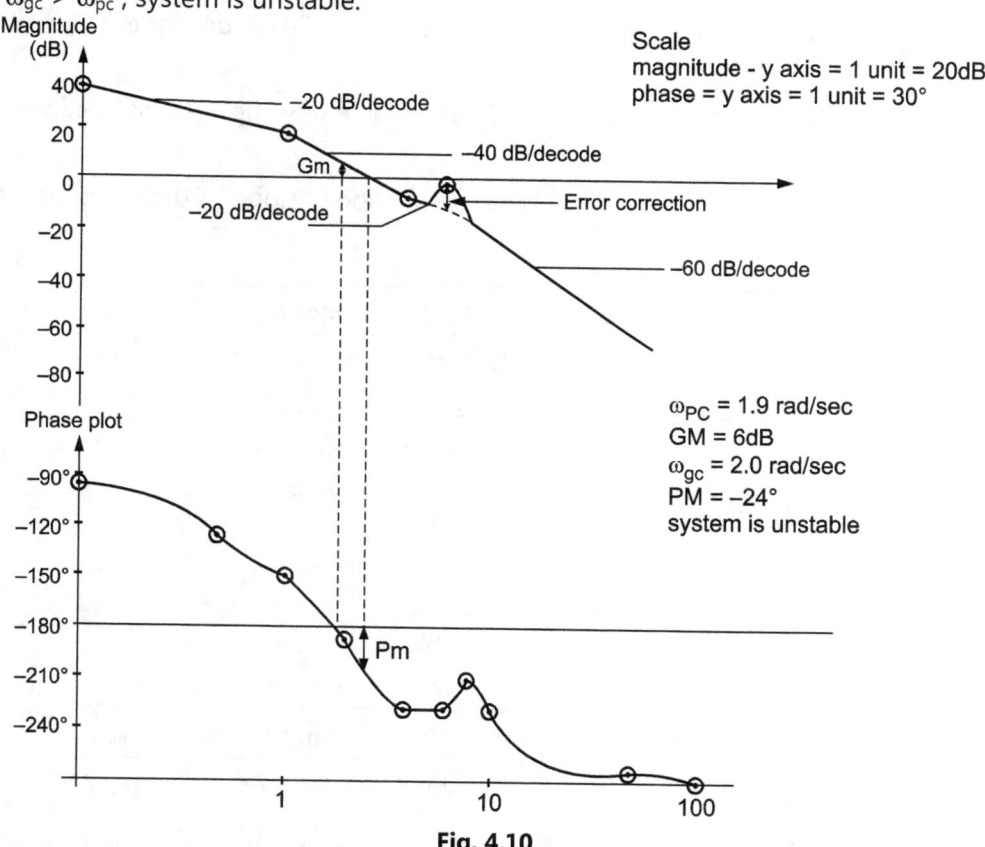

Fig. 4.10

Example 4.9 : For a unity feedback system with open loop transfer

$$G(s) = \frac{40 (s + 5)}{s (s + 10) (s + 2)}$$

Draw the bode plot. Determine G.M., P.M., ω_{gc}, ω_{pc}, comment on stability of the system.

Solution :

$$G(s) = \frac{40 (s + 5)}{s (s + 10) (s + 2)}$$

$$= \frac{40 \times 5 (1 + s/5)}{s \times 10 \times 2 \left(1 + \frac{s}{10}\right)\left(1 + \frac{s}{2}\right)} = \frac{10 (1 + 0.25)}{s (1 + 0.15) (1 + 0.55)}$$

Factors :

- $K = 0$, $20 \log K = 20 \log_{10} = 20$ dB

- $\dfrac{1}{s}$ one pole at origin. Straight line slope $-$ 20 dB/dec passing through intersection of $\omega = 1$.

- $\dfrac{1}{(1 + 0.55)}$ $T_F = \omega_{cl} = \dfrac{1}{T_1} = 2$ rad/s straight line of slope = $-$ 20 dB/dec for $\omega > 2$.

- $(1 + 0.2s)$ simple zero, $T_2 = 0.2$, $\omega_{c_2} = \dfrac{1}{T_2} = 5$ straight line of slope + 20 dB/dec for $\omega > 5$.

- $\dfrac{1}{(1 + 0.1s)}$ simple pole, $T_3 = 0.1$, $\omega_{c_3} = 10$ rad straight line of slope $-$ 20 dB/dec for $\omega > 10$.

Resultant Slope :

Range of ω	Resultant Slope
$0 \angle \omega \angle \omega_c$ (2)	$-$ 20 dB/dec (pole at origin)
$2 \angle \omega \angle \omega_c$ (5)	$-$ 20 $-$ 20 = $-$ 40 dB
$5 \angle \omega \angle \omega_c$ (10)	$-$ 40 + 20 = $-$ 20 dB/dec
$10 \angle \omega \angle \infty$	$-$ 20 $-$ 20 = $-$ 40 dB/dec

Phase angle table

$$G(j\omega)\, H(j\omega) \;=\; \frac{10\,(1 + 0.2\, j\omega)}{j\omega\,(1 + 0.1\, j\omega)\,(1 + 0.5\, j\omega)}$$

Table 4.7

ω	$1/j\omega$	$-\tan^{-1} 0.5\,\omega$	$\tan^{-1} 0.2\,\omega$	$-\tan^{-1} 0.1\,\omega$	ϕ_R
0.2	$-$ 90	$-$ 5.71°	+ 2.29°	$-$ 1.14°	$-$ 94.56°
5	$-$90	$-$68.19°	+ 45°	$-$26.56°	$-$139.57°
10	$-$90	$-$78.69°	+ 63.43°	$-$45°	$-$150.11°
50	$-$90	$-$87.71	+ 84.29°	$-$78.69°	$-$172.11°
∞	$-$90	$-$90°	+ 90°	$-$90°	$-$180°

ω_{gc} = 4.4 rad/sec

ω_{pc} = ∞

GM = + ∞ dB

PM = + 42°

As GM = + ∞ dB, the system is absolutely stable in nature.

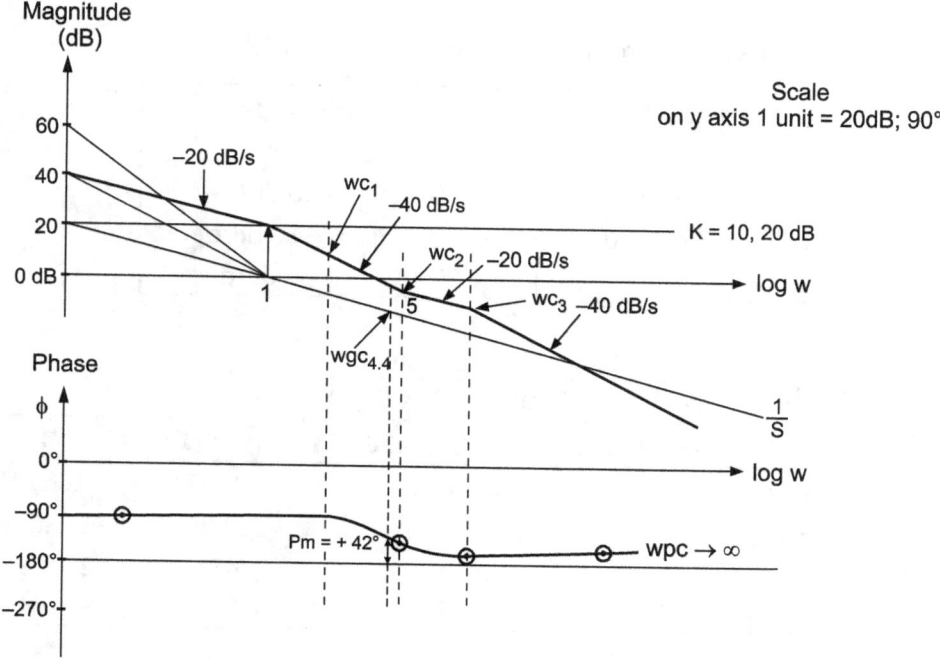

Fig. 4.11

Example 4.10 : A unity F.B control system has $G(s) = \dfrac{20\,(s+10)}{s^2\,(s+2)\,(s+7)}$ sketch bode plot determine G.M., P.M. comment on the stability.

Solution : $G(s) \cdot H(s)$ is the time constant form

$$G(s)\,H(s) \;=\; \frac{20 \times 10\left(1 + \dfrac{s}{10}\right)}{s^2 \times 2 \times \left(1 + \dfrac{s}{2}\right) \times 7 \times \left(1 + \dfrac{s}{7}\right)}$$

$$=\; \frac{14.2857\,(1 + 0.1\,s)}{s^2\,(1 + 0.5\,s)\,(1 + 0.1428s)}$$

Factors :

- $K = 14.2875$, $20 \log K = 23.09$ dB

- $1/s^2$, 2 pools at origin straight line of slope $-$ 40dB/dec passing through intersection of 0 dB and $\omega = 1$ lines.

- $\omega_{c1} = \dfrac{1}{T_1} = \dfrac{1}{0.5} = 2$, simple pole, slope $-$ 20 dB/dec

- $\omega_{c2} = \dfrac{1}{T_2} = \dfrac{1}{0.1428} = 7$, simple pole, slope $-$ 20 dB/dec

---

- $\omega_{c3} = \dfrac{1}{T_3} = \dfrac{1}{0.1} = 10$, simple zero, slope + 20 dB/dec

Frequency Range	Resultant Slope
$0 \angle \omega \angle 2$	– 40 dB/dec
$2 \angle \omega \angle 7$	– 40 – 20 = – 60 dB/dec
$7 \angle \omega \angle 10$	– 60 + (–20) = – 80 dB/dec
$10 \angle \omega \angle \infty$	– 80 + 20 = – 60 dB/dec

Phase Angle :

$$G(j\omega)\, H(j\omega) = \frac{14.2857\,(1 + 10.1\, j\omega)}{(j\omega)^2\,(1 + 0.5\, j\omega)\,(1 + 0.1428\, j\omega)}$$

ω	$1/(j\omega)^2$	$-\tan^{-1} 0.5\,\omega$	$-\tan^{-1} 0.1428\,\omega$	$\tan^{-1} 0.1\,\omega$	ϕR
0.2	–180	–5.71°	–1.6359°	1.1457°	–186.2°
2	–180	–45°	–15.93°	11.3°	–229.63°
10	–180	–78.69°	–55°	45°	–268.69°
∞	–180	–90°	–90°	90°	–270°

$\omega_{gc} = 2.9$ rad/s

$\omega_{pc} = 0$ rad/s

PM $= -60°$

GM $= -\infty$ dB

Unstable system.

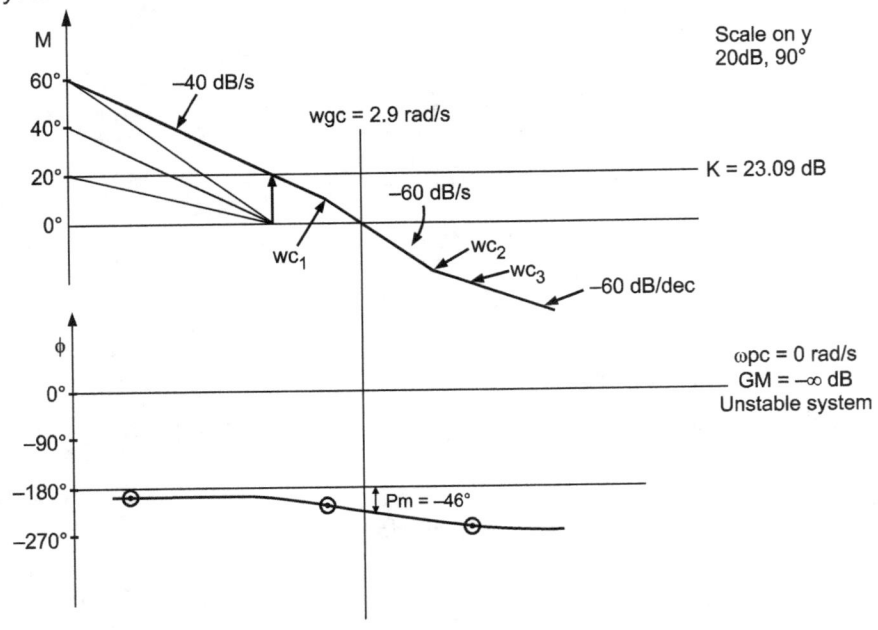

Fig. 4.12

4.6 POLAR PLOT

In polar plot, the magnitude of $G(j\omega) \cdot H(j\omega)$ is plotted against the phase angle of $G(j\omega) \cdot H(j\omega)$ for various values of ω varied from 0 to ∞.

$$M = |G(j\omega) H(j\omega)| = \text{Magnitude}$$
$$\phi = \angle G(j\omega) \cdot H(j\omega) = \text{Phase}$$

We can obtain values of M and ϕ by varying the input frequency ω from 0 to ∞.

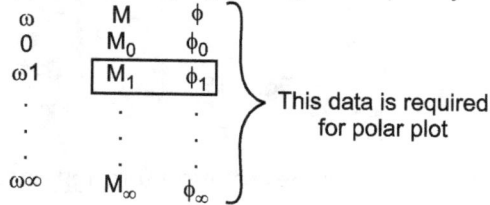

ω	M	ϕ
0	M_0	ϕ_0
$\omega 1$	M_1	ϕ_1
.	.	.
.	.	.
.	.	.
$\omega\infty$	M_∞	ϕ_∞

This data is required for polar plot

Fig. 4.13

Each value of M and ϕ corresponding to particular frequency ω decides a point as per the polar co-ordinate system.

*   Polar co-ordinates $M_1 < \phi_1$.
*   This is the point which is tip of the phasor of magnitude M1 plotted at an angle ϕ_1.
*   Paragraph sheet has concentric circles and radial lines. A concentric circle represents the magnitude whereas a radial line represents the phase angles.

The positive angles are measured anticlockwise while the negative angles are measured in clockwise direction.

Definition : Polar plot is the locus of tips of the phasors of various magnitudes plotted at the corresponding phase angles for different values of frequencies form 0 to ∞.

Polar plot starts at $\omega = 0$; while terminates at $\omega = \infty$.

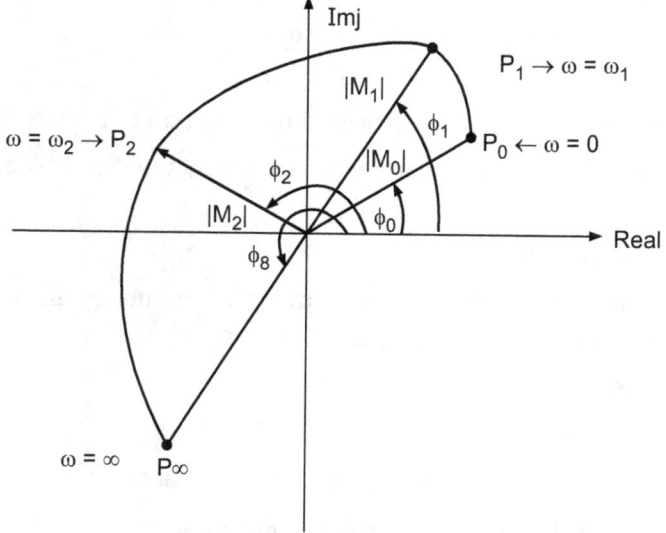

Fig. 4.14 : Polar plot

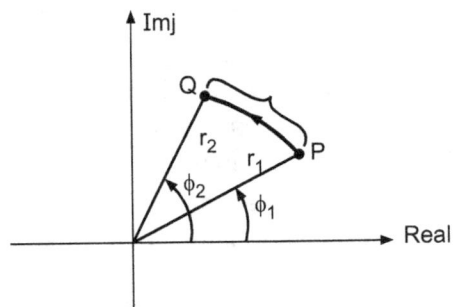

Fig. 4.15

Consider two points $r_1 < \phi_1$ and $r_2 < \phi_2$.

When point P moves to point Q it undergoes rotation through angle $\phi_2 - \phi_2$.

- If $\phi_2 - \phi_1 \rightarrow + ve \rightarrow$ rotation is anticlockwise

- If $\phi_2 - \phi_1 \rightarrow - ve \rightarrow$ rotation is clockwise

So $\omega \rightarrow 0$ $M_0 < \phi_0 \rightarrow$ Starting point

$\omega \rightarrow \infty$ $M_\infty < \phi_\infty \rightarrow$ Terminating point

$\phi_\infty - \phi_0$ = Rotation of starting point to reach to the terminating point.

Keynote

- +ve phase angle is measured in anticlock wave from 0.

- −ve phase angle is measured in clock wave from 0.

Principle of Argument :

Function q(s) can be expressed as

$$q(s) = \frac{(s - \alpha_1)(s - \alpha_2) \ldots (s - \alpha_m)}{(s - \beta_1)(s - \beta_2) \ldots (s - \beta_n)} \qquad \ldots(1)$$

q(s) → said to be analytic in the s-plane provided the function and all its derivatives exist.

Singular Point : The point in the s-plane where the function (or its derivatives) does not exist.

Procedure to Draw Polar Plot :

To sketch the polar plot of $G(j\omega)$ for the entire range of frequency ω, i.e., from 0 to infinity, there are four key points that usually need to be known:

- The start of plot where $\omega = 0$,

- The end of plot where $\omega = \infty$,

- Where the plot crosses the real axis, i.e., $Im(G(j\omega)) = 0$, and

- Where the plot crosses the imaginary axis, i.e., $Re(G(j\omega)) = 0$.

4.7 NYQUIST PLOT

The Nyquist stability criterion relates the location of the roots of the characteristic equation to the open-loop frequency response of the system. In this, the computation of closed-loop poles is not necessary to determine the stability of the system and the stability study can be carried out graphically from the open-loop frequency response. Therefore experimentally determined open-loop frequency response can be used directly for the study of stability; when the feedback path is closed. The Nyquist criterion has the following features that make it an alternative method that is attractive for the analysis and design of control systems. 1. In addition to providing information on absolute and relative.

Nyquist criterion is not interested in the exact shape of the q(s) – plane contour; H only concerns us in the encirclement of the origin by the q(s)-plane contour.

For any non-singular point s in the s-plane contour, there corresponds a point q(s) on the q(s) plane contour.

The point q(s) is given as

$$|q(s)| = \frac{|s - \alpha_1|\ |s - \alpha_2|\ \ldots}{|s - \beta_1|\ |s - \beta_2|\ \ldots}$$

$$\angle q\ (s) = \angle\ (s - \alpha_1) + \angle\ (s - \alpha_2) + \ldots - \angle\ (s - \beta_1) - \angle\ (s - \beta_2) \ldots$$

If the contour in the s-plane does not enclose any zero or pole, the corresponding contour in the q(s)-plane then will not encircle the origin.

For each zero of q(s) enclosed by the s-plane contour, the corresponding q(s)-plane contour encircles the origin once in the clockwise direction.

Since the pole term (s-β_1) is in the denominator of q (s), the q(s) –plane contour experiences an angle change of + 2π, which means one counter clockwise encirclement of the origin.

If P-poles and z-zeros, then q(s) plane contour must encircle the origin z times in the clockwise direction and p times in the counterclockwise direction, resulting in a net encirclement of the origin (p-z) times in a counter clockwise direction.

Example : z – 2, P = 4.

• Net encirclement of origin by the q(s) – plane contour is 2π(4 – 2) = 4π rad, i.e. 2 counterclockwise revolution.

In general poles of the function are its singularities.

Encirclements : For closed path, it is necessary to understand the concept of an encirclement.

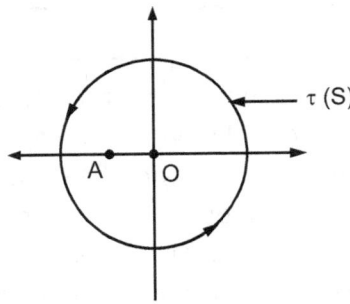

Fig. 4.16

A point is said to be encircled by a closed path if it is found to lie inside that closed path.

In Fig. 4.15 points O, A and all which are inside the path are encircled by that path.

Counting Encirclements :

- Draw a vector from a point whose encirclements are to be determined, in such a way to join any direction. Avoid confusing directions.

- Identify the number of intersections of this vector with a closed path.

- Mark these interactions with small arrow on the same vector indicating direction of closed path at the time of intersection.

- Cancel the oppositely directed encirclements. The remaining arrow gives us the number of encirclement of that point.

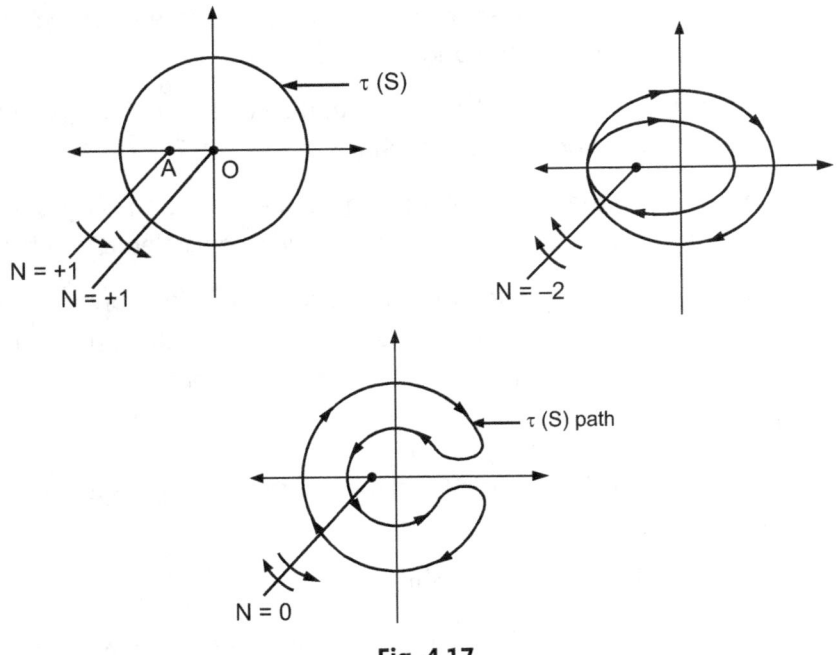

Fig. 4.17

Example 4.11 : Sketch the Nyquist plot for system with

$$G(s)\,H(s) \;=\; \frac{(1 + 0.5s)}{s^2\,(1 + 0.1\,s)\,(1 + 0.02s)}$$

Comment on the stability.

Solution : Nyquist Path

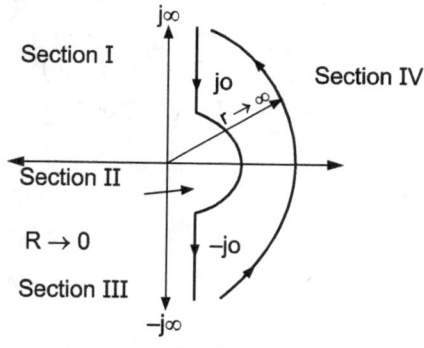

Fig. 4.18

Step 1 : P = 0

Step 2 : N = –P = 0 for stability

Step 3 : Two poles at origin.

Step 4 : $G\,(j\omega)\,H(j\omega) = \dfrac{1 + 0.5\,j\omega}{(j\omega)\,(j\omega)\,(1 + 0.1j\omega)\,(1 + 0.02\,j\omega)}$

Section I : $S = j\infty + 0s = j0$

Starting point

$\omega \to +\infty,\; \dfrac{0 \angle 90°}{90°.90°.90°.90°} = 0 \angle -270°$

Terminating point

$\omega \to 0,\; \infty \angle \dfrac{0°}{90°\;90°\;0°\;0°} = \infty \angle - 180°$

$\therefore\qquad - 180° - (-270°) \;=\; 90°$

Anticlockwise rotation

Section II : $S = j_0$ to $s = - j_0$

Starting point

$$\omega = 0,\, \infty \angle - 180°$$

Terminating point

$\omega \to - 0,\; \infty \dfrac{\angle 0°}{-90° - 90°\; 0°\; 0°} = \infty \angle 180°$

$\therefore\qquad 180° - (- 180°) \;=\; 360°$

Anticlockwise rotation.

Section III : Is mirror image of section I

Section IV : Is not required.

Step 5 : $G(j\omega)\, H(j\omega) \;=\; \dfrac{(1 + 0.5\, j\omega)}{(-\omega^2)\,(1 + 0.1\, j\omega)\,(1 + 0.02\, j\omega)}$

Rationalizing $G(j\omega) \cdot H(j\omega)$ and separating real and imaginary parts, we get

$$G(j\omega)\, H(j\omega) \;=\; \frac{(1 + 0.5\, j\omega)\,[1 - 0.12\, j\omega - 0.002\, j\omega^2]}{(-\omega^2)\,(1 + 0.01\,\omega^2)\,(1 + 0.0004\omega^2)}$$

$$=\; \frac{(1 + 0.058\omega^2)}{D} \;+\; j\omega\,\frac{[0.38 - 0.001\,\omega^2]}{D}$$

Equating imaginary parts, we get

$\omega\,(0.38 - 0.001\,\omega^2) \;=\; 0$

$\therefore$ $\omega^2 \;=\; \dfrac{0.38}{0.001} = 380$ $\omega_{pe} \;=\; 19.4935\ \text{rad/sec}$

Substituting in real parts

$$P + Q \;=\; \frac{(1 \times 0.058 \times 380)}{(-380)\,(1 + 0.01 \times 380)\,(1 + 0.0004 \times 380)} \;=\; -\,0.0109$$

Step 6 : The section I starts from origin tangential to $-270°$ and crossing $-$ve real axis at point $Q = -0.109$ and is terminating at $\infty\, \angle -180°$ i.e. mapping of $S = j_0$. So rotation of plot in section I is 90° anticlockwise but it is crossing $-$ve real axis while during so. Nuquist plot is

Step 7 : Critical point $-1 + j0$ is getting encircled once in clockwise and once in anticlockwise.

$\therefore$ $W = 0$

This satisfies the stability criterion

$\therefore$ System is stable.

$$GM \;=\; 20\log\frac{1}{|04|} \;=\; 20\log\left|\frac{1}{0.0109}\right|\ dB = 39.19\ dB$$

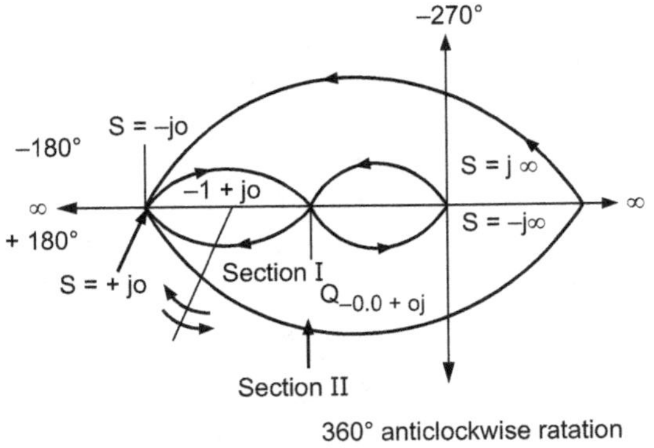

360° anticlockwise ratation

Fig. 4.19

Example 4.12 : Find if the system is stable. Using Nyquist plot

$$G(s)\,H(s)\;=\;\frac{1}{s\,(s+1)}$$

Solution :

Step 1 : No open loop pole in right half of s-plane hence p = 0.

Step 2 : According to Nyquist criteria , N = – P = 0 for stability.

Step 3 : Due to pole at origin, the Nyquist path is as shown.

Step 4 : Analysis of section

$$G(j\omega)\,H\,(j\omega)\;=\;\frac{1}{j\omega\,(1+j\omega)}$$

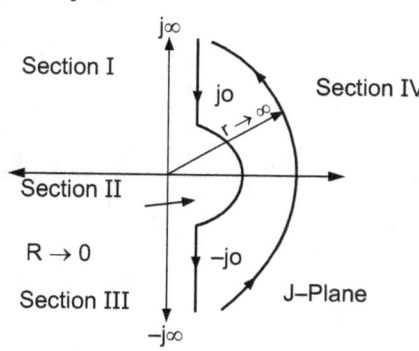

Fig. 4.20

Section I : S = j∞ to s = j0

Starting point

$$\omega \to \infty\; 0 \angle \frac{0°}{90°\;90°}\;=\;0\angle-180°$$

Terminating point

$$\omega \to 0\;\infty \angle \frac{0°}{90°\;0°}\;=\;\infty\angle-90°$$

$$-90° - (-180°)\;=\;90° \;...Anticlockwise$$

Section II :   s = j∞ to s = –j$_0$

Starting point ω.

$$W \to +\,0,\;\infty\;=\;\angle-90°$$

Terminating point

$$W \to -0,\;\infty\;=\;\angle\,90°$$

$$90° - (-90°)\;=\;+\,180° \text{ anticlockwise}$$

Unit IV | 4.37

Section III : Mirror image of section I about real axis.

Section IV : Not required for closed loop stability.

Section V : Intersection with negative real axis.

$$G(j\omega)\, H(j\omega) \;=\; \frac{(-j\omega)\,(1 - j\omega)}{(j\omega)\,(-j\omega)\,(1 + j\omega)\,(1 - j\omega)}$$

Rationalize

$$=\; \frac{-\,\omega^2 - j\omega}{\omega^2\,(1 + \omega^2)} = \frac{-1}{1 + \omega^2}$$

Thus imaginary part is zero for $\omega = 0$ but $\omega = 0$ is not on the Nyquist plot hence the Nyquist plot does not interest the negative real axis at finite point.

Section VI : Nyquist plot shown

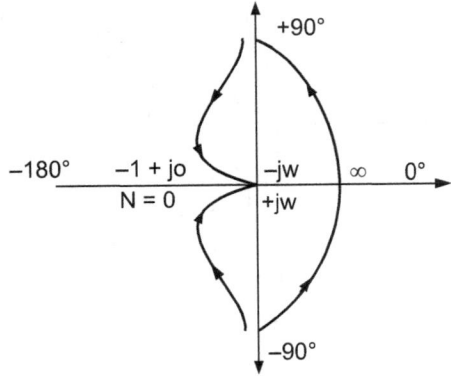

Fig. 4.21

Section VII : The Nyquist plot does not encircle $-1 + j_0$ hence N = 0. This matches with the criteria in step 2. Thus, the given system is stable in nature.

SUMMARY

- For marginally stable systems,
  - ➤ $\omega_{gc} = \omega_{pc}$
  - ➤ G(j)H(j) at $\omega = \omega_{pc} = 1$
  - ➤ GM = 0 dB
- For Unstable systems,
  - ➤ $\omega_{gc}\, \omega_{pc}$
  - ➤ G(j)H(j) at $\omega = \omega\, pc > 1$
  - ➤ GM = in negative dB
  - ➤ Gain is to be reduced to make the system stable

EXERCISE

1. The open-loop transfer function of a control system is $G(s)H(s) = \dfrac{10}{s(1 + 0.5S)(1 + 0.1S)}$

2. Draw the Bode plot and determine the gain crossover frequency, and phase and gain margins

3. Write notes on correlation between time & Frequency response of a second order system

4. Derive expressions for M_r, w_r, ω_b of the second order system

5. Explain Gain and Phase Margin in detail.

SOLVED UNIVERSITY PROBLEMS

Example 4.1 : Obtain resonance peak and resonance frequency if;

$G(s).H(s) = \dfrac{21}{s(s + 5)}$ with $H(s) = 1$ **[Dec. 2014]**

Solution : $G(s).H(s) = \dfrac{21}{s(s + 5)}$

Comparing with second order system standard equation

$$\frac{C(s)}{R(s)} = \frac{\omega_n^2}{s^2 + 2\xi\omega_n s + \omega_n^2}$$

We get, $\omega_n = \sqrt{21} = 4.58$

$2\xi\omega_n = 5$ $\therefore$ $\xi = 0.54$

Step 1 : Resonance peak (M_r)

$$M_r = \frac{1}{2\xi\sqrt{1 - \xi_2}} = \frac{1}{\tau \times 0.54\sqrt{1 - 0.54^2}} = 1.104$$

Step 2 : Resonance frequency $\omega_r = \omega_n\sqrt{1 - 2\xi^2}$

$\therefore$ $\omega_r = 4.58\sqrt{1 - 2 \times 0.54^2} = 2.956$ rad/s.

Example 4.2 : If $G(s).H(s)$

Find Resonance peak and resonance frequency

$$G(s).H(s) = \frac{1}{s(s + 1)}$$ **[June 2015]**

Solution : $G(s).H(s) = \dfrac{1}{s(s + 1)}$

Comparing it with standard second order system equation.

$$\frac{C(s)}{R(s)} = \frac{\omega_n^2}{s^2 + 2\xi\omega_n s + \omega_n^2}$$

We   get $\omega_n = \sqrt{1} = 1$

$$2\xi\omega_n = \xi = 0.5$$

Step 1 : Resonance peak (M_r)

$\therefore$ $M_r = \dfrac{1}{2\xi\sqrt{1-\xi^2}} = \dfrac{1}{2 \times 0.5\sqrt{1-(0.5)^2}} = 1.154$

$\therefore$ $M_r = 1.154$

Step 2 : Resonance frequency (ω_r)

$\therefore$ $\omega_r = \omega_n\sqrt{1-2\xi^2}$

$\therefore$ $\omega_r = 1\sqrt{1-2 \times 0.5^2} = 0.707$ rad/s

$\therefore$ $\omega_r = 0.707$ rad/s

Example 4.3 : If $G(s)\,H(s) = \dfrac{24}{s(s+2)(s+12)}$. Construct bode plot and calculate gain cross-over frequency, phase crossover frequency gain margin, phase margin and comment on stability.   **[May 14] [8M]**

Ans.: $G(s)\,H(s) = \dfrac{24}{s(s+2)(s+12)}$

1. $G(s)\,H(s) = \dfrac{1}{s(1+0.5s)(1+0.0833s)}$ ... time constant form

2.   Factors:

• $K = 1$, 20 log K = 0 dB, no effect on bode plot.

• $\dfrac{1}{s}$, one pole at origin, straight line of slope – 20 dB/dec. Passing through intersection point of $\omega e = 1$ and 0 dB.

• $\dfrac{1}{1+0.5s}$, simple pole, $T_1 = 0.5$, $\omega_{C1} = \dfrac{1}{T_1} = 2$, straight line of slope – 20 dB/dec for $\omega \geq 2$.

• $\dfrac{1}{1+0.0833s}$, simple pole, $T_2 = 0.0833$, $\omega_{C2} = \dfrac{1}{T_2} = 12$ straight line of slope – 20 dB/dec for $\omega \geq 12$. The resultant slope table is.

Range of ω	$0 < \omega < 2$	$2 \leq \omega < 12$	$12 \leq \omega < \infty$
Resultant slope	– 20 dB/dec	– 20 – 20 = – 40 dB/dec	– 40 – 20 = – 60 dB/dec

3. Phase angle table:

$$G(j\omega)\,H(j\omega) = \dfrac{1}{j\omega(1+0.5\,j\omega)(1+0.0833\,j\omega)}$$

ω	$\dfrac{1}{j\omega}$	$-\tan^{-1}0.5\omega$	$-\tan^{-1}0.0833\,\omega$	ϕ_R
2	– 90°	– 45°	– 9.46°	– 144.46°
4	– 90°	– 63.43°	– 18.43°	– 171.86°
5	– 90°	– 68.19°	– 22.62°	– 180.8°
12	– 90°	– 80.53°	– 45°	– 215.5°
∞	– 90°	– 90°	– 90°	– 270°

4. Fig. 4.22 shows the bode plot along with its various specifications.

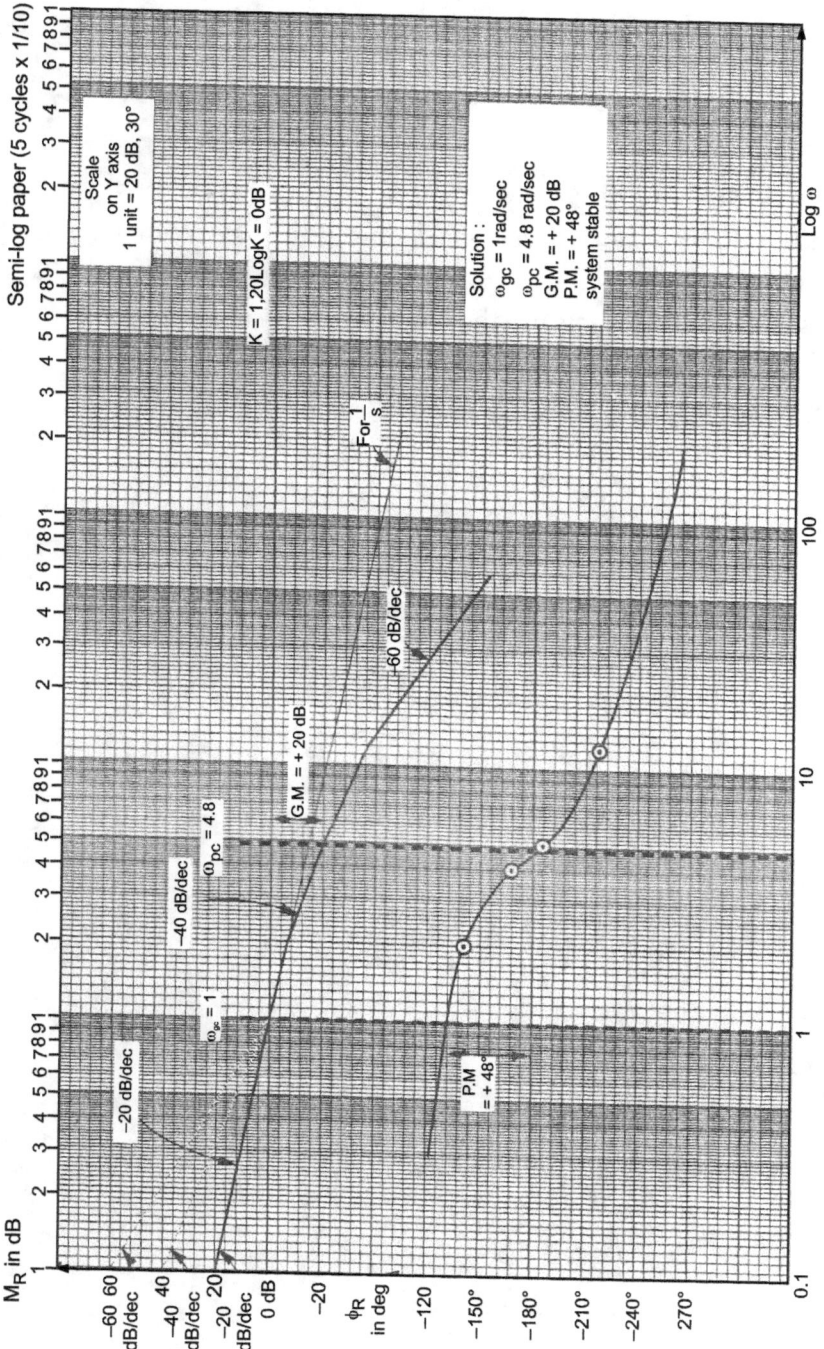

Fig. 4.22

Example 4.4 : Construct Nyquist plot and find phase crossover frequency and gain margin if

: $G(s) \cdot H(s) = \dfrac{1}{s(\, + 1)\,(s + 2)}$. Also comment on stability.   **[Dec. 14] [8M]**

Ans. :

1. Position of poles : s = 0, s = – 1, s = – 2.

As there are no poles on the RHS, P = 0.

Hence for stability, number of encirclements in the counter clockwise direction about (– 1 + 0 j) point should be zero, N = 0.

2. As there is a pole at origin, lets use the modified Nyquist plot.

The Nyquist paths are,

(i) Path a – b;   s = jω

(ii) Path b – c – d; $s = \displaystyle\lim_{R \to \infty} R e^{j\theta}, \quad 90° \le \theta \le 90°$

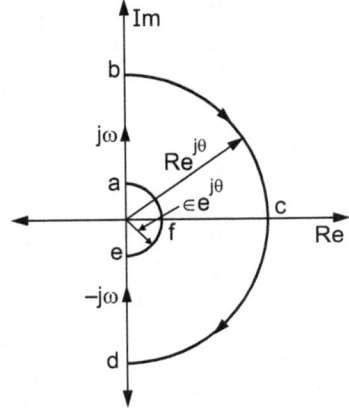

Fig. 4.23

(iii) Path d – e;   s = – jω

(iv) Path e – f – a; $s = \displaystyle\lim_{\epsilon \to 0} \epsilon e^{j\theta}, \quad -90° \le \theta \le 90°$

3. Path a – b :

Here s = jω. This is the polar plot of the system.

$$G(j\omega)\,H(j\omega) = \frac{1}{j\omega\,(j\omega + 1)\,(j\omega + 2)}$$

$$|G(j\omega)\,H(j\omega)| = \frac{1}{\omega \cdot \sqrt{\omega^2 + 1} \cdot \sqrt{\omega^2 + 4}}$$

$$\angle\, G(j\omega)\,H(j\omega) = -90° - \tan^{-1}(\omega) - \tan^{-1}\left(\frac{\omega}{2}\right)$$

$$\text{At } \omega = 0$$

$$|G(j\omega)\,H(j\omega)| = \infty$$

$$\angle\, G(j\omega)\,H(j\omega) = -90°$$

$$\text{At } \omega = \infty$$

$$|G(j\omega)\,H(j\omega)| = 0°$$

$$\angle\, G(j\omega)\,H(j\omega) = -90° - 90° - 90° = -270°$$

Fig. 4.24 show the polar plot.

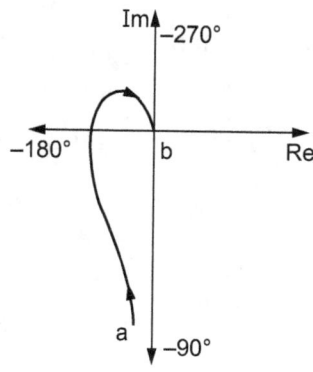

Fig. 4.24

4. **Path b – c – d :**

Here $\qquad s = \lim\limits_{R \to \infty} Re^{j\theta} \qquad G(s)\,H(s) = \dfrac{1}{Re^{j\theta}\,(Re^{j\theta} + 1)\,(Re^{j\theta} + 2)}$

$\because \qquad\qquad R \to \infty$

$\therefore \qquad\qquad G(s)\,H(s) = 0$

This path will map as a dot on the origin.

5. **Path d – e :**

Here $\qquad s = -j\omega$

This is mirror image of path a – b.

6. **Path e – f – a :**

$$s = \lim\limits_{\epsilon \to 0} \epsilon\, e^{j\theta}$$

$$G(s)\,H(s) = \lim\limits_{\epsilon \to 0} \dfrac{1}{\epsilon\, e^{j\theta}\,(\epsilon\, e^{j\theta} + 1)(\epsilon\, e^{j\theta} + 2)} = \dfrac{1}{2\,\epsilon\, e^{j\theta}} = \dfrac{1}{\epsilon\, e^{j\theta}} = \infty\, e^{-j\theta}$$

This will be a semi circle of infinite radius from e to a in the clockwise direction.

As P = 0, for stability N = 0 i. e. there should be no encirclement about the (– 1 + 0j) point.

$\therefore$ X should be less than 1.

At X, $\angle G(j\omega) H(j\omega) = -180°$

As it is phase cross over frequency.

$\therefore \quad \angle G(j\omega) H(j\omega)\Big|_{\omega = \omega_{pc}} = -180°$

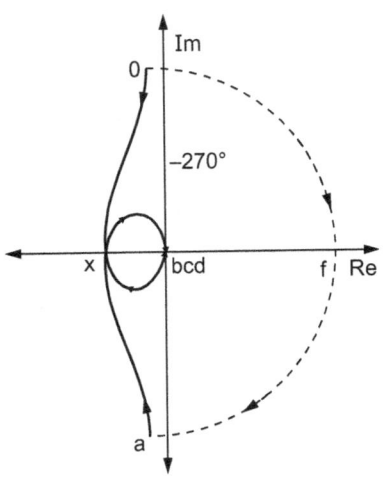

$\therefore \quad -90° - \tan^{-1}(\omega) - \tan^{-1}\left(\dfrac{\omega}{2}\right) = -180°$

$\therefore \qquad\qquad 90° = \tan^{-1}(\omega) + \tan^{-1}\left(\dfrac{\omega}{2}\right)$

Let $\qquad\qquad A = \tan^{-1}(\omega),\ B = \tan^{-1}\left(\dfrac{\omega}{2}\right)$

$\therefore \qquad\qquad 90° = A + B$

Taking   tan   on   both   sides

Fig. 4.25

$\qquad\qquad \tan 90° = \tan(A + B)$

$\qquad\qquad \infty = \dfrac{\tan A + \tan B}{1 - \tan A \cdot \tan B}$

This is true.

$\qquad\qquad 1 - \tan A \cdot \tan B = 0$

$\therefore \qquad \tan A \cdot \tan B = 1$

$\therefore \quad \tan(\tan^{-1}(\omega)) \cdot \tan^{-1}\left(\tan^{-1}\left(\dfrac{\omega}{2}\right)\right) = 1$

$\therefore \qquad\qquad \omega \cdot \dfrac{\omega}{2} = 1 \qquad\qquad \omega^2 = 2$

$\therefore \qquad\qquad \omega = \pm 1.414$

As ω has to be positive,

$\qquad\qquad \omega = \omega_{pc} = \mathbf{1.414.}$

Substituting this in the magnitude condition.

$$G(s) H(s)\Big|_{\omega_{pc} = 1.414} = X = \frac{1}{1.414 \cdot \sqrt{(1.414)^2 + 1} \cdot \sqrt{(1.414)^2 + 4}}$$

$\therefore \qquad\qquad X = \mathbf{0.166}$

As X < 1, there are no encirclements. Hence the given system is stable.

Example 4.5 : Using Routh's criteria, comment on stability if characteristics equation is $s^5 + 2s^4 + 3s^3 + 8s^2 + s + 1 = 0$.   **[May 15] [4 M]**

Ans. :

s^5	1	3	1
s^4	+ 2	8	1
s^3	− 1	0.5	0
s^2	+ 9	1	0
s^1	0.6111	0	
s^0	1		

Example 4.6 : Construct bode plot and calculate GM, PM, ω_{qc} and ω_{pc} if

$G(s) = \dfrac{200 (s + 20)}{s(s + 1) (s + 40)}$ and H(s) = 1.   **[Dec. 15] [8 M]**

Ans.: 1. G(s) H(s) in time constant form is given as,

$$G(s) \, H(s) = \frac{100 (1 + 0.05 \, s)}{s(1 + 2s) (1 + 0.025s)}$$

2. Factors:

- K = 100, 20 log K = 40 dB, straight line parallel to log ω axis.

- $\dfrac{1}{s}$, one pole at origin, straight line of slope − 20 dB/dec.

- $\dfrac{1}{1 + 2s}$, simple pole, $T_1 = 2$, $\omega_{C1} = \dfrac{1}{T_s} = 0.5$, straight line of slope − 20 dB/dec for $\omega \geq 0.5$.

- (1 + 0.05s), simple zero, $T_2 = 0.05$, $\omega_{C2} = \dfrac{1}{T_2} = 20$, straight line of slope + 20 dB/dec for $\omega \geq 20$.

- $\dfrac{1}{1 + 0.025s}$, simple pole, $T_3 = 0.025$, $\omega_{C3} = \dfrac{1}{T_3} = 40$, straight line of slope − 20 dB/dec for $\omega \geq 40$.

Range of ω	0 < ω < 0.5	0.5 ≤ ω < 20	20 ≤ ω < 40	40 ≤ ω < ∞
Resultant slope in dB/dec	− 20	− 20 − 20 = − 40	− 40 + 20 = − 20	− 20 − 20 = − 40

3. Phase angle table, $G(j\omega) \, H(j\omega) = \dfrac{100 (1 + 0.05 \, j\omega)}{j\omega (1 + 2 \, j\omega) (1 + 0.025 \, j\omega)}$

ω	$\dfrac{1}{j\omega}$	$- \tan^{-1} 2\omega$	$+ \tan^{-1} 0.05\omega$	$- \tan^{-1} 0.025 \, \omega$	ϕ_R
0.5	−90°	− 45°	+ 1.43°	− 0.72°	− 134.2°
10	−90°	− 87.1°	+ 26.56°	− 14.1°	− 164.5°
40	−90°	− 89.3°	+ 63.43°	− 45°	− 160.8°
100	−90°	− 89.7°	+ 78.69°	− 68.19°	− 169.2°
∞	−90°	− 90°	+ 90°	− 90°	− 180°

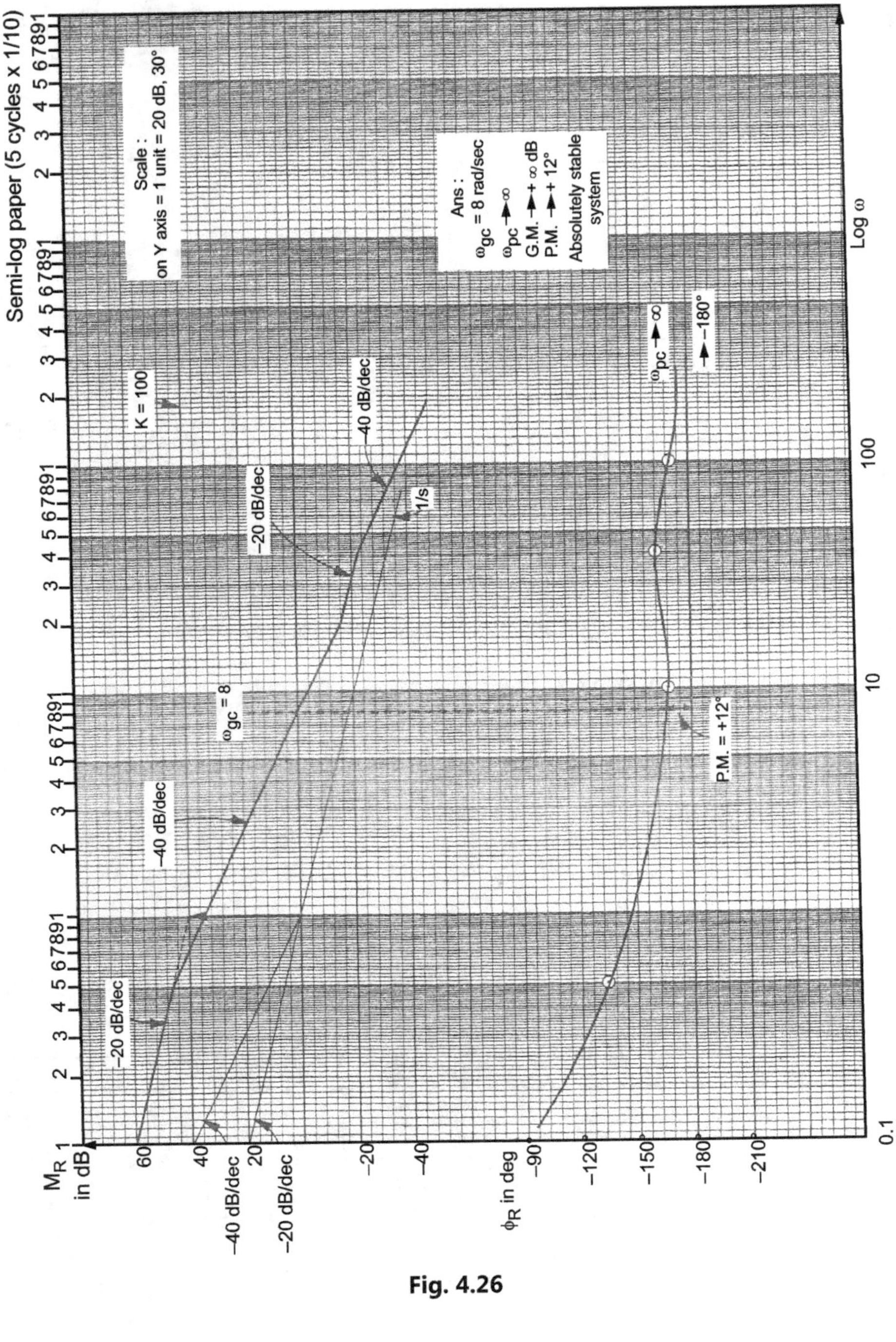
Semi-log paper (5 cycles x 1/10)
Scale :
on Y axis = 1 unit = 20 dB, 30°
Ans :
ωgc = 8 rad/sec
ωpc → ∞
G.M. → + ∞ dB
P.M. → + 12°
Absolutely stable system
K = 100
−40 dB/dec
−20 dB/dec
1/s
ωpc → ∞
→ −180°
ωgc = 8
P.M. = +12°
Log ω
0.1
10
100
MR in dB
60
40
20
−20
−40
φR in deg
−90
−120
−150
−180
−210

Fig. 4.26

◈◈◈

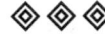

STATE VARIABLE ANALYSIS

5.1 INTRODUCTION

- Systems in which the output is not only dependent on the input but also on the initial conditions are called the systems with memory or dynamic systems.

- Also, the systems in which the output of the system depends only on the input applied at t = 0 are called systems with zero memory or static systems.

- The initial conditions i.e. memory affects the system characterization and subsequent behavior.

- The initial conditions describe the status or state of the system at $t = t_0$.

The state can be regarded as a compact and concise representation of the past history of the system. So the state of the system in brief separates the future from the past history of the system, so that state contains all the information concerning the past history of the system.

- State of the system is actually the combined effect of the values of all the different elements of the system which are associated with initial conditions. So state can be defined as vector x(t) called state vector.

- This x(t), i.e. state at any time 't' is 'n' dimensional vector i.e. column matrix $n \times 1$ as indicated below

$$x(t) = \begin{bmatrix} x_1(t) \\ x_2(t) \\ \vdots \\ \vdots \\ x_n(t) \end{bmatrix}$$

Now these variables $x_1(t)$, $x_2(t)$,...$x_n(t)$ which constitutes the state vector x(t) are called the state variables of the system.

If state at $t = t_1$ is to be decided then we must know $x(t_0)$ and knowledge of the input applied between $t_0 \rightarrow t_1$.

The new state will be $x(t_1)$; which will be acting as a initial state; to find out the state at any time $t > t_1$.

This is called updating of the state.

Advantages of State Space Analysis over Classical Control :

- The use of vector matrix notation simplifies the mathematical representation of the equation

- The transfer function approach assumes zero initial conditions and hence initial conditions cannot be included in the design, where as the state space method allows inclusion of the initial conditions

- Transfer function can be used to represent only linear time invariant systems. But state space technique can be used to represent non-linear and time variant systems as well

- State space method can be more conveniently used than transfer function which explicitly specify the derivatives of all sate variables

- The systems represented in state space can be easily designed for optimizing many performance indices whereas using transfer function approach there is limited scope to design optimal control systems

- The analysis in state space can be carried out for a class of inputs without much complexity

- State space method is more conveniently used compared to Transfer function method

- State space model implements optimal designs of control systems

- Transfer function method cannot be applied to MIMO systems; while state space cab be applied to MIMO systems.

Terminology of State Space Representation :

1. State :

The state of a dynamic system is a smallest set of variables such that the knowledge of these variables at time $t = t_0$, together with the knowledge of inputs for $t \geq t_0$, completely determines the output response of the system for any time $t \geq t_0$.

2. State Variables :

The state variables of dynamic systems are the variables making up a smallest set of variables that determines the state of a dynamic system.

If 'n' variables $x_1, x_2, \dots x_n$ are required to completely describe the behavior of the dynamic system, then 'n' such variables are state variables.

3. State Vector :

It is a vector whose 'n' components are the 'n' state variables. It is the 'n' dimensional column vector and is denoted as;

$$x = [x_1, x_2, \dots x_n]^T$$

4. State Space :

The 'n' dimensional space whose co-ordinate axes are the state variables $x_1, x_2, \dots x_n$ is called as state space

5. State Space Equation :

The state space equations for continuous time linear time invariant systems are :

$$x(t) = Ax(t) + Du(t) \qquad \text{... State Equation}$$

$$y(t) = Cx(t) + Du(t) \qquad \text{... Output Equation}$$

5.1.1 State Model of Linear Systems

Consider multiple input multiple output system as shown in Fig. 5.1 below

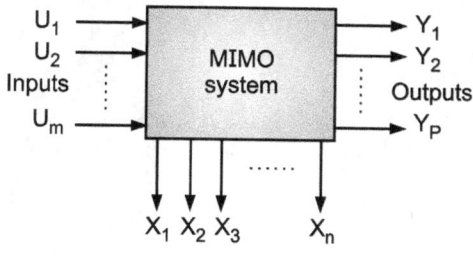

Fig. 5.1

Number of inputs= m

Number of outputs = p

$$U(t) = \begin{bmatrix} u_1(t) \\ u_2(t) \\ : \\ : \\ u_m(t) \end{bmatrix} ; x(t) = \begin{bmatrix} X_1(t) \\ X_2(t) \\ : \\ : \\ X_n(t) \end{bmatrix}$$

$$Y(t) = \begin{bmatrix} Y_1(t) \\ Y_2(t) \\ : \\ : \\ Y_n(t) \end{bmatrix}$$

All columns are vectors having orders m × 1, n × 1 and p × 1 respectively.

For such system state variable representation can be arranged in the form of 'n' first order differential equations.

The state space method is based on the description of nth order system in terms of 'n' first order differential equations of state variables.

In contrast to conventional control theory, the state variable technique involves three types of variables as;

1. Input variables (u)
2. Output variables (y)
3. State variables (x)

$$\frac{dx_1(t)}{dt} = x_i(t) = f_1 (x_1, x_2, \ldots , x_n, u_1, u_2, \ldots u_m)$$

$$\frac{dx_2(t)}{dt} = x_2(t) = f_2 (x_1, x_2, \ldots , x_n, u_1, u_2, \ldots u_m)$$

$$\vdots$$
$$\vdots$$

$$\frac{dx_n(t)}{dt} = x_n(t) = f_n (x_1, x_2, \ldots , x_n, u_1, u_2, \ldots u_m)$$

where f, is the functional operator

$$f = \begin{bmatrix} f_1 \\ f_2 \\ \vdots \\ \vdots \\ f_n \end{bmatrix}$$

Integrating above equation,

$$x_i(t) = x_i(t_0) + \int_{t_0}^{t} f_i (x_1, x_2, \ldots x_n, u_1, u_2, u_m) \, dt$$

where $i = 1, 2, \ldots n$

Thus, n state variables and hence state vector at any time 't' can be determined uniquely.

Hence, any 'n' dimensional time invariant system has state equations in the functional form as;

$$x'(t) = f(x, u)$$

while outputs of such system are dependent on the state of system and the instantaneous inputs.

$\therefore$ Functional output equation can be written as;

$$Y(t) = g(x, u)$$

where, g is the functional operator.

For time variant system, the same equation can be written as

$$x'(t) = f(x, u, t) \ldots \text{state equation}$$
$$Y(t) = g(x, u, t) \ldots \text{output equation}$$

5.1.2 Broad Classification of State Space Representation

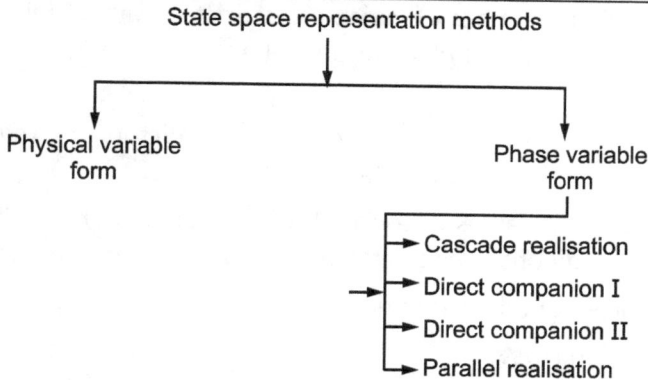

The direct companion-I form is also called as controllable canonical form.

The direct companion-II form is also called as observable canonical form.

The parallel realization form is also called as Diagonal / Jordan canonical form.

5.2 STATE VARIABLE REPRESENTATION USING PHYSICAL VARIABLES

State variables are associated with all the initial conditions of the system for all the state models, it is necessary that the number of state variables is equal and minimal.

The number 'n' indicates the order of the system.

Example : For second order minimum two state variables.

Many times, physical quantities are itself selected as the state variables.

For the electrical systems, the currents through various inductors and the voltage across the various capacitors are selected to be the state variables.

In mechanical systems, the displacements and velocities of energy storing elements such as spring and friction are selected as the state variables.

In general, physical variables associated with all initial conditions of the system associated with energy storing elements, are selected as the state variable of system.

In physical variable form, states chosen are physical variables of the system.

Process :

* Obtain the state model of the given electrical system

* In the electrical network, to Obtain State Model :

$$\dot{X} = A\, x(t) \cdot B\, u\,(t)$$
$$Y = C\, x(t) \cdot D\, u\,(t)$$

To obtain state model, it is necessary to select state variables.

State variables are minimal number of variables associated with all initial conditions of the system. Many a times, the various physical quantities of system itself are selected as state variables.

For the electrical systems, the currents through various indictors and the voltage across the various capacitors are selected to be the state variables.

In general, the physical variables associated with energy storing elements, which are responsible for initial conditions, are selected as state variables of the given system.

- Select state variables from the network.

- Predict the order of the system.

- Solve the network using KVL, KCL.

- Equate the equation in terms of differential form.

$$\therefore \qquad \dot{X} = A\,X(t) + B\,U(t)$$

SOLVED EXAMPLES

Example 5.1 : Obtain the state model of the given electrical system.

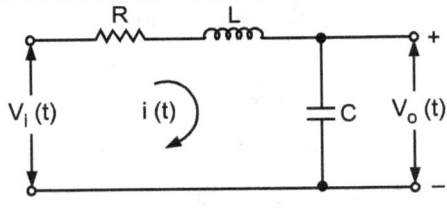

Fig. 5.2

Solution :

In the above network, two energy storage elements L and C. So the two state variables are current through indicator $i(t)$ and voltage across capacitor i.e. $V_0(t)$.

$$\therefore \qquad X_i(t) = i(t) \text{ and } X_2(t) = V_0(t)$$

and $\qquad U(t) = V_i(t) = $ Input variable

Applying KVL to the loop,

$$V_i(t) = i(t) \cdot R + L \cdot \frac{di(t)}{dt} + V_0(t)$$

Arrange it for $di(t)/dt$,

$$\therefore \qquad \frac{di(t)}{dt} = -\frac{R}{L}x_1(t) - \frac{1}{L}V_0(t) + \frac{1}{L}V_i(t)$$

but $\qquad \dfrac{di(t)}{dt} = x_i(t)$

i.e. $\qquad$ $x_i(t) = -\dfrac{R}{L} x_1(t) - \dfrac{1}{L} x_2(t) + \dfrac{1}{L} U(t)$ $\qquad$ ...(1)

while, $\qquad$ $V_o(t) =$ Voltage across capacitor

$\qquad\qquad\qquad = \dfrac{1}{C} \int i\,(t)\,dt$

$\therefore \qquad \dfrac{dv_o(t)}{dt} = \dfrac{1}{C} i\,(t)$

but $\qquad \dfrac{dv_o(t)}{dt} = X_2^{\cdot}\,(t)$

$\therefore$ i.e. $\qquad X_2^{\cdot} = \dfrac{1}{C} i\,(t)$ $\qquad$ ...(2)

The equation (1) and (2) give required state equations

$$\begin{bmatrix} X_1^{\cdot}(t) \\ \\ X_2^{\cdot}(t) \end{bmatrix} = \begin{bmatrix} -R/L & -1/L \\ 1/C & 0 \end{bmatrix} \begin{bmatrix} x_1(t) \\ x_2(t) \end{bmatrix} + \begin{bmatrix} 1/L \\ 0 \end{bmatrix} u(t)$$

i.e. $\qquad X^{\cdot}\,(t) = Ax(t) + Bu(t)$

while, $\qquad Y(t) = V_o(t) = X_2(t)$

$\therefore \qquad Y(t) = [0\ \ 1] \begin{bmatrix} X_1 \\ X_2 \end{bmatrix} + [0] \cdot U(t)$

This is the required state model. As n = 2, it is a second order system.

Example 5.2 : Consider an example of electrical network,

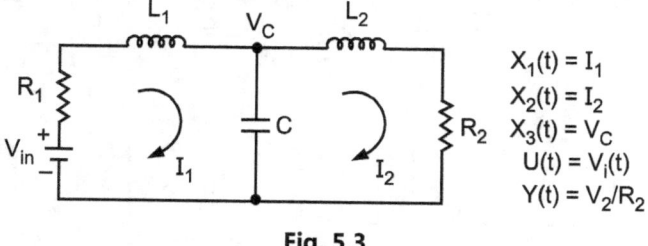

$X_1(t) = I_1$
$X_2(t) = I_2$
$X_3(t) = V_C$
$U(t) = V_i(t)$
$Y(t) = V_2/R_2$

Fig. 5.3

Solution :

The above electrical network consists of three energy storage elements. Hence the history of the network can be completely specified by capacitor voltage and inductor currents at t = 0.

Thus, if capacitor voltage (V_c) and inductor currents (I_1, I_2) are known at t = 0, then for the input V_{in} for time t ≥ 0, the system behavior can be completely determined.

Hence, we have to choose I_1, I_2 and V_c as the state variables.

Applying KVL to loop-I, we get

$$V_{in} - I_1 R_1 - L_1 \frac{dI_1}{dt} - V_c = 0$$

$$\frac{dI_1}{dt} = \frac{1}{L_1}(V_{in} - I_1 R_1 - V_c) \qquad \qquad ...(1)$$

Applying KVL to loop – II

$$V_C - \frac{L_2\, dI_2}{dt} - I_2 R_2 = 0$$

$$\therefore \qquad \frac{dI_2}{dt} = \frac{1}{L_2}[V_C - I_2 R_2] \qquad \qquad ...(2)$$

Now, applying KCL at node V_c

$$I_1 - I_2 - C \cdot \frac{dv_c}{dt} = 0$$

$$\therefore \qquad \frac{dv_c}{dt} = \frac{1}{C}[I_1 - I_2] \qquad \qquad ...(3)$$

Let current through R_2 and voltage across R_2 be the output variables

$$\therefore \qquad \qquad V_2 = I_2 R_2$$

Then the state model is,

State Equation

$$
\begin{bmatrix} x_i' \\ x_2' \\ x_3' \end{bmatrix} =
\begin{bmatrix} \dfrac{dI_1}{dt} \\ \dfrac{dI_2}{dt} \\ \dfrac{dv_c}{dt} \end{bmatrix} =
\begin{bmatrix} -\dfrac{R_1}{L_1} & 0 & -\dfrac{1}{L_1} \\ 0 & -\dfrac{R_2}{L_2} & \dfrac{1}{L_2} \\ \dfrac{1}{C} & -\dfrac{1}{C} & 0 \end{bmatrix}
\begin{bmatrix} I_2 \\ I_2 \\ V_c \end{bmatrix} + V_{in}
$$

Output Equation

$$
\begin{bmatrix} y_1 \\ y_2 \end{bmatrix} =
\begin{bmatrix} I_2 \\ V_2 \end{bmatrix} =
\begin{bmatrix} 0 & 1 & 0 \\ 0 & R_2 & 0 \end{bmatrix}
\begin{bmatrix} I_1 \\ I_2 \\ V_c \end{bmatrix}
$$

In this example, the variables I_1, I_2 and V_c are choosen as state variables which are physically available for the measurement.

Selecting physical variables for state space formulation gives direct relevance to the physical system.

However, sometimes with the choice of physical variables the solutions of state equations becomes difficult.

Example 5.3 : Find the state model of the network.

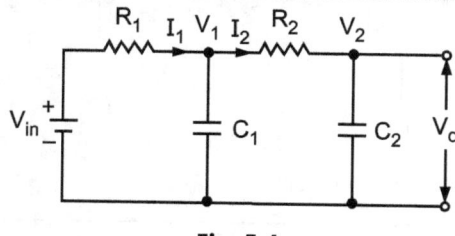

Fig. 5.4

Solution : Above network consists of two energy storage elements C_1 and C_2; hence we select two state variables as V_1 and V_2.

The input variable $V_{in} = U_1(t)$

The output variable $V_2 = Y(t)$

Applying KCL at node V_1, we get

$$I_1 - I_2 - C_1 \frac{dv_1}{dt} = 0$$

$\therefore$
$$\frac{dv_1}{dt} = \frac{1}{C_1}[I_1 - I_2] = \frac{1}{C_1}\left[\frac{V_{in} - V_1}{R_1} - \frac{V_1 - V_2}{R_2}\right]$$

$$\frac{dv_1}{dt} = \frac{1}{C_1}\left[\frac{V_{in}}{R_1} - \frac{V_1}{R_1} - \frac{V_1}{R_2} + \frac{V_2}{R_2}\right] \qquad \ldots(1)$$

Also,
$$I_2 = C_2 \frac{dv_2}{dt}$$

i.e. KCL at v_2

$$I_2 - C_2 \frac{dv_2}{dt} = 0$$

$\therefore$
$$I_2 = C_2 \frac{dv_2}{dt}$$

$\therefore$
$$\frac{dv_2}{dt} = \frac{1}{C_2} I_2 = \frac{1}{C_2}\left[\frac{V_1 - V_2}{R_2}\right] \qquad \ldots(2)$$

$$= \frac{1}{C_2}\left[\frac{V_1}{R_2} - \frac{V_2}{R_2}\right]$$

Then the state model is,

State equation,

$$\begin{bmatrix} x_1' \\ x_2' \end{bmatrix} = \begin{bmatrix} \dfrac{dv_1}{dt} \\ \dfrac{dv_2}{dt} \end{bmatrix}$$

$$= \begin{bmatrix} \dfrac{1}{R_1C_1} - \dfrac{1}{R_2C_1} & \dfrac{1}{R_2C_1} \\[3mm] \dfrac{1}{R_2C_2} & -\dfrac{1}{R_2C_2} \end{bmatrix} \begin{bmatrix} v_1 \\[2mm] v_2 \end{bmatrix} + \begin{bmatrix} \dfrac{1}{R_1C_1} \\[2mm] 0 \end{bmatrix} V_{in}$$

Output equation,　　　　$y = V_2 = [0 \; 1] \begin{bmatrix} v_1 \\ v_2 \end{bmatrix}$

Example 5.4 : Obtain the state model of the given electrical network in a standard form.

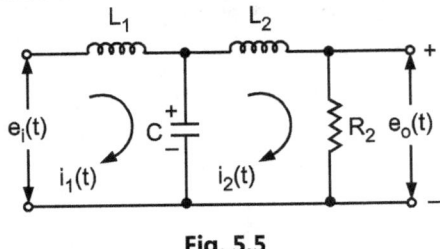

Fig. 5.5

Solution :

In the above network, three energy storage elements are present; hence we can select three state variables.

$$X_1 = I_1$$
$$X_2 = I_2$$
$$X_3 = V_c$$
$$U(t) = e_i(t)$$

- Applying KVL to the first loop,

$$-L_1 \frac{dI_1}{dt} - V_c(t) + e_i(t) = 0$$

i.e.　　　　$\dfrac{dI_1}{dt} = \dfrac{-1}{L_1} V_c(t) + \dfrac{1}{L_1} e_i(t)$　　　　... (1)

- Applying KVL to second loop :

$$-L_2 \frac{dI_2(t)}{dt} - I_2R_2 + V_c(T) = 0$$

i.e.　　　　$\dfrac{dI_2(t)}{dt} = -\dfrac{R_2}{L_2} I_2(t) + \dfrac{1}{L_2} V_c(t)$　　　　...(2)

At node V_c apply KCL

$\therefore$　　　$I_1(t) - I_2(t) - C \dfrac{dv_c(t)}{dt} = 0$

$\therefore$ $\qquad$ $[I_1(t) - I_2(t)] \dfrac{1}{C} = \dfrac{dv_c(t)}{dt}$ $\qquad\qquad\qquad$ ...(3)

For output across $e_0(t)$

$$e_0(t) = I_2(t) \cdot R_2$$

Formulating state model,

Use state variables as

$x_1 = I_1(t),\ x_2 = I_2(t),\ x_3 = V_c(t)$

State Equations :

$$
\begin{bmatrix} x_1' \\ x_2' \\ x_3' \end{bmatrix}
=
\begin{bmatrix}
0 & 0 & \dfrac{-1}{L_1} \\
0 & -\dfrac{R_2}{L_2} & \dfrac{1}{L_2} \\
\dfrac{1}{C} & -\dfrac{1}{C} & 0
\end{bmatrix}
\begin{bmatrix} x_1 \\ x_2 \\ x_3 \end{bmatrix}
+
\begin{bmatrix} \dfrac{1}{L_1} \\ 0 \\ 0 \end{bmatrix} U(t)
$$

Output Equations :

$$
Y = [0\ 1\ 0] \begin{bmatrix} x_1 \\ x_2 \\ x_3 \end{bmatrix}
$$

5.3 PHASE VARIABLE FORM

Phase variable forms are used when the system model in the form of differential equation or transfer function is known. These forms result in simplicity in formulation.

But the states are generally not available for the measurement.

The phase variables are those state variables which are obtained by assuming one of the system variables as a state variable and other state variables are the derivatives of the selected system variable.

5.3.1 Phase Variable Forms Obtained by Companion I (Controllable Canonical Form)

Consider a differential equation for n^{th} order LIT system.

$y^{(n)} + a_1 y^{(n-1)} + a_2 y^{(n-2)} + \dots a_{n-1} y' + a_n y = b_0 u^{(m)} + b_1 u^{(m-1)} + \dots + b_{m-1} u' + b_m u;\ m \leq n$

with all initial conditions; expressed as

$Y(0),\ Y'(0),\ Y''(0),\ \dots y^{(n-1)}(0)$

Considering zero initial conditions, the transfer function can be obtained as;

$$G(s) = \frac{Y(s)}{U(s)} = \frac{b_0 s^m + b_1 s^{m-1} + \dots b_{m-1} s + b_m}{s^n + a_1 s^{n-1} + \dots a_{n-1} s + a_n}$$

Let, $$\frac{Y(s)}{U(s)} = \frac{Z(s)}{U(s)} \cdot \frac{Y(s)}{Z(s)}$$

Let z; be the auxillary variable with,

$$\frac{Z(s)}{U(s)} = \frac{1}{s^n + a_1 s^{n-1} + \dots a_{n-1} s + a_n}$$

and $$\frac{Y(s)}{Z(s)} = b_0 s^m + b_1 s^{m-1} + \dots b_{m-1} s + b_m$$

For $\frac{Z(s)}{U(s)}$; we can write

$$[s^n + a_1 s^{n-1} + \dots a_{n-1} s + a_n]\, z(s) = U(s)$$

Taking Laplace inverse of above equation

$$\therefore \quad z^n + a_1 z^{(n-1)} + \dots a_n + z + a_n z' = U$$

$$\therefore \qquad z^{(n)} = u - a_1 z^{(n-1)} - \dots - a_{n-1} z' - a_n z'$$

The last equation can be represented in block diagram as,

Choice of state variables is generally output variable Y(t) itself and other state variables are derivatives of the selected state variable Y(t).

$$\therefore \qquad X_1(t) = Y(t)$$

$$\therefore \qquad X_2(t) = Y'(t) = x'(t)$$

$$\therefore \qquad X_3(t) = Y''(t) = x_1'(t) = x_2(t)$$

Thus above state equations are,

$$x_1'(t) = x_2(t)$$

$$x_2'(t) = x_3$$

$$\therefore \qquad x_{n-1}'(t) = x_n(t)$$

Hence, the equation,

$$z^n = u - a_1 z^{(n-1)} - \dots a_{n-1} z' - a_n z$$

The above equation can be represented using block diagram

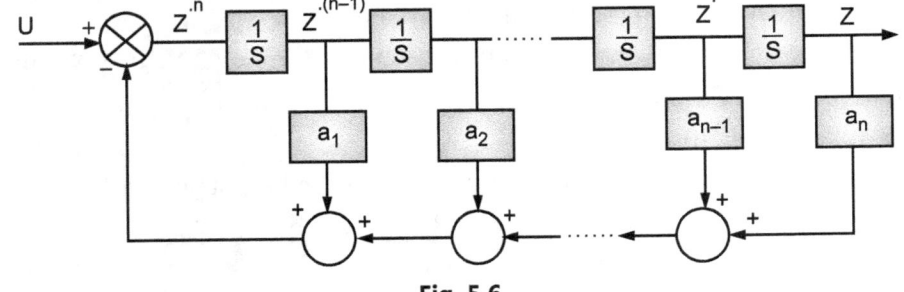

Fig. 5.6

Now, consider $\dfrac{Y(s)}{Z(s)} = b_0 s^n + b_1 s^n + \dots b_n s + b_n$

For m = n case

$\therefore$ $\qquad\qquad\qquad\qquad Y = b_0 z^{(n)} + b_1 z^{(n-1)} + \dots b_n + z + b_n z$

Hence. $\dfrac{Y(s)}{Z(s)}$ can be represented as;

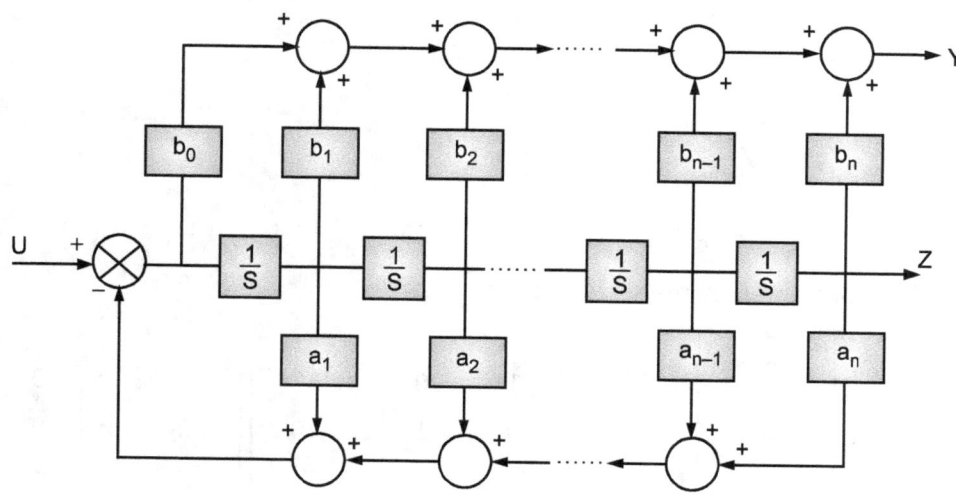

Fig. 5.7

The same can be represented with state assignments

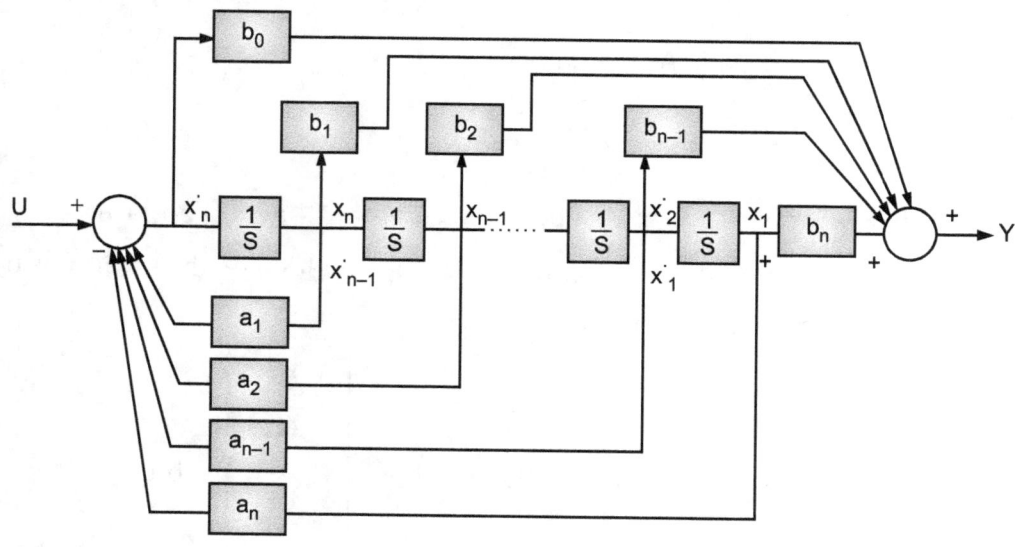

Fig. 5.8

The representation is controllable canonical because the resulting model is guranted to be controllable (i.e. because the control enters a chain of ρ) and it has ability to move in every stable.

State Equations :

$$\dot{x_1} = x_2$$

$$\dot{x_2} = x_3$$

$$\vdots$$

$$\dot{x_{n-1}} = x_n$$

$$\dot{x_n} = u - a_1 x_n - a_2 x_{n-1} \dots a_{n-1} x_2 - a_n x_1$$

which can be represented by matrix form as

$$
\begin{bmatrix} \dot{x_1} \\ \dot{x_2} \\ \vdots \\ \dot{x_{n-1}} \\ \dot{x_n} \end{bmatrix}
=
\begin{bmatrix}
0 & 1 & 0 & \dots & 0 \\
0 & 0 & 1 & \dots & 0 \\
\vdots & \vdots & \vdots & & \\
0 & 0 & 0 & \dots & 1 \\
-a_n & -a_{n-1} & -a_{n-2} & \dots & a_1
\end{bmatrix}
\begin{bmatrix} x_1 \\ x_2 \\ \vdots \\ x_{n-1} \\ x_n \end{bmatrix}
+
\begin{bmatrix} 0 \\ 0 \\ \vdots \\ 0 \\ 1 \end{bmatrix} U
$$

$$\dot{X} = Ax(t) + Bu(t)$$

Output Equation :

$$Y = b_n x_1 + b_{n-1} x_2 + \dots b_2 x_{n-1} + b_1 x_n + b_0 \dot{x_n}$$

$$= b_n x_1 + b_{n-1} x_2 + \dots b_2 x_{n-1} + b_1 x_n + b_1 x_n + b_0 [a_n x_1 - a_{n-1} x_2 - a_1 x_n + u]$$

$$= (b_n - b_0 a_n) x_1 + (b_{n-1} - b_0 a_{n-1}) x_2 + \dots + (b_2 - b_0 a_2) x_{n-1} + (b_1 - b_0 a_1) x_n + b_0 u$$

which can be represented in matrix form as;

$$y = [b_n - b_0 a_n \quad b_{n-1} - b_0 a_{n-1} \dots b_2 - b_0 a_2 \quad b_1 - b_0 a_1]
\begin{bmatrix} x_1 \\ x_2 \\ \vdots \\ x_{n-1} \\ x_n \end{bmatrix}
+ b_0 u$$

If m > n, D matrix is not available.

If m = n; D matrix is available.

$$Y(t) = [1, 0, ..., 0] \begin{bmatrix} x_1(t) \\ x_2(t) \\ : \\ : \\ x_n(t) \end{bmatrix}$$

$$y(t) = x(t) \text{ where } d = 0$$

Companion I :

Phase model used when differential equation or transfer function is known.

Steps to Solve :

- If equation given in differential form, Using Laplace Transfer (L.T.) reduce it to transfer function form.
- After transfer function represent in block diagram format.
- From block diagram, find out equations for state variables.
- From the equations from the matrices of state equation and output equation.

Example 5.5 : Obtain the controllable canonical state model of

$$\dddot{y} + 6\ddot{y} + 11\dot{y} + 6y = 0$$

Solution : We have the differential equation

$$\dddot{y} + 6\ddot{y} + 11\dot{y} + 6y = 0$$

Taking laplace transform on both sides with zero initial conditions we get

$$[s^3 + 6s^2 + 11s + 6] \cdot Y(s) = U(s)$$

$$\therefore \qquad \frac{Y(s)}{U(s)} = \frac{1}{s^3 + 6s^2 + 11s + 6}$$

$$\therefore \qquad = \frac{b_0 s^m + b_1 s^{m-1} + ... b_m}{s^n + a_1 s^{n-1} + ... a_n}$$

This transfer function can be represented as

$$\therefore \qquad \dot{x}_1 = x_2$$

$$\dot{x}_2 = x_3$$

$$\dot{x}_3 = U - 6x_1 - 11x_2 - 6x_3$$

$$y = x_1$$

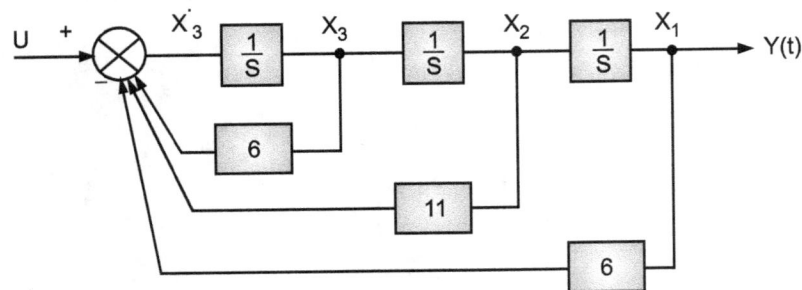

Fig. 5.9

State Equation :

$$\begin{bmatrix} \dot{x_1} \\ \dot{x_2} \\ \dot{x_3} \end{bmatrix} = \begin{bmatrix} 0 & 1 & 0 \\ 0 & 0 & 1 \\ -6 & -11 & -6 \end{bmatrix} \begin{bmatrix} x_1 \\ x_2 \\ x_3 \end{bmatrix} + \begin{bmatrix} 0 \\ 0 \\ 1 \end{bmatrix} u$$

Output Equation :

$$y = [1 \ 0 \ 0] \begin{bmatrix} x_1 \\ x_2 \\ x_3 \end{bmatrix}$$

Example 5.6 : Obtain the state model of given transfer function in controllable canonical form

$$G(s) = \frac{s^2 + 3s + 3}{s^3 + 2s^2 + 3s + 1} \quad m \le n$$

Solution : We have,

$$G(s) = \frac{Y(s)}{U(s)} = \frac{s^2 + 3s + 3}{s^3 + 2s^2 + 3s + 1}$$

$$= \frac{b_0 s^m + b_1 s^{m-1} + \dots + b_m}{s^n + a_1 s^{n-1} + \dots a_n}$$

This can be represented as

$$\therefore \qquad \dot{x_1} = x_2$$

$$\dot{x_2} = x_3$$

$$\dot{x_3} = U - x - 3x_2 - 2x_3$$

$$y = 3x_1 + 3x_2 + x_3$$

State Equation :

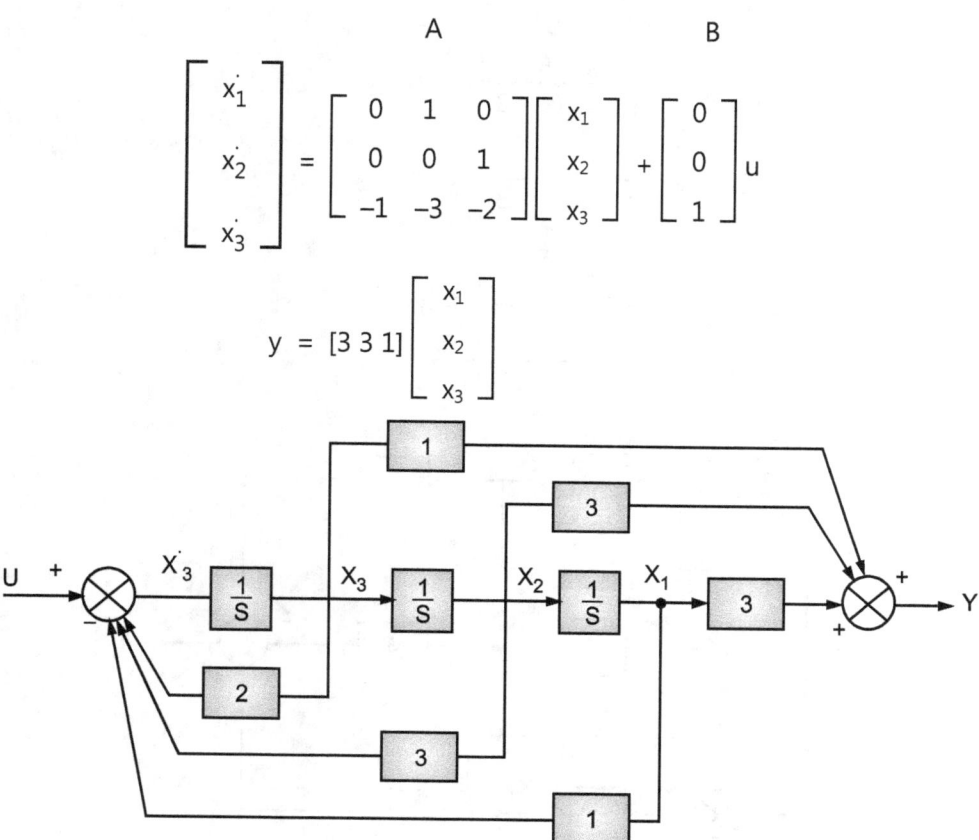

$$\begin{bmatrix} \dot{x}_1 \\ \dot{x}_2 \\ \dot{x}_3 \end{bmatrix} = \overset{A}{\begin{bmatrix} 0 & 1 & 0 \\ 0 & 0 & 1 \\ -1 & -3 & -2 \end{bmatrix}} \begin{bmatrix} x_1 \\ x_2 \\ x_3 \end{bmatrix} + \overset{B}{\begin{bmatrix} 0 \\ 0 \\ 1 \end{bmatrix}} u$$

$$y = \begin{bmatrix} 3 & 3 & 1 \end{bmatrix} \begin{bmatrix} x_1 \\ x_2 \\ x_3 \end{bmatrix}$$

Fig. 5.10

5.3.2 Companion II (Observable Canonical Form)

- The matrix 'A' in observable canonical form is A^T in controllable and vice-versa.

- The matrix 'B' in observable canonical form is C^T in controllable form and vice-versa.

- The matrix 'C' in observable is BT in canonical form and vice-versa.

- D is same in both forms.

If controllable canonical form is determined, the observable canonical form can be determined directly without block diagram realization.

Example 5.7 :	$\dfrac{y(s)}{u(s)} = \dfrac{s + 5}{s^3 + 6s^2 + 11s + 6}$

Solution : We have, $\quad G(s) = \dfrac{y(s)}{u(s)} = \dfrac{s + 5}{s^3 + 6s^2 + 11s + 6} = \dfrac{s + 5}{(s + 1)(s + 2)(s + 3)}$

$\therefore$

$$G(s) = \frac{A}{s+1} + \frac{B}{s+2} + \frac{C}{s+3}$$

where

$$A = \left.\frac{s+5}{(s+2)(s+3)}\right|_{s=-1} = 2$$

$$B = \left.\frac{s+5}{(s+1)(s+3)}\right|_{s=-2} = -3$$

$$C = \left.\frac{s+5}{(s+1)(s+2)}\right|_{s=-3} = 1$$

$\therefore$

$$G(s) = \frac{2}{s+1} - \frac{3}{s+2} + \frac{1}{s+3}$$

which can be realized as,

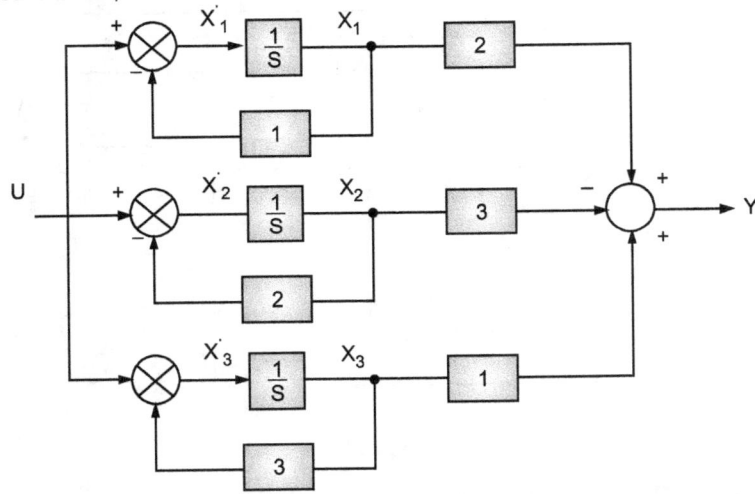

Fig. 5.11

From the above diagram we get,

$$\dot{x_1} = u - x_1$$

$$\dot{x_2} = u - 2x_2$$

$$\dot{x_3} = u - 3x_3$$

$$y = 2x_1 - 3x_2 + x_3$$

$$\begin{bmatrix} \dot{x_1} \\ \dot{x_2} \\ \dot{x_3} \end{bmatrix} = \begin{bmatrix} -1 & 0 & 0 \\ 0 & -2 & 0 \\ 0 & 0 & -3 \end{bmatrix} \begin{bmatrix} x_1 \\ x_2 \\ x_3 \end{bmatrix} + \begin{bmatrix} 1 \\ 1 \\ 1 \end{bmatrix} u$$

$$y = [2\,{-}3\;1] \begin{bmatrix} x_1 \\ x_2 \\ x_3 \end{bmatrix}$$

Observation :

The transfer function of the blocks in the various feedback paths are the coefficients existing in the original differential equation.

Output of each integrator is a state variable.

If the differential equation consists of the derivatives of the input control force u(t) then this method is not useful. In such case the state model is to be obtained from the transfer function.

Example 5.8 : Obtain the controllable canonical state model of

$$\dddot{y} + 6\ddot{y} + 11\dot{y} + 6y = u$$

Solution : We have differential equation,

$$\dddot{y} + 6\ddot{y} + 11\dot{y} + 6y = u$$

Taking laplace transform on both sides with zero initial conditions, we get

$$[s^3 + 6s^2 + 11s + 6]\,Y(s) = U(s)$$

$$\therefore \quad \frac{Y(s)}{U(s)} = \frac{1}{s^3 + 6s^2 + 11s + 6} = \frac{b_0 s^m + b_1 s^{m-1} + \dots b_m}{s^n + a_1 s^{n-1} + \dots a_n}$$

This transfer function can be represented as;

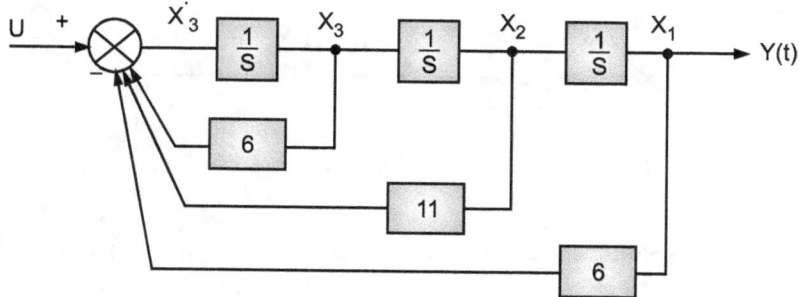

Fig. 5.12

5.3.3 Phase Variable form Obtained by Parallel Realization (Diagonal / Jordon Canonical Form)

In parallel realization, the transfer function is represented as a sum of transfer functions using partial fraction.

Every such transfer functions is realized using direct companion – I realization and then they are added to get y.

- Transfer function is represented as a sum of transfer functions using partial fractions. Every such transfer function is realized using direct companion form I realization and then they are added to get y.

Step 1 : Deduce the T.F in P.F form

Step 2 : Represent in parallel form : B.D.R

Step 3 : Form equations from diagram

Step 4 : Form matrices from the equations.

Example 5.9 : $\dfrac{Y(s)}{U(s)} = \dfrac{s + 5}{s^3 + 6s^2 + 11s + 6}$

Solution : We have,

$$G(s) = \frac{Y(s)}{U(s)} = \frac{s + 5}{s^3 + 6s^2 + 11s + 6} = \frac{s + 5}{(s + 1)(s + 2)(s + 3)}$$

$$G(s) = \frac{A}{s + 1} + \frac{B}{s + 2} + \frac{C}{s + 3}$$

where,

$$A = \left.\frac{s + 5}{(s + 2)(s + 3)}\right|_{s = -1} = 2$$

$$B = \left.\frac{s + 5}{(s + 1)(s + 3)}\right|_{s = -2} = -3$$

$$C = \left.\frac{s + 5}{(s + 1)(s + 2)}\right|_{s = -3} = 1$$

$\therefore \qquad G(s) = \dfrac{2}{s + 1} - \dfrac{3}{s + 2} + \dfrac{1}{s + 3}$

which can be realized as,

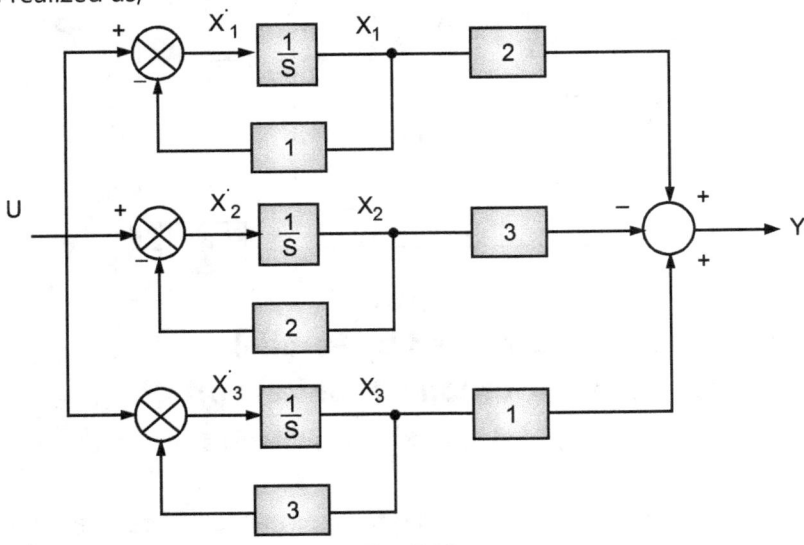

Fig. 5.13

From the above diagram, we get

$$\dot{x}_1 = u - x_1$$

$$\dot{x}_2 = u - 2x_2$$

$$\dot{x}_3 = u - 3x_3$$

$$y = 2x_1 - 3x_2 + x_3$$

$$\begin{bmatrix} \dot{x}_1 \\ \dot{x}_2 \\ \dot{x}_3 \end{bmatrix} = \begin{bmatrix} -1 & 0 & 0 \\ 0 & -2 & 0 \\ 0 & 0 & 3 \end{bmatrix} \begin{bmatrix} x_1 \\ x_2 \\ x_3 \end{bmatrix} + \begin{bmatrix} 1 \\ 1 \\ 1 \end{bmatrix} u$$

$$y = \underset{A \quad B \quad C}{[2 \ -3 \ 1]} \begin{bmatrix} x_1 \\ x_2 \\ x_3 \end{bmatrix}$$

5.4 STATE TRANSITION MATRIX

5.4.1 Properties of State Transition Matrix

1. $\phi(0) = I$

    Proof : $\phi(t) = e^{At}$

    $\therefore$ $\phi(0) = e^{A0}$

    $= e^{0}$

    $= I$

2. $\phi(t) = [\phi(-t)]^{-1}$ or $[\phi(t)]^{-1} = \phi(-t)$

    Proof : $\phi(t) = e^{At}$

    $\therefore$ $\phi(-t) = e^{-At}$

    $\therefore$ $\phi(-t) = [e^{-At}]^{-1}$

3. $\phi(t_1 + t_2) = \phi(t_1) \phi(t_2) = \phi(t_2) \phi(t_1)$

    Proof : $\phi(t_1 + t_2) = e^{A(t_1 + t_2)}$

    $= e^{At_1} e^{At_2}$

    $= \phi(t_1) \phi(t_2)$

4. $[\phi(t)]^n = \phi(nt)$

    Proof : $[\phi(t)^n] = [e^{At}]^n$

    $= e^{Ant}$

    $= \phi(nt)$

5. $\phi(t_2 - t_1) \phi(t_1 - t_0) = \phi(t_2 - t_0)$

   Proof : $\phi(t_2 - t_1) = e^{A(t_2 - t_1)}$

   $= e^{At_2} e^{At_1}$

   $\phi(t_1 - t_0) = e^{A(t_1 - t_0)}$

   $= e^{At_1} e^{At_0}$

   $\therefore \quad \phi(t_2 - t_1) \phi(t_1 - t_0) = e^{At_2} - e^{At_1} e^{At_1} e^{-At_0}$

   $= e^{At_2} e^{-At_0}$

   $= e^{A(t_2 - t_0)}$

5.4.2 Computation of State Transition Matrix (S.T.M.)

State transition matrix can be computed by

1. Using inverse Laplace transform.
2. Similarity transformations
3. Using Caley Hamilton theorem and Sylvester's interpolation.
4. e^{At} as infinite power series.

Computation of S.T.M. using inverse Laplace transform

Consider the homogeneous state equation

$$\dot{x} = Ax$$

Taking Laplace transform on both sides we get,

$$sx(s) - x(0) = Ax(s)$$

$\therefore \qquad [sI - A] x(s) = x(0)$

$\therefore \qquad x(s) = [sI - A]^{-1} x(0)$

$\therefore \qquad x(t) = L^{-1} \{[sI - A]^{-1}\} x(0)$

Also we have, $x(t) = e^{At} x(0) = \phi(t) x(0)$

$\therefore \qquad$ S.T.M. $= \phi(t) = e^{At} = L^{-1} \{[sI - A]^{-1}\}$

- **Conversion of State Model into Transfer Function :**

   State model :

   $$\dot{X} = Ax + Bu$$
   $$Y = Cx + Du$$

Transfer Function :

$$\frac{Y(s)}{U(s)} = C [sI - A]^{-1} B + D$$

Inverse of matrix :

$$A^{-1} = \frac{1}{\det A} \text{ (adjoint of A)}$$

or

$$A^{-1} = \frac{1}{\det A} \text{ (cofactor matrix of A)}^{\mathsf{T}}$$

State Transition Matrix :

Homogeneous equations :

$$\dot{X} = Ax \text{ with } x(0) \text{ as initial state}$$

A is constant and input control forces are zero.

$$x(t) = e^{At} \cdot x(0)$$

$$\phi(t) = e^{At} \quad \rightarrow \quad \text{S.T.M.}$$

Computation using inverse Laplace transforms.

$$\therefore \qquad \text{S.T.M.} = \phi(t) = e^{At} = L^{-1}\{[sI - A]^{-1}\}$$

Example 5.10 : Find the transfer function of the system with state space model matrices.

Solution : The transfer function is;

$$G(s) = C[sI - A]^{-1}B + D$$

Now,

$$A = \begin{bmatrix} -2 & -2 \\ 0 & -1 \end{bmatrix} \quad B = \begin{bmatrix} 3 \\ 1 \end{bmatrix}, C = \begin{bmatrix} 1 & 0 \end{bmatrix}, I = \begin{bmatrix} 1 & 0 \\ 0 & 1 \end{bmatrix}$$

$$\therefore \qquad [sI - A] = \begin{bmatrix} s & 0 \\ 0 & s \end{bmatrix} - \begin{bmatrix} -2 & -2 \\ 0 & -1 \end{bmatrix} = \begin{bmatrix} s+2 & 2 \\ 0 & s+1 \end{bmatrix}$$

$$[sI - A]^{-1} = \frac{1}{\det [sI - A]^{-1}} \begin{bmatrix} s+1 & -2 \\ 0 & s+2 \end{bmatrix} = \frac{\begin{bmatrix} s+1 & -2 \\ 0 & s+2 \end{bmatrix}}{(s+2)(s+1)}$$

$$\therefore \qquad G(s) = \frac{[1 \ 0] \begin{bmatrix} s+1 & -2 \\ 0 & s+2 \end{bmatrix} \begin{bmatrix} 3 \\ 1 \end{bmatrix}}{(s+1)(s+2)}$$

$$= \frac{[s+1 \ -2] \begin{bmatrix} 3 \\ 1 \end{bmatrix}}{(s+1)(s+2)} = \frac{3(s+1)-2}{(s+1)(s+2)} = \frac{3s+3-2}{(s+1)(s+2)}$$

$$= \frac{3s+1}{(s+1)(s+2)}$$

Example 5.11 : Find the transfer function of the system with state model.

$$A = \begin{bmatrix} 0 & 1 & 0 \\ 0 & 0 & 1 \\ -6 & -11 & -6 \end{bmatrix} ; B = \begin{bmatrix} 0 \\ 0 \\ 1 \end{bmatrix} ; C = [1 \ 0 \ 0]$$

Solution : $G(s) = [sI - A]^{-1}B + D$

$$A = \begin{bmatrix} 0 & 1 & 0 \\ 0 & 0 & 1 \\ -6 & -11 & -6 \end{bmatrix}$$

$$sI - A = s\begin{bmatrix} 1 & 0 & 0 \\ 0 & 1 & 0 \\ 0 & 0 & 1 \end{bmatrix} - \begin{bmatrix} 0 & 1 & 0 \\ 0 & 0 & 1 \\ -6 & -11 & -6 \end{bmatrix} = \begin{bmatrix} s & -1 & 0 \\ 0 & s & -1 \\ 6 & 11 & s+6 \end{bmatrix}$$

$$[sI - A]^{-1} = \frac{1}{\det A} \cdot adj \ (sI - A)^{+}$$

$$= \frac{1}{\det A} [\text{cofactor of matrix of } (sI - A)]^{+}$$

Cofactor of A = [sI – A]

$$= \begin{bmatrix} s & -1 & 0 \\ 0 & s & -1 \\ 6 & 11 & s+6 \end{bmatrix}$$

$$A_{11} = \begin{vmatrix} s & -1 \\ 11 & s+6 \end{vmatrix} = s^2 + 6s + 11$$

$$A_{12} = \begin{vmatrix} 0 & -1 \\ 6 & s+6 \end{vmatrix} = -6$$

$$A_{13} = \begin{vmatrix} 0 & s \\ 6 & 11 \end{vmatrix} = -6s$$

$$\therefore \quad \text{Cofactor of } [sI - A] = \begin{bmatrix} s^2 + 6s + 11 & -6 & -6s \\ s+6 & s^2 + 6s & -11s - 6 \\ -1 & s & s^2 \end{bmatrix}$$

$\therefore \qquad [sI - A]^T = \begin{bmatrix} s^2 + 6s + 11 & s + 6 & 1 \\ -6 & s^2 + 6s & s \\ -6s & -11s - 6 & s^2 \end{bmatrix}$

$\therefore \qquad [sI - A]^{-1} = \dfrac{\begin{bmatrix} s^2 + 6s + 11 & s + 6 & 1 \\ -6 & s^2 + 6s & s \\ -6s & -11s - 6 & s^2 \end{bmatrix}}{s[s^2 + 6s + 11] + 6}$

$\qquad\qquad = \dfrac{\begin{bmatrix} s^2 + 6s + 11 & s + 6 & 1 \\ -6 & s^2 + 6s & s \\ -6s & -11s - 6 & s^2 \end{bmatrix}}{s^3 + 6s^2 + 11s + 6}$

$G(s) = C[sI - A]^{-1} B + D$

$\qquad = \dfrac{[1\ 0\ 0] \begin{bmatrix} s^2 + 6s + 11 & s + 6 & 1 \\ -6 & s^2 + 6s & s \\ -6s & -11s - 6 & s^2 \end{bmatrix} \begin{bmatrix} 0 \\ 0 \\ 1 \end{bmatrix}}{s^3 + 6s^2 + 11s + 6}$

$G(s) = \dfrac{1}{s^3 + 6s^2 + 11s + 6}$

5.5 SOLUTION OF NON-HOMOGENEOUS STATE EQUATION

The non-homogeneous state equation is

$$\dot{x} = Ax + Bu \rightarrow \text{(input term is also available)}$$

Its solution is given by,

$$x(t) = \underset{\text{Natural}}{e^{At} \cdot x(0)} + \underset{\text{forced}}{\int_0^t e^{A(t-T)} \cdot B\,u\,(T)\,dt}$$

$$= \phi(t)\,x(0) + \int_0^t \phi(t - T)\,Bu(t)\,dT \ \dots \text{ time consuming solution}$$

$$= \phi(t) \cdot x(0) + \int_0^t \phi(t - T) \cdot Bu(t)\,dt$$

The same can be obtained using inverse laplace transform

We have $\qquad \dot{x} = Ax + Bu$

$\therefore \qquad sx(s) - x(0) = Ax(s) + Bu(s)$

$\qquad [sI - A] \cdot x(s) = x(0) + Bu(s)$

$\therefore \qquad x(s) = [sI - A]^{-1} x(0) + [sI - A]^{-1} \cdot Bu(s)$

$\therefore \qquad x(t) = L^{-1} \{[sI - A]^{-1} [X(0) \cdot Bu(s)]\}$

$\qquad y(t) = C.x(t) + D.u(t)$

In the term $\qquad x(t) = \phi(t) \cdot x(0) + \int_{0}^{t} \phi(t - T) \, Bu(t) \, dt$

$\phi(t) \cdot x(0)$ is the natural response and $\int_{0}^{t} \phi(t - T) \cdot B \, u(t) \, dt$ is the forced response.

Examples 5.12 : Find the solution of state equation $\dot{x} = Ax + Bu$; if

$$A = \begin{bmatrix} 0 & 1 \\ -2 & -3 \end{bmatrix} ; B = \begin{bmatrix} 0 \\ 2 \end{bmatrix}$$

$$u(t) = 1 \; ; t \geq 0 \qquad x(0) = \begin{bmatrix} 0 \\ 1 \end{bmatrix}$$

$$= 0 \; ; t < 0$$

Solution : Laplace transform approach;

$$x(t) = L^{-1} \{[sI - A]^{-1} [x(0) \cdot Bu(s)]\}$$

$$A = \begin{bmatrix} 0 & 1 \\ -2 & -3 \end{bmatrix}$$

$$[sI - A] = \begin{bmatrix} s & -1 \\ 2 & s + 3 \end{bmatrix}$$

$$[sI - A]^{-1} = \frac{\begin{bmatrix} s + 3 & 1 \\ -2 & s \end{bmatrix}}{s^2 + 3s + 2}$$

$$u(t) = 1 ; \quad t \geq 0$$

$$= 0 ; \quad t < 0$$

$$\therefore \qquad u(s) = \frac{1}{s}$$

$$\therefore \qquad Bu(s) = \begin{bmatrix} 0 \\ 2/3 \end{bmatrix}$$

$$x(0) + Bu(s) = \begin{bmatrix} 0 \\ 1 \end{bmatrix} \begin{bmatrix} 0 \\ 2/s \end{bmatrix}$$

5.6 SOLUTION OF HOMOGENEOUS STATE EQUATION

Homogeneous state equation, its solution and state transition matrix,

The homogeneous state equation is,

$$\dot{x} = Ax \text{ with } x(0) \text{ as initial state.}$$

Solution of homogeneous state equation,

Let,

$$x(t) = e^{At}k \text{ be the solution of differential equation}$$

$$\dot{x}(t) = Ax(t)$$

$$\because \qquad x(t) = e^{At}K$$

$$\dot{x}(t) = Ae^{At}K$$

$$= Ax(t) \qquad\qquad \dots (1)$$

To evaluate the value of k substitute t = 0 in equation (1) to get,

$$x(0) = K$$

$\therefore$ The solution x(t) is,

$$x(t) = e^{At} x(0)$$

Hence if state x(t) at t = 0 is known, any state x(t) can be computed with the help of matrix e^{At}.

Hence matrix e^{At} is called as State Transition Matrix (STM) and is denoted by $\phi(t)$.

$$\phi(t) = e^{At}$$

5.7 CONTROLLABILITY AND OBSERVABILITY

Controllability and Observability represent two major concepts of modern control system theory.

5.7.1 Controllability

In order to be able to do whatever we want with the given dynamic system under control, input the system is controllable.

Definition : A system with interval state vector x is called controllable if and only if the system states can be changed by changing the system input.

A system x_0 is controllable at time to if for some finite time t_1 there exists an input u(t) that transfers the state x(t) from x_0 to the origin at time t_1.

A system is called controllable at time t_0 if every state x_o in the state-space is controllable.

A system is said to be completely state controllable if it is possible to transfer the system from any initial state to any desired state in a finite time interval with the help of unconstrained control vector u(t).

or

A system is said to be completely state controllable if there exists an unconstrained control vector u(t) which transfers any initial state x(0) to any desired state x_d in a finite time.

Condition for Complete State Controllability

A continuous time system described by,

$$\dot{x} = A_x + B_u$$

is completely state controllable; if rank of the matrix

$$M = [B \ AB \ A^2B \ldots A^{n-1}B] \text{ is n! = order of the system}$$

The matrix $[B \ AB \ A^2B \ldots A^{n-1}B]$ is called as controllability matrix.

5.7.2 Observability

In order to see what is going on inside the system under observable, the system must be observable.

It is well known that a solvable system of linear algebraic equations has a solution if and only if the rank of the system matrix is full.

If things cannot be directly observed for any of the reasons above, it can be necessary to calculate or estimate the values of the internal state variables; using only input-output relation of the system.

In other words, we must ask whether or not it is possible t_0 determine what the inside of the system (the internal system states); by only observing the outside performance of the system.

Definition : A system with an initial state x (t_0) is observable if and only if the value of the initial state can be determined from the system output y(t) that has been observed through the time interval to < t < t_f.

If the initial state cannot be so determined the system is unobservable.

A system is said to be completely state observable if every initial state x(0) can be determined from the observation of y(t) and control vector u(t) over a finite time interval.

Condition for Complete State Observability :

The continuous time LTI system described by,

$$\dot{x} = Ax + Bu$$
$$y = Cx$$

is completely state observable if rank of matrix

$$[C^T \ A^T C^T \ A^{T^2} C^T \ ... \ A^{T^{n-1}} \ C^T] \text{ is n!}$$

The matrix $[C^T \ A^T C^T \ A^{T^2} C^T \ ... \ A^{T^{n-1}} \ C^T]$ is called as observability matrix.

5.7.3 Obervability and Controllability Tests will be Connected to the Rank of Matrices

Controllability and observability have been introduced in the state space domain as pure time domain concepts. It is interesting to point out that in frequency domain there exists a very powerful and simple theorem that gives a single condition for both the controllability and the observability of a system.

Let H(s) be the transfer function of a single-input, single-output system.

$$H(s) = C \ (sI - A)^{-1} \ b$$

Note that H(s) is defined by ratio of two polynomials containing the corresponding system poles and zeros.

Theorem :

- If there are no pole-zero cancellation in the transfer function of a SISO, then the system is both controllable and observable. If the zero-pole constellation occurs in H(s), then the system is either uncontrollable or unobservable or both uncontrollable and unobservable.

- The concept of controllability refers to the ability of a controller to arbitrarily alter the functionality of the system plant.

- The state variable of a system x, represents the internal workings of the system that can be separate from the regular input-output relationship of the system. This also need to be measured, or observed.

- The term observability describes whether the internal state variables of the system can be externally measured.

Complete state controllability describes the ability of an external input to move the internal state of a system from any initial state to any other final state in a finite time in interval.

Example 5.13 : Investigate for complete state controllability and complete state observability for the system with state model materials.

Solution :

$$A = \begin{bmatrix} 0 & 1 & 0 \\ 0 & 0 & 1 \\ 0 & -2 & -3 \end{bmatrix}, B = \begin{bmatrix} 0 \\ 0 \\ 1 \end{bmatrix}, c = [10 \ 0 \ 0]$$

in the state model $\dot{x}$ = Ax + Bu

$\qquad\qquad\qquad$ y = Cx

The controllability matrix is,

$$M = [B \quad AB \quad A^2B]$$

$$AB = \begin{bmatrix} 0 & 1 & 0 \\ 0 & 0 & 1 \\ 0 & -2 & -3 \end{bmatrix} \begin{bmatrix} 0 \\ 0 \\ 1 \end{bmatrix} = \begin{bmatrix} 0 \\ 1 \\ -3 \end{bmatrix}$$

$$A^2B = AAB \begin{bmatrix} 0 & 1 & 0 \\ 0 & 0 & 1 \\ 0 & -2 & -3 \end{bmatrix} \begin{bmatrix} 0 \\ 1 \\ -3 \end{bmatrix} = \begin{bmatrix} 1 \\ -3 \\ 7 \end{bmatrix}$$

$\therefore \qquad\qquad M = [B \quad AB \quad A^2B]$

$$M = \begin{bmatrix} 0 & 0 & \phi \\ 0 & 1 & -3 \\ 1 & -3 & 7 \end{bmatrix} \rightarrow \text{Controllable matrix}$$

$\therefore \qquad\qquad |M| = \begin{vmatrix} 0 & 0 & 1 \\ 0 & 1 & -3 \\ 1 & -3 & 7 \end{vmatrix} = -1 \neq 0$

$\therefore \qquad\qquad$ Rank of M = 3 = n

$\therefore$ The system is completely state controllable.

The observability matrix is.

$$N = \begin{bmatrix} C^T A^T C^T A^{T^2} C^T \end{bmatrix}$$

$$A^T C^T = \begin{bmatrix} 0 & 0 & 0 \\ 1 & 0 & -2 \\ 0 & 1 & -3 \end{bmatrix} \begin{bmatrix} 10 \\ 0 \\ 0 \end{bmatrix} = \begin{bmatrix} 0 \\ 10 \\ 0 \end{bmatrix}$$

$$A^{T^2} C^T = A^T A^T C^T = \begin{bmatrix} 0 & 0 & 0 \\ 1 & 0 & -2 \\ 0 & 1 & -3 \end{bmatrix} \begin{bmatrix} 0 \\ 10 \\ 0 \end{bmatrix} = \begin{bmatrix} 0 \\ 0 \\ 10 \end{bmatrix}$$

$\therefore \qquad\qquad N = \begin{bmatrix} 10 & 0 & 0 \\ 0 & 10 & 0 \\ 0 & 0 & 10 \end{bmatrix}$

$$\therefore \qquad |N| = \begin{bmatrix} 10 & 0 & 0 \\ 0 & 10 & 0 \\ 0 & 0 & 10 \end{bmatrix} = 1000 \neq 0$$

$\therefore$ Rank of N = 3 = n

$\therefore$ The system is completely state observable.

Matrices Rules :

1. Inverse of Matrix :

For $\qquad A = \begin{bmatrix} a & b \\ c & d \end{bmatrix}$

$$A^{-1} = \frac{1}{\det + A} \begin{bmatrix} d & -b \\ -c & a \end{bmatrix}$$

$$= \frac{1}{ad - bc} \begin{bmatrix} d & -b \\ -c & a \end{bmatrix}$$

Property, $\qquad AA^{-1} = A^{-1}A = I$

2. Adjoint Method :

$$A^{-1} = \frac{1}{\det + A} \text{ (Adjoint of A)}$$

or, $\qquad A^{-1} = \frac{1}{\det + A} \text{ (Cofactor matrix of A)}^T$

3. Cofactor of Matrix :

$$A = \begin{bmatrix} 1 & -2 & 3 \\ 0 & 4 & -5 \\ 1 & -0 & 6 \end{bmatrix}$$

$A_{11} = \begin{vmatrix} 4 & 5 \\ 0 & 6 \end{vmatrix} = 24 \qquad A_{12} = -\begin{vmatrix} 0 & 5 \\ 1 & 6 \end{vmatrix} = 5 \qquad A_{13} = \begin{vmatrix} 0 & 4 \\ 1 & 0 \end{vmatrix} = -4$

$A_{21} = -\begin{vmatrix} 2 & 3 \\ 0 & 6 \end{vmatrix} = -12 \qquad A_{22} = \begin{vmatrix} 1 & 3 \\ 1 & 6 \end{vmatrix} = 3 \qquad A_{23} = -\begin{vmatrix} 1 & 2 \\ 1 & 0 \end{vmatrix} = 2$

$A_{31} = \begin{vmatrix} 2 & 3 \\ 4 & 5 \end{vmatrix} = -2 \qquad A_{32} = -\begin{vmatrix} 1 & 3 \\ 0 & 5 \end{vmatrix} = -5 \qquad A_{33} = \begin{vmatrix} 1 & 2 \\ 0 & 4 \end{vmatrix} = 4$

$$\text{The cofactor matrix is } = \begin{bmatrix} 24 & 5 & -4 \\ -12 & 3 & 2 \\ -2 & -5 & 4 \end{bmatrix}$$

3×3 matrix

$$A^{-1} = \frac{1}{\det(A)} \text{ adj}(A)$$

Example 5.14 : A matrix given $\dot{x}(t) = Ax(t)$. Find $x(t)$ if $x(0) = [\ ]$

Solution : Use standard formula;

$$\phi(t) = L^{-1}\{[sI-A]^{-1}\}$$

$$x(t) = \phi(t) \cdot x(0)$$

Non-Homogeneous equations :

$$\dot{x} = Ax + Bu$$

$\therefore \qquad x(t) = L^{-1}\{[sI - A]^{-1}\}[x(0) + B u(s)]$

Observability and controllability :

1.   Controllability Matrix :

$$\dot{x} = Ax + Bu$$

$$M = [B \; AB \; A^2B \; \ldots \ldots \; A^{n-1}B]$$

If order of system = Rank of matrix

Hence matrix is controllable.

2.   Observability Matrix :

$$\dot{x} = Ax + Bu$$

$$Y = Cx$$

$$N = [C^TA^T \quad C^T A^{+2} \quad C^T A^{t^{n-1}}]$$

Same condition as above for observable.

Example 5.15 : Investigate the complete state controllability and complete state observability

$$\dot{x} = \begin{bmatrix} -2 & 1 \\ 1 & -2 \end{bmatrix} x + \begin{bmatrix} 0 \\ 1 \end{bmatrix} u$$

$$Y = [1 - 1] x$$

Solution :

The controllability matrix is,

$$M = [B \quad AB]$$

$$AB = \begin{bmatrix} -2 & 1 \\ 1 & -2 \end{bmatrix} \begin{bmatrix} 0 \\ 1 \end{bmatrix} = \begin{bmatrix} 1 \\ -2 \end{bmatrix}$$

$$\therefore \qquad M = \begin{bmatrix} 0 & 1 \\ 1 & -2 \end{bmatrix}$$

$$\therefore \qquad |M| = \begin{vmatrix} 0 & 1 \\ 1 & -2 \end{vmatrix} = -1 \neq 0$$

∴ Rank of M = 2 = n ≠ order of system

∴ The system is completely controllable.

The observability matrix is,

$$N = [C^T \quad A^T C^T]$$

$$A^T C^T = \begin{bmatrix} -2 & 1 \\ 1 & -2 \end{bmatrix} \begin{bmatrix} 1 \\ -1 \end{bmatrix} = \begin{bmatrix} -3 \\ 3 \end{bmatrix}$$

$$\therefore \qquad N = \begin{bmatrix} 1 & -3 \\ -1 & 3 \end{bmatrix}$$

$$\therefore \qquad |N| = \begin{bmatrix} 1 & -3 \\ -1 & 3 \end{bmatrix} = 0$$

∴ Rank of N ≠ 2

∴ Rank of N ≠ n

∴ The system is not completely state observable.

Example 5.16 : Investigate for complete state controllability and complete state observability of the system.

$$\dot{x} = \begin{bmatrix} 0 & 1 & 0 \\ 0 & 0 & 1 \\ -1 & 0 & 3 \end{bmatrix} x + \begin{bmatrix} 0 & 0 \\ 0 & 1 \\ 1 & 0 \end{bmatrix} u$$

$$y = \begin{bmatrix} 1 & -1 & 0 \end{bmatrix} u$$

Solution :

The controllability matrix is,

$$M = [B \quad AB \quad A^2B]$$

$$AB = \begin{bmatrix} 0 & 1 & 0 \\ 0 & 0 & 1 \\ -1 & 0 & 3 \end{bmatrix} \begin{bmatrix} 0 & 0 \\ 0 & 1 \\ 1 & 0 \end{bmatrix} = \begin{bmatrix} 0 & 1 \\ 1 & 0 \\ 3 & 0 \end{bmatrix}$$

$$A^2B = A.AB = \begin{bmatrix} 0 & 1 & 0 \\ 0 & 0 & 1 \\ -1 & 0 & 3 \end{bmatrix} \begin{bmatrix} 0 & 1 \\ 1 & 0 \\ 3 & 0 \end{bmatrix} = \begin{bmatrix} 1 & 0 \\ 3 & 0 \\ 9 & -1 \end{bmatrix}$$

$$= \begin{bmatrix} 0 & 0 & 0 & 1 & 1 & 0 \\ 0 & 1 & 1 & 0 & 3 & 0 \\ 1 & 0 & 3 & 0 & 9 & -1 \end{bmatrix}$$

Since, m is not a square matrix, we have to find MMT to get a square matrix of dimensions n×n. Also Rank (m) and rand of (mm^t) are same.

$$mm^t = \begin{bmatrix} 0 & 0 & 0 & 1 & 1 & 0 \\ 0 & 1 & 1 & 0 & 3 & 0 \\ 1 & 3 & 3 & 0 & 9 & -1 \end{bmatrix} \begin{bmatrix} 0 & 0 & 1 \\ 0 & 1 & 3 \\ 0 & 1 & 3 \\ 1 & 0 & 0 \\ 1 & 3 & 9 \\ 0 & 0 & -1 \end{bmatrix} = \begin{bmatrix} 2 & 3 & 9 \\ 3 & 11 & 30 \\ 9 & 30 & 92 \end{bmatrix}$$

$$mm^t = \begin{vmatrix} 2 & 3 & 9 \\ 3 & 11 & 30 \\ 9 & 30 & 92 \end{vmatrix} = 125 \neq 0$$

∴   Rank (m) = Rank (mm^t) = 3 = n

∴   The system is completely state controllable.

The observability matrix is,

$$N = [C^T \quad A^TC^T \quad A^{T^2}C^T]$$

$$A^TC^T = \begin{bmatrix} 0 & 0 & -1 \\ 1 & 0 & 0 \\ 0 & 1 & 3 \end{bmatrix} \begin{bmatrix} 1 \\ -1 \\ 0 \end{bmatrix} = \begin{bmatrix} 0 \\ 1 \\ -1 \end{bmatrix}$$

$$A^{T^2} C^T = A^T A^T C^T = \begin{bmatrix} 0 & 0 & -1 \\ 1 & 0 & 0 \\ 0 & 1 & 3 \end{bmatrix} \begin{bmatrix} 0 \\ 1 \\ -1 \end{bmatrix} = \begin{bmatrix} 1 \\ 0 \\ -2 \end{bmatrix}$$

$$\therefore \quad N = \begin{bmatrix} 1 & 0 & 1 \\ -1 & 1 & 0 \\ 0 & -1 & -2 \end{bmatrix}$$

$$\therefore \quad |N| = \begin{bmatrix} 1 & 0 & 1 \\ -1 & 1 & 0 \\ 0 & -1 & -2 \end{bmatrix}$$

$$\therefore \quad |N| = \begin{bmatrix} 1 & 0 & 1 \\ -1 & 1 & 0 \\ 0 & -1 & -2 \end{bmatrix} = -1 \neq 0$$

$\therefore$ Rank of $N = 3 = n$

$\therefore$ The system is completely state observable.

Problem 5.17 : Find the transfer function of the system with state space model matrices.

$$A = \begin{bmatrix} 0 & 1 \\ -2 & 3 \end{bmatrix}, B = \begin{bmatrix} 0 & 1 \\ 1 & 1 \end{bmatrix}, C = [1 \ 0]$$

Solution :

$$A = \begin{bmatrix} 0 & 1 \\ -2 & 3 \end{bmatrix}$$

$$[sI - A] = \begin{bmatrix} s & -1 \\ 2 & s+3 \end{bmatrix} \qquad (\because \ AA^{-1} = A^{-1}A = I)$$

$$[sI - A]^{-1} = \frac{\begin{bmatrix} s+3 & 1 \\ -2 & s \end{bmatrix}}{s^2 + 3s + 2}$$

$$G(s) = C[sI - A]^{-1} B + D$$

$$= \frac{[1 \ 0] \begin{bmatrix} s+3 & 1 \\ -2 & s \end{bmatrix} \begin{bmatrix} 0 & 1 \\ 1 & 1 \end{bmatrix}}{s^2 + 3s + 2} = \frac{[s+3 \ \ 1] \begin{bmatrix} 0 & 1 \\ 1 & 1 \end{bmatrix}}{s^2 + 3s + 2}$$

$$= \frac{[1 \ \ s+4]}{s^2 + 3s + 2}$$

$$G(s) = \begin{bmatrix} \dfrac{1}{s^2 + 3s + 2} & \dfrac{s+4}{s^2 + 3s + 2} \end{bmatrix}$$

Problem 5.18 : Find state transition matrix if-

$$A = \begin{bmatrix} 0 & 1 \\ -2 & -3 \end{bmatrix} \text{ in } \dot{X}(t) = AX(t)$$

Also find X(t), if $X(0) = \dot{X} \begin{bmatrix} 0 \\ 1 \end{bmatrix}$

Solution : We have,

$$\phi(t) = L^{-1}\{[sI - A]\}$$

Now,

$$A = \begin{bmatrix} 0 & 1 \\ -2 & -3 \end{bmatrix}$$

$$[sI - A] = \begin{bmatrix} s & -1 \\ 2 & s+3 \end{bmatrix}$$

$$[sI - A]^{-1} = \frac{\begin{bmatrix} s+3 & 1 \\ -2 & s \end{bmatrix}}{s^2 + 3s + 2}$$

$$\therefore \quad [sI - A]^{-1} = \begin{bmatrix} \dfrac{s+3}{(s+1)(s+2)} & \dfrac{1}{(s+1)(s+2)} \\ \dfrac{-2}{(s+1)(s+2)} & \dfrac{s}{(s+1)(s+2)} \end{bmatrix}$$

$$= \begin{bmatrix} \dfrac{A_1}{s+1} + \dfrac{B_1}{s+2} & \dfrac{A_2}{s+1} + \dfrac{B_2}{s+2} \\ \dfrac{A_3}{s+1} + \dfrac{B_3}{s+2} & \dfrac{A_4}{s+1} + \dfrac{B_4}{s+2} \end{bmatrix}$$

Where,

$$A_1 = \frac{s+3}{s+2}\bigg|_{s=-1} = 2$$

$$B_1 = \frac{s+3}{s+1}\bigg|_{s=-2} = -1$$

$$A_2 = \frac{1}{s+2}\bigg|_{s=-1} = 1$$

$$B_2 = \frac{1}{s+1}\bigg|_{s=-2} = -1$$

$$A_3 = -2A_2 = -2$$

$$B_3 = -2B_2 = 2$$

$$A_4 = \frac{s}{s + 2}\bigg|_{s = -1} = -1$$

$$B_4 = \frac{s}{s + 1}\bigg|_{s = -2} = 2$$

∴ $$[sI - A]^{-1} = \begin{bmatrix} \dfrac{2}{s + 1} - \dfrac{1}{s + 2} & \dfrac{1}{s + 1} - \dfrac{1}{s + 2} \\ \dfrac{-2}{s + 1} + \dfrac{2}{s + 2} & \dfrac{-1}{s + 1} + \dfrac{2}{s + 2} \end{bmatrix}$$

∴ $$\phi(t) = L^{-1}\{[sI - A]^{-1}\}$$

$$= \begin{bmatrix} 2e^{-t} - e^{-2t} & e^{-t} - 2e^{-t} \\ 2e^{-2t} - 2e^{-t} & 2e^{-2t} - e^{-t} \end{bmatrix}$$

$$X(t) = \phi(t)\,x(0)$$

$$= \begin{bmatrix} 2e^{-t} - e^{-2t} & e^{-t} - e^{-2t} \\ 2e^{-2t} - 2e^{-t} & 2e^{-t} - e^{-t} \end{bmatrix}\begin{bmatrix} 0 \\ 1 \end{bmatrix}$$

$$X(t) = \begin{bmatrix} e^{-t} - e^{-2t} \\ 2e^{-2t} - e^{-t} \end{bmatrix}$$

Example 5.19 : Solve using Jordan form $G(s) = \dfrac{5}{(s + 1)^2 (s + 2)}$

Solution : The given transfer function is

$$\in (s) = \frac{5}{(s + 1)^2 (s + 2)}$$

$$= \frac{A}{(s + 1)^2} + \frac{B}{s + 1} + \frac{C}{s + 2}$$

where,

$$A = \frac{s}{s + 2}\bigg|_{s = -1} = 5$$

$$B = \frac{d}{ds}\left[\frac{s}{s + 2}\right]_{s = -1} = \frac{-s}{(s + 2)^2}\bigg|_{s = -1} = -5$$

$$C = \frac{s}{(s + 1)^2}\bigg|_{s = -2}$$

$$G(s) = \frac{s}{(s + 1)^2} - \frac{s}{s + 1} + \frac{s}{s + 2}$$

This can be represented as,

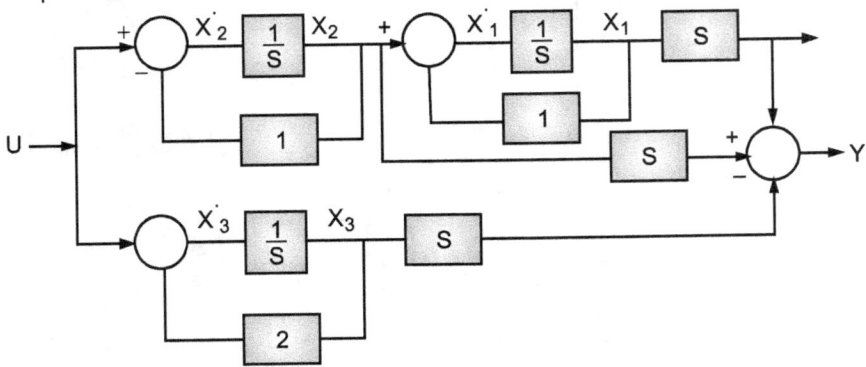

Fig. 5.14

$$\dot{x}_1 = x_2 - x_1$$

$$\dot{x}_2 = U - x_2$$

$$Y = 5x_1 - sx_2 + 5x_3$$

Then the state model is

$$\begin{bmatrix} \dot{x}_1 \\ \dot{x}_2 \\ \dot{x}_3 \end{bmatrix} = \begin{bmatrix} -1 & 1 & 0 \\ 0 & -1 & 0 \\ 0 & 0 & -2 \end{bmatrix} \begin{bmatrix} X_1 \\ X_2 \\ X_3 \end{bmatrix} + \begin{bmatrix} 0 \\ 1 \\ 1 \end{bmatrix} u$$

$$Y = [5 - 5 \ \ 5] \begin{bmatrix} X_1 \\ X_2 \\ X_3 \end{bmatrix}$$

∴

Example 5.20 : Obtain the state space model in physical variable system in Fig. 5.15 below.

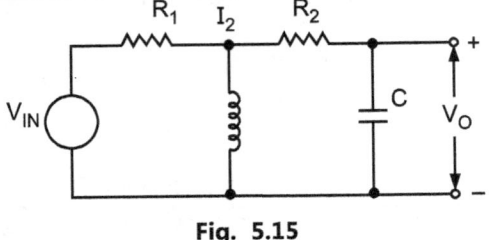

Fig. 5.15

Applying KVL to first loop,

$$Vin_2 \ i_1R_1 + \frac{Ld}{Cdt} (i_1 - i_2) \qquad \qquad \dots (1)$$

Applying KVL to loop 2

$$R_2I_2 + V_C + Ld/dt \ (i_2 - i_1) \qquad \qquad \dots (2)$$

From (1) and (2)

$$\frac{V}{L} - i_1 \frac{R_1}{L} = X_i \qquad \qquad \dots (3)$$

$$\frac{Riz}{l} + \frac{x_2}{L} = Xi$$

$$V = \frac{1}{L} \int i_2 dt = iz = cdv_o/dt$$

Now,

$$x_1 + i_2 = i_1$$

$$\frac{V}{L} - X_1 \frac{R_1}{L} - I_2 \frac{R_1}{C} = X_i$$

Put $\qquad \qquad i_2 = Cx_2$

$$\frac{V}{L} - X_i \frac{R_1}{C} - C (\dot{X}_2) \frac{R_1}{L} = X_i$$

$$\frac{-X_2}{L} + \frac{RL}{L} (C\dot{X}_2) = X_i$$

$$\frac{V}{L} - \frac{V_3}{2} - \frac{X_1 F_1}{L} - \frac{C\dot{X}_2}{L} (R_1 + R_2))$$

$$U - X_2 - X_1 R_1 = C\dot{X}_2 (R_1 + R_2)$$

$$\frac{1}{C(R_1 + R_2)} (u - X_2 - X_i F_i) = X_i$$

Put values of $\dot{X}_2$ in any of (2) equations for X_i

$$X_i - \frac{XL}{L} \left(\frac{R_1}{R_1 + R_2} \right) + \frac{VR_2}{L(R_1 + R_2)} - \frac{XR_1 R_2}{C(R_1 + R_2)}$$

$$X_i = \begin{bmatrix} X_1 \\ X_2 \end{bmatrix} = \begin{bmatrix} \dfrac{R_1 R_2}{V_c CR_1 + R_2} & \dfrac{R_1}{(L R_1 + R_2)} \\ \dfrac{-R}{C(R_1 + R_2)} & \dfrac{-1}{R_1 + R_2} \end{bmatrix} \begin{bmatrix} X_1 \\ X_2 \end{bmatrix} + \begin{bmatrix} \dfrac{1}{R_1 + R_2} \\ 1 \end{bmatrix} V.$$

Example 5.21 : Obtain the state model of the system with transfer function

$$G(s) = \frac{(s + 1) (s + 2) (s + 5)}{(s + 4)^2 (s + 6)}$$

(a) Controllable canonocal form.

(b) Observable canonical form

(c) Jordan canonical form

Solution : $G(s) = \dfrac{(s + 1)(s + 2)(s + 5)}{(s^2 + 8s + 16)(s + 6)} = \dfrac{(s^2 + 3s + 2)(s + 5)}{(s^3 + 8s^2 + 16s + 6s^2 + 48s + 96)}$

$= \dfrac{s^3 + 3s^2 + 2s + 5s^2 + 15s + 10}{s^3 + 14s^2 + 54s + 96}$

$G(s) = \dfrac{Y(s)}{V(s)} = \dfrac{s^3 + 8s^2 + 17s + 10}{s^3 + 14s^2 + 54s + 96} = \dfrac{b_0 s^m + b_1 s^{m-1} + \ldots + b_m}{s^n + a_1 s^{n-1} + \ldots + a_n}$

This can be represented as :

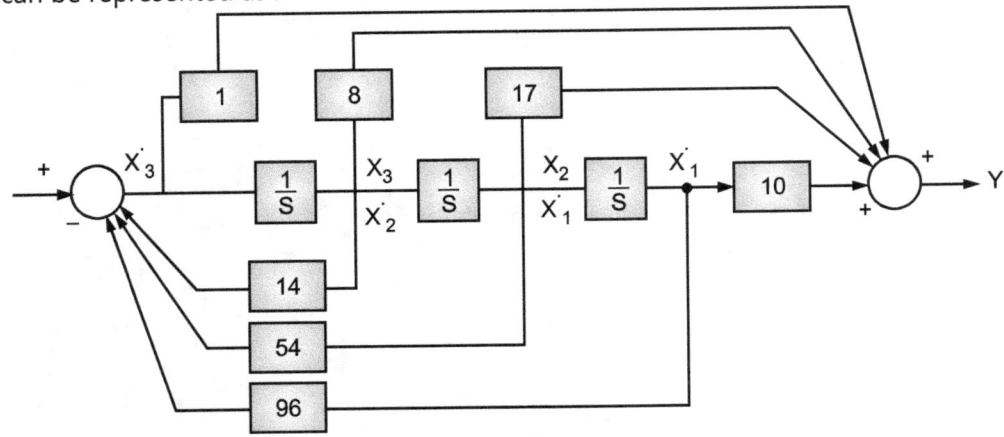

Fig. 5.16

$\dot{X_1} = X_2$

$\dot{X_2} = X_3$

$\dot{X_3} = 4 - 96\, x_1 - 54\, x_2 - 14\, x_3$

$y = 10x_1 + 17x_2 + 8\, x_3 + x_4$

(1) $\dot{X} = A\,(x(t) + Bu(t))$

$$\begin{bmatrix} \dot{X_1} \\ \dot{X_2} \\ \dot{X_3} \end{bmatrix} = \begin{bmatrix} 0 & 1 & 0 \\ 0 & 0 & 1 \\ -96 & -54 & -14 \end{bmatrix} \begin{bmatrix} X_1 \\ X_2 \\ X_3 \end{bmatrix} + \begin{bmatrix} 0 \\ 0 \\ 1 \end{bmatrix} u$$

$Y(t) = CX(t)$

$$Y = \begin{bmatrix} 10 & 17 & 8 & 1 \end{bmatrix} \begin{bmatrix} X_1 \\ X_2 \\ X_3 \\ X_4 \end{bmatrix}$$

∴ By controllable canonical form

$$\begin{bmatrix} \dot{X_1} \\ \dot{X_2} \\ \dot{X_3} \end{bmatrix} = \begin{bmatrix} 0 & 1 & 0 \\ 0 & 0 & 1 \\ -96 & -54 & -14 \end{bmatrix} \begin{bmatrix} X_1 \\ X_2 \\ X_3 \end{bmatrix} + \begin{bmatrix} 0 \\ 0 \\ 1 \end{bmatrix} u$$

2. The controllable canonical model obtained earlier is

$$\begin{bmatrix} \dot{X_1} \\ \dot{X_2} \\ \dot{X_3} \end{bmatrix} = \begin{bmatrix} 0 & 1 & 0 \\ 0 & 0 & 1 \\ -96 & -54 & -14 \end{bmatrix} \begin{bmatrix} X_1 \\ X_2 \\ X_3 \end{bmatrix} + \begin{bmatrix} 0 \\ 0 \\ 1 \end{bmatrix} u$$

$$Y = \begin{bmatrix} 10 & 17 & 8 & 1 \end{bmatrix} \begin{bmatrix} X_1 \\ X_2 \\ X_3 \\ X_4 \end{bmatrix}$$

Hence observable canonical form is

$$\begin{bmatrix} \dot{X_1} \\ \dot{X_2} \\ \dot{X_3} \end{bmatrix} = \begin{bmatrix} 0 & 0 & -96 \\ 1 & 0 & -54 \\ 0 & 1 & -14 \end{bmatrix} \begin{bmatrix} X_1 \\ X_2 \\ X_3 \end{bmatrix} + \begin{bmatrix} 1 \\ 0 \\ 0 \end{bmatrix} u$$

$$Y = \begin{bmatrix} 1 & 8 & 17 & 10 \end{bmatrix} \begin{bmatrix} X_1 \\ X_2 \\ X_3 \\ X_4 \end{bmatrix}$$

Example 5.22 : Find the T.F of system with the system with space model matrices.

$$A = \begin{bmatrix} 0 & 1 \\ -2 & -3 \end{bmatrix}, B = \begin{bmatrix} 0 & 1 \\ s & 1 \end{bmatrix} C = \begin{bmatrix} 1 & 0 \end{bmatrix}$$

Solution : The transfer function is $U(s) = C [sI - A]^{-1} B + D$

Now,

$$A = \begin{bmatrix} 0 & 1 \\ -2 & -3 \end{bmatrix}$$

$$sI - A = s \begin{bmatrix} 1 & 0 \\ 0 & 1 \end{bmatrix} - \begin{bmatrix} 0 & 1 \\ -2 & -3 \end{bmatrix}$$

$$= \begin{bmatrix} s & -1 \\ +2 & s+3 \end{bmatrix} - \begin{bmatrix} s+3 & 2 \\ 1 & s \end{bmatrix}^{T}$$

$$[sI - A]^{-1} = \frac{\begin{bmatrix} s+3 & +1 \\ -2 & s \end{bmatrix}}{s(s+3)+2} = \frac{\begin{bmatrix} s+3 & +1 \\ -2 & s \end{bmatrix}}{s^2 + 3s + 2}$$

$$U(s) = C[sI-A]^{-1}B + D$$

$$= \frac{[1 \quad 0] \begin{bmatrix} s+3 & 1 \\ -2 & s \end{bmatrix} \begin{bmatrix} 0 & 1 \\ 1 & 1 \end{bmatrix}}{s^2 \; 3s + 2}$$

$$= \frac{[s+3 \quad 1] \begin{bmatrix} 0 & 1 \\ s & 1 \end{bmatrix}}{s^2 + 3s + 2}$$

$$= \frac{\begin{bmatrix} 0 & s+3 \\ 1 & 1 \end{bmatrix}}{s^2 + 3s + 2}$$

$$= \begin{bmatrix} \dfrac{s+4}{s^2+3s+2} & \dfrac{1}{s^2+3s+2} \end{bmatrix}$$

$$T(s) = \frac{X(s)}{U(s)} \begin{bmatrix} \dfrac{s+4}{s^2+3s+2} & \dfrac{1}{s^2+3s+2} \end{bmatrix}$$

Example 5.23 : Find the SIM of,

$$A = \begin{bmatrix} 0 & 1 \\ -2 & -3 \end{bmatrix} \text{ in } x(t) = A\, x(t)$$

Find re(t) if $x(0) = \begin{bmatrix} 0 \\ 1 \end{bmatrix}$

Solution

We know, $\phi(t) = C^{-1}[(sI-A)]^{-1}$

$$A = \begin{bmatrix} 0 & 1 \\ -2 & -3 \end{bmatrix}$$

$$sI - A = s \begin{bmatrix} 1 & 0 \\ 0 & 1 \end{bmatrix} - \begin{bmatrix} 0 & 1 \\ -2 & -3 \end{bmatrix}$$

$$= s \begin{bmatrix} 5 & -1 \\ 2 & s+3 \end{bmatrix}$$

$$[sI - A]^{-1} = \frac{\begin{bmatrix} s+3 & 1 \\ -2 & 5 \end{bmatrix}}{s^2 + 3s + 2}$$

$$= \frac{\begin{bmatrix} s+3 & 1 \\ -2 & s \end{bmatrix}}{(s+1)(s+2)}$$

$$[sI - A]^{-1} = \frac{\begin{bmatrix} s+3 & 1 \\ -2 & 5 \end{bmatrix}}{s^2 + 3s + 2} = \frac{\begin{bmatrix} s+3 & 1 \\ -2 & s \end{bmatrix}}{(s+1)(s+2)}$$

$$[sI - A]^{-1} = \begin{bmatrix} \dfrac{s+3}{(s+1)(s+2)} & \dfrac{1}{(s+1)(s+2)} \\ \dfrac{-2}{(s+1)(s+2)} & \dfrac{s}{(s+1)(s+2)} \end{bmatrix}$$

$$= \begin{bmatrix} \dfrac{A_1}{s+1} + \dfrac{B_1}{s+2} & \dfrac{A_2}{s+1} + \dfrac{B_2}{s+2} \\ \dfrac{A_3}{s+1} + \dfrac{B_3}{s+2} & \dfrac{A_4}{s+1} + \dfrac{B_4}{s+2} \end{bmatrix}$$

Where, when $\quad s = -1, -2$

$$A_1 = \frac{s+3}{s+2} \Big|_{s=-1} = 2 \qquad\qquad A_2 = 1$$

$A_3 = -2$ $\qquad\qquad\qquad\qquad A_4 = -1$

$B_1 = -1$ $\qquad\qquad\qquad\qquad B_2 = -1$

$B_3 = -2$ $\qquad\qquad\qquad\qquad B_4 = -2$

$$[sI - A]^{-1} = \begin{bmatrix} \dfrac{2}{(s+4)} - \dfrac{1}{(s+2)} & \dfrac{1}{s+1} - \dfrac{1}{s+2} \\ \dfrac{-2}{s+1} + \dfrac{2}{s+2} & \dfrac{-1}{s+1} + \dfrac{2}{s+2} \end{bmatrix}$$

Example 5.24 : Solve using Jordon forms

$$G(s) = \frac{5}{(s+1)^2(s+2)}$$

Solution : $G(s) = \frac{5}{(s+1)^2(s+2)}$

$$= \frac{A}{(s+1)^2} + \frac{B}{s+1} + \frac{C}{s+2}$$

Where, $s = -1$

$$A = \frac{5}{s+2}\bigg|_{s=-1} = 5$$

$$B = \frac{d}{ds}\left[\frac{s}{s+2}\right]_{s=-1} = -5$$

$$C = \frac{5}{(s+1)^2} = 5$$

$$G(s) = \frac{5}{(s+1)^2} = \frac{5}{s+1} + \frac{5}{s+2}$$

This can be represented as,

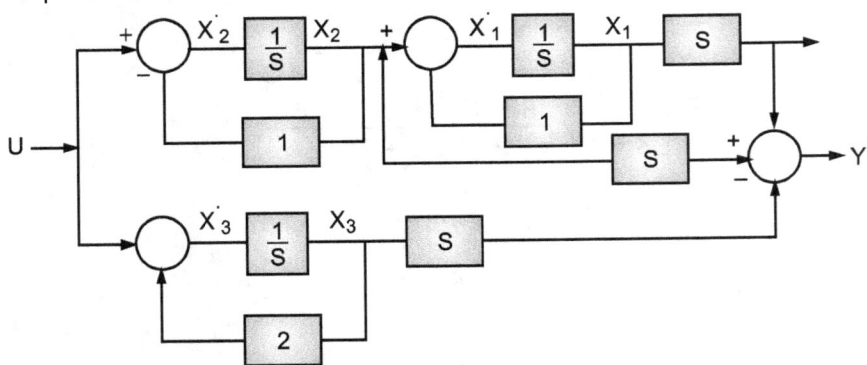

Fig. 5.17

$$\dot{X_1} = x_2 - x_1$$

$$\dot{X_2} = U - x_2$$

$$\dot{X_1} = U - 2x_2$$

$$y = 5x_1 - 5x_2 + 5x_3$$

Then the state model is

$$
\begin{bmatrix} \dot{X_1} \\ \dot{X_2} \\ \dot{X_3} \end{bmatrix} = \begin{bmatrix} -1 & 0 & 0 \\ 0 & -1 & 0 \\ 0 & 0 & -2 \end{bmatrix} \begin{bmatrix} X_1 \\ X_2 \\ X_3 \end{bmatrix} + \begin{bmatrix} 0 \\ 1 \\ 1 \end{bmatrix} u
$$

$$
Y = \begin{bmatrix} 5 & -5 & 3 \end{bmatrix} \begin{bmatrix} X_1 \\ X_2 \\ X_3 \end{bmatrix}
$$

SUMMARY

- The state of a system refers to the past, present, and future conditions of the system.
- The number of state elements in a state vector is referred to as the order of the system.
- Transfer Function approach is called conventional or classical approach and the state variable approach is called the modern approach.
- Classical design methods are based on trial and error procedures and do not result in optimal and adaptive systems.
- State variable approach is applicable to linear as well as non-linear systems, time-invariant as well as time-varying systems, and SISO as well as MIMO systems.
- The transfer function formulation requires the Laplace transform for continuous data control systems and z- transform for discrete-data control systems, but state variable approach offers us a way to look at both the continuous systems and the discrete data systems with the same formulation.
- State variable approach can be used to solve higher order differential equations.
- **A** is called system matrix and **D** is called output matrix.
- The number of state variables of a system is equal to the number of integrators present in the system.
- The STM Depends only on the length (t-t_0) and not on the initial time t_0.

EXERCISE

1. Discuss the advantage of state space techniques over the transfer function techniques of analyzing the control system   **[6]**

2. Determine the state variable representation of the system whose transfer function is given as $\dfrac{Y(s)}{U(s)} = \dfrac{2s^2 + 8s + 7}{(s + 2)^2 (s + 1) (16)}$ **[7]**

3. Explain state space representation for discrete time system **[5]**

4. Given the transfer function of a system, determine a state variable representation for the system $\dfrac{Y(s)}{U(s)} = \dfrac{1}{(s + 2)\,(s + 3)\,(s + 4)\,(16)}$ **[7]**

5. Explain the importance of controllability and Observability of the control system model in the design of the control system. **[6]**

6. Derive an expression for the solution of a homogeneous state equation **[6]**

7. Obtain transfer function of a system from its state model **[6]**

SOLVED UNIVERSITY PROBLEMS

Example 5.1 :

   Obtain controllable and observable canonical state model if.
$$G(s) = \frac{y(s)}{u(s)} = \frac{s^3 + 2s^2 + 5s + 1}{s^4 + 4s^3 + 4s^2 + 7s + 2}$$

Solution :

Given transfer function :
$$G(s) = \frac{s^3 + 2s^2 + 5s + 1}{s^4 + 4s^3 + 4s^2 + 7s + 2}$$

Controllabel canonical form for 4th order system
$$G(s) = \frac{b_0 s^4 + b_1 s^3 + b_2 s^2 + b_3 s + b_4}{s^4 + a_1 s^3 + a_2 s^2 + a_3 s + a_4}$$

$$
\begin{bmatrix} \dot{x}_1 \\ \dot{x}_2 \\ \dot{x}_3 \\ \dot{x}_4 \end{bmatrix}
=
\begin{bmatrix}
0 & 1 & 0 & 0 \\
0 & 0 & 1 & 0 \\
0 & 0 & 0 & 1 \\
-a_4 & -a_3 & -a_2 & -a_1
\end{bmatrix}
=
\begin{bmatrix} x_1 \\ x_2 \\ x_3 \\ x_4 \end{bmatrix}
+
\begin{bmatrix} 0 \\ 0 \\ 0 \\ 1 \end{bmatrix} u
$$

$$
y = [\,b_4 - a_4 b_0 \quad b_3 - a_3 b_0 \qquad b_2 - a_2 b_0 \quad b_1 - a_1 b_0\,]
\begin{bmatrix} x_1 \\ x_2 \\ x_3 \\ x_4 \end{bmatrix}
+ b_0 u
$$

From given transfer function

$b_0 = 0;$ $b_1 = 1,$ $b_2 = 2,$ $b_3 = 5,$ $b_4 = 1$

$a_1 = 2;$ $a_2 = 4,$ $a_3 = 7,$ $a_4 = 2$

Controllable canonical form

$$
\begin{bmatrix} \dot{x}_1 \\ \dot{x}_2 \\ \dot{x}_3 \\ \dot{x}_4 \end{bmatrix} = \begin{bmatrix} 0 & 1 & 0 & 0 \\ 0 & 0 & 1 & 0 \\ 0 & 0 & 0 & 1 \\ -2 & -7 & -4 & -4 \end{bmatrix} = \begin{bmatrix} x_1 \\ x_2 \\ x_3 \\ x_4 \end{bmatrix} + \begin{bmatrix} 0 \\ 0 \\ 0 \\ 1 \end{bmatrix} u
$$

$$
y = [1, 2, 5, 1] \begin{bmatrix} x_1 \\ x_2 \\ x_3 \\ x_4 \end{bmatrix}
$$

Observable canonical form for 4th order system.

$$
\begin{bmatrix} \dot{x}_1 \\ \dot{x}_2 \\ \dot{x}_3 \\ \dot{x}_4 \end{bmatrix} = \begin{bmatrix} 0 & 0 & 0 & -a_4 \\ 1 & 0 & 0 & -a_3 \\ 0 & 1 & 0 & -a_2 \\ 0 & 0 & 1 & -a_1 \end{bmatrix} \begin{bmatrix} x_1 \\ x_2 \\ x_3 \\ x_4 \end{bmatrix} + \begin{bmatrix} b_4 - a_4 b_0 \\ b_3 - a_3 b_0 \\ b_2 - a_2 b_0 \\ b_1 - a_1 b_0 \end{bmatrix} u
$$

$$
y = [0\,0\,0\,1] \begin{bmatrix} x_1 \\ x_2 \\ x_3 \\ x_4 \end{bmatrix} + b_0 u
$$

Observable canonical form :

$$
\begin{bmatrix} \dot{x}_1 \\ \dot{x}_2 \\ \dot{x}_3 \\ \dot{x}_4 \end{bmatrix} = \begin{bmatrix} 0 & 0 & 0 & -2 \\ 1 & 0 & 0 & -7 \\ 0 & 1 & 0 & -4 \\ 0 & 0 & 1 & -4 \end{bmatrix} = \begin{bmatrix} x_1 \\ x_2 \\ x_3 \\ x_4 \end{bmatrix} + \begin{bmatrix} 1 \\ 5 \\ 2 \\ 1 \end{bmatrix} u
$$

$$y = [0\,0\,0\,1] \begin{bmatrix} x_1 \\ x_2 \\ x_3 \\ x_4 \end{bmatrix}$$

Example 5.2 : Find controllability and observability if :

$$A = \begin{bmatrix} -2 & 1 & 0 \\ 1 & -3 & 2 \\ 10 & 0 & -8 \end{bmatrix}, B = \begin{bmatrix} 0 \\ 0.1 \\ 1 \end{bmatrix}, C = [1\ 0\ 1]\ D = [0]$$

Solution :

Step 1 : To check whether the system is controllable

A nth order LIT system may be represented by its state equation as

$$\dot{x}(t) = A\,x(t) + Bu(t)$$

Here, A is a n × n matrix

The necessary and sufficient condition for controllability is that rank of the composite matrix Q_c is n, Where n is the rank of the matrix A.

And $\qquad\qquad Q_c = [B : AB : A_2B : \ldots\ldots A^{n-1}B)$

By comparing we get,

$$A = \begin{bmatrix} -2 & 1 & 0 \\ 1 & -3 & 2 \\ 10 & 0 & -8 \end{bmatrix} B = \begin{bmatrix} 0 \\ 0.1 \\ 1 \end{bmatrix}$$

Therefore A is a 3 × 3 matrix, thus n = 3

$$\therefore \qquad AB = \begin{bmatrix} -2 & 1 & 0 \\ 1 & -3 & 2 \\ 10 & 0 & -8 \end{bmatrix} \begin{bmatrix} 0 \\ 0.1 \\ 1 \end{bmatrix} = \begin{bmatrix} 0.1 \\ 1.7 \\ -8 \end{bmatrix}$$

$$\therefore \qquad A^2B = A(AB) = \begin{bmatrix} -2 & 1 & 0 \\ 1 & -3 & 2 \\ 10 & 0 & -8 \end{bmatrix} \begin{bmatrix} 0.1 \\ 1.7 \\ -8 \end{bmatrix} = \begin{bmatrix} 1.5 \\ 21 \\ 65 \end{bmatrix}$$

$$\therefore \qquad Q_c = [B\ AB\ A^2B]$$

$$\therefore \qquad Q_c = \begin{bmatrix} 0 & 0.1 & 1.5 \\ 0.1 & 1.7 & -21 \\ 1 & -8 & 65 \end{bmatrix}$$

Now, we calculate the determinant of Q_c

$$\begin{vmatrix} 0 & 0.1 & 1.5 \\ 0.1 & 1.7 & -21 \\ 1 & -8 & 65 \end{vmatrix} = -6.5$$

i.e. determinant of Q_c is non-zero

Hence the Rank of Q_c = n = 3

Since, the Rank of Q_c = n

Hence the system is controllable.

Step 2 : To check operability of the system

N^{th} order MIMO LTI system can be represented by state variables as;

$$\dot{x}(t) = Ax(t) + Bu(t) \text{ and}$$
$$y(t) = Cx(t) + Du(t)$$

But $\qquad\qquad\qquad D = [0]$

Where $\qquad\qquad y(t) = p \times 1 \qquad\qquad$ output vector

$\qquad\qquad\qquad C = 1 \times n$ is the matrix

A system is completely observable if and only if the rank of the composite matrix Q_o is n

Where, $\qquad\qquad Q_o = [c^T : ATCT : \quad (A^T)^{n-1} C^T]$

In this order of the system is 3, thus n = 3

Now $\qquad\qquad\qquad A = \begin{bmatrix} -2 & 1 & 0 \\ 1 & -3 & 2 \\ 10 & 0 & -8 \end{bmatrix}$ and c = [1, 0, 1]

$\therefore \qquad\qquad A^T = \begin{bmatrix} -2 & 1 & 10 \\ 1 & -3 & 0 \\ 0 & 2 & -8 \end{bmatrix}$ and $\qquad c^t = \begin{bmatrix} 1 \\ 0 \\ 1 \end{bmatrix}$

$\therefore \qquad A^T C^T = \begin{bmatrix} -2 & 1 & 10 \\ 1 & -3 & 0 \\ 0 & 2 & -8 \end{bmatrix} \begin{bmatrix} 1 \\ 0 \\ 1 \end{bmatrix} = \begin{bmatrix} 8 \\ 1 \\ -8 \end{bmatrix}$

$\therefore \quad (A^T)^2 C^T = A^T (A^T C^T) = \begin{bmatrix} -2 & 1 & 10 \\ 1 & -3 & 0 \\ 0 & 2 & -8 \end{bmatrix} = \begin{bmatrix} 8 \\ 1 \\ -8 \end{bmatrix} = \begin{bmatrix} -95 \\ 5 \\ 66 \end{bmatrix}$

$$Q_o = [C^T A^T C^T \quad (A^T)^2 \qquad C^T]$$

$$\therefore \quad Q_o = \begin{bmatrix} 1 & 8 & -95 \\ 0 & 1 & 5 \\ 1 & 8 & 66 \end{bmatrix}$$

Now we calculate the determinant of Q_o

$$\begin{vmatrix} 1 & 8 & -95 \\ 0 & 1 & 5 \\ 1 & 8 & 66 \end{vmatrix} = 241$$

i.e. determinant of Q_o is non – zero

Hence the Rank of Q_o = n = 3

Since, Rank of Q_o = n

Hence, the system is completely observable.

Example 5.3 : Find controllability and observability of the state model.

$$A = \begin{bmatrix} 1 & 0 & 1 \\ 0 & 1 & 1 \\ 1 & 1 & 1 \end{bmatrix}, B = \begin{bmatrix} 1 \\ 1 \\ 1 \end{bmatrix}, C = [1\ 1\ 1]\ D= [\ 0]$$

[June 2015]

Solution :

Ans. : To check controlability : The rank of the composite matrix Qc is n = 3, which is necessary and sufficient condition for controllability where n is the size of matrix A.

$$Q_c = [B : ..... A^{n-1} B]$$

Since n = 3.

$$\therefore \qquad Qc = [B : AB : A^2 B]$$

Here,

$$B = \begin{bmatrix} 1 \\ 1 \\ 1 \end{bmatrix}$$

$$AB = \begin{bmatrix} 1 & 0 & 1 \\ 0 & 1 & 1 \\ 1 & 1 & 1 \end{bmatrix} \begin{bmatrix} 1 \\ 1 \\ 1 \end{bmatrix} \begin{bmatrix} 1 + 0 + 1 \\ 0 + 1 + 1 \\ 1 + 1 + 1 \end{bmatrix}$$

$$\therefore \qquad AB = \begin{bmatrix} 2 \\ 2 \\ 3 \end{bmatrix}$$

$$A^2B = A(AB) = \begin{bmatrix} 1 & 0 & 1 \\ 0 & 1 & 1 \\ 1 & 1 & 1 \end{bmatrix} \begin{bmatrix} 2 \\ 2 \\ 2 \end{bmatrix} = \begin{bmatrix} 2+0+3 \\ 0+2+3 \\ 2+2+3 \end{bmatrix}$$

$\therefore \qquad A^2B = \begin{bmatrix} 5 \\ 5 \\ 7 \end{bmatrix}$

$\therefore \qquad Q_c = [B : AB : A^2B] \begin{bmatrix} 1 & 2 & 5 \\ 1 & 2 & 5 \\ 1 & 3 & 7 \end{bmatrix}$

To find the determinant of Q_C

$|\therefore \qquad Q_0 = \begin{bmatrix} 1 & 2 & 5 \\ 1 & 2 & 5 \\ 1 & 2 & 7 \end{bmatrix} = 0$

$\therefore \qquad |Q_C| = 0$

As determinant is zero, the rank of Q_c is 3 ≠ n. Thus, system is **not controllable.**

To check or observability :

A system is completely observable if and only if the rank of composite matrix Q_o is n (in this case n = 3). Here

$$Q_0 = [C^T : A^T C^T : ... (A^T)^{n-1} C^T]$$

Since n = 3

$\therefore \qquad Q_0 = [C^T : A^T C^T : ... (A^T)^2 C^T]$

We have

$$C^T = \begin{bmatrix} 1 \\ 1 \\ 1 \end{bmatrix} \quad A^T C^T = \begin{bmatrix} 1 & 0 & 1 \\ 0 & 1 & 1 \\ 1 & 1 & 1 \end{bmatrix} \begin{bmatrix} 1 \\ 1 \\ 1 \end{bmatrix}$$

$\therefore \qquad A^T C^T = \begin{bmatrix} 1+0+1 \\ 0+1+1 \\ 1+1+1 \end{bmatrix} \begin{bmatrix} 2 \\ 2 \\ 3 \end{bmatrix}$

Now,

$$(A^T)^2 C^T = A^T \{A^T C^T\} = \begin{bmatrix} 1 & 0 & 1 \\ 0 & 1 & 1 \\ 1 & 1 & 1 \end{bmatrix} \begin{bmatrix} 2 \\ 2 \\ 3 \end{bmatrix} = \begin{bmatrix} 2+0+3 \\ 0+2+3 \\ 2+2+3 \end{bmatrix}$$

$$\therefore \qquad (A^T)^2 C^T = \begin{bmatrix} 5 \\ 5 \\ 7 \end{bmatrix}$$

$$\therefore \qquad Q_0 = \begin{bmatrix} 1 & 2 & 5 \\ 1 & 2 & 5 \\ 1 & 3 & 7 \end{bmatrix}$$

We now compute the determinant of Q_0

$$\therefore \qquad |Q_0| = \begin{vmatrix} 1 & 2 & 5 \\ 1 & 2 & 5 \\ 1 & 3 & 7 \end{vmatrix} = 0$$

Since $\qquad |Q_0| = 0$.

$\therefore$ Rank of $Q_0 \neq 3 \neq n$.

$\therefore$ System is **not observable.**

Example 5.4 : Find controllability and observability of the system given by state model :

$$A = \begin{bmatrix} 1 & 1 & 5 \\ 1 & -2 & 2 \\ 5 & 2 & 8 \end{bmatrix}, B = \begin{bmatrix} 5 \\ 1 \\ 10 \end{bmatrix}, C = [10 \ 15 \ 11]$$

$$D = [0] \qquad\qquad \text{[May 2014]}$$

Solution :

Step 1 : To check whether system is controllable.

A nth order LIT system may be represented by its state equation as

$$\dot{x}(t) = Ax(t) + b\,u(t)$$

Here, A is a $n \times n$ matrix

The necessary and sufficient condition for controllability $\rightarrow$ the rank of the matrix Q_c should be n; where n is the size of matrix A.

$$Q_c = [B : AB : A^2B : ... \ A^{n-1} B]$$

By comparing we get,

$$A = \begin{bmatrix} 1 & 1 & 5 \\ 1 & -2 & 2 \\ 5 & 2 & -8 \end{bmatrix}, B = \begin{bmatrix} 5 \\ 1 \\ 10 \end{bmatrix}$$

Therefore, A is a 3×3 matrix, Thus n = 3

$\therefore \qquad AB = \begin{bmatrix} 1 & 1 & 5 \\ 1 & -2 & 2 \\ 5 & 2 & -8 \end{bmatrix} \begin{bmatrix} 5 \\ 1 \\ 10 \end{bmatrix} = \begin{bmatrix} 56 \\ 23 \\ -53 \end{bmatrix}$

$\therefore \qquad A^2B = A(AB) = \begin{bmatrix} 1 & 1 & 5 \\ 1 & -2 & 2 \\ 5 & 2 & -8 \end{bmatrix} \begin{bmatrix} 56 \\ 23 \\ -53 \end{bmatrix} = \begin{bmatrix} -186 \\ -96 \\ 750 \end{bmatrix}$

$\therefore \qquad Q_c = [B\ AB\ A^2B]$

$\therefore \qquad Q_c = \begin{bmatrix} 5 & 56 & -186 \\ 1 & 23 & -96 \\ 10 & -53 & 750 \end{bmatrix}$

Step 2 : Calculate determinant of Q_c

$\therefore \qquad Q_c = \begin{bmatrix} 5 & 56 & -186 \\ 1 & 23 & -96 \\ 10 & -53 & 750 \end{bmatrix} = 17688$

The determinant of Q_c is non-zero,
Hence, the rank of Q_c = n = 3
Since Rank of Qc = n (size of matrix)
Hence the system is controllable

Step 3 : To check whether system is observable.
n^{th} order MIMO LIT system can be represented by its state variable as ;

$$\dot{x}(t) = Ax(t) + Bu(t)\ \text{and}$$
$$y(t) = Cx(t) + Du(t)$$

The system is completely observable if and only if the rank of composite matrix Q_o is n.
Where, $Q_o = [C^T : A^TC^T : ... (A^T)^{n-1}\ C^T]$
Here order of system is 3, thus n = 3

$$A = \begin{bmatrix} 1 & 1 & 5 \\ 1 & -2 & 2 \\ 5 & 2 & -8 \end{bmatrix} \text{ and } C = [10\ 15\ 11]$$

$\therefore \qquad A^T = \begin{bmatrix} 1 & 1 & 5 \\ 1 & -2 & 2 \\ 5 & 2 & -8 \end{bmatrix} \text{ and } c^T = \begin{bmatrix} 10 \\ 15 \\ 11 \end{bmatrix}$

$\therefore$
$$A^T C^T = \begin{bmatrix} 1 & 1 & 5 \\ 1 & -2 & 2 \\ 5 & 2 & -8 \end{bmatrix} \begin{bmatrix} 10 \\ 15 \\ 11 \end{bmatrix} = \begin{bmatrix} 80 \\ 2 \\ -8 \end{bmatrix}$$

$\therefore$
$$(A^T)^2 C^T = A^T (A^T C^T)$$

$$= \begin{bmatrix} 1 & 1 & 5 \\ 1 & -2 & 2 \\ 5 & 2 & -8 \end{bmatrix} \begin{bmatrix} 80 \\ 2 \\ -8 \end{bmatrix} = \begin{bmatrix} 42 \\ 60 \\ 468 \end{bmatrix}$$

$$Q_o = [C^T \; A^T C^T \; (A^T)^2 C^T]$$

$\therefore$
$$Q_o = \begin{bmatrix} 10 & 80 & 42 \\ 15 & 2 & 60 \\ 11 & -8 & 468 \end{bmatrix}$$

Step 4 : To calculate determinant of Q_o

$$Q_o = \begin{vmatrix} 10 & 80 & 42 \\ 15 & 2 & 60 \\ 11 & -8 & 467 \end{vmatrix} = -500604$$

Q_o is non zero. Hence Rank of matrix $Q_o = n = 3$, Since rank of $Q_o = n$

Hence system is completely **observable.**

Example 5.5 : Obtain the state space representation of system whose differential equation is

$$\frac{d^3y}{dt^3} + 2\frac{d^2y}{dt^2} + 3\frac{dy}{dt} + 6y = \frac{d^2u}{dt^2} - \frac{du}{dt} + 2u$$

Also find the controllability and observability of the system. Assume zero initial conditions.

Solution :

Given :
$$\frac{d^3y}{dt^3} + 2\frac{d^2y}{d_t^2} + 3\frac{dy}{dt} + 6y = \frac{d^2u}{d_t^2} - \frac{du}{dt} + 2u$$

Apply laplace by taking initial conditions as zero, we get,

$$(s^3 + 2s^2 + 3s + 6) \, Y(s) = (s^2 - s + 2) \, u(s)$$

Transfer function is

$$\frac{Y(s)}{u(s)} = \frac{s^2 - s + 2}{s^3 + 2s^2 + 3s + 6}$$

Transfer function equation be split as;

$$\frac{Y(s)}{X(s)} = s^2 - s + 2 \text{ and } \frac{x(s)}{u(s)} = \frac{1}{s^3 + 2s^2 + 3s + 6}$$

$$\therefore \quad \frac{x(s)}{u(s)} = \frac{1}{s^3 + 2s^2 + 3s + 6}$$

$$u(s) = s^3 x(s) + 2s^2 x(s) + 3s x(s) + 6 x(s)$$

Apply inverse laplace we get,

$$u = \overset{..}{x} + 2\overset{..}{x} + 3\dot{x} + 6x \tag{1}$$

$$x_1 = x(2)$$
$$x_2 = \dot{x}(3)$$
$$x_3 = x_2(4)$$

Substitute equations (2), (3), (4) in equation (1)
Hence, we get

$$\dot{x}_3 = u - 2x_3 - 3x_2 + 6x_1 \tag{5}$$

From equation (3), (4), (5) we can form matrix as;

$$\begin{bmatrix} \dot{x_1} \\ \dot{x}_2 \\ \dot{x_3} \end{bmatrix} = \begin{bmatrix} 0 & 1 & 0 \\ 0 & 0 & 1 \\ -6 & -3 & -2 \end{bmatrix} = \begin{bmatrix} x_1 \\ x_2 \\ x_3 \end{bmatrix} + \begin{bmatrix} 0 \\ 0 \\ 1 \end{bmatrix} u$$

$$Y(s) = s^2 x(s) - s x(s) + 2 x(s)$$

Apply inverse laplace,

$$Y = \overset{..}{x} - \dot{x} + 2x$$
$$Y = x_3 - x_2 + 2x_1$$

$$Y = [2 \; -1 \; 1] \begin{bmatrix} x_1 \\ x_2 \\ x_3 \end{bmatrix}$$

Hence, the State Space Model is

$$\begin{bmatrix} \dot{x_1} \\ \dot{x}_2 \\ \dot{x_3} \end{bmatrix} = \begin{bmatrix} 0 & 1 & 0 \\ 0 & 0 & 1 \\ -6 & -3 & -2 \end{bmatrix} = \begin{bmatrix} x_1 \\ x_2 \\ x_3 \end{bmatrix} + \begin{bmatrix} 0 \\ 0 \\ 1 \end{bmatrix} u$$

$$Y = [2 \; -1 \; 1] \begin{bmatrix} x_1 \\ x_2 \\ x_3 \end{bmatrix}$$

Example 5.6 : Obtain the state transition matrix ifl

(i) $\qquad \dfrac{dx}{dt} = \begin{bmatrix} 0 & 1 \\ -1 & 0 \end{bmatrix} x$

(ii) $\qquad \dfrac{dx}{dt} = \begin{bmatrix} 0 & 1 \\ 0 & 0 \end{bmatrix} x$ **[Dec. 2010]**

Solution : Using laplace transform

Given, $\qquad \dfrac{dx}{dt} = \begin{bmatrix} 0 & 1 \\ -1 & 0 \end{bmatrix} x$

We have homogeneous equation; $\dfrac{dx}{dt} = Ax$ by

Comparing we get;

$$A = \begin{bmatrix} 0 & 1 \\ -1 & 0 \end{bmatrix}$$

State transition matrix is $e^{At} = L^{-1}[\{sI - A\}^{-1}]$

Where, $\qquad I = \begin{bmatrix} 1 & 0 \\ 0 & 1 \end{bmatrix}$ $\qquad$ Identity Matrix

Hence, $\qquad [(sI - A)] = \left[s\begin{bmatrix} 1 & 0 \\ 0 & 1 \end{bmatrix} - \begin{bmatrix} 0 & 1 \\ -1 & 0 \end{bmatrix} \right]$

$$= \begin{bmatrix} s & -1 \\ 1 & s \end{bmatrix}$$

$$[\{sI - A\}^{-1}] = \dfrac{adj\ (sI - A)}{det\ (sI - A)}$$

$$adj\ (sI - A) = \begin{bmatrix} s & -1 \\ 1 & s \end{bmatrix}$$

$$det\ (sI - A) = (s^2 + 1)$$

Now, $\qquad [(sI - A)^{-1}] = \dfrac{\begin{bmatrix} s & 1 \\ -1 & s \end{bmatrix}}{s^2 + 1}$

$$L^{-1}[\{sI - A\}^{-1}] = L^{-1}\begin{bmatrix} \dfrac{s}{s^2 + 2} & \dfrac{1}{s^2 + 1} \\ \dfrac{-1}{s^2 + 1} & \dfrac{s}{s^2 + 1} \end{bmatrix}$$

From the laplace transform formula,

$$L^{-1} = \left[\frac{a}{s^2 + a^2}\right] = \sin(at)$$

$$L^{-1} = \left[\frac{a}{s^2 + a^2}\right] = \cos(at)$$

Hence the state transition matrix is,

$$e^{At} = \begin{bmatrix} \cos t & \sin t \\ -\sin t & \cos t \end{bmatrix}$$

(ii) Given

$$\frac{dx}{dt} = \begin{bmatrix} 0 & 1 \\ 0 & 0 \end{bmatrix} x$$

We have homogeneous equation

$$\frac{dx}{dt} = ax \ by$$

Comparing we get

$$A = \begin{bmatrix} 0 & 1 \\ 0 & 0 \end{bmatrix}$$

State transition matrix is

$$e^{At} = L^{-1}[\{sI - A\}^{-1}]$$

where,

$$I = \begin{bmatrix} 1 & 0 \\ 0 & 1 \end{bmatrix} \quad \text{Identity matrix}$$

now

$$(sI - A) = s\begin{bmatrix} 1 & 0 \\ 0 & 1 \end{bmatrix} - \begin{bmatrix} 0 & 1 \\ 0 & 0 \end{bmatrix} = \begin{bmatrix} s & -1 \\ 0 & s \end{bmatrix}$$

$$(sI - A)^{-1} = \frac{adj(sI - A)}{det(sI - A)} =$$

$$Adj\,(sI - A) = \begin{bmatrix} s & -1 \\ 0 & s \end{bmatrix}$$

$$det = (sI - A) = s^2$$

Hence,

$$L^{-1}[\{sI - A\}^{-1}] = L^{-1}\left(\frac{\begin{bmatrix} s & 1 \\ 0 & s \end{bmatrix}}{s^2}\right)$$

The Inverse laplace is given by,

$$L^{-1}\left(\frac{1}{s}\right) = L^{-1}\left(\frac{1}{s^n}\right) = \frac{1}{(n-1)!}\ t^{n-1}$$

$\therefore$

$$e^{At} = \begin{bmatrix} \dfrac{s}{s^2} & \dfrac{1}{s^2} \\[2ex] 0 & \dfrac{s}{s^2} \end{bmatrix}$$

Therefore the state transition matrix is

$$e^{At} = \begin{bmatrix} 1 & t \\ 0 & t \end{bmatrix}$$

◇ ◇ ◇

CONTROLLERS AND DIGITAL CONTROL SYSTEMS

6.1 INTRODUCTION TO PLC

Initially industries used relays to control the manufacturing processes. The relay control panels had to be regularly replaced, consumed lot of power and it was difficult to figure out the problems associated with it. To sort these issues, Programmable logic controller (PLC) was introduced.

6.1.1 What is PLC?

Programmable Logic Controller (PLC) is a digital computer used for the automation of various electro-mechanical processes in industries. These controllers are specially designed to survive in harsh situations and shielded from heat, cold, dust, and moisture etc. The purpose of a PLC was to directly replace electromechanical relays as logic elements, substituting instead a solid-state digital computer with a stored program, able to emulate the interconnection of many relays to perform certain logical tasks. PLC consists of a microprocessor which is programmed using the computer language.

The program is written on a computer and is downloaded to the PLC via cable. These loaded programs are stored in non – volatile memory of the PLC. During the transition of relay control panels to PLC, the hard wired relay logic was exchanged for the program fed by the user. A visual programming language known as the Ladder Logic was created to program the PLC.

6.1.2 History

Programmable Logic Controllers were discovered by the automotive industry to substitute the re-wiring of the machine's control panel.

Prior to the invention of PLC, automobiles were manufactured using plenty of relays, cam timers, and closed loop controllers. The electricians had to re-wire every part of the machine daily which was time consuming and highly expensive on the financial front.

Later in the year 1968, a request for an electronic device for the hard-wired relay systems was made by GM hydramatic. Bedford Associates won the proposal and started a new company to develop, fabricate, sell, and service this new launched product. The first PLC launched was designated 084 as it was the eighty fourth projects of Bedford Associates. Dick Morley worked on this project and is being considered as the Father of PLC. In the year 1977, the brand invented by Modicon was sold to Gould Electronics. The Gould Electronics later sold it to German Company AEG which was later taken over by French Schneider Electric.

The first 084 model of PLC was revealed in North Andover, Massachusetts at the Modicon headquarters. The automotive industry is one of the largest users of PLC.

6.2 WORKING OF PLC (PROGRAMMABLE LOGIC CONTROLLER)

The Programmable logic controller functions in four steps.

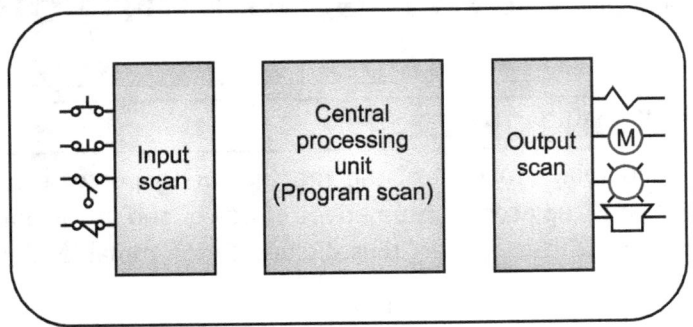

Fig. 6.1

- **Input Scan :** The state of the input is scanned which is connected externally. The inputs include switches, pushbuttons, and proximity sensors, limit switches, pressure switches. Ideally, they are transformers and not relays.

- **Program Scan :** The loaded program is executed to carry out the function appropriately.

- **Output Scan :** The input sources have a control over the output ports to energize or de-energize them. The outputs include solenoids, valves, motors, actuator, and pumps. Depending on the model of PLC, these relays can be transistors, triacs or relays.

- **Housekeeping**

6.3 BLOCK DIAGRAM

Block Diagram of PLC

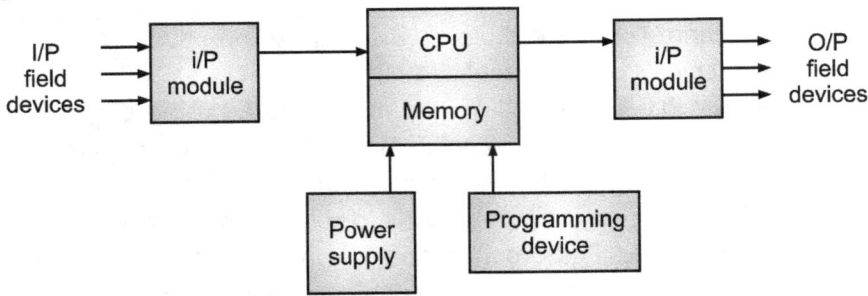

Fig. 6.2 : Block diagram of PLC

The block diagram of PLC is shown in Fig. 6.2. The PLC consist of following elements.

1. CUP (Processor)
2. Memory
3. Programming device
4. Input module
5. Output module
6. Power supply.

1. **CPU :** All programmable Logic controller contains a central processing unit. This is the microprocessor that controls and supervises the entire process. The CPU executes users program and status of output devices. During the program execution the process takes input, read input values and according to user's program depending on input values it makes and updates status of output devices.

2. **Memory :** Memory is used to store program result of input output operations. PLC memory is divided in two categories.

   - System memory
   - Application memory

   System program is stored in ROM and application program is stored in RAM.

3. **Programming Device :**

- The PLC is programmed by using programming devices. Programmer can enter, or edit program by using programming device.
- The basic elements of a programming device are keyboard, display, communication cable.
- The programming device is connected to programmable controller during programming or during troubleshooting of control system. Otherwise it is disconnected from the system.
- The most common programming devices are
   - ➢ Handheld programming unit
   - ➢ Industrial programming unit
   - ➢ Personal computer

4. **Input Module :**

- Input module creates link between input field devices and CPU of PLC. Each module has terminal block for attaching Input wiring from each individual field input device.
- The main function of Input module is to take input field device signal, convert this signal into signal which is compatible with CPU i.e. CPU can work on this signal.
- Input module and CPU are electrically isolated. Optocouplers are used for isolation.
- Typical Input modules have either 8, 16 or 32 Input terminals.

5. **Output Module :**

- Output module is a electronic circuit which interfaces field input devices to CPU of PLC.
- Each module has a terminal block for attaching output wiring to each individual field output device.
- The main function of output module is controlled signal from CPU, electrically isolate and energize or de-energize the modules switching device to turn on or turn off the output field device.
- Typical output modules have either 8, 16 or 21 output terminals.

6. Power Supply :

It supplies power to PLC

Selection Criteria for PLC :

- Number of logic inputs & Outputs
- Memory
- Number of special I/O Modules
- Scan Time
- Communications
- Software

Advantages of PLC :

- **Small Size :** They are usually very compact and do not have large space requirement
- **Rugged Construction :** It is rugged enough to operate in industrial environment.
- **Greater Reliability :** According to logic in program the operations are performed by it.
- **Easy Interfacing :** Input devices are easily interfaced with PLC by using input output module.
- It can be easily reprogrammed.
- Ability to communicate with computers, another PLC's.
- Relatively inexpensive than hardwired relay control.

Disadvantages :

- It is a tedious job when replacing or bringing any changes to it.
- Skilful work force is required to find its errors.
- Lot of effort is put to connect the wires.
- The holdup time is usually indefinite when any problem arises.

Applications of PLC :

The simple suitable application is a conveyor system. The requirements of the conveyor systems are as follows :

- A programmable logic controller is used to start and stop the motors of the conveyor belt.
- The conveyor system has three segmented conveyor belts. Each segment is run by a motor.
- To detect the position of a plate, a proximity switch is positioned at the segment's end.
- The first conveyor segment is turned ON always.
- The proximity switch in the first segment detects the plate to turn ON the second conveyor segment.
- The third conveyor segment is turned ON when the proximity switch detects the plate at the second conveyor.
- As the plate comes out of the detection range, the second conveyor is stopped after 20 sec.
- When the proximity switch fails to detect the plate, the third conveyor is stopped after 20 sec.

6.4 LADDER LOGIC FOR PLC

Ladder logic was originally a written method to document the design and construction of relay racks as used in manufacturing and process control. Each device in the relay rack would be represented by a symbol on the ladder diagram with connections between those devices shown. In addition, other items external to the relay rack such as pumps, heaters, and so forth would also be shown on the ladder diagram.

Ladder logic has evolved into a programming language that represents a program by a graphical diagram based on the circuit diagrams of relay logic hardware. Ladder logic is used to develop software for programmable logic controllers (PLCs) used in industrial control applications. The name is based on the observation that programs in this language resemble ladders, with two vertical rails and a series of horizontal rungs between them.

The language itself can be seen as a set of connections between logical checkers (contacts) and actuators (coils). If a path can be traced between the left side of the rung and the output, through asserted (true or "closed") contacts, the rung is true and the output coil storage bit is asserted (1) or true. If no path can be traced, then the output is false (0) and the "coil"

Ladder logic has contacts that make or break circuits to control coils. Each coil or contact corresponds to the status of a single bit in the programmable controller's memory. Unlike electromechanical relays, a ladder program can refer any number of times to the status of a single bit, equivalent to a relay with an indefinitely large number of contacts.

So-called "contacts" may refer to physical ("hard") inputs to the programmable controller from physical devices such as pushbuttons and limit switches via an integrated or external input module, or may represent the status of internal storage bits which may be generated elsewhere in the program.

Each rung of ladder language typically has one coil at the far right. Some manufacturers may allow more than one output coil on a rung.

- **Rung Input :** Checkers (contacts)
  - ➤ $-[\ ]-$ Normally open contact, closed whenever its corresponding coil or an input which controls it is energized. (Open contact at rest)
  - ➤ $-[\backslash]-$ Normally closed ("not") contact, closed whenever its corresponding coil or an input which controls it is not energized. (Closed contact at rest)
- **Rung Output :** Actuators (coils)
  - ➤ $-(\ )-$ Normally inactive coil, energized whenever its rung is closed. (Inactive at rest)
  - ➤ $-(\backslash)-$ Normally active ("not") coil, energized whenever its rung is open. (Active at rest)

The "coil" (output of a rung) may represent a physical output which operates some device connected to the programmable controller, or may represent an internal storage bit for use elsewhere in the program.

A way to recall these is to imagine the checkers (contacts) as a push button input, and the actuators (coils) as a light bulb output. The presence of a slash within the checkers or actuators would indicate the default state of the device at rest.

Rules of Ladder Diagram :

- The vertical line, which is at left represent power line (left rail)
- The vertical line, which is at right represent neutral line (right rail)
- Input device connected to left rail (Power line)
- Output devices are connected towards right rail (Neutral line)
- Horizontal line represents (rung) step of a ladder.
- Horizontal line or rungs labblled numerically from top to bottom.
- Ladder diagram programme is read from left to right and from top to bottom.
- Many input device can be connected in a rung.
- Generally only one output device is connected in a rung.
- N.O. contact are closed, when the device that control is energized.
- N.C. contact is opened, when the device that control is de-energized.
- Address or numbers are given to the input output device.
- The last rung of a ladder diagram is "end" which terminates the programme.

6.4.1 PLC Applications with Ladder Diagram

    1. Bottle filling   2. Elevator

    3. Motor Control 4. Digital Logic

1. Ladder Diagram for Bottle Filling Plant :

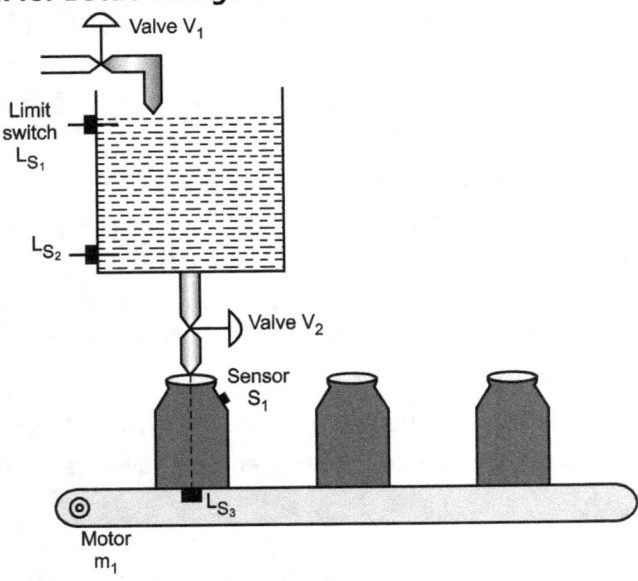

Fig. 6.3 : Bottle filling plant system

Logic :

- When start push button is pressed process should start and when stop button is pressed whole process should stop.
- When process starts, motor turns ON and conveyer belt moves.
- Position of bottle is sensual by limit switch L_{s3}. When bottle is exactly below the value outlet, liquid filled in bottle by opening value V_2.
- Liquid level in bottle is sensed by sensor when bottle level is full then valve V_2 is closed.
- Limit switch L_s, and L_{s2} are used to sense liquid level in tank. When liquid level is low it is sensed by L_{s2} and valve V_1 is turned on (Opened) to fill the liquid in tank.
- When liquid in tank is full then valve V_1 is turned off. (closed)

Input/Output List :

Input List :

1.	Start push button $\rightarrow$ No $\rightarrow$	PB_1
2.	Stop push button $\rightarrow$ Nc $\rightarrow$	PB_2
3.	Limit switch to sense high level of liquid in tank $\rightarrow$ Nc $\rightarrow$	LS_1
4.	Limit switch to sense low level of liquid in tank $\rightarrow$ No $\rightarrow$	LS_2
5.	Limit switch to sense position of bottle below the value $V_2 \rightarrow$ No $\rightarrow$	LS_3
6.	Sensor to sense liquid level in bottle $\rightarrow$ No $\rightarrow$	S_1

Output List :

1. Motor m_1
2. Valve V_1 to Fill liquid in tank
3. Valve V_2 to fill liquid in bottle.

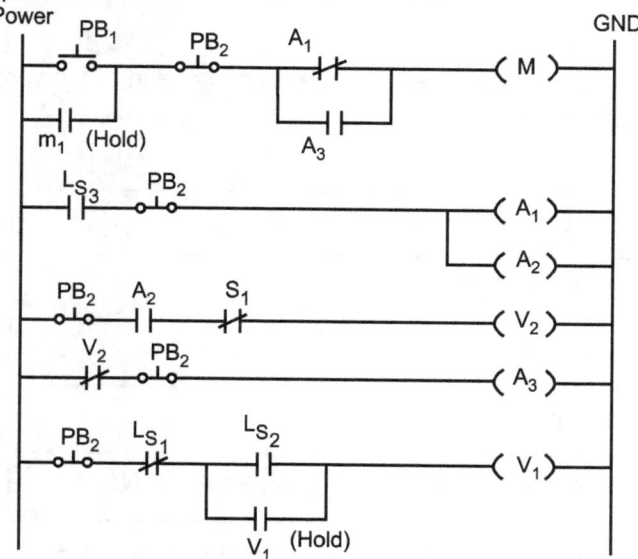

Fig. 6.4 : Ladder logic for bottle filling

2. Ladder Diagram for Elevator Control :

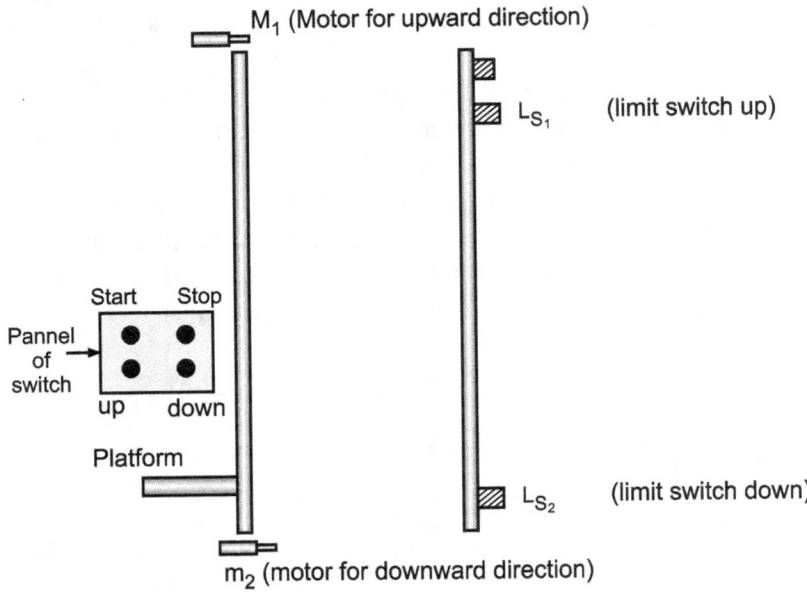

Fig. 6.5 : Elevator control system

Logic :

- When we press 'start' push button, the platform moves in downward direction.

- When we press 'stop' push button, the platform stops moving.

- When 'up' push button is pressed, the platform moves in upward direction if it is not moving downward.

- When down push button is pressed, the platform move in downward direction if it is not moving upward direction.

Input List :

1.	Start push button $\rightarrow$ No $\rightarrow$	$\dashv\!\!\downarrow\!\!\vdash$ PB$_1$
2.	Stop push button $\rightarrow$ Nc $\rightarrow$	$\dashv\!\!\downarrow\!\!\vdash$ PB$_2$
3.	'Up' push button $\rightarrow$ No $\rightarrow$	$\dashv\!\!\downarrow\!\!\vdash$ PB$_3$
4.	'down' push button $\rightarrow$ No $\rightarrow$	$\dashv\!\!\downarrow\!\!\vdash$ PB$_4$
5.	Limit switch to sense platform position at Top $\rightarrow$ Nc $\rightarrow$	$\dashv\!\!\mid\!\!\vdash$ LS$_1$
6.	Limit switch to sense platform position at down $\rightarrow$ Nc $\rightarrow$	$\dashv\!\!\mid\!\!\vdash$ LS$_2$

Output List :

- Motor M_1 for upward motion
- Motor M_2 for downward motion

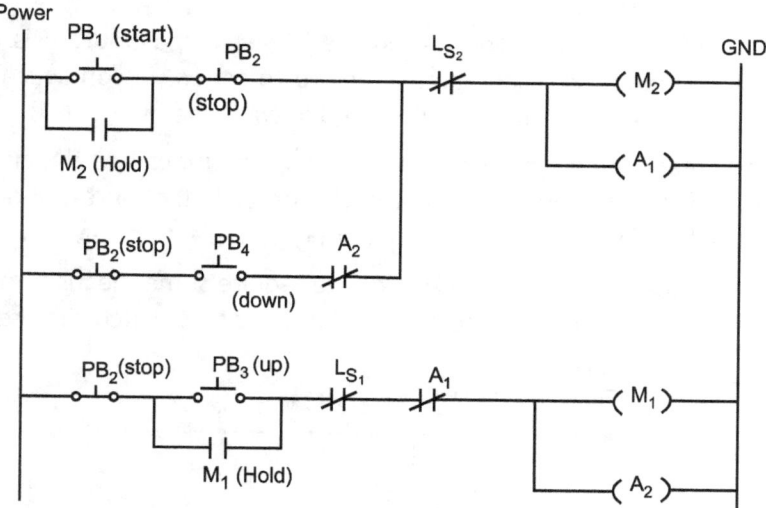

Fig. 6.6 : Ladder logic for elevator control system

3. Motor Control Circuits :

- The interlock contacts installed in the previous section's motor control circuit work fine, but the motor will run only as long as each push button switch is held down. If we wanted to keep the motor running even after the operator takes his or her hand off the control switch (es), we could change the circuit in a couple of different ways : we could replace the pushbutton switches with toggle switches, or we could add some more relay logic to "latch" the control circuit with a single, momentary actuation of either switch. Let's see how the second approach is implemented, since it is commonly used in industry.

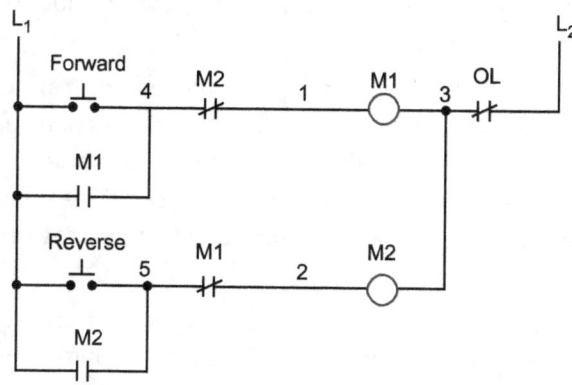

Fig. 6.7

- When the "Forward" pushbutton is actuated, M_1 will energize, closing the normally-open auxiliary contact in parallel with that switch. When the pushbutton is released, the closed M_1 auxiliary contact will maintain current to the coil of M_1, thus latching the "Forward" circuit in the "on" state.

- The same sort of thing will happen when the "Reverse" pushbutton is pressed. These parallel auxiliary contacts are sometimes referred to as *seal-in* contacts, the word "seal" meaning essentially the same thing as the word *latch* as seen in Fig. 6.7.

- However, this creates a new problem : how to *stop* the motor! As the circuit exists right now, the motor will run either forward or backward once the corresponding pushbutton switch is pressed, and will continue to run as long as there is power.

- To stop either circuit (forward or backward), we require some means for the operator to interrupt power to the motor contactors. We'll call this new switch, *Stop* seen in Fig. 6.8.

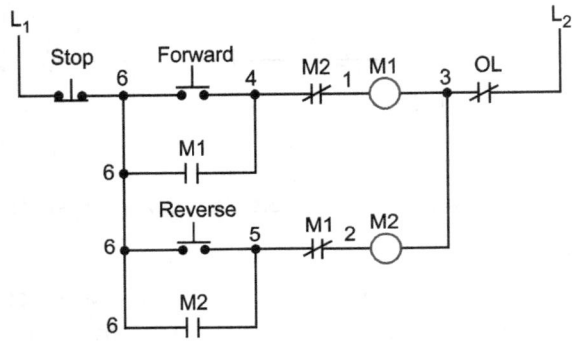

Fig. 6.8

- Now, if either forward or reverse circuits are latched, they may be "unlatched" by momentarily pressing the "Stop" pushbutton, which will open either forward or reverse circuit, de-energizing the energized contactor, and returning the seal-in contact to its normal (open) state.

- The "Stop" switch, having normally-closed contacts, will conduct power to either forward or reverse circuits when released.

- Let's consider another practical aspect of our motor control scheme before we quit adding to it. If our hypothetical motor turned a mechanical load with a lot of momentum, such as a large air fan, the motor might continue to coast for a substantial amount of time after the stop button had been pressed. This could be problematic if an operator were to try to reverse the motor direction without waiting for the fan to stop turning.

- If the fan was still coasting forward and the "Reverse" pushbutton was pressed, the motor would struggle to overcome that inertia of the large fan as it tried to begin turning in reverse, drawing excessive current and potentially reducing the life of the motor, drive mechanisms, and fan.

- What we might like to have is some kind of a time-delay function in this motor control system to prevent such a premature startup from happening.

- Let's begin by adding a couple of time-delay relay coils, one in parallel with each motor contactor coil. If we use contacts that delay returning to their normal state, these relays will provide us a "memory" of which direction the motor was last powered to turn.

- What we want each time-delay contact to do is to open the starting-switch leg of the opposite rotation circuit for several seconds, while the fan coasts to a halt.

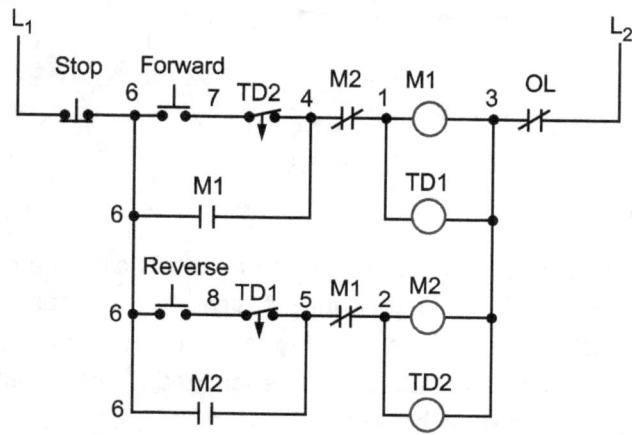

Fig. 6.9

- If the motor has been running in the forward direction, both M_1 and TD_1 will have been energized. This being the case, the normally-closed, timed-closed contact of TD_1 between wires 8 and 5 will have immediately opened the moment TD_1 was energized. When the stop button is pressed, contact TD_1 waits for the specified amount of time before returning to its normally-closed state, thus holding the reverse pushbutton circuit open for the duration so M_2 can't be energized. When TD_1 times out, the contact will close and the circuit will allow M_2 to be energized, if the reverse push button is pressed. In like manner, TD_2 will prevent the "Forward" push button from energizing M_1 until the prescribed time delay after M_2 (and TD_2) have been de-energized.

- The careful observer will notice that the time-interlocking functions of TD_1 and TD_2 render the M_1 and M_2 interlocking contacts redundant. We can get rid of auxiliary contacts M_1 and M_2 for interlocks and just use TD_1 and TD_2's contacts, since they immediately open when their respective relay coils are energized, thus "locking out" one contactor if the other is energized.

- Each time delay relay will serve a dual purpose : preventing the other contactor from energizing while the motor is running, and preventing the same contactor from energizing until a prescribed time after motor shutdown.

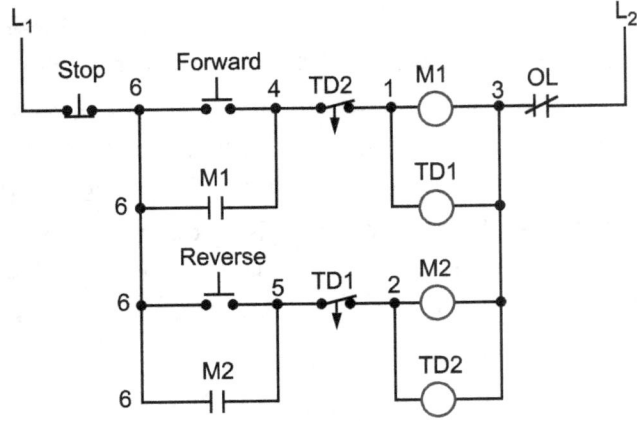

Fig. 6.10

4. Digital Logic Functions :

- We can construct simply logic functions for our hypothetical lamp circuit, using multiple contacts, and document these circuits quite easily and understandably with additional rungs to our original "ladder." If we use standard binary notation for the status of the switches and lamp (0 for un-actuated or de-energized; 1 for actuated or energized), a truth table can be made to show how the logic works :

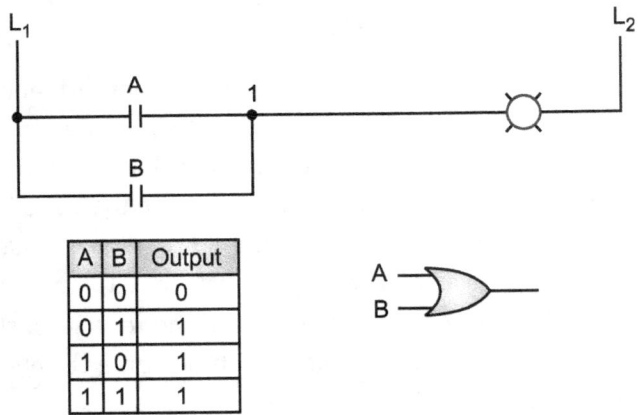

A	B	Output
0	0	0
0	1	1
1	0	1
1	1	1

Fig. 6.11 : Ladeder logic for OR gate

- Now, the lamp will come on if either contact A or contact B is actuated, because all it takes for the lamp to be energized is to have at least one path for current from wire L_1 to wire 1. What we have is a simple OR logic function, implemented with nothing more than contacts and a lamp.

- We can mimic the AND logic function by wiring the two contacts in series instead of parallel :

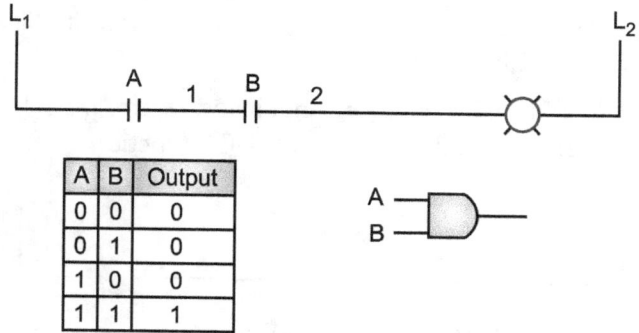

Fig. 6.12 : Ladder logic for AND gate

- Now, the lamp energizes only if contact A and contact B are simultaneously actuated. A path exists for current from wire L_1 to the lamp (wire 2) if and only if both switch contacts are closed.

- The logical inversion, or NOT, function can be performed on a contact input simply by using a normally-closed contact instead of a normally-open contact :

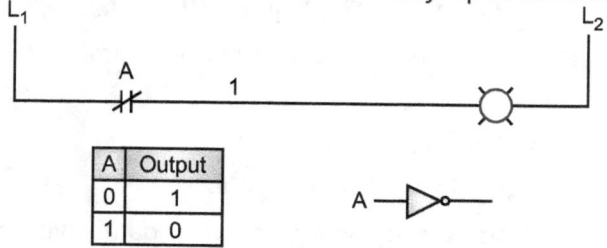

Fig. 6.13 : Ladder logic for inverter

- Now, the lamp energizes if the contact is *not* actuated, and de-energizes when the contact *is* actuated.

- If we take our OR function and invert each "input" through the use of normally-closed contacts, we will end up with a NAND function. In a special branch of mathematics known as Boolean algebra, this effect of gate function identity changing with the inversion of input signals is

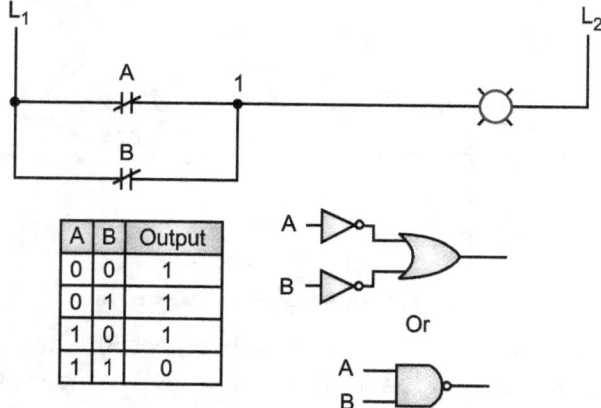

Fig. 6.14 : Ladder logic for NAND gate

- The lamp will be energized if *either* contact is un-actuated. It will go out only if both contacts are actuated simultaneously.

- Likewise, if we take our AND function and invert each "input" through the use of normally-closed contacts, we will end up with a NOR function

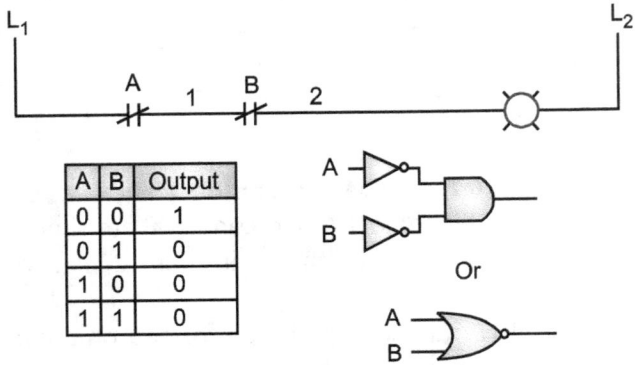

Fig. 6.15 : Ladder logic for NOR gate

A pattern quickly reveals itself when ladder circuits are compared with their logic gate counterparts :

- ➤ Parallel contacts are equivalent to an OR gate.

- ➤ Series contacts are equivalent to an AND gate.

- ➤ Normally-closed contacts are equivalent to a NOT gate (inverter).

We can build combinational logic functions by grouping contacts in series-parallel arrangements, as well. In the following example, we have an Exclusive-OR function built from a combination of AND, OR, and inverter (NOT) gates :

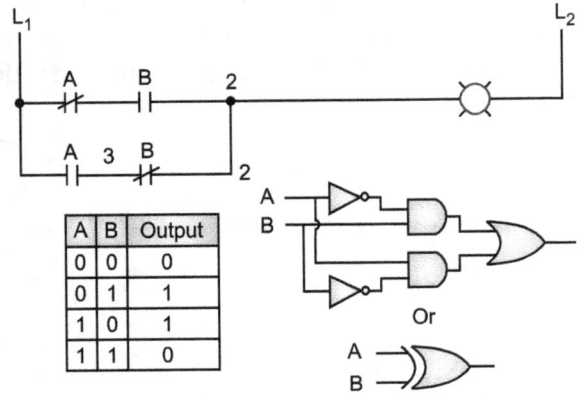

Fig. 6.16 : Ladder logic for XOR gate

- The top rung (NC contact A in series with NO contact B) is the equivalent of the top NOT/AND gate combination. The bottom rung (NO contact A in series with NC contact B) is the equivalent of the bottom NOT/AND gate combination. The parallel connection between the two rungs at wire number 2 forms the equivalent of the OR gate, in allowing either rung 1 or rung 2 to energize the lamp.

- To make the Exclusive-OR function, in Fig. 6.16 we had to use two contacts per input : one for direct input and the other for "inverted" input.

- The two "A" contacts are physically actuated by the same mechanism, as are the two "B" contacts.

- The common association between contacts is denoted by the label of the contact.

- There is no limit to how many contacts per switch can be represented in a ladder diagram, as each new contact on any switch or relay (either normally-open or normally-closed) used in the diagram is simply marked with the same label.

- Sometimes, multiple contacts on a single switch (or relay) are designated by a compound labels, such as "A-1" and "A-2" instead of two "A" labels.

- This may be especially useful if you want to specifically designate which set of contacts on each switch or relay is being used for which part of a circuit. For simplicity's sake.

- If you see a common label for multiple contacts, you know those contacts are all actuated by the same mechanism.

- If we wish to invert the output of any switch-generated logic function, we must use a relay with a normally-closed contact. For instance, if we want to energize a load based on the inverse, or NOT, of a normally-open contact, we could do this :

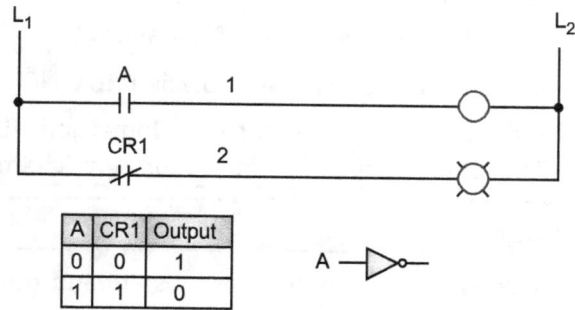

A	CR1	Output
0	0	1
1	1	0

Fig. 6.17

- We will call the relay, "control relay 1," or CR_1. When the coil of CR_1 (symbolized with the pair of parentheses on the first rung) is energized, the contact on the second rung *opens*, thus de-energizing the lamp.

- From switch A to the coil of CR_1, the logic function is non-inverted. The normally-closed contact actuated by relay coil CR_1 provides a logical inverter function to drive the lamp opposite that of the switch's actuation status.

- Applying this inversion strategy to one of our inverted-input functions created earlier, such as the OR-to-NAND, we can invert the output with a relay to create a non-inverted function :

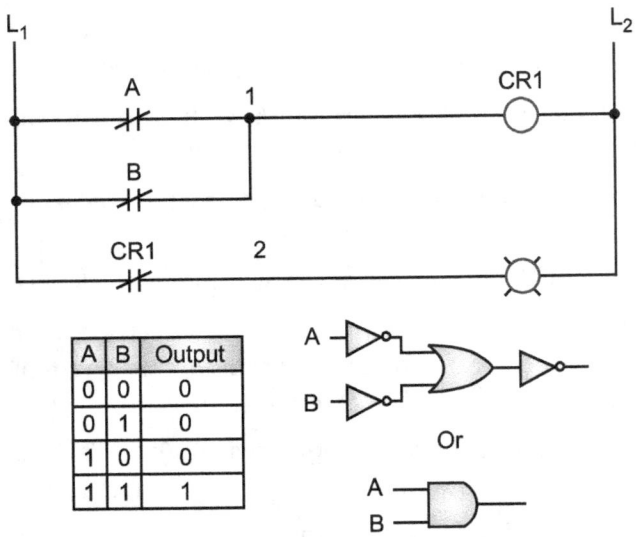

Fig. 6.18

From the switches to the coil of CR_1, the logical function is that of a NAND gate. CR_1's normally-closed contact provides one final inversion to turn the NAND function into an AND function.

Keynote :

- Parallel contacts are logically equivalent to an OR gate.
- Series contacts are logically equivalent to an AND gate.
- Normally closed (N.C.) contacts are logically equivalent to a NOT gate.
- A relay must be used to invert the *output* of a logic gate function, while simple normally-closed switch contacts are sufficient to represent inverted gate *inputs*.

6.5 PID CONTROLLER

A controller is a device which is used to control steady state and transient response as per the requirement. The best system demands the smallest transient response, smallest t_s, smallest e_{ss} and smallest M_p, which is not possible without PID controller.

Block diagram with controller shown in Fig. 6.19.

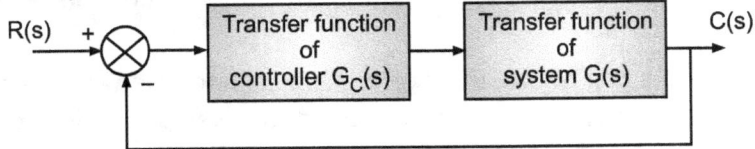

Fig. 6.19 : Basic controller

An automatic controller compares the actual value of the system output with the reference input, determines the deviation and produces a control signal that will reduce deviation to zero or a small value. The manner in which automatic controller produces the control signal is called the control action.

Proportional, integral and derivative (PID) control is referred to as 3-term control. P action is the basis for PID control, any I or D action is always superimposed on the P action.

An equation for PID control is first developed in analog form, as used in pneumatic and electron controllers. This is then translated into a discrete form for implementation of an algorithm in a digital controller. The ideal continuous time domain PID controller for a SISO process is expressed in the Laplace domain as follows :

$$U(s) = G_c(s).\, E(s)$$

Where, $U(s) \rightarrow$ controller output

          $G_c \rightarrow$ controller (P, PI, PID)

          $E(s) \rightarrow$ error (difference between expected output and set point)

Thus, the transfer function of PID controller has the general form

$$G_c(s) = k_p + \frac{k_i}{s} + kds \qquad \qquad \text{... (6.1)}$$

$$= \frac{k_p s + k_i + kds^2}{s}$$

$$= \frac{k_d \left[s^2 + \frac{K_p}{k_d}s + \frac{k_i}{k_d} \right]}{s} \qquad \qquad \text{... (6.2)}$$

Where, the proportional term designated as k_p integral term designated as $\frac{k_i}{s}$ and the derivative term designated as sk_d.

PID controllers area also expressed as follows.

$$G_c(s) = k_p \left[1 + \frac{1}{T_i s} + T_d s \right] \qquad \qquad \text{... (6.3)}$$

Where, $T_i = \frac{k_p}{k_i}$ and $T_d = \frac{k_d}{k_p}$

Where, T_i = integration time const.

          T_d = derivative or rate time const.

The block diagram of PID controller is shown in Fig. 6.20. The transfer function of PID controller involves one pole at the origin and two zeros whose position depends upon the parameters K_p, K_i and K_d or T_i and T_d.

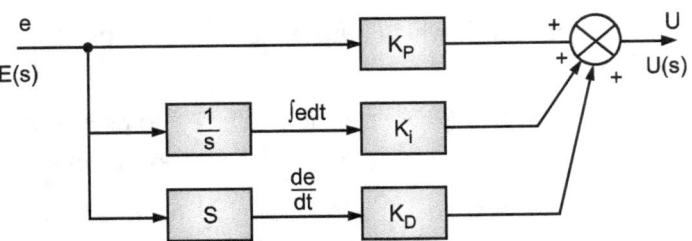

Fig. 6.20 : PID controller structure

- A PID controller has a parallel structure with these three actions (proportional-integrative-derivative) The three constants can be tuned to adjust the relative strength of each action.

- The proportional action is the main action, and other two actions are add-ons to improve the control. Often one sees a P-only controller, i.e. a controller with only Kp. Often on sees a PID controller with one action – integral or derivative – turned off. Thus the most common variants are a P controller, PI controller, PD controller or the full blown PID controller.

6.5.1 Proportional Control

The most common of all continuous industrial process control action is proportional control action. One almost never sees a PID controller without P-action.

For a controller with proportional control action, the relationship between the output of the controller u(t) and the actuating error signal e(t) is :

$$U(t) \ = \ k_p \, e(t) \qquad\qquad \dots (6.4)$$

Where, k_p is the proportional gain

In Laplace form, $\dfrac{u(s)}{E(s)} \ = \ k_p$ $\qquad\qquad \dots (6.5)$

Whatever the actual mechanism may be, the proportional controller is essentially an amplifier with an adjustable gain. The block diagram of proportional controller is shown in Fig. 6.21.

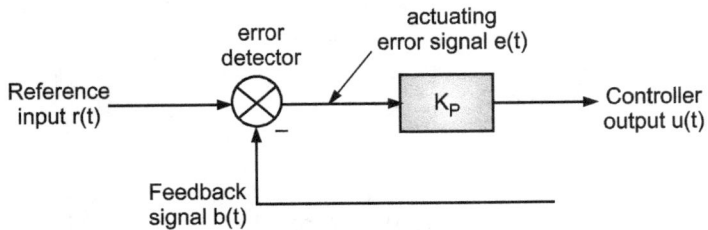

Fig. 6.21 : Block diagram of proportional controller

The controller sees the error as input. If the error is small, the controller should suggest a small action, a nudge, to the actuator to get the plant back on track and reduce the error to 0. If the error is large, that means the actual value has drifted far away from the desired value. The controller needs to suggest a large action to the actuator to bring the plant in line with the desired value. Such a strategy means the controller should be proportional to the error, i.e. P action.

The proportional gain, K_p can be regarded as the sensitivity of the controller, how great an action it will suggest for a given deviation of actual from desired. The controller is very sensitive. If K_p is small, the reaction of the controller to a deviation of actual from desired is gentle.

Keynote :

- Proportional control is based on the current value of the error i.e. present values.
- Integral action is based on the past.
- Derivative action is based on the future.

Example for Proportional Controller :

Let us consider the system $G(s) = \dfrac{1}{s(s + 10)}$

To change transient response as per the requirement transfer function of P controller is k_p.

$$\Rightarrow \frac{C(s)}{R(s)} = \frac{1}{s^2 + 10s + 1}$$

Comparing with standard second order equation $\omega_n = 1$

$$\xi = 5 \rightarrow \text{overdamped}$$

With controller, the transfer function will be.

$$G(s) = \frac{k_p}{s(s + 10)}$$

$$\frac{C(s)}{R(s)} = \frac{k_p}{s^2 + 10s + 1}$$

If $k_p = 100;$ $\omega_n = 10$

$$\xi = 0.5 \rightarrow \text{under damped.}$$

If $k_p = 25 \; ;$ $\omega_n = 5$

$$\xi = 1 \rightarrow \text{critically damped.}$$

The main disadvantage in p-controller is as k_p value increases, % M_p increases.

As % Mp increases, the system becomes less stable.

6.5.2 Integral Action and P + I

Integral action is used to get rid of stead-state error. A system's type is not enough, so one uses a PI controller to add a free integrator to the open-loop transfer function. The integral term acts, not on the error itself but rather on the integral of the error i.e. on the accumulated error produced over time.

The value of the controller output u(t) is changed at a rate proportional to the actuating error signal e(t) given by equation (6.6)

$$\frac{du(t)}{d(t)} = kie(t)$$

Or
$$u(t) = ki \int_o^t e(t)\, dt \qquad \qquad ... (6.6)$$

Where, k_i is an adjustable constant.

The transfer function of integral controller is,

$$\frac{u(s)}{E(s)} = \frac{k_i}{s} \qquad \qquad ...(6.7)$$

If the value of e(t) is doubled, then u(t) varies twice as fast. For zero actuating error, the value of u(t) remains stationary. The integral action is also called reset control. Fig. 6.22 shows block diagram of the integral controller.

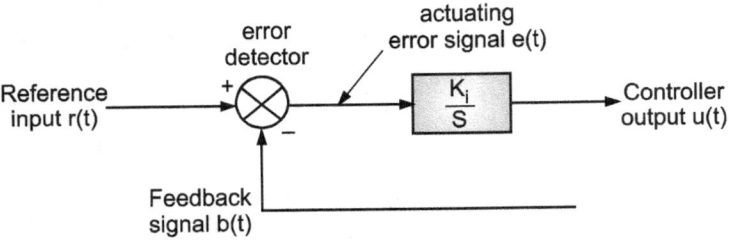

Fig. 6.22 : Block diagram of an integral action

Noteworthy is that the integral action will continue to accumulate until the error is 0. Once the error is 0, there is no proportional action. Note that with e=0, the integral action is not 0, it just doesn't accumulate anymore.

Control engineers in the field often use the term reset to characterize the strength of integral action. Reset is also called integral time T_i (in the process industry, this variable is often expressed as R. This is not the same R used for input or reference value in the standard control loop). This is a comparison of integral action with proportional action. If a PI controller were subjected to a steady input signal, the reset time is the time it would take for the integral action to reach the level of proportional action. So, with an input signal of 1, the proportional action would be K_p.

The integral action would be

$$K_I \int 1 \cdot dt = K_I t$$

At
$$t = T_1, K_p = k_1 T_1. \text{ So } T_1 = k_p/k_1$$

Since, T_1 is a measure of how long it takes the integral action to develop, the higher T_1 is, the lower k_1 is and the more gentle the integral action.

Since, the integral action accumulates over time, what is important to it is the history of error over time, integral action "remembers" what has happened, so it is an action based upon past experience.

6.5.2.1 Proportional – Plus – Integral Control Action

The control action of a proportional – plus – integral controller is defined by

$$u(t) = k_p \, e(t) + \frac{k_p}{T_i} \int_{o}^{t} e(t) \, dt$$

The transfer function of the controller is

$$\frac{u(s)}{E(s)} = k_p \left[1 + \frac{1}{Ti(s)} \right]$$

Where, K_p = proportional gain.

                     T_i = integral time which are adjustable.

The integral time adjusts the integral control action, while change in proportional gain affects both the proportional and integral action. The inverse of integral time is called reset rate. The reset rate is number of times per minute that a proportional part of control action is duplicated. Fig. 6.23. shows the block diagram of the proportional plus-integral controller. For an actuating error of unit step input, the controller output is shown in Fig. 6.24.

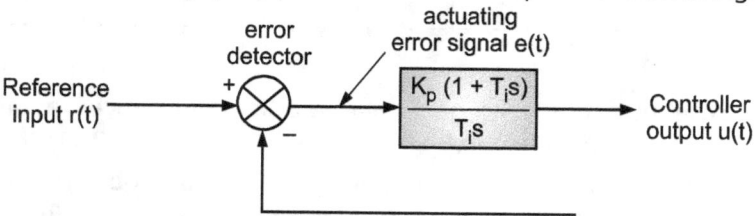

Fig. 6.23 : Block diagram of proportional plus integral control system

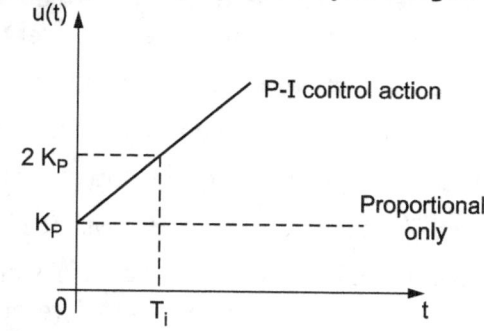

Fig. 6.24 : Response of PI controller to unit actuating error signal

Example of Integral Controller :

Purpose : To decrease steady state error. The transfer function of Integral controller is $\frac{k_i}{s}$ I – controller add one pole at origin hence type is increased.

As the type of the system is increased, the steady state error decreases but the system stability is affected.

Consider, $G(s) = \dfrac{1}{s(s + 10)}$ (without controller)

Type of system = 1

Characteristic equation = $s^2 + 10s + 1$ stable.

With controller;

$$G(s) = \dfrac{k_i}{s^2(s + 10)}$$

Now type of system = 2

∴   Characteristic equation = $s^3 + 10 s^2 + k_i = 0$ unstable

---

Keynote :

- To decrease steady state error without affecting stability.

- PI controller add one pole at origin hence type is increased. As type of system increases steady state error (e_{ss}) decreases.

- PI controller add one finite zero in left half OP s-plane, which avoids effect on stability.

6.5.2.2 Reset Wind Up

It is often the case that the solving of one problem introduces another. While the introduction of the integral mode has solved the problem of offset, it has introduced another worry that has to do with the very nature of integral mode. The fact that integral looks at the past history of the error and integrates it is good and useful when the loop is operational, but it can be a problem when the loop is idle. When the plant is shut down for the night, the controllers do not need to integrate the error under the error curve.

The other cases where the integration of error is undesirable includes :

- A selective control system, when a particular controller is not selected for operation.

- In cascade master, if the operator has switched the loop off cascade.

- In this case, the integrator will saturate and its output will be either zero or maximum.

Once saturated, the controller will not be ready to take control when called upon. In all such situations, the controller must be provided with external reset, which protects it from becoming idle or with an anti-reset windup which protects it from saturating in idle state.

6.5.3 Derivative Active and P + D

Derivative action is predictive in nature. It operates on the rate of change of error, not on the error itself.

In Fig. 6.25 a supply tank has a level controller on it. As the liquid in the tank is needed, an outlet valve opens to supply more to a downstream process. If the tank starts off at a steady state and then a sudden demand for more liquid downstream occurs, the outlet valve opens quickly, and the level in the tank starts to drop. The trouble with proportional control is that it really does not react until the error has developed. So there is a lag time before the proportional action comes into play, since it can only react to current error, error that has already occurred. This is unfortunate, because with the valve open and the error developing rapidly, It was entirely predictable that the error would develop it did develop. The idea behind derivative control lies in this phrase " with the error developing rapidly". The rate of change of error is high. That means the error is developing rapidly and there is no reason why the controller shouldn't react to that before the error develops. So a strong deviation action at the start, before the error develops, ensures that less error will actually develop.

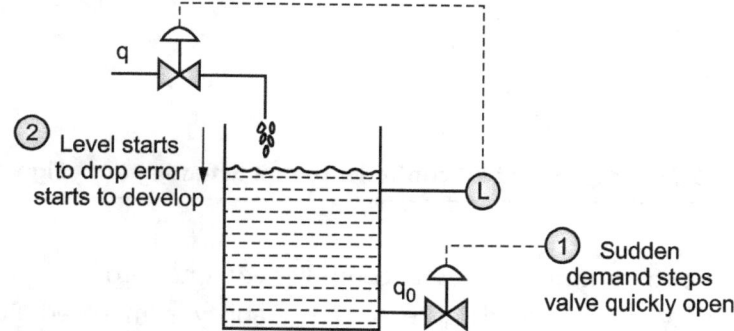

Fig. 6.25 : Level regulator experiencing sudden increase in demand.

Proportional - Plus Derivative Control Action :

The control action of proportional plus derivative controller is defined by

$$U(t) = k_p.e(t) + k_pT_d \frac{de(t)}{dt} \qquad\qquad ... (6.8)$$

The transfer function is

$$\frac{U(s)}{E(s)} = k_p(1 + Tds) \qquad\qquad ... (6.9)$$

Where, k_p is the proportional gain

T_d is derivative time constant

Both k_p and T_d are adjustable. The derivative control action is also called as rate control. In rate controller, the output is proportional to the rate of change of actuating error signal. The derivative time T_d is the time interval by which the rate action advances the effect of the proportional control action. The derivative control is anticipatory in nature and amplifies the noise effect. Fig. 6.26 shows the block diagram of proportional plus derivative control for an actuating error of unit ramp input, the controller output is shown in Fig. 6.27.

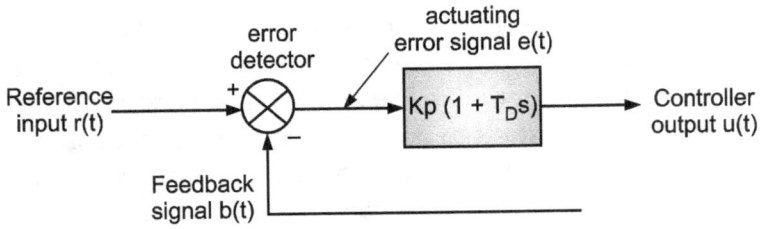

Fig. 6.26 : Block diagram of propositional plus derivative controller.

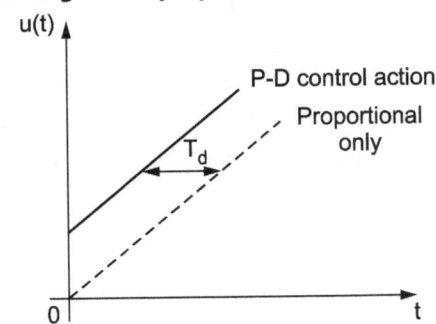

Fig. 6.27 : Response of PD controller to unit actuating error signal

---

Keynote :

Transfer function of d-controller is $k_D.S$. D-controller add one zero at origin hence type is decreased. As the type of system is deceased the stability is improved. But steady state error is increased.

Example of Derivative Action :

Consider, $G(s) = \dfrac{1}{s^2(s + 10)}$

Characteristic equation = $s^3 + 10s^2 + 1 = 0 \Rightarrow$ unstable

With considering d-controller,

$$G(s) = \frac{k_D s}{s^2 (s + 10)}$$

Type of system = 1

Characteristic equation = $s^2 + 10s + 1 < D = 0 \Rightarrow$ stable.

6.5.3.1 P + D controller

To improve stability without affecting steady state error.

Transfer function of PD controller is $k_p + k_D s$. PD controller add only one finite zero in the left of s-plane hence system stability is improved.

No change in type with PD controller, hence no effect on steady state error.

ξ value with PD-controller is,

$$\xi_{pD} = \xi + \frac{\omega_n k_D}{2}$$

As ξ_{pD} incereases, % Mp also increase and hence more stable is the system.

6.5.3.2 Proportional – Plus Integral –Plus Derivative Control Action

It is a combination of proportional control action, integral control action and derivative control action. The equation of controller is.

$$u(t) = k_p e(t) + \frac{k_p}{T_i} \int_0^t e(t)\, dt + k_p T_d \frac{de(t)}{dt} \qquad \dots (6.10)$$

or the transfer function is

$$\frac{u(s)}{E(s)} = k_p \left[1 + \frac{1}{T_i s} + T_d s \right] \qquad \dots (6.11)$$

Where, K_p is the proportional gain, T_i is the integral time, and T_d is the derivative time. The block diagram of PID controller is shown in Fig. 6.28 for an actuating error of unit ramp input, the controller output is shown in Fig. 6.29.

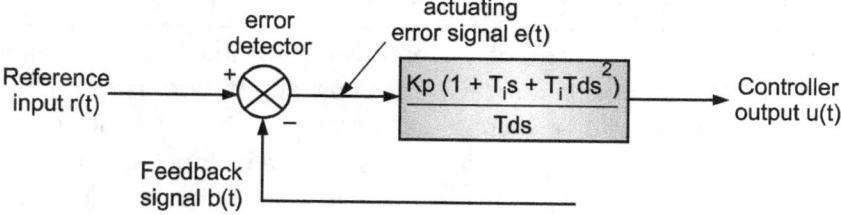

Fig. 6.28 : Block Diagram of PID controller

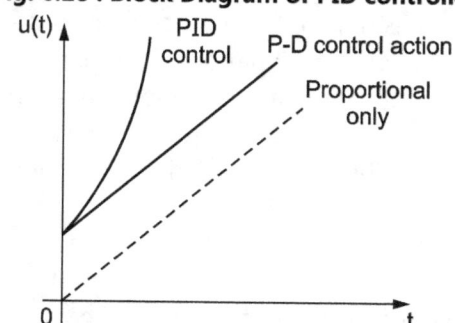

Fig. 6.29 : Response of PID controller to unit actuating error signal

Example of PID Controller :

Purpose : To improve stability as well as to decrease steady state error.

Transfer function of PID = $K_p + \frac{k_i}{s} + k_D s$

PID, adds one pole of origin which in creases type of system, hence deceases steady state error, PID adds two finite zeros in the left hand side. One finite zero avoid effect on system stability and the other zero improve stability of the system.

The effects of increasing each of the controller parameters KP,

Note: KI and KD can be summarized as

Response S	Rise Time	Overshoot	Settling Time	S-S Error
K_p	Decrease	Increase	NT	Decrease
K_I	Decrease	Increase	Increase	Eliminate
K_D	NT	Decrease	Decrease	NT

How Do We Use the Table?

Typical steps for designing a PID controller are

1. Determine what characteristics of the system needs to beimproved.
2. Use KP to decrease the rise time.
3. Use KD to reduce the overshoot and settling time.
4. Use KI to eliminate the steady-state error.

6.6 DIGITAL PID CONTROLLER

In digital, technology, the concept of a controller is probably a misnomer. Although standalone devices (single loop controllers) exist that perform control computation using their own microprocessors rather than a pneumatic or electronic analog circlljtry· the situation is to have a multi-loop digital processor, such as a distributed control system (DCS) or a programmable logic controller (PLC}. Here both the section of code performing the control computation and the provisions for human machine interface (HMI) are shared by many loops. The only thing that is unique to a particular loop is a data record in memory the contains an identification of the loop, designation of the particular subroutine to use for the control calculation, pointers to other memory locations as sources for its input values, and memory locations for holding tuning parameter, manual-automatic status parameter, configuration options and so on. The heart of a digital controller is the control algorithm this is the section of code that performs the computation that mimics one of the PID forms. Because of the versatility of a digital processor, however many functions that were impossible with analog controllers, such as automated bumpless transfer, wind-up prevention, and interblock status communications, can now be performed as a part of a digital controller.

6.6.1 PID Position Algorithm

The non-interacting PID form was given by equation below.

$$\mu = Kc \left(e + \frac{1}{T_1} \int edt + T_D \frac{de}{dt} \right) \qquad \dots (6.12)$$

We will develop an analogous digital algorithm that operates repetitively in a sampling environment. The sampling interval is ΔT (such as 1/60 minute); everything is related to the nth sampling instant. Corresponding to the proportional mode term e, is the error at the nth sampling instant $e_n = r_n - c_n$. The term $\int edt$ will be approximated by summing the errors at each sampling instant If s_{n-1} represents the previously accumulated sum, then,

$$S_n = S_{n-1+e}$$

And the integral mode term is

$$\frac{\Delta T}{T1} S_n$$

Putting these all together, the digital algorithm corresponding to Equation (14) is

$$\mu_n = Kc \left[e_n + \frac{\Delta T}{T_1} S_n + \frac{T_D}{\Delta T} (e_n - e_{n-1}) \right] \qquad \dots (6.13)$$

The terms $K_c.T_1$ and T_D represent the conventional tuning parameters controller gain reset time in minutes/repeat and derivative time in minutes, ΔT represents the sampling interval. A similar approach can be used for the paralled (independent gains) form of PID.

$$\mu_n = K_c e_n + K_1 S_n \Delta T + K_D \frac{e_n - e_{n-1}}{\Delta T} \qquad \dots (6.14)$$

Where K_c, K_1 and K_D re the proportional gain, integral gain, and derivative gain, respectively. Equations (6.13) and (6.14) are called position algorithms because they compute the required position of the final actuator, μ_n at the nth sampling instant.

6.6.2 PID Velocity Algorithm

A capability unavailable in analog control systems is that of velocity algorithms. Previously discussed algorithms have been positional. They calculated μ_n, the required position of the valve or other final actuator. Velocity algorithms, on the other hand, calculate $\Delta\mu_n$, the increment by which the position of the final actuator should change. (Incremental algorithms would be better terminology, however, the term velocity is in traditional usage).

Velocity algorithms were developed during the time of supervisory control when a computer output set the set point of an analog controller, A stepping motor was often used to drive the analog controller set point. The controller output $\Delta\mu$ was converted to a pulse train that incremented the stepping motor by the required amount. Even though that technology is rarely used today, velocity algorithms are retained and offer certain advantages as well as disadvantages. To develop a velocity algorithm that is the counterpart of Equation (16) the equation will first be rewritten for the previous calculation cycle. That is the subscript n will be replaced by n − 1 wherever it appears.

$$\mu_n = K_c \left[e_{n-1} + \frac{\Delta T}{T_1} S_{n-1} + \frac{T_D}{\Delta T} (e_{n-1} - e_{n-2}) \right] \qquad \dots (6.15)$$

The required incremental change is given by $\Delta\mu_n = \mu_n - \mu_{n-1}$. Hence, to develop an equation for $\Delta\mu_n$, the right-hand side of Equation (6.15) will be subtracted from the right-hand side of Equation (6.13). In doing so the term $S_n - S_{n-1}$ is encountered. By Equation (6.12) however, this is simply equal to e_n. Hence the final results are

$$\mu_n = K_c\left[e_n - e_{n-1} + \frac{\Delta T}{T_1} e_{n-1} + \frac{T_D}{\Delta T}(e_n - 2 e_{n-1} + e_{n-2})\right] \qquad \dots \text{(6.16)}$$

In digital control systems that use velocity algorithms today, the previous required position of the final actuator μ_{n-1}, is stored in a separate memory location. After the velocity algorithm computes the required incremental change, this increment is added to the previous position, and the new required position overwrites the previous value in the memory location. The new value is then converted to an analog value, such as 4-10mA, for transmission to the final actuator This operation is described by Equation (6.17).

$$\mu_n \leftarrow \mu_{n-1} + \Delta\mu_n \qquad \dots \text{(6.17)}$$

An examination of Equation (6.16) reveals that it contains no into greater that is subject to windup. Therefore, advantage of the velocity algorithm is what it doesn't windup. Whereas that is true of the algorithm itself, it does not mean that there cannot be windup in the overall control system. Suppose there is a sustained error, the situation that cause windup in position algorithm Each time the velocity algorithm is processed it calculates an output change $\Delta\mu_n$. These incremental changes accumulate in the output memory location due to equation (6.17) so the windup occurs in the memory location, not in the algorithm itself. If the incremental change were applied to on external stepping motor, then the stepping motor would wind up. Therefore a better description of the velocity algorithm is it moves the windup to some place else.

6.7 ZEIGLER NICHOLAS METHOD

What is Tuning?

Tuning is adjustment of control parameters to the optimum values for the desired control response. Stability is a basic requirement. However, different systems have different behavior, different applications have different requirements, and requirements may conflict with one another. PID tuning is a difficult problem, even though there are only three parameters and in principle is simple to describe, because it must satisfy complex criteria within the limitations of PID control. There are accordingly various methods for loop tuning, some of them :

- Manual tuning method,
- Ziegler–Nichols tuning method,
- PID tuning software methods

Ziegler-Nichols

J.G. Zeigler and N.B. Nichols published two tuning methods for PID Controllers in 1942

- The Ultimate cycling method
- The Process Reaction-curve, often called the Zeigler-Nochols Open-Loop tuning method.

The Ziegler-Nichols tuning algorithm was developed primarily for regulator control loops in the process industry (power generation station, chemical plants, refineries, etc.). As regulators, these loops' purpose is *disturbance rejection* that is keeping a desired quantity at a certain level despite disturbing influences that try to change it. Ziegler-Nichols is probably the best known and most widely used of the heuristic tuning methods for tuning PID controllers. "Heuristic" simply means "based on experimentation" or "based on trial-and-error". Such methods do not depend on the development of a system model. They are field tuning methods, in that one can apply them to the real system and tune it in place.

In Ziegler-Nichols tuning, tuning parameters K_p, K_D, K_I are based on K_u and P_u. K_u is the gain that causes a system with a P-only controller to be marginally stable. ("u" stands for "ultimate".) You can find the ultimate gain by a trial and error process. One sets K_p to some low value (K_I and K_D are 0 at this stage). Test the system with this K_p to see if it oscillates continuously (marginally stable). If the oscillations decay, keep increasing K_p. If the oscillations increase in amplitude (unstable system), reduce K_p. Do this until the system is marginally stable. When you arrive at this point, you have found K_u, the gain that got you there. P_u is the period of the non-decaying oscillations at this point of marginal Stability.

Often you will not be able to reach a system's ultimate gain because the system actuator will saturate. This is a situation where the controller demands more of the actuator than it can provide. Remember the actuator gets a command input from the controller and sends a "force" signal to the plant. The actuator is limited in the amount of "force" it can send to the plant. For a valve/tank level-control system, the valve cannot open more than 100%, nor can it close more than 0%.

First step : Find K_u

Find K_u by increasing K_p until the system oscillates without a decay. While you are monitoring the loopoutput, monitor the actuator at the same time to see whether or not it is saturating. Continue toincrease K_p until you find Ku or the actuator saturates.

If the actuator saturates, you will not be able to get Ku. In this case use another method to get K_q("q" stands for quarter). Adjust the P - only gain until you have quarter - cycle damping. This is a measurement for a second - order, underdamped system. On the response plot look at the first two humps (the first hump is where the %OS is measured). K_q is the value of K_p that makes the height of the second hump 1/4 the height of the first hump. Use the final output value as the reference for measuring the hump heights.

Now K_u can be determined from K_q. It is : $K_u = 2 \cdot K_q$.

Second step : Find P_u

P_u is the ultimate period of oscillation. You can find this out from the response plot with $K_P = K_u$, if you were able to find it. If you found K_u from K_q, get P_q. We assume that $P_u = P_q$. This is close enough.

Third Step : Find Controller Gains

Now the suggested Ziegler Nichols settings for P, PI, and PID controllers are :

P : $KPID = 0.5 \cdot K_u$

PI : $KPID = 0.45 \cdot K_u; \; TI = 1.2/P_u$

PID : $KPID = 0.6 \, K_u; \; TI = 2/P_u; \; TD = P_u/8$

Ziegler-Nichols in this example. It applies to plants with neither integrators nor dominant complex-conjugate poles, whose unit-step response resemble an S-shaped curve with no overshoot. This S-shaped curve is called the reaction curve depicted in Fig. 6.30.

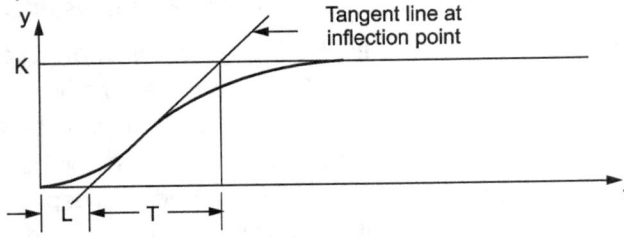

Fig. 6.30

The S-shaped reaction curve can be characterized by two constants, delay time L and time constant T, which are determined by drawing a tangent line at the inflection point of the curve and finding the intersections of the tangent line with the time axis and the steady-state level line.

The Ziegler-Nichols Tuning Rule Table

Using the parameters L and T, we can set the values of K_P, K_I and K_D according to the formula shown in the table below.

Table

Controller	K_p	K_I	K_D
P	$\dfrac{T}{L}$	0	0
PI	$0.9\dfrac{T}{L}$	$0.27\dfrac{T}{L^2}$	0
PID	$1.2\dfrac{T}{L}$	$0.6\dfrac{T}{L^2}$	$0.6T$

These parameters will typically give you a response with an overshoot about 25% and good settling time. We may then start fine-tuning the controller using the basic rules that relate each parameter to the response characteristics.

6.8 INTRODUCTION TO DIGITAL CONTROL SYSTEMS

Digital control is a branch of control theory that uses digital computers to act as a system controllers. Depending upon the requirements, a digital control system can take the form of a microcontroller to an ASIC to a standard desktop computer. Since, a digital computer is a discrete system, the laplace transform is replaced with z transform.

Digital controllers can be implemented either in hardware or software on a microcomputer. But their bit size introduces various sources of error which affect controller performance. The error depends on many factors including the way an algorithm is implemented to a program, the number system used to implement the control laws and the mathematical operations employed in implementation.

Digital control systems are used in many applications for machine tools, metal working process, chemical process, aircraft control, automatic traffic control, radar tracking system and a space satellite.

6.8.1 Necessity of Digital Control Systems

Software fault tolerance and hardware fault tolerance need to evolve to solve a design fault problem, as more large-scale digital control systems are designed and built, especially, safety critical systems.

The field of control systems started essentially in the ancient world. Modern control methods were introduced in the early 1950s, as a way to bypass some of the shortcomings of the classical methods. Modern control methods became increasingly popular after 1957 with the invention of the computer and the start of the space program.

Computers created the need for digital control methodologies, and the space program required the creation of some 'advanced' control techniques such as 'optimal control', 'robust control' and 'non-linear control'.

6.8.2 Features of Digital Control System

- **Accuracy :** Digital signals are more accurate than their analog counterparts.
- **Flexibilty :** Reliability in implementation; i.e you can simply modify(reprogrammed) the control function in software without any extra cost.
- **Implementation :** Complex function can be implemented in software easily rather than hardware (Hardware is replaced by software, which is effective)
- **Usage :** Computers can be used in Data logging (monitoring), supervisory control and control multiple loops simultaneously as the computers are well fast.
- **Speed :** Digital computers may yield superior performance at very high speeds.
- **Cost :** Digital Computers are more cost effective than analog computers.
- **Decision :** High decision making and logic capability.
- **Design :** Can be designed easily and tested for simulations.

6.9 SAMPLED DATA CONTROL SYSTEMS

It is a digital control system which uses a computer or a micro-controller as a digital controller. Fig. 6.31 below shows block diagram of sampled data control system.

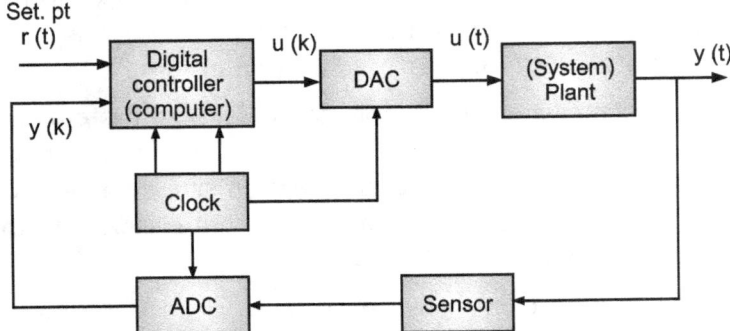

Fig. 6.31

Digital controller is a chip where control algorithm is written to accept the input (set point) through user interface. The system input y(t) is passed back to the digital controller (fed back) and measured using sensor. Using ADC block, the output of sensor is converted into digital form and is applied to the computer. The control signal is then converted into continuous signal u(t) and is applied to the system. This, in turn, keeps y(t) as close as possible to set point r(t).

The overall accuracy of this control system depends on :

* Sampling rate of ADC
* Resolution of DAC
* Accuracy of sensors, actuators and
* Control algorithm

The analytical block diagram of sampled data control system is as shown in the Fig. 6.32 below :

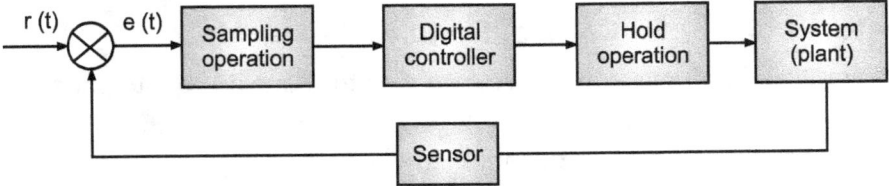

Fig. 6.32

In this diagram, the ADC and DAC blocks are replaced as :

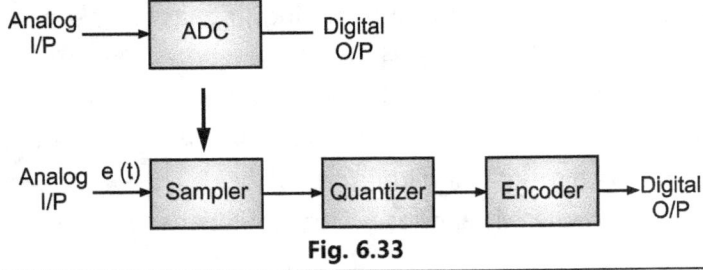

Fig. 6.33

Unit VI | 6.32

Here, if the speed of operation is very high, the effects of quantizer can be neglected. The encoder in ideal cases has the transfer gain equal to unity. Hence the ADC can be replaced by the sampler.

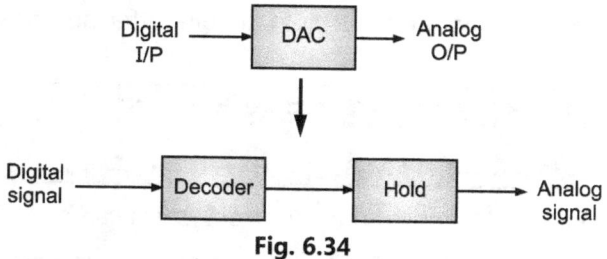

Fig. 6.34

Transfer gain of decoder is unity and hence DAC can be replaced by the Hold device.

6.9.1 Discrete Data System

When the signal or information at any or some points in a system is in the form of discrete pulses, then the system is called discrete data system.

6.9.2 Sampling Theorem

A band limited continuous time signal with highest frequency f_m Hertz can be uniquely recovered from its samples provided that the sampling rate F_s is greater than or equal to $2f_m$ samples per second.

6.9.3 Sample and Hold

The signal given to a digital controller is a sampled data signal and in turn, the controller gives the controller output in digital form. But the system to be controlled needs an analog control signal as input. Therefore the digital output of controllers must be converted into digital form.

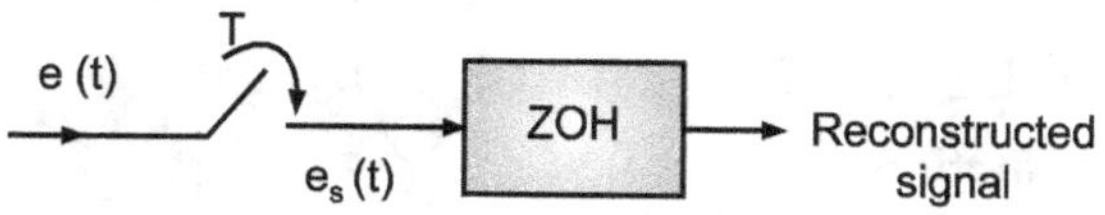

Fig. 6.35

This can be achieved by means of various types of hold circuits. The simplest hold circuits are the zero order hold (ZOH). In ZOH, the reconstructed analog signal acquires the same values as the last received samples for the entire sampling period.

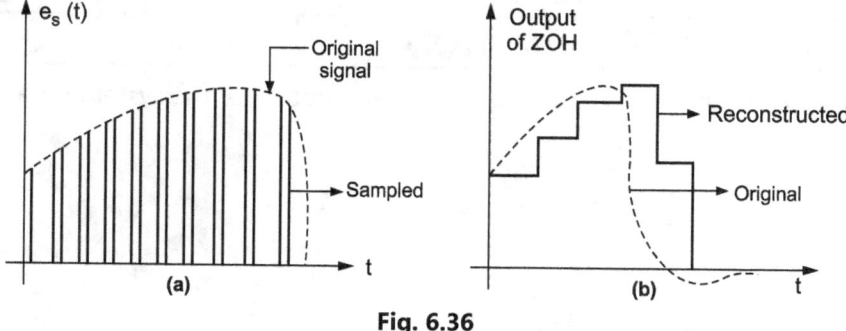

Fig. 6.36

The high frequency noises present in the reconstructed signal are automatically filtered out by the control system component which behaves like low pass filters. In a first order hold circuit, the last two signals for the current sampling period. Similarly, higher order hold circuit can be devised. First or higher order hold circuits offer no particular advantage over the zero order hold.

6.10 MATHEMATICAL MODEL OF SAMPLED DATA CONTROL SYSTEM

The analytical block diagram of sampled data control system can be represented as :

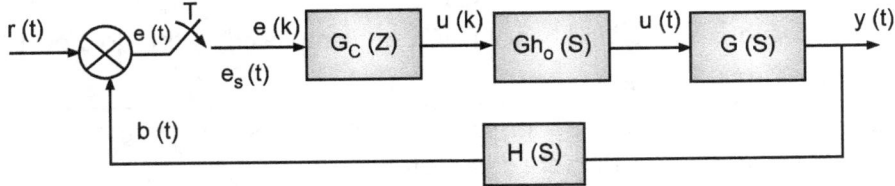

Fig. 6.37

The transfer function $G_c(z)$ is ,

$$G_c(z) = \frac{u(z)}{E(z)}$$

Also from the analytical block diagram we get,

$$Y(z) = G_c(z) = [G_{ho}(s) . G(s)]. E(z)$$
$$E(z) = R(z) - B(z)$$
$$B(z) = E(z) G_c(z)^2 = [G_{ho}(s) G(s). H(s)]$$
$$\therefore \quad R(z) = E(z) [1 + G_c(z). z [G_{ho}(s). G(s). H(s)]]$$

∴ P.T.F. (Pulse Transfer function)

$$= \frac{y(z)}{R(z)} = \frac{G_c(z). z[G_{ho}(s).G(s)]}{1 + G_c(z).x[G_{ho}(s). G(s).H(s)]}$$

$$= \frac{G_c(z).G_{ho} G(z)}{1 + G_c(z).G_{ho}.GH(z)]}$$

6.11 PULSE TRANSFER FUNCTION

For any linear time invariant discrete time system, the output of the system for any input can be determined as

$$y(n) = \sum_{k=0}^{\infty} r(k).h(n-k); \quad k \geq 0$$

Where $r \rightarrow$ Input

$h \rightarrow$ impulse response of the system

Using convolution property of z transform,

$$Y(z) \ = \ R(z) . \ H(z)$$

$$\frac{Y(z)}{R(z)} \ = \ H(z) \quad \text{Pulse transfer function.}$$

With $H(z) \ = \ z \ [h(k)]$

The pulse transfer function is the ration of z transform of output sequence to z transform of input sequence with zero initial conditions.

Note :

Important S – z pairs :

Laplace transform	Z-Transform
$\dfrac{1}{s}$	$\dfrac{z}{z-1}$
$\dfrac{1}{s^2}$	$\dfrac{T^2}{(z-1)^2}$
$\dfrac{1}{s^3}$	$\dfrac{T^2 \ Z(z+1)}{2(z-1)^3}$
$\dfrac{1}{s+a}$	$\dfrac{z}{Z - e^{-eat}}$

With T = sampling period

- Starred laplace transform = it is discrete variation of laplace transform

  For 'n' system with transfer function, $H_1(s)$, $H_2(s)$, ... $H_n(s)$ the P.T.F. is,

$$H(z) \ = \ z \ [H_1(s), H_2(s), \ ... \ H_n(s)] \neq H_1(z) \ H_2(z) \ ... \ H_n(z)$$

- Obtaining pulse transfer function of sampled data control systems using first principle (using starred laplace transform)

SOLVED EXAMPLES

Example 6.1 : Obtain the pulse transfer function of the system shown below .

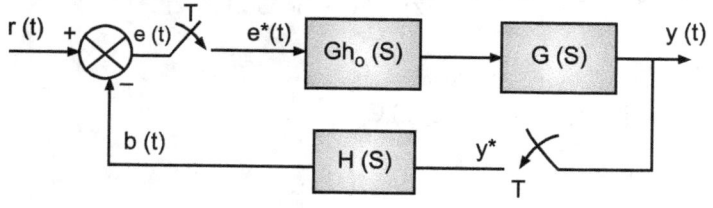

Fig. 6.38

Solution :

System is represented in block diagram

Sampling time $= T$

We have,　　　　　　　　$e(t) = r(t) - b(t)$

Taking laplace transform,

$\therefore$　　　　　　　　　　$E(s) = R(s) - B(s)$

Taking starred laplace transform (after samples)

$\therefore$　　　　　　　　　$E^*(s) = R^*(s) - B^*(s)$

Taking z – transform,

$\therefore$　　　　　　　　　$E(z) = R(z) - B(z)$

　　　　　　　　　$Y(s) = G_{ho}(s).G(s). E^*(s) \ldots$　　$E^*(t) = E^*(s)$

$\therefore$　　　　　　　$Y^*(s) = G_{ho}(S) G(s).E^*(s) \ldots$taking starred laplace

$\therefore$　Now taking Z-transfer m of above equation

$\therefore$　　　　　　　　$Y(z) = G_{ho} G(z).E(z)$

Now,　　　　　　　　$B(s) = y^*(s).H(s)$

　　　　　　　　　　$= Y^*(s) H^*(s)$

Substituting value of $Y^*(s)$ in B(s)

$\therefore$　　　　　　　$B(s) = E^*(s) [G_{ho}(s).G(s)]^*H(s)$

Taking starred laplace transform

$\therefore$　　　　　　　$B^*(s) = E^*(s) [G_{ho}G^*(s)] H^*(s)$

Taking Z-transform,

$\therefore$　　　　　　　$B(z) = E(z) G_{ho}G(Z).H(z)$

$\therefore$　　　　　　　$E(z) = R(z) - E(z) G_{ho}(z).H(z)$

$\therefore$　　　　　　　$R(z) = E(z) [1 + G_{ho} G(z) .H(z)]$

$\therefore$　　Pulse transfer function $= \dfrac{Y(z)}{R(z)} = \dfrac{G_{ho}G(z)}{1 + G_{ho}G(z) .H(z)}$

Property :

　　　　　$Z[G_1(s).G_2(s)] \neq G_1(z).G_2(z)$

But in starred laplace transform

　　　　　$z[G_1^*(s). G_2^*(s)] = G_1(z).G_2(z)$

Example 6.2 : Obtain the pulse transfer function of

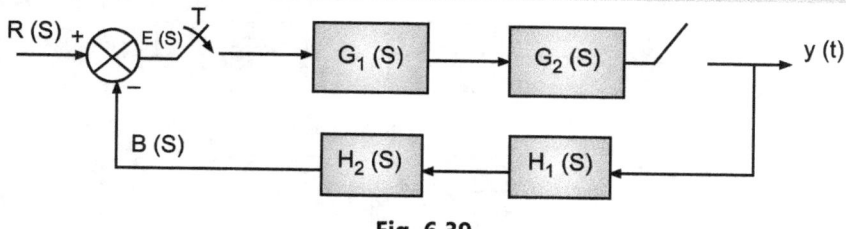

Fig. 6.39

Solution :

Sampling Time = T

We have; $\qquad E(s) = R(s) - B(s)$

   Obtaining starred Laplace

$\therefore \qquad E^*(s) = R^*(s) - B^*(s)$

$\therefore \qquad E(z) = R(z) - B(z)$

$\qquad Y(s) = E^*(s) \, [G_1(s) . G_2(s)]^*$

$\qquad Y^*(s) = E^*(s) . G_1G_2^*(s)$

$\therefore \qquad Y(z) = E(z) \, G_1G(z)$

$\qquad B(s) = E^*(s) \, G_1G_2^*(s) . H_1(s) . H_2(s)$

$\qquad B^*(s) = E^*(s) \, G_1G_2(s) \, H_1H_2^*(s)$ Taking starred LT

$\therefore \qquad B(z) = E(z) \, G_1G_2(z) \, H_1H_2(z)$ …Taking ZT

$\therefore \qquad R(z) = E(z) \, [1 + G_1G_2(z) . H_1H_2(z)]$

$\therefore \qquad \text{P.T.F.} = \dfrac{Y(z)}{R(z)} = \dfrac{G_1G_2(z)}{1 + G_1G_2(z) \, H_1H_2(z)}$

$$= \dfrac{G_1G_2(z)}{1 + G_1G_2H_1H_2(z)}$$

- Z transform of impulse and step inputs.

  $\delta(k) = 1,$ $K = o$ $u(k) = 1,$ $K \geq o$

      $= o,$ $K \neq o$ $= o,$ $K < o$

  $\delta(z) = 1$ $u(z) = \dfrac{z}{z-1}$

The transfer function of ZOH

$$G_o(s) = \frac{1}{s} - \frac{1}{s} \, e^{-ST} = \frac{1 - e^{-st}}{s}$$

- System with zero order Hold :

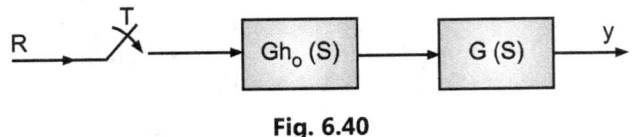

Fig. 6.40

$$\text{P.T.F.} = \frac{Y(z)}{R(z)} = z[G_{ho}(s).G(s)]$$

$$= Z\left[\frac{1-e^{-ST}}{S}G(s)\right]$$

$$\therefore \qquad = (1-z^{-1})\,z\left[\frac{G(s)}{s}\right]$$

$$= \left[\frac{z-1}{z}\right]z\left[\frac{G(s)}{s}\right]$$

Examples 6.3 : Find the pulse transfer function, impulse response and step response of

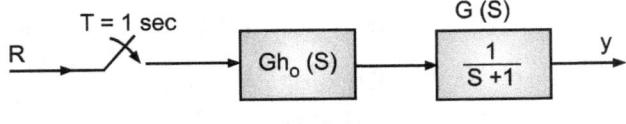

Fig. 6.41

Solution : The pulse transfer function is

$$\text{P.T.F.} = \frac{Y(z)}{R(z)} = z\,[G_{ho}(s).G(s)]$$

$$= z\left[\frac{1-e^{-ST}}{S}\frac{1}{s+1}\right]$$

$$= \left[\frac{z-1}{z}\right]z\left[\frac{1}{s\,(s+1)}\right]$$

$$= \left[\frac{z-1}{z}\right]z\left[\frac{A}{s}+\frac{B}{s+1}\right]$$

$$A = \left.\frac{1}{s+1}\right|_{s=0} = 1$$

$$\therefore \qquad A = 1$$

$$B = \left.\frac{1}{s}\right|_{s=-1}$$

$$\therefore \qquad B = -1$$

$$\therefore \quad \frac{Y(z)}{R(z)} = \left[\frac{z-1}{z}\right] z \left[\frac{1}{s} - \frac{1}{s+1}\right]$$

$$= \left[\frac{z-1}{z}\right]\left[\frac{z}{z-1} - \frac{z}{z-e^{-T}}\right]$$

$$= \left[\frac{z-1}{z}\right]\left[\frac{z}{z-1} - \frac{z}{z-0.3679}\right] \quad \cdots T = 1 \text{ sec}$$

$$= \left[\frac{z-1}{z}\right]\left[\frac{z-(z-0.3679) - z(z-1)}{(1-z)(z-0.3679)}\right]$$

$$= \left[\frac{z-1}{z}\right]\frac{z^2 - 0.3679z - z^2 + 2}{(z-1)(z-0.3679)}$$

$$= \frac{(z-1)}{z}\left[\frac{0.6321z}{(z-1)(z-0.3679)}\right]$$

$$= \frac{0.6321}{z - 0.3679}$$

For Impulse response, R(z) = 1

$$\therefore \qquad Y(z) = \frac{0.6321z}{z(z-0.3679)}$$

$$\therefore \qquad y(k) = 0.6321\,(0.3679)^{k-1}\,u(k) \qquad \qquad \cdots(1)$$

For step response, $\qquad R(z) = \dfrac{z}{z-1}$

$$\therefore \qquad Y(z) = \frac{0.6321\,z}{(z-1)(z-0.3679)}$$

$$\therefore \qquad \frac{Y(z)}{z} = \frac{0.6321}{(z-1)(z-0.3679)}$$

$$= \frac{A}{z-1} + \frac{B}{z-03679}$$

$$A = \frac{0.6321}{z - 0.3679}\Bigg|_{z=1} = 1$$

$$B = \frac{0.6321}{z-1}\Bigg|_{z=0.3679} = -1$$

$$\therefore \qquad Y(z) = \frac{z}{z-1} - \frac{z}{z-0.3679}$$

$$\therefore \qquad Y(k) = [1 - (0.3679)^k]\,u(k)$$

Example 6.4 : Find pulse transfer function, impulse response and step response of

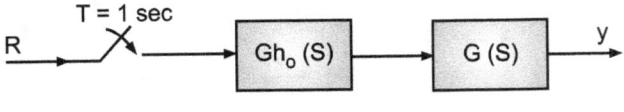

T = 1 sec

R → / → $Gh_o(S)$ → $G(S)$ → y

Fig. 6.42

Solution : The pulse transfer function is,

$$P.T.F. = \frac{Y(z)}{R(z)} = z\,[G_{ho}(s)\,G(s))]$$

$$= z\left[\frac{1-e^{-ST}}{s}\,\frac{1}{s\,(s+1)}\right]$$

$$= \left[\frac{z-1}{z}\right] z\left[\frac{1}{s^2\,(s+1)}\right]$$

$$= \left[\frac{z-1}{z}\right] z\left[\frac{A}{s^2}+\frac{B}{s}+\frac{C}{s+1}\right]$$

$$A = \left.\frac{1}{s+1}\right|_{s\,=\,0} = 1$$

$$B = \left.\frac{d}{ds}\left[\frac{1}{s+1}\right]\right|_{s\,=\,0} - \left.\frac{1}{(s+1)^2}\right|_{s\,=\,0} = -1$$

$$C = \left.\frac{1}{s^2}\right|_{s\,=\,-1} = 1$$

$$\therefore \qquad \frac{Y(z)}{R(z)} = \left[\frac{z-1}{z}\right] z\left[\frac{1}{s^2}-\frac{1}{s}+\frac{1}{s+1}\right]$$

$$= \left[\frac{z-1}{z}\right]\left[\frac{z}{(z-1)^2}-\frac{z}{z-1}+\frac{z}{z-e^{-T}}\right]$$

$$= \frac{1}{z-1}-1+\frac{z-1}{z-0.3679}$$

$$= \frac{0.3679\,z+0.2642}{(z-1)\,(z-0.3679)}$$

For impulse response, R(z) = 1

$$\therefore \qquad Y(z) = \frac{0.3679\,z+0.2642}{(z-1)\,(z-0.3679)}$$

$$\therefore \qquad \frac{Y(z)}{z} = \frac{0.3679z+0.2642}{z\,(z-1)\,(z-0.3679)}$$

$$= \frac{A}{z} + \frac{B}{z-1} + \frac{C}{z-0.3679}$$

$$A = \left. \frac{0.3679z + 0.2642}{(z-1)(z-0.3679)} \right|_{z=0} = 0.7181$$

$$B = \left. \frac{0.3679z + 0.2642}{z(z-0.3679)} \right|_{z=1} = 1$$

$$C = \left. \frac{0.3679z + 0.2642}{z(z-1)} \right|_{z=0.3679} = -1.7181$$

$$\therefore \quad \frac{Y(z)}{z} = \frac{0.7181}{z} + \frac{1}{z-1} - \frac{1.7181}{z-0.3679}$$

$$\therefore \quad Y(z) = 0.7181 + \frac{z}{z-1} - \frac{1.7181z}{z-0.3679}$$

$$Y(k) = 0.7181\,\delta(k) + u(k) - 1.7181\,(0.3679)^k\,u(k)$$

Similarly step response can be obtained by taking $R(z) = \dfrac{z}{z-1}$ in $\dfrac{Y(z)}{R(z)}$ to get,

$$Y(z) = \frac{(0.3679 + 0.2642)z}{(z-1)^2(z-0.3679)}$$

$$\frac{Y(z)}{z} = \frac{(0.3679z + 0.2642)}{(z-1)^2(z-0.3679)}$$

$$= \frac{A}{(z-1)^2} + \frac{B}{z-1} + \frac{C}{z-0.3679}$$

$$A = \left. \frac{0.3679z + 0.2642}{z-0.3679} \right|_{z=1} = 1$$

$$B = \left. \frac{d}{dz}\left[\frac{0.3679z + 0.2642}{z-0.3679} \right] \right|_{z=1} = -1$$

$$= \left. \frac{(z-0.3678)(0.3679) - (0.36792 + 0.2642)}{(z-0.3679)^2} \right|_{z=1}$$

$$C = \left. \frac{0.3679z + 0.2642}{(z-1)^2} \right|_{z=0.3679} = 1.5820$$

$$\therefore \quad \frac{Y(z)}{z} = \frac{z}{(z-1)^2} - \frac{1}{z-1} + \frac{1.5820}{z-0.3679}$$

$$\therefore \quad Y(z) = \frac{z}{(z-1)^2} - \frac{z}{z-1} + \frac{1.5820\,z}{z-0.3679}$$

$$\therefore \quad Y(k) = ku(k) - u(k) + 1.5820\,(0.3679)^k\,u(k)$$

Example 6.5 : Find pulse transfer function of

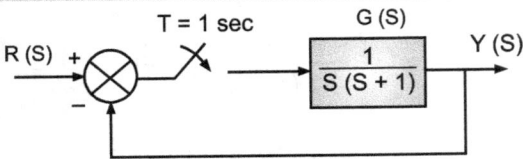

R (S)   +
T = 1 sec   G (S)
$\dfrac{1}{S\,(S+1)}$ Y (S)

Fig. 6.43

Solution : The P.T.F. of the given system is.

$$\frac{Y(z)}{R(z)} = \frac{G(z)}{1+6(z)} = \frac{z\left[\dfrac{1}{s(s+1)}\right]}{1+z\left[\dfrac{1}{s\,(s+1)}\right]}$$

$$G(z) = z\left[\frac{A}{s} + \frac{B}{s+1}\right] \quad A = \left.\frac{1}{s+1}\right|_{s=0} = 1$$

$$= z\left[\frac{1}{s} - \frac{1}{s+1}\right] \quad B = \left.\frac{1}{s}\right|_{s=-1} = -1$$

$$= \frac{z}{z-1} - \frac{z}{z-e}$$

$$\therefore \quad G(z) = \frac{z}{z-1} - \frac{z}{z-0.3679}$$

$$= \frac{0.6321z}{(z-1)\,(z-0.3679)}$$

$$\therefore \quad \text{P.T.F.} = \frac{\dfrac{0.6321z}{(z-1)\,(z-0.3679)}}{1 + \dfrac{0.6321\,z}{(z-1)\,(z-0.3679)}}$$

$$= \frac{0.6321z}{(z-1)\,(z-0.3679) + 0.6321z}$$

$$\therefore \quad = \frac{0.6321z}{z^2 - 1.3679z + 0.3679 + 0.6321z}$$

$$= \frac{0.6321z}{z^2 - 0.7358\,z + 0.3679}$$

Note : Please refer the z transform and inverse z transfer of standard functions and properties of z transfer.

SUMMARY

- A systematic approach to the writing of programs can improve the chances of high-quality programs being generated in a short time as possible.

- PLC's can be used in applications ranging from vending machine controls and packaging machinery to roller coasters and complex camera positioning systems.

- PLC scan time is the time in which the PLC runs through the program taking in data and updating outputs this is typically a few milliseconds.

- Proportional and integrative modes are also used as single control modes, a derivative mode is rarely used on it's own in control systems.

- When P controller is used, large gain is needed to improve steady state error.

- D mode is used when prediction of the error can improve control or when it necessary to stabilize the system.

- PID controller is often used in industry, but also in the control of mobile objects.

- Tuning is adjustment of control parameters to the optimum values for the desired control response. Stability is a basic requirement.

EXERCISE

1. Write short notes on the following :   **[3+3]**

   (i) Controller tuning   (ii) P Controller

2. Considering a typical feedback control system, give the advantages of a P+I controller as compared to a purely proportional controller.   **[4]**

3. Draw ladder logic for traffic light controller   **[5]**

4. Explain Ladder logic for Digital circuits   **[7]**

5. Explain PID Controller in detail   **[6]**

6. Give Advantages, Disadvantages and Applications of PLC   **[6]**

SOLVED UNIVERSITY PROBLEMS

Example 6.1 : Obtain pulse transfer function of the system shown in Fig. 6.44 using first principle.   **[May 14] [7 M]**

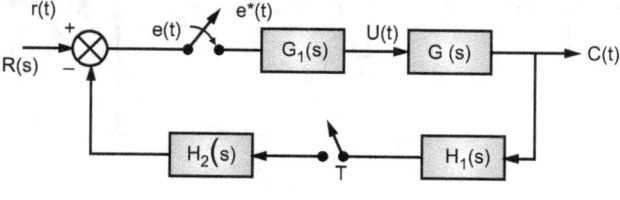

Fig. 6.44

Solution :　　　　$E(s) = R(s) - B(s)$　i.e.　$B^*(s) = R^*(s) - B^*(s)$　　　　　... (1)

$B(s) = M^*(s) H_2(s)$　and　$M(s) = C(s) H_1(s)$

∴　　　$M^*(s) = CH_1^*(s)$　i.e.　$B(s) = CH^*(s) H_2(s)$　　　　　... (2)

$C(s) = E^*(s) G(s) G(s)$　i.e.　$C^*(s) = E^*(s) G_1 G^*(s)$　　　　　... (3)

Put equation (2) and (3) in equation (1),

$$\frac{C^*(s)}{G_1 G^*(s)} = R^*(s) - CH_1^*(s) H_2^*(s)$$

∴　　　$C^*(s) = R^*(s) G_1 G^*(s) - CH_1^*(s) H_2^*(s)$

∴　　　$C(z) = R(z) G_1 G(z) - CH_1(z) H_2(z)$

Example 6.2 : Find pulse transfer function and impulse response for the system shown in Fig. 6.45.　　　　　**[Dec. 14] [6 M]**

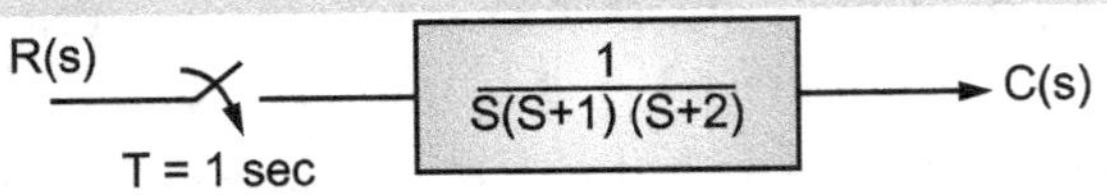

$R(s)$ ⟍ $\frac{1}{S(S+1)(S+2)}$ → $C(s)$

$T = 1$ sec

Fig. 6.45

Solution :　　$\dfrac{C(z)}{R(z)} = \dfrac{C^*(s)}{R^*(s)} = \dfrac{1}{s(s+1)(s+2)} = z\left[\dfrac{1}{s(s+1)(s+2)}\right] L^{-1}\left[\dfrac{1}{s(s+1)(s+2)}\right]$

$$= L^{-1}\left[\frac{0.5}{s} - \frac{1}{s+1} + \frac{0.5}{s+2}\right] = 0.5 - e^{-t} - 0.5e^{-2t}$$

$$z\left[\frac{1}{(s+1)(s+2)}\right] = z[0.5 - e^{-t} - 0.5e^{-2t}] = z[0.5 - e^{-kT} - 0.5e^{-2kT}]$$

$$= \frac{0.5z}{z-1} - \frac{z}{z-e^{-T}} - \frac{0.5z}{z-e^{-2T}} = \frac{0.5z}{z-1} - \frac{z}{z-0.3678} - \frac{0.5z}{z-0.1353}$$

∴　　$\dfrac{C(z)}{R(z)} = \dfrac{z[-z^2 + 1.5676z - 0.2943]}{(z-1)(z-0.3678)(z-0.1353)}$

This is pulse response.

The impulse response is z^{-1} of $C(z)$.

$$C(k) = z^{-1}\left[\frac{0.5z}{z-1} - \frac{z}{z-0.3678} - \frac{0.5z}{z-0.1353}\right]$$

∴　　$C(k) = 0.5(1)^k - (0.3678)^k - 0.5(0.1353)^k$

Example 6.3 : Find pulse transfer function of　　　　　**[May 15] [7 M]**

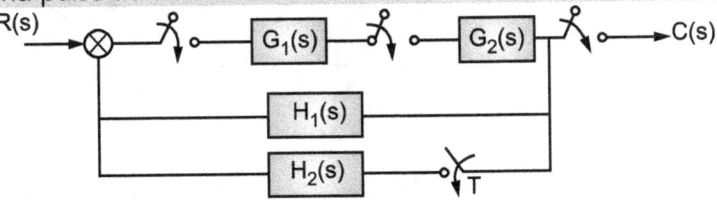

Fig. 6.46

Solution :　　$E(s) = R(s) - B(s)$ i.e. $E^*(s) = R^*(s) - B^*(s)$　　　　　... (1)

$$B(s) = C(s) H_1(s) + C^*(s) H_2(s) \qquad \dots (2)$$

$$C(s) = [E^*(s) G_1(s)]^* G_2(s) = E^*(s) G_1^*(s) G_2(s) \qquad \dots (3)$$

$$\therefore \qquad C^*(s) = E^*(s) G_1^*(s) G_2^*(s) \qquad \dots (4)$$

Using equation (3) and (4) in equation (2).

$$\therefore \qquad B(s) = E^*(s) G_1^*(s) G_2(s) H_1(s) + E^*(s) G_1^*(s) G_2^*(s) H_2(s)$$

Taking star on both sides,

$$\therefore \qquad B^*(s) = E^*(s) G_1^*(s) [G_2 H_1(s)]^* + E^*(s) G_1^*(s) G_2^*(s) H_2^*(s) \qquad \dots (5)$$

Using equation (5) in equation (1).

$$\therefore \qquad E^*(s) = R^*(s) - E^*(s) G_1^*(s) [G_2 H_1(s)]^* - E^*(s) G_1^*(s) G_2^*(s) H_2^*(s)$$

$$\therefore \qquad E^*(s) = \frac{R^*(s)}{1 + G_1^*(s) [G_2 H_1(s)]^* + G_1^*(s) G_2^*(s) H_2^*(s)} \qquad \dots (6)$$

Put equation (6) in equation (4),

$$\therefore \qquad C^*(s) = \frac{R^*(s) G_1^*(s) G_2^*(s)}{1 + G_1^*(s) [G_2 H_1(s)]^* + G_1^*(s) G_2^*(s) H_2^*(s)}$$

Pulse   T.F. $= \dfrac{C(z)}{R(z)} = \dfrac{G_1(z) G_2(z)}{1 + G_1(z) G_2 H_1(z) + G_1(z) G_2(z) H_2(z)}$

Example 6.4 : Obtain unit step response of the system shown in Fig. 6.47.   **[May 15]**

Fig. 6.47

Solution : For zero order hold,

$$G_{ho}(s) = \frac{1 - e^{-Ts}}{s} = \frac{1 - e^{-s}}{s}$$

$$\therefore \qquad (s) = R^*(s) \left[\frac{1 - e^{-s}}{s} \times \frac{1}{s + 1} \right]$$

$$\therefore \qquad C^*(s) = R^*(s) \left[\frac{1 - e^{-s}}{s} \times \frac{1}{s + 1} \right]$$

$$\frac{e^*(s)}{R^*(s)} = 1 - e^{-s} \left[\frac{1}{s(s + 1)} \right]$$

$$\left[\frac{1}{s(s + 1)} \right]^* = z \left[\frac{1}{s(s + 1)} \right]$$

$$L^{-1} \left[\frac{1}{s(s + 1)} \right] = L^{-1} \left[\frac{1}{s} - \frac{1}{s + 1} \right] = 1 - e^{-t}$$

$$\therefore \quad z\left[\frac{1}{s(s+1)}\right] = z[1 - e^{-kt}] = \frac{z}{z-1} - \frac{z}{z-e^{-1}} = z\left[\frac{1}{z-1} - \frac{1}{z-e^{-1}}\right]$$

$$= \frac{z(1-e^{-1})}{(z-1)(z-e^{-1})} = \frac{0.6321z}{(z-1)(z-0.3678)}$$

$$\frac{C^*(s)}{R^*(s)} = \frac{C(z)}{R(z)} = \frac{(1-z^{-1})\,0.6321z}{(z-1)(z-0.3678)} = \frac{0.6321}{z-0.3678}$$

For unit step input,

$$R(z) = \frac{z}{z-1}$$

$$\therefore \quad C(z) = \frac{0.6321z}{(z-1)(z-0.3678)}$$

$$\frac{C(z)}{z} = \frac{0.6321}{(z-1)(z-0.3678)} = \frac{1}{z-1} - \frac{1}{z-0.3678}$$

$$C(z) = \frac{z}{z-1} - \frac{z}{z-0.3678}$$

$$\therefore \quad C(k) = z^{-1}[C(z)] = (1)^k - (0.3678)^k$$

Example 6.5 : Obtain pulse transfer function of the system shown in Fig. 6.48 with $\alpha = 1$.

[Dec. 15] [6 M]

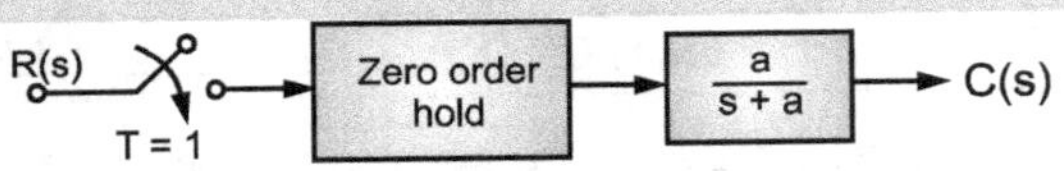

Fig. 6.48

Solution : The transfer function of a zero hold system is $\left[\dfrac{1 - e^{-Ts}}{s}\right]$

Thus we have

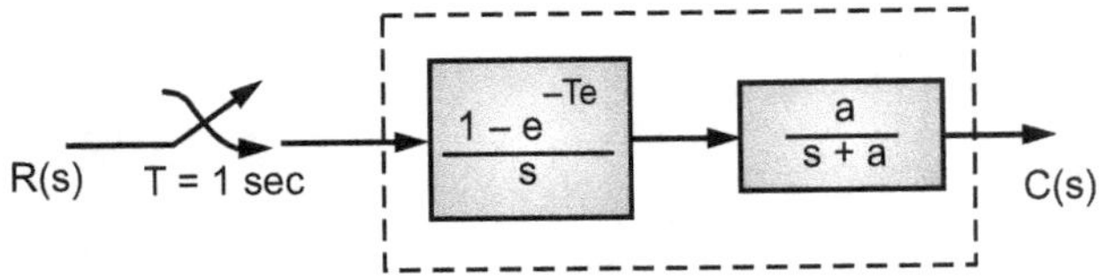

Fig. 6.49

$$G(s) = \frac{1 - e^{-Ts}}{s} \cdot \frac{a}{s+a}$$

Since $a = 1$ (given)

$$\therefore \quad G(s) = \frac{1 - e^{-Ts}}{s} \cdot \frac{1}{s+1}$$

$$\therefore \quad G(s) = (1 - e^{-Ts})\frac{G_1(s)}{s},$$

where $\quad G_1(s) = \dfrac{1}{s+1}$

◇ ◇ ◇

SAMPLE QUESTION PAPER – I

End-Sem. Theory Examination

Time : 1 Hour   **Max. Marks : 50**

INSTRUCTIONS :

1. Answer Q.No.1 or Q.No.2, Q.No.3 or Q.No.4, Q.No.5 or Q.No.6, Q.No.7 or Q.No.8.
2. Neat diagrams must be drawn whenever necessary.
3. Figures to the right indicate full marks.
4. Assume suitable data, if necessary.

1. (a) Define open loop and closed loop control systems with suitable examples. **[6]**

(b) Write the system equations for the given system in Fig. 1. **[6]**

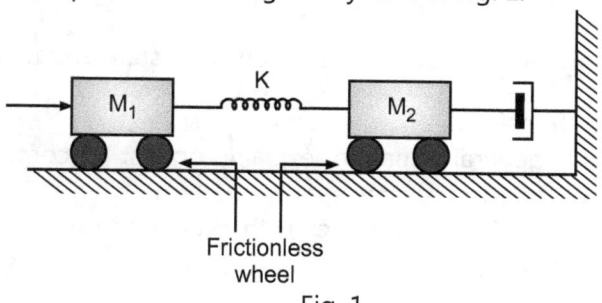

Frictionless
wheel

Fig. 1   **OR**

2. (a) A unity feedback control system has an open-loop transfer functions $G(s) = \dfrac{20}{s(5+s)}$.

Find rise time, peak time and percentage overshoot for a unit step input. **[6]**

(b) Obtain the transfer function of the system shown in fig. 2. **[6]**

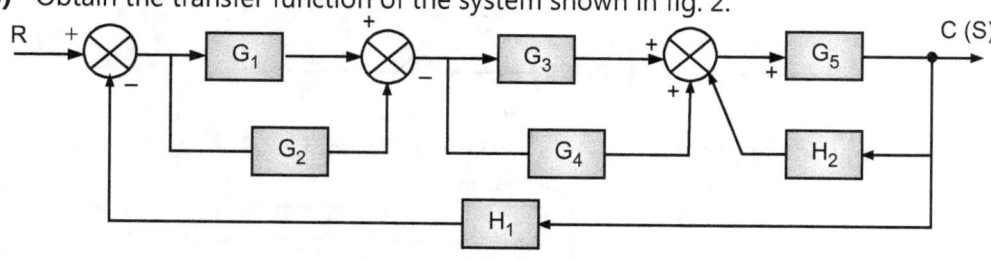

Fig. 2

3. (a) Comment on the stability of a system using Routh's stability criteria whose characteristics equation is $s^4 + 2s^3 + 4s^2 + 6s + 8 = 0$. How many poles of system lie in the right half of S- plane. **[4]**

(b) Draw the Bode plot and obtain gain margin, phase margin, gain crossover frequency, and phase crossover frequency if, **[8]**

$$G(s).H(s) = \frac{20}{s(1+0.05s)(s+0.5s)}$$ **OR**

4. (a) If $G(s).H(s) = \dfrac{K}{s(s^2+5s+10)}$. Sketch the complete Root locus, and comment on the

stability. **[8]**

(b) If $G(s).H(s) = \dfrac{1}{s(s + 1)}$ **[4]**

Find Resonance peak and Resonance frequency.

5. (a) State any three advantages of state space approach over classical approach. Determine an expression to obtain transfer function from a state model.   **[7]**

(b) Find controllability and observability of the state model.   **[6]**

$$A = \begin{bmatrix} 1 & 0 & 1 \\ 0 & 1 & 1 \\ 1 & 1 & 1 \end{bmatrix}, B = \begin{bmatrix} 1 \\ 1 \\ 1 \end{bmatrix}, C = [1,\ 1,\ 1],\ D = [0]$$ **OR**

6. (a) Obtain state transition matrix for the system with state equation $\begin{bmatrix} \dot{x} \end{bmatrix} = \begin{bmatrix} 0 & 1 \\ -8 & -9 \end{bmatrix}$

[x] using laplace transform.   **[6]**

(b) With the help of general equation, explain concept of controllable canonical and observable canonical form of state space.   **[7]**

7. (a) Write the equation of PID controller with sketch of output of P. PI. PID, and PD controller for step input.   **[6]**

(b) Find the pulse transfer function of Fig. 3.   **[7]**

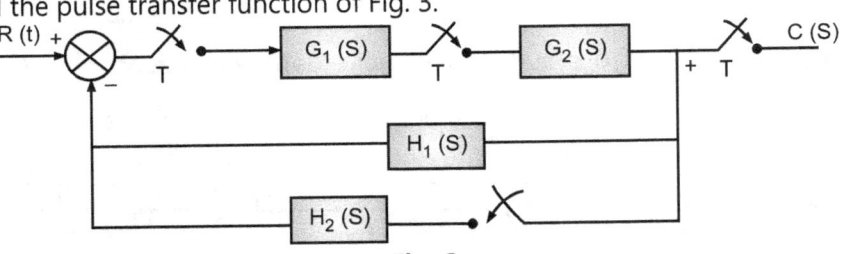

Fig. 3   **OR**

8. (a) Explain any one application of PLC with ladder diagram.   **[6]**

(b) Obtain unit step response of the system in fig.4.   **[7]**

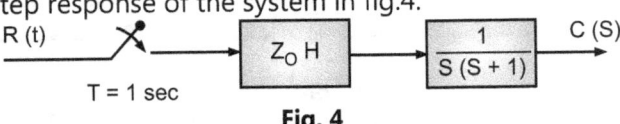

Fig. 4

✻ ✻ ✻

SAMPLE QUESTION PAPER – II

End-Sem. Theory Examination

Time : 1 Hour   **Max. Marks : 50**

1. (a) A unity Feedback system has open loop transfer function.

$G(s) = \dfrac{K}{s(s + 5)}$ Determine the 'K' so that damping factor is 0.5 for this value 'K'

Determine (i) location of closed loop poles. (ii) Peak overshoot (iii) Peak time Assume input is unit step.   **[6]**

(b) Find the overall transfer function $\frac{c(s)}{R(s)}$ for the signal flow graph below by Mason's Rule.   **[6]**

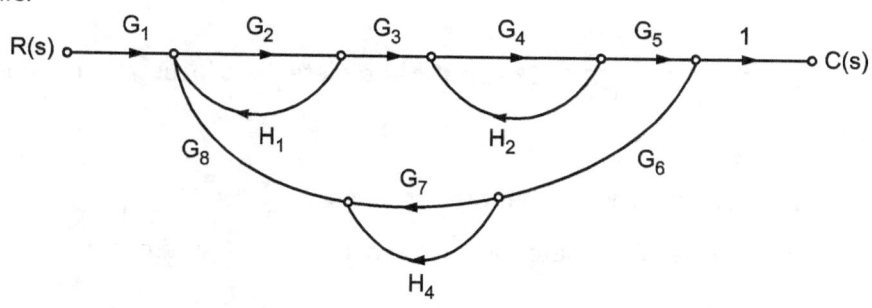

Fig. 1   **OR**

2. (a) Determine the ratio for the system shown in Fig. 2 by block reduction method.   **[6]**

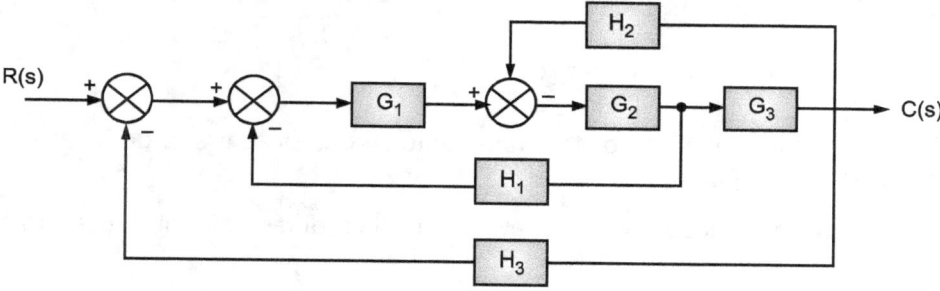

Fig. 2

(b) Draw the electrical analogous circuit (use F-v analogy) and derive their transfer function.   **[6]**

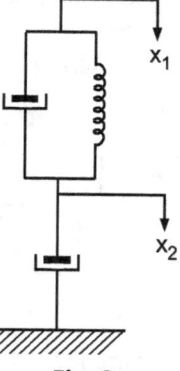

Fig. 3

3. (a) Discuss the advantages and limitations of frequency response method of analysis for control systems in detail.   **[6]**

(b) Define the following terms in reference to Bode plot for a given transfer functions.
   (i)   Phase crossover for equation   (ii) Gain crossover for equation
   (iii) Phase margin   (iv) Gain margin   **[6] OR**

4. (a) Determine the range of K over which the following characteristic polynomials belong to stable system. **[4]**

(i) $s^4 + 5s^3 + 9s^2 + 20s + K$

(b) If $G(s).H(s) = \dfrac{K}{s(s + 5)(s + 10)}$. Sketch the complete Root locus, and comment on the stability. **[4]**

5. (a) A system is characterized by the transfer function $\dfrac{Y(s)}{u(s)} = \dfrac{2}{s^3 + 6s^2 + 11s + 6}$. obtain state space model and determine whether or not system is controllable and observable. **[7]**

(b) Discuss the advantages of state-space representations of systems. Point out the significance of state transition matrix in solving equations. **[6] OR**

6. (a) Obtain the state transition matrix if $\dot{x} = \begin{bmatrix} 0 & 1 \\ -11 & -12 \end{bmatrix} x$ **[6]**

(b) Write the state equation for the non-Homogenous system and derive the equation for finding its solutions. **[7]**

7. (a) Explain ladder concept in PLC. Draw and explain different symbol used to contract ladder. **[6]**

(b) Find the pulse transfer function and impulse response for the system in Fig. 4. **[7]**

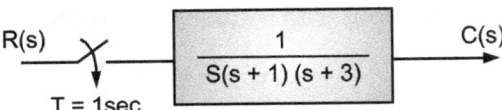

R(s)   T = 1sec $\dfrac{1}{S(s + 1)(s + 3)}$ C(s)

Fig. 4   **OR**

8. (a) Obtain pulse transfer function of the system shown in Fig. 5 with $\alpha = 1$. **[6]**

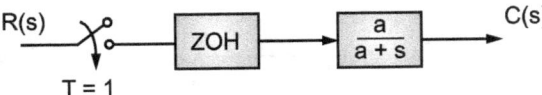

R(s)   T = 1   ZOH $\dfrac{a}{a + s}$ C(s)

Fig. 5

(b) Write short notes on: **[6]**

(a) Advantages of Digital system over analog control system

(b) Application of PLC is elevator.

❊ ❊ ❊